The Phantom's Melody

Australia D. Kincannon

Copyright © 2024 by Australia Kincannon

All rights reserved.

No part of this publication may be reproduced, distributed, or transmitted in any form or by any means, including photocopying, recording, or other electronic or mechanical methods without the prior written permission of the publisher, except as permitted by U.S. copyright law. For permission requests, contact AustraliaD.KincannonAuthor@hotmail.com

The story, all names, characters, locations, buildings, and incidents portrayed in this production are fictitious and based on the works of Gaston Leroux, which are public domain. No identification with actual persons (living or deceased), or products is intended or should be inferred.

Ebook ISBN: 979-8-9902189-0-1

Paperback ISBN: 979-8-9902189-1-8

Hardcover ISBN: 979-8-9902189-2-5

Cover Artist: Australia Kincannon

Illustrator: Australia Kincannon

Editor: Jyl Glenn

Interior Formatting: Australia Kincannon

First Edition 2024 Revised

Dedication

For all the other tired little weirdos who need an escape. And like masked men.

Help Index

- How to pronounce: Erique (Er-eek) or (Erik)

- Monsieur (mister/sir) will be replaced with M. in front of several names throughout the book.

- There is use of the French and Italian language within a few of the chapters. You are meant to feel as lost as Melody, the main character who doesn't speak those languages..

If you would like to read the translations, please visit the link below where you will find page numbers for the corresponding translation.

www.Australiadkincannon.bigcartel.com

Contents

1. Chapter I — 1
2. Chapter II — 13
3. Chapter III — 22
4. Chapter IV — 31
5. Chapter V — 38
6. Chapter VI — 46
7. Chapter VII — 54
8. Chapter VIII — 61
9. Chapter IX — 67
10. Chapter X — 76
11. Chapter XI — 82
12. Chapter XII — 87
13. Chapter XIII — 97
14. Chapter XIV — 110
15. Chapter XV — 117
16. Chapter XVI — 122
17. Chapter XVII — 127
18. Chapter XVIII — 139
19. Chapter XIX — 147
20. Chapter XX — 156

21. Chapter XXI	163
22. Chapter XXII	173
23. Chapter XXIII	182
24. Chapter XXIV	188
25. Chapter XXV	195
26. Chapter XXVI	202
27. Chapter XXVII	217
28. Chapter XXVIII	218
29. Chapter XXIX	223
30. Chapter XXX	231
31. Chapter XXXI	244
32. Chapter XXXII	252
33. Chapter XXXIII	260
34. Chapter XXXIV	269
35. Chapter XXXV	277
36. Chapter XXXVI	286
37. Chapter XXXVII	296
38. Chapter XXXVIII	306
39. Chapter XXXIX	314
40. Chapter XXXX	323
41. Chapter XXXXI	329
42. Chapter XXXXII	341

43. Epilogue	354
Aknowledgements	359
About the Author	361

"The Opera ghost really existed. He was not, as was long believed, a creature of the imagination of the artists, the superstition of the managers, or a product of the absurd and impressionable brains of the young ladies of the ballet, their mothers, the box-keepers, the cloakroom attendants or the concierge. Yes, he existed in flesh and blood, although he assumed the complete appearance of a real phantom, that is to say, of a spectral shade."

- Gaston Leroux

The Phantom of the Opera

Chapter I

Melody

Fear is the enemy of all. Change its companion. To change means overcoming fear. Venture into the unknown, venture outside of one's comfort. We fear what we can't change. Because the unknown is terrifying.

Maybe second to having someone else take your photo.

Fear didn't have me tonight, though. At least that's what I kept telling myself as I readied for the occasion I had been dreaming about since I was sixteen.

Nope. Tonight, I was in New York City for the first time, and about to see one of the greatest shows ingrained into every band, choir and theater kid since the '80s. And no, not *CATS*.

"Come on, Melody," Sarah, my younger sister, said from across the table of our small hotel room. "Let me do your makeup. Please?"

"That brush has seen better days," I said as I wiped the partially laid foundation from my face. "It was like Freddy Krueger was giving me a facial."

Makeup wasn't something I did in my day-to-day for no other reason than it wasn't my hobby, so the abuse was unnecessary.

She sighed and set the brush down. "We're all getting dressed up, Mel. You should want to look as beautiful as possible for Phantom tonight."

She said it like I had forgotten why I had taken this trip across the country in the first place. Like I wasn't in desperate need of some sort of "magic". To feel something other than the drying of the well that was my life.

It seemed so stupid to think a show I knew so well could be that magic, maybe. But, after thirty-five years on Broadway, Andrew Lloyd Webber's *The Phantom of the Opera* was closing. And I already had too many regrets to add that one to the list.

I huffed and turned to the dining table covered in Sarah's makeup and other random things we'd pulled out for the night, including three homemade Phantom masks I had brought. One was black and silver, another silver and blue, and of course, the classic all white. "I'm wearing a mask, anyway. Just focus on you," I said, running my fingers over the smooth surfaces of each one.

"You still have half a face to show off. Maybe…" Sarah wiggled her eyebrows suggestively, "it could get you some attention."

Even when well intentioned, the notion that I had to be something other than myself to get someone's "attention," irked me.

I'm always beautiful when I'm someone else… And I hate it.

I picked up the white mask and held it to my face. "I'll stay ugly. Thank you."

"*Cute*," Sarah quipped, and rolled her eyes.

"And unless he's a mask-wearing tortured soul who's completely obsessed with me and musically inclined, I don't want it," I said. A deep chuckle rumbled within my chest as I set the mask down. "We're also leaving tomorrow, remember?"

"At least let me do your eyeliner," she said.

I reluctantly took a seat in the chair opposite her. "Fine."

As the tip of the black liquid liner touched my skin, I held back any remnants of the chuckle I had. Never in a million years would I have thought my sister would be the best person to go on vacation with. This trip had been more than just an escape from my empty reality. We had connected like we hadn't in a long time. Or maybe ever.

Chapter I

The past few days as we walked the city, and I daydreamed about moving to a place like this - a hub for creatives, we planned our next trip. Europe! We would do all the Phantom inspired things in Paris. See the original show in London, the works! Maybe I would even find myself a boyfriend along the way.

Ha.

It was only thanks to the generosity of my boss that I could even afford to get us out here in the first place.

It's amazing how an extra few hundred dollars can change someone's life. Even for a moment.

Guess it was lucky for Mom that another trip or moving couldn't happen. She was almost too fragile to fly to NYC. Europe would be out of the question, and there wasn't anyone to stay with her if I just left.

Sometimes I wonder what life would be like if she didn't wake up…

Sick at the reoccurring thought the moment it crossed my mind, I sighed, trying to relieve the sudden tension in my shoulders coupled with an instant headache.

"I'm just saying. It's been like what, four years since your last relationship? It's time to get out there," Sarah said.

"Excuse you. I've been out there," I said.

She let out one of those high pitched "huh" sounds, like she didn't believe me.

It's not her fault, though. She's been married to the same amazing man for eleven years with whom she built a flourishing business with, that afforded them whatever they wanted. Kids. A white picket fence. Everything. The "perfect" life.

I mean, I knew it wasn't really perfect. They have their issues, but they always pull through.

I had always wondered what that would be like to have someone love you so much that they choose to grow with you. That they choose you.

Then there's me. An overweight thirty-five-year-old cashier who failed at the two things I loved most. All while struggling to keep my head above water as the soul-crushing weight of capitalism and failed relationships stomped out any hopes and dreams of living a creative, love filled, content life with enough time or energy to take care of myself, as it pushed its spike soled boots down on my neck.

I'm tired.

"No one wants anything real. I would rather just sit at my computer and write stories no one will ever see when I'm not taking care of our mother. Plus, men are terrible. Just look at Mom."

Luckily, Mama was still asleep in the bed nearby when we glanced over. Sarah and I have had so much fun, we almost forgot she was with us. She'd been asleep for most of the trip.

"Not everyone's like that," Sarah said. "So… you're still writing, then? I thought you gave up?"

Stupid big mouth.

"No?..."

She set the tube of liner down and twisted up her lips. "Well, anyway, there! You're all done."

Eagerly, I turned to the mirror. My brown eyes popped at the center of the black liner and mascara. "Wow. You really killed this! I never get the wings right." Having hooded eyes made it seem futile. Yet here my sister was, making it look so easy.

"I know. The perfect wings," she said, pleased with herself. "Are you sure you don't want blush or something? You're just so pale."

I placed the back of my hand against my forehead dramatically, "I'm sorry that my dying Victorian child-like complexion is hard to look at."

"You should go outside more often, hun," Mama chimed in as if she wasn't dead asleep moments ago.

"Oh, you've got jokes. Like either of you are Miss California Sunshine," I said, marveling at the big audacity in the tiny room. It was good to hear Mama laugh, though. Especially because it was rare anymore.

"My turn!" she said, trying to push herself up from the bed.

I hurried to her side. "Here, let me help, Mama." She squeezed my hands, holding on with all the strength she had to steady herself. "How are you feeling?"

The wrinkles of time crept at the corners of worn eyes that hid behind a tired smile. "Less pain today," she said. "It's almost Phantom time! I'm so excited. Sing to me, my Angel!"

Choking back the lingering guilt behind a smile, I settled her in at the table with Sarah.

Chapter I

"So, anyway, men suck. Gotcha," Sarah said. "But like there's someone out there just waiting for you to trip into them and then tell them to fuck off."

"Can we please talk about anything else?" I asked.

Just as I pulled away, the grip on my forearm tightened.

"We should be here to see one of your movies. It's not fair," Mama said so affectionately I wanted to vomit. *Great. This again.*

"Let's go back to talking about the disaster that is my love life…" I started, when the faintest brush of—something, like an echo from a memory, stopped me.

I turned back to the mirror, looking for the source that I had only felt in my dreams. But just my reflection stared back.

"You know the playwright you're named after was French," Mama said, ignoring my plea for redirection and pulling my attention to a story I've heard a million times before. There's nothing worse than a famous namesake you couldn't live up to. Especially one you don't even remember listening to.

"Yes, Mama," I grumbled.

"Melody Rena…Rena…" she stumbled, trying to say the name she used to say with ease, one of the side effects of her condition being memory loss.

"Renaître," I answered.

"*Oui Oui!* Yes," she said, proud of herself. "Her and her husband wrote musicals, like operas and stuff. When I was pregnant with you–"

"Yes Mama, I know." *Well, that's two things I'll never have. Thank you for the reminder.* My eyes saw the back of my skull. "The only channel we had was PBS and they played their work over and over, and it was the only thing that soothed me."

I stepped away to fish out my super discounted pair of beautiful, black, rhinestone-covered strappy heels by Michael Kors from beneath the table.

"Mom, stop moving please," Sarah begged.

"Remember, hun, her career didn't even take off until she was almost forty," Mama said, ignoring Sarah's plea.

As I fastened my straps, I bit the inside of my cheek, determined not to let the brewing bitterness fuck up the rest of the night.

In an attempt to derail the previous subjects, I returned to the masks on the table, fiddling with each one. "Hey! You guys know the original story, right?" I asked.

"Uh uh," Mama said.

"Not really, actually," Sarah answered. "Is it much different?"

My mind lit up like the fourth of July, and I beamed with glee. "Yes! So, the author of the original 1909 story, Gaston Leroux, took elements from real life. Places, people, etc. Some things were a little inaccurate, like the year the *Palais Garnier* opera house actually opened, but you know, for drama."

"That's cool…" Sarah replied, to humor me. Only one of us was into history or reading. It wasn't her.

"Right? Anyway, there's nothing sexy about the original Phantom at all. He was off his rocker, basically. Like, Christine tries to kill herself when he kidnaps her, mostly because he's so ugly and won't stop crying and begging for her love. Then he basically plans a murder suicide. But then he doesn't go through with it and tells his 'friend', the Daroga, that he let Christine and Raoul go. But no one ever hears from them again. Then he dies of a 'broken heart'."

Sarah's mouth hung open in utter horror. "What the actual fuck?"

"Yeah! It's a better depiction of obsession than at least most adaptations, which is cool. I personally think he killed them and then overdosed. It's gothic horror, so that makes sense."

"Well. I didn't know that," Mama said, wincing.

"That sounds terrifying," Sarah added.

"I'm still hot under the collar for the version we're seeing tonight, though," I said.

Sarah giggled. "Oh yeah? Same."

As my sister continued working on Mom, I grabbed the black and silver mask and put it on for my final outfit check. It had been a long time since I felt beautiful. It had to be perfect tonight. And it was.

I couldn't be happier with the black off the shoulder, long sleeve dress with slits in the skirt that stopped just below the crease of my belly, accentuating the tattoo on my leg. A beautiful piece done of roses and the overture from Phantom, wrapped around an ornate pipe organ. My favorite tattoo. Well, tied with the one on my forearm, dedicated to

Chapter I

Beethoven's *Moonlight Sonata*.

However, my favorite part was the way the dress fell off my belly and didn't cling to it for dear life, screaming, "Here I am!".

"I could definitely take home a phantom in this," I joked.

"You wouldn't know what to do with him," Sarah said, followed by a very throaty laugh.

"Yeah, well…," I said, half-heartedly.

"Jesus, Mel. God himself could literally hand you the person specifically made for you and tell you 'this is the one' and you would still be like… 'Eh. No. I don't believe you.' And then you boo hoo that you're single." Her mocking tone cut like an old razor.

"I don't boo hoo." *Not really, anyway.*

"Leave her alone, hun," Mama scolded.

As I opened my mouth for a fight, I stopped mid-breath as goose pimples rose along my neck and arms. The sensation from earlier was stronger this time. Like someone had walked through my body and grabbed onto my soul.

The voices trying to repair a broken bridge dissipated, and the room slipped away when I peered into the mirror, and saw nothing. It was empty yet calling as my heart beat faster in anticipation for a presence that dwelled somewhere within. *Am I awake?*

A flash of white behind the woman in the mirror yanked my focus. Beneath the fabric of a dress shirt, a chest heaved as though the man it belonged to had been running like his life depended on it.

Fidgeting hands danced at his side, and bewildered, piercing eyes, one emerald green, the other, stone gray, stared through the eyeholes of a white mask that spanned his face.

The craving within my very being held me in place. Like it knew something I didn't.

A little odd, even for my fantasy.

Cautiously, as if approaching a wild animal, he stepped closer with a hypnotic gaze locked on mine. Without warning, the warmth from his body forced a silent gasp from me as it hit my back.

I shouldn't be able to feel my imaginary boyfriend.

With a glint of wonder in his eyes, he glanced from the mirror to me as if he wasn't alone like I was. His pale hand raised with intent, but hesitated, hovering over the round of my bare shoulder. His jaw rocked as he stared, contemplating something.

Heat radiated from his flesh as he moved towards my cheek, hesitating again. Without touching, I melted, and my eyelids grew heavy. A tingling flowed down my arm when his fingertips finally made contact and traveled towards my wrist. With sweet desperation in a voice I had never heard before, he strained, "Are you real?"

Unable to concentrate, my lips parted to answer. But the murmur of another voice stifled my thoughts. His head snapped in the direction from which it came, like he had heard it too.

Sarah's voice called again. Clearer this time. "Hello…?"

As though he could feel the connection fading as well, his gentle grip around my wrist tightened. "No…" he shouted, yet his voice somehow was lower than a whisper.

I turned like I would actually find him there. But I was standing in the hotel room with my family staring at me like I was a lunatic.

"Earth to Melody!" Sarah called out, waving her hands again.

"Huh?" I said, scanning the room. The sensations were gone, but the heat on my wrist still lingered.

Maybe I'd finally let my imagination run a bit too wild. I should probably get therapy. Lord knows I needed it.

"I was just saying, you look hot tonight," Sarah said with sincerity. "Meanwhile, I'm over here looking like the penguin from Batman Returns…" In her black Spanx, she turned to the side and slumped over, really adding to the bit. "You're coming with me!"

"Oh my God, shut up!" I cracked, forcing my mind from the delusional break from reality, or ignoring it all together.

"No. Hun," Mama said as we continued to laugh.

It was a real Hallmark moment. But…

"As great as this is, time's a slippin'. And I swear to God, if I miss my crazy pants basement dwelling boyfriend, I'll hang you both from the catwalk myself!" I threatened, "Okay? Okay!"

It was mostly a joke.

"I got Mom's hair. Get dressed, Penguin," I said and tossed Sarah her blue velvet dress.

***

Chapter I

The hotel was only a ten-minute walk to the Majestic Theater. *Best planning ever.* Unfortunately, cutting through the busy night life of Times Square—which smells like assholes by the way and is riddled with them—was the quickest way to get there.

I pushed through the crowd with the weird sense of power and strength my amazing outfit and matching black and silver mask gave me. Especially as peddlers weaved in and out of our little group, giving "compliments" as they tried to sell their shitty CDs.

As we finally turned onto 6th Avenue, the bright lights and unmistakable blue marquee, donning the iconic white mask and long stem rose, washed away the stress and stench of tourism. A shiver of thrill mixed with the memory of my strange mirror fantasy trickled in, and kick started my adrenaline. I reached into my pocket for my phone and froze. "Oh shit."

"What?" Sarah asked. "Don't tell me you forgot your phone?"

"Aren't the tickets on the phone?" Mama asked.

The little Smith & Wesson pocket knife I always carried was still in my pocket. It wouldn't normally be an issue, but concealed weapons scanners stood outside the doorway, and I didn't want to have to go back to the hotel. I'd die if I missed this.

"Uh. Nothing. Everything's good." I took a deep breath and exhaled before turning back to the line. My heart palpitated, threatening to burst from my chest as I tried not to shit myself.

Please. Please. Please. Don't see me. . .

"Have a good time," the security guard said as he ushered me towards the door.

Ignoring that part of me that was suspicious as to how I made it through the scanner, relief rolled off my shoulders and the urge to shit subsided. "Come on!" I said, waving down my companions.

With five minutes to spare, we stepped into the soft glow of the lobby. Unfortunately, there wasn't any time to appreciate the beautiful details throughout the place as we hurried up to our overpriced balcony seats.

However, the red curtains trimmed in gold, the bronze angels that framed the stage, and the setup for the opening scene were worth the rush.

Was this the magic that I was looking for? The magic of the stage? Something to help me find the courage to try again?

"This is the most beautiful place," Mama said and squeezed my hand just in time to watch the lights dim.

"Yeah. It is." *I wish I didn't have to go back home.*

***

"Ladies and gentlemen, we will take a twenty-minute intermission and will return to the music of the night, shortly," the intercom announcement said as the curtain fell.

Every detail was exactly as I hoped it'd be. I wanted to be there. Be the girl with the voice of an angel that the unhinged Phantom desired and the whiny Vicomte swooned over. It was too bad my bladder had other ideas. "Oh God, I have to pee so bad," I said, getting to my feet.

"The Phantom is so sexy and so manly! His voice!" Mama sang.

Apparently, she was just as entranced as I was. Made sense. Toxic men followed us everywhere.

Honestly, he'd still probably be a better partner than any I've had.

"The singing is phenomenal!" Sarah said.

"Totally!" I said, as I slid by. "Be right back. Make sure mom doesn't slide off her seat."

"Ew," they said, simultaneously.

Oh, the delight I derived from their discomfort.

After navigating through another crowd of people, eventually I found the back of the line to the restroom. Why was there always a line the length of a football field for the women's restroom?

As I waited with the several other unrelieved ladies, many commented on my outfit. I twisted my fingers in the hem of my skirt as I uncomfortably took their compliments. It wasn't until then, I realized that Mom, Sarah and I were the only ones that had dressed up.

I mean, I was the queen of comfort, but it's Broadway. Even more so, it's Phantom. To dress up was in the name. Why was everyone wearing jeans and t-shirts?

"Finally!" I shrieked, when it was my turn.

My shorts had just hit my knees when the overture blared from the speaker above, nearly knocking me off the seat with its five-minute warning.

Chapter I

I was suddenly a horse in the final stretch of the Kentucky Derby. I'd never cleaned up so fast in my life. "Excuse me," I said, weaving through the still very long line of women at the doorway.

Whoa...

Like ocean waves against a boulder, dizziness crashed into me the second I stepped through the threshold into the hallway.

"Holy fuck." *Please don't vomit,* I begged myself. My brain spun on a tilt-a-whirl at full speed while the rest of me turned into marble.

The lights dimmed, and with no relief in sight, I forced myself onward, determined not to miss anything. Groans and comments from the owners of the feet I tripped over in the aisle fell on uncaring ears before I finally crashed into my seat.

"Do you have anything for a headache?" I asked, leaning into Mom.

The applause was on the highest setting as the music started up. There might as well have been a drum line of kindergartners in my head. My vision blurred and my head pounded worse the more I concentrated on the stage and the odd music playing. "Mama, please? Anything?" I asked, grabbing her arm. I recoiled when I found a confused man staring back at me. "Oh. I'm sorry."

The dizzy wave hit me again, and I squeezed my face, taking a few deep breaths before turning to my sister. In her place was a woman surrounded by a sea of similarly disgusted faces in nice suits and gowns. A huge change from all the jeans and t-shirts.

I snapped back to the stage, which was clearer now. The air in the room was gone and my chest caved into my stomach when I noticed the bronze angels were gone, and the theater was much larger. I staggered to my feet, and made my way back down the aisle, tripping over dress hems and polished shoes once again.

"*Madame, restez à votre place,*" the usher said as I pushed past him.

I clung onto the railings in the hallway, trying not to fall as blurred faces stepped away, probably thinking I had gone rabid.

The hallway finally opened up into an enormous foyer, where I stared down a grand staircase lined with tall statues and candles as far as the eye could see. At the bottom were large wooden doors to what I hoped was the outside.

Screams and the sounds of a million glasses shattering erupted in the distance behind me urging me onward, but with every step my reprieve seemed further away.

The thick night air slapped me as I burst through the heavy wooden door, and everything I had ingested within the last year tore my throat as it came back up. My head pulsed and tensed as people bumped into me trying to get past as they exited the building, taking me farther away from it.

I looked up into the sky, trying to catch my breath, and to my surprise, no more swirling or blurred vision. The stars twinkled and stayed put as they should.

"*Hors du chemin!*" a man's voice called out.

Wide eyed, I jumped back just as a horse-drawn buggy raced past, barely missing me.

"What the shit is this?"

Chapter II
Melody

What looked like gas-powered lamps illuminated cobblestone streets. Clacking hooves and creaking carriage wheels turned my stomach again. People in Victorian clothing glared, as if I were some sort of pus leaking leper.

I turned back to where I had just emerged from. Enormous golden angels stared down from the white building that looked like it belonged in another time. The very building I had told my mom and Sarah about earlier in the night.

It can't be. The Palais Garnier…

Like a punishment, the dizziness returned. My hands flew to my stomach and my knees locked to keep me upright.

Before I knew it, my Michael Kors heels had me moving along the sidewalk absentmindedly. Maybe if I walked long enough, I'd wake from this absolutely fucking nightmare.

It could be just a different part of NYC? Like, Central Park has horse-drawn carriages, right? But the lack of trees and tall buildings told me otherwise. Was I drugged? Was this a hallucination and I was just out walking the streets of New York but… No. That'd be one hell of a hallucination. And I hadn't ingested anything.

Was I dying?

Confusion leaked down my face as my feet carried me. Nothing was familiar nor were there any signs of rational thoughts in sight.

"*Hey, jolie dame,*" a man's voice called from a distance. Jumping onto the sidewalk, a man with a skinny mustache and another with curly red hair bee-lined for me with smiles on their faces.

Something in those smiles set off alarm bells. I turned on my heels, trying not to break an ankle, and started back the way I came.

They caught up quickly, grabbing at me like I was a toy. "*Hey, jolie dame,*" the one with the mustache said again.

"*Pourquoi es-tu seule, ma fille?*" the other asked.

"Get off me!" I pushed against them, breaking free.

They laughed and grabbed at me again. Red was unfazed by my nails in his flesh as his hand slid up the opening in my skirt. Skinny Mustache ran his tongue over a toothy grin as he watched in delight.

My elbow met the sternum of the man holding me against my will, and yelled more gibberish before letting me loose.

Whack!

Skinny mustache rushed to his friend, shouting at the police officer who'd hit him with a club. They yelled back and forth for a moment, as the baton bounced in the cop's palm.

The two roaches flipped him off and scurried away as if someone had switched on the lights.

I had never been so happy to see a cop. But nowhere near relieved.

The officer grabbed my arm. Curious dark eyes raked over me, like all the faces since I had stepped out of the restroom. "*Vous allez bien, mademoiselle?*"

I shook in his grip even with the sincere smile resting on his boyish face. He tipped his hat and gestured down the road, "*Ça ira bien. Par ici.*"

With lack of a better option, I nodded and walked along with him.

My mind hurt as it tried to make sense of everything. What was I going to do once we got to the station? I'm sure they totally had a phone that would call the 21st century. *Wait, was I actually in another century?*

I hissed as the back of my head met something solid.

Ripped from the chaos in my mind and into the dark alley, I was unaware we'd turned down, the man who had helped me had forced me

Chapter II

against a wall. His mouth mashed to mine and his hands mauled at my hip, trying to get under my skirt as I clawed at him. His rank tongue tried to slide between my closed lips as I pushed against him, hit him, tried to wriggle away, but it just seemed to egg him on.

He threw me to the ground, knocking the wind from my lungs. I coughed, inhaling some of the dry dirt from the plume caused by the fall. I shouted for help, but even without gasping for air, I wasn't very loud. I might as well have been invisible—like every day of my life.

The buttons of his uniform snagged on my dress as he ascended my body and forced my legs apart with his. He was heavier than he looked. I was paralyzed beneath him as he pinned my hands down. In the dark, his wild face contorted like a demon breaking free of the human flesh it had stolen. A face my mother had seen so many times before.

The rattling of a belt being undone was the last thing I heard before darkened eyes that had instilled fear, widened in surprise.

His hand flew to the one I had pressed against his throat. Liquid splattered onto my face as he coughed. Then, like a broken dam, his life pumped out between his fingers as I pulled my stubby knife from him.

I thought I was going to drown with how much hit me.

His bloody hand fumbled at a whistle hanging around his neck as he stumbled away. The gurgling it made stilled my soul until the whistle fell silent and empty eyes stared from across the alley.

What did I do?

I loved horror movies. I never wanted to live in one.

Shouting from men in the distance started, followed by shadows dancing within a glow of bouncing light against the walls.

With no time to think about what had just happened, I cut the straps to my once beautiful shoes, and staggered to my bare feet. Before I was fully upright, I was already moving away from the voices.

I hadn't seen the inside of a gym since before the Covid lockdown, even then, in my best athletic shape, I'd never had the lungs for long distance. They already burned and my chest ached as I ran. Every breath was like someone had a hold on my throat while running razors along it.

But if I stopped…

The thought of getting caught by a gang of angry men was enough to keep me going until I blacked out, at least.

My heart pounded like an alien trying to burst out through my chest. I don't know how many alleys I'd run down, or corners I'd turned. Everything looked the same and unfamiliar all at once.

Blurry vision and tired legs that tried so hard to keep me moving, weakened with every step.

I turned what had to be my last corner and nearly collapsed into the darkness of a doorway. My body shook so violently that I almost couldn't muffle the wheezing, while the other hand frantically grasped the doorknob.

It was unlocked!

I slipped in, and shut it quietly, as I peered through the window in the door. No sign of them, but their voices were growing loud again. I rushed to the door at the other end of the entryway, only to find luck hadn't struck twice.

"SHIT!"

I pushed against it, trying to force it open. Nothing happened.

My tired eyes fell to an iron gate in the floor next to it. Moonlight reached just far enough to show a bit of stairway beneath the bars.

Shadows ran across the surrounding walls again. *They were here.*

I lifted the heavy gate with haste and squeezed underneath.

As I backed down the stairs, I watched for them to come, dreading when they'd bust through the door.

The pads of my aching feet hit the hard packed ground at the bottom of the stairs. Black tunnels stretched in every direction. If this was the catacombs beneath the city, I was fucked, no matter which way I chose. Still a better option than what waited for me above.

Abruptly, a firm, gloved hand covered my mouth, and another wrapped around my waist, cutting off my thoughts. Then faster than humanly possible, I was flipped around and snatched again. With my arms pinned at my sides and drained of any strength, I was powerless to fight back. I was done.

Light glinted in what I assumed were eyes staring down at me. "*Que fais-tu ici, petite souris?*" the man in the shadows growled in a low tone.

The door above crashed into the wall, stealing his attention. Shouts and stomping from boots echoed through the cold, stale air. A silent cry escaped my lips. My heart seized and my eyelids slammed shut.

Chapter II

The people I loved. The life I wouldn't have. Everything I did and didn't do ran through my mind in a flash.

This was it. *This* was the end.

The man's grip tightened and, like I weighed nothing, my feet lifted and barely grazed the dirt as he moved us around the corner.

His grip loosened for a split second, and I took the opportunity. I only got one step away before he was wrapped around me again, pulling us into the wall. Cold dragged across my back as we crammed farther inside, until the light around us was gone.

Voices bounced off the walls, making it impossible to pinpoint how close they were. I shook and wiggled, trying to break away again. Like a snake, his grip only constricted more with every movement. "*Non*," he whispered with warning. The hand on my mouth lifted and a single finger pressed against my lips. "Shh."

It was apparent my attempts to break free were pointless. He wasn't letting up. I gripped the lapels of his jacket and buried my face as far within as possible. My temple strained against his collarbone as I tried to crawl inside him and hide.

A calm heartbeat met my face through a barely rising chest. Was he not worried about being found? Or that I might have just killed us both?

In an attempt to calm myself, I inhaled deeply. A familiar scent emanated from him. Damp, cold–wrapped in a sulfur blanket, laced in cedar, maybe? Like a campfire in the forest after a rainfall.

If this was it, I was going to be thinking of something that made me happy.

I fell into memories of camping as a child. Sarah was a brat, as always. Mama was so young and full of life, before all the bad. She'd wrap us up in a blanket so we didn't freeze as we sat under the tarp watching the fire dance and the rain fall.

I focused so hard on that memory; I almost didn't notice the officer walking past us.

Almost.

My temporary savior's cheek pressed to the top of my head as I tried to step further into the dark. His grip was unwavering as the hand at my nape moved in a small gentle motion. Somewhat soothing, but not enough.

The cop's feet drug against the dirt and flickering light from the torch brightened through my closed eyes, pulling me from the safety of the memory.

The glow crept up the arm of the man that held me. My nails dug through the layers of fabric into the palms of my hands, causing a pain to concentrate on. We had nowhere left to go.

"*Quelqu'un l'a vue!*" someone yelled in the distance.

Oh god, they found us!

The glow lingered for a few moments longer and the pulsing in my ears grew louder with the thumping in my heart.

Then the light vanished, followed by a herd of footsteps.

When the door slammed shut, I jolted against the stranger, and we were left in silence.

I don't know how long we stayed there — too scared to move.

The thought of what this man had done or could still do filled me with a deep sense of dread, but the thought of leaving too soon was even more petrifying. They could be outside the door. Waiting.

Ease and panic shot through me when he adjusted his grip.

Still holding my knife, I let go of his lapels and ripped myself away. I backed out through the opening where he hid us, trembling as I pointed my blade at him.

We weren't far from the place where he had grabbed me. The fact they didn't find us was a miracle.

I watched him like a hawk as I backed towards the stairs that led to the gate. It was like being stalked by Michael Myers. No sound. Only a shape, a shadow in the dark, inching towards me, seemingly getting closer, though I was moving faster.

Moonlight reflected off his black shoes and matching slacks as he stepped into it.

"Stop!" I commanded.

At his side, fidgeting, gloved fingers raised slowly. "You're hurt." His voice was warm, almost worried.

A stabbing pain demanded my attention to the dirt-crusted blood that covered my foot. I lifted it to find a shard of broken glass wedged into my skin. I winced as I touched it, then yanked out the shard and tossed it. The relief only lasted for a moment and then an unfamiliar

Chapter II

pain emerged and threatened to double me over.

"No! Don't!" I shouted, noticing he had inched closer again.

I had already made the mistake of trusting someone that sounded safe. That was supposed to be safe. How could I give that to a man hiding in the dark?

The light halted at his chest, revealing a white dress shirt that was covered in the same color of death as my hands.

Was I afraid of him? He's the one who should be afraid. I had killed someone. It was all over me. And now him.

"I just wanna go home," I cried, taking another step upwards.

The gate slammed closed behind me, and I rushed past the bloody footprints to the door. I had literally left a map to where I was.

With no cop in sight. No one, actually, I twisted the knob and opened the door, ready to run into the night.

Don't turn around.

Against my better judgment, I did.

At the bottom of the stairs stood my temporary savior. My "Basement Angel". But for how long, though?

His fingers moved curiously at his side again. Like they were fighting to reach out or controlling another urge of some kind.

It didn't matter what it was. I wasn't sticking around to find out.

Run, run little mouse. Before this monster changes its mind.

The door latched as she left me, startling me in a way it shouldn't have. She had slipped into the night and left this creature with his thoughts. Where I should have been celebrating the fall of *le Garnier's* grand chandelier as the vermin scurried below, I was left empty, staring at the space the little mouse had occupied only moments ago.

What hid beneath that silver and black mask? No horror worse than my own?

The urge to grab her again, take her below to my world of night, gnawed at me like a starving dog on a fleshless bone. It would have been so easy to subdue the scared little thing. If she had waited any longer to reach the top, that may have been her fate. Yet, I'd been stilled in my actions. Turned me from all things planned. *Interesting*.

The affection I have for my pupil, my rising star, the one who would take the world, and in time, know me and love me as I do her. Yes, my love for Christine must have stopped me, no doubt.

'Is that so?' the *Ghost* that dwells within my mind taunted.

A draft from the tunnels scraped over this body, threatening to erase the moment which passed too quickly. My lungs had forgotten their purpose, and pathetically, my hands rushed to my chest. For the first time, my heart pulsated between them, attempting to jolt them to life.

Never in this treacherous existence have I held another. *Alive*. The warmth where she laid her head lingered, yet also threatened to fade in the cool air with every passing moment. Hands, with which I laid a finger upon her lips, boiled within the tailored leather they're wrapped, trying to preserve the memory a bit longer.

How would her hair have felt entwined in these fingers had they been bare?

The sole of my shoe touched down onto the ground step of the stairway. The other followed behind and planted on the one above it.

Though frightened as she was, part of this creature wondered if she would have come willingly. Her final glance was certainly debating whether to depart from the man who saved her. *Saved*.

I took another step, looking upon hands that have taken many men from this world.

'You lie to yourself, Erique. She only ensured that you were far from her. You may have done worse had the Gendarmerie not come. Remember, there's only one that will bring you what you want. Without Christine, we are lost.'

My jaw clenched as I fought to bare teeth at the voice that's always haunted me with the truth I never desired to see.

However, on this night, these same hands that take life chose to protect, and in return, received rewards beyond what dreams could grant.

'This girl's of no significance. Leave thoughts of her behind in this place and go where you are meant to be. Christine's our hope and only a short time away. Waiting for you while her grandmother sleeps. Waiting for her teacher. Her Angel.'

She would be in wait. To please me with her voice as our lessons

Chapter II

resumed. To listen as I told her of the accident that fell upon the stage tonight. And how her father in heaven missed her.

Unredeemable, not only were my hands.

'Erique. Go to Christine.'

My fingers wrapped around the iron bars of the gate.

'You will regret this detour if you continue,' the *Ghost* warned.

"It is only to repay a debt in which I do not wish the weight of."

'Liar.'

Chapter III
Melody

At least "toilet" was basically the same in most languages. In my best mouse impression, I rushed towards the toilettes sign at the back of the nearly empty pub. The bartender and a few men that were huddled around the bar were too immersed in whatever story to notice the embodiment of distress running past.

To my relief, the restroom was unoccupied, and the door had a deadbolt.

It wasn't the freshest bathroom, but it was private and, for the moment, somewhere that I could clean up and think.

Even though my foot was still furious from the abuse it had endured during the night, I lunged at the sink.

The water pressure was low and the water freezing, but I was thankful for the indoor plumbing. The cold water stung my hands as the red stains swirled down the drain. I got my foot into the basin, ignoring the blaring bruise on my hip as it stretched. My teeth gnashed together through the pain as the water bit at the wound I hoped wasn't infected already.

Every pass of soap erased a little more evidence of the night's terror.

Chapter III

Visibly, at least. Until I looked in the mirror and saw the evidence across my face.

I thought maybe for a moment, it was all a dream.

The sight of my homemade mask and perfect wings seemed so silly now. What hadn't rubbed off on the Basement Angel's shirt, dried into the cracks of the custom design. Red splotches stained where my mask didn't cover. I looked like the final girl in every horror movie you'd ever seen.

I ripped the mask off and dove into my hands, scrubbing until my skin hurt and the water ran clear.

No more perfect wings.

No stupid romanticized theater night.

No more Mom and Sarah.

But no matter how many times my hands passed over my face or through my hair, it wouldn't wash away the monster's eyes that stared into mine until life left them.

You couldn't wash that kind of memory away.

"It was self-defense," I whispered, over and over. Even though it was true, it didn't make it any easier to digest.

The spiraling thoughts were catching up again. I stumbled back against the wall and slid to the floor. "What's happening? Where am I?"

My arms crossed my midsection, and I rocked back and forth wishing for home. But of course, when I opened my eyes, I was still fucking there, in that bathroom, crying on the floor.

A partially crumbled newspaper laid at my feet, obviously meant for the trash. I wiped the fear from my face and reached for it.

The moment I unraveled it, my throat closed. What I hoped wouldn't be confirmed, stared back at me.

17th Janvier 1880.

"January 17th 1880."

Frantically, I pulled the trash bin down, not caring what else had been tossed inside. Papers and alike rolled onto the ground. I grabbed the first one I saw and unfolded it. *14th Janvier 1880.*

"No... No... No. No. No."

One after the other, a similar date was printed.

The room spun and I couldn't keep up with it. How could I be where these papers said I was?

In the same moment, the doorknob twisted and rattled. "*Sors de là maintenant!*" A man yelled through the door as he continued his attempts to get inside.

My body leapt with every heavy knock. Further into the wall, I tried to melt. *Just a few more minutes, please.*

The pounding on the door doubled when another voice joined in the shouting. I knew I couldn't stay in this room forever, especially with my fucking foot bleeding out like the end of a *SAW* movie.

My knees came up as far as they could go. I closed my eyes and covered my ears. Trying to focus on anything but this.

The faint smell of the Basement Angel still lingered. I concentrated harder, trying to hold the memory of false safety. Even trying to fall back into the camping memory it brought on. Nothing worked.

The possibility of this ending badly was very high, and I was here wishing I had never left a stranger's arms on the off chance he wasn't an awful person like everyone else seemed to be.

I'm fucking manic.

Then the pounding halted. The sudden silence left me even more uneasy as I sat and listened for signs of life.

Cautiously, I uncoiled my body and reluctantly pulled myself from the floor. Every bit of me trembled as I walked to the door.

Had they given up? Or had they gone to get some help?

The pulsing in my ears grew louder when I pressed it against the wood. I waited for something to tell me that someone was right outside, or that they were still nearby.

Nothing.

The stinging in my foot begged for relief again, and the voice in my head told me how stupid I was for wanting to leave the safety of the restroom.

It felt like a trap. A too-good-to-be-true moment. I unlatched the door anyway. I couldn't stay.

The creaking from the hinges might as well have been a tornado siren, alerting everyone I was coming out. But I was greeted by an empty space.

I had almost wished there was someone waiting. It was eerie.

Chapter III

I stuck my head out just enough to scan the room and found it empty. Even the bartender was gone.

There was a man at the far end of the bar, but he didn't seem focused on me, and kept his head beneath the brim of a hat.

I took the bit of luck presented to me and slipped out through a backdoor not too far from where I was.

***

The eyes of every passerby burned with disgust for me. I suppose I did look strange. Bare-footed and dressed sort of like a lady of the night for their time. Which my brain still couldn't wrap around.

Their time.

1880… Paris. 1880…

That at least explained the gibberish. It was French.

How was this even possible? Was it even real? It sure as shit felt real.

My mind was an unrelenting whirlwind of thoughts. What should I do? Where do I go? I wouldn't even fathom trying for a hotel. With no means to pay for it, they'd run me away.

My bottom lip quivered from the cold and the attempt to hold back the dam of emotions as I stared at a row of garbage bins in an alley.

The smell was awful, more potent than the city overall. But the exhaustion was worse than any smell. I sort of wished I remembered the way back to the place underground. At least no one would find me there.

Well, almost no one.

Nearly collapsing, I hit the ground too tired to even care that I was sleeping behind trash cans. My arms wrapped around myself, and my legs curled up. I sobbed as silently as I could while I clamped my eyes shut.

Everything played on a loop. From the beautiful night with my family, to killing the cop, and being "saved" by the man below the city.

I worried for Mom and Sarah. Especially Mom. What did they think happened to me? Did they even know? Or did something happen to them, too?

Finally, the weight of the Sandman's blanket began to take effect. Any thoughts softened and fell away, and I sank further into the ground as the surrounding cold didn't feel so bad anymore.

"*Ça va, ma chérie?*" a woman's voice snuck through.

My eyes snapped open, and I jerked away from the older woman standing over me.

"*Chérie?*" she asked, stretching her hand out. "*Tu peux venir avec nous.*"

I froze, going back and forth between her and the elderly man she was with.

"*Viens?*" she asked. Gesturing towards herself and her companion.

"No *français,*" I answered. Really hoping that's how you said 'no French'.

Her brows knitted and a pitiful smile crossed her face. "English?"

I nodded, almost like I wasn't even sure.

The man pulled her back and said something as he looked around, like he was afraid someone would see them.

She cut him off and returned her attention to me. "Come," she said. "Stay."

After watching too many crime shows, and being well aware of the historical mistreatment of women, I was naturally hesitant and stayed put. "No money," I said.

The man snapped more things at her I couldn't catch. She shushed him again and reached back out. "*S'il te plaît.* Please."

What were the odds this was a random act of kindness? What other options did I have, though? Maybe not get murdered by an old couple.

I removed my favorite dress up accessory, a fake diamond necklace I only wore a few times, and handed it to her, "*Faux.*"

She looked at the jewelry and nodded. With the same pitiful smile she started with, the woman took my hand and helped me to my feet.

"*Je m'appelle,* Antoinette," she said. Then pointed to the man. "Old Louis."

"Melody," I replied.

"Come, Melody," she said, and led me away.

***

Relief washed over me when we entered the small lobby of *Hôtel des Anges.*

I still wasn't sure this wasn't some trick or something. The idea of there being good people in this place baffled me. Since everyone's been pretty awful.

Mostly everyone.

Chapter III

The couple left me standing on a rug in the middle of the lobby. My foot was finally numb. Which I was sure wasn't actually a good sign. But a relief, nonetheless.

Louis sat down in a nearby chair. The light from the simple hanging fixture bounced off the skin of his head as he hunched over and reached for a paper on the table.

The place was small, but nice. A little worn down from the years, maybe a little outdated too, but well kept.

Then again, I guess I couldn't be sure what was outdated here.

"*Sept nuits*," Antoinette said, holding up seven fingers and a room key.

"Seven nights?" I asked, feeling a spark of hope. Something in her wrinkled smile reassured me I was safe for now. Hopefully, I wouldn't need that much time.

After signing the ledger, Antoinette led me up the stairway. My guard still hadn't dropped, but I was so tired, and it was slipping.

At least the bathroom was cleaner than the one I had washed up in earlier. She sat me on a bench near a small metal bathtub, which didn't look like it got much use.

She knelt down with a fresh pot of water she had filled in the sink and lifted my foot into it.

"It's ok. I can do that," I said, trying to stop her.

Antoinette pushed my hands away, saying something I for sure didn't understand, and continued cleaning the area around the gash.

The water was chilly like before, but the pain felt different. Almost good.

We didn't try talking while she tended my wound. Which was good, since my mind fazed in and out, replaying every moment since I had stepped out of that stupid bathroom and into this place. And kept going back to the man below.

Why did he sound concerned? And in English? I had to be remembering that part wrong.

It was probably best that I couldn't tell anyone about my situation anyway. They wouldn't believe me. And who wanted to be thrown into an asylum in the 1800s? Or any year.

Whatever it was, I was in France. In the past? Like a rift in time?

An alternate universe? A hallucination given to me by the aliens who abducted me?

To be honest, that last one probably made the most sense.

In any case, I was somewhere I didn't belong.

Pain zapped through my foot, ripping me from the rabbit hole my imagination was taking me down.

Freshly bandaged and cleaned up, I was shown my tiny room. A twin-size bed, loveseat and table with a chair. Simple. Everything anyone could want and more. I don't think I've ever felt so thankful in my life and still so scared.

"*Thank you*," I said. At least I knew that much French.

Her eyes were sad as she stared. Like she knew everything already. Honestly, I probably still had it written all over my face.

"*Bed*"*à demain*," she said. "Tomorrow."

I locked the door behind her and limped to the bed. It wasn't the most comfortable mattress, but anything was better than the cold ground behind trash cans in an alley.

The moon glowed through the window near the bed. It had to be late. The streets were bare, at least from where I could see, and it was a clear, beautiful, quiet night.

I hated the quiet.

At any point in my day, there was always some sort of noise. Music. Movies. Talking. A small escape from my reality. I needed some of that now. Anything to dull my mind for a moment.

Memory smacked me when I realized I still had my phone, and intact to my surprise!

As it powered up, the message alerts sounded. I ignored them and opened my phone book without hesitation.

The signal bars were an "x". It was futile, but I called Sarah anyway, because Mom never answered the phone.

Incomplete call.

I tried again… a few more times before I was finally defeated and thumbed over to the unread messages from Sarah.

Chapter III

> **Where are you? Get me a soda if you're getting snacks.**

> **Dude, Mom won't stop talking about how manly the Phantom is. Hurry.**

I couldn't help but chuckle at Sarah's texts. Poor girl had to deal with Mom now.

There was another from my friend back home, that had me wishing I could actually laugh.

> **How's New York? You're seeing Phantom tonight, right?? Let me know how it is. And keep your whore hands to yourself. Or not.**

Knowing it wouldn't actually reach him, I texted him back anyway just to torture myself.

> **10/10 wouldn't recommend getting thrown back in time, if you can help it. It's scary as fuck.**

In a last stitch of effort to find something to ease the situation, I opened the YouTube Music app and scrolled through my downloaded favorites filled with artists like Pink. Cher. Nickelback. Blink 182. Reba McEntire. Etc.

My current repeat was *Waiting For The Night* cover by GHOST. But not even that sounded good.

Moonlight Sonata by Beethoven was always my go to when I needed peace. And if ever there was a time, this was it.

I stared out the window, trying to get lost in the stars above as the tension slowly disappeared. Wishing on them like I did when I was a little girl. I never believed in magic or whatever, but if I was really where I was, then maybe wishing on a star could reverse it? *Stupid.*

Tomorrow, I'd have to figure out how to get home. Where would I even start? Could I even get home? Should I find work until then? A place to stay?

Sarah wasn't going to be able to handle Mom for long.

The tension in my shoulders returned and my lids closed as the migraine clawed its way in.

A few hours ago I was having the time of my life for the first time in a long time, and then it turned into a literal nightmare. And I was alone.

For some reason, the man from the catacombs entered my mind again. I wondered what he thought about our encounter? It must have been so terrifying for him too. Then again, he was the one hiding. I can't imagine he was down there for anything good. Hell, he could have been some Jack the Ripper type, *Jacque ze Ripper* 'cause we're in France, and was hiding bodies or something. The blood on his shirt might not have even been from me.

Ugh. I didn't want to think about any of it anymore. I made light of it all, but the truth is, I was petrified.

When I said I needed some magic in my life, this was not what I meant.

Chapter IV
Melody

Waking up to find that this wasn't a dream is some bullshit.

I spent the better part of my morning crying into my pillow until I couldn't anymore. Knowing my bandage needed changing and my bladder needed relieving was the only reason I even got out of bed.

What a relief it was not to be using chamber pots or something. I limped into the hallway from the bathroom to find a plate of food sitting on top of a box next to my door.

My stomach growled as I stared at the plate of flakey bread with some sort of jam and chunks of meat. I knew I should eat, but the thought of food made me nauseous again.

I picked up the gifts and took them back to bed, not trying to upset the couple that took me in.

Even though the food was cold, it was delicious. But after not eating for a day, anything probably would have hit the spot.

While I forced down the meal, I eyed the dark brown box that came along with it.

Eventually, curiosity got the best of me. I gripped the lid and pulled it off to find a pair of gently worn women's laced-up brown shoes.

They were ugly, to be honest, and I couldn't wait to wear them.

I put them back in the box and pulled my phone out. I wanted to tell my sister all about this.

Still no signal or messages. *Wishful thinking.*

God, they must be going out of their minds. My freakin' mother's already a mess. Something like this could just speed that up.

I needed to get the fuck home. Wishing for something and it actually happening were two very different things. I already felt shitty enough as it was for just thinking.

How would I deal with the possibility of never going home? What would I do?

Even if Antoinette and Louis let me stay…

Stay.

I was a lost child. What a terrible feeling. When you understood nothing and hoped that someone else had all the answers.

I couldn't force myself to eat anymore, and grabbed the blanket to burrito up again. It was a short-lived comfort when a knock at the door startled me upright.

Still wearing the bedding, I opened the door to a very kind smile on the other side. "*Hello,* Melody," Antoinette said.

"*Hello.*"

Antoinette eyed the half-eaten plate, then the blanket I wore. Contorting her mouth like she was in deep thought, she walked past me into the room and picked up the shoe box.

"They are good?" she asked.

"Oh! Yes, *thank you.* Thank you so much," I said, realizing I hadn't even thought to thank her yet.

"*Merveilleux.*" Taking my hand and dragging me to the bed, Antoinette's manner turned giddy. *"Mettez-les! Et c'est parti!"* she said as I plopped down on the very springy bed.

"What's happening?" I asked as she pulled the shoes from the box and undid the laces on one. "I get it, ok."

It only took a few minutes to get both on. Luckily, they were a bit big, which never happened. My feet were wide and shoes hated them. However, it surprised me they fit at all with the added volume of the bandage.

Chapter IV

"We will go now," she said and jumped to her feet. She grabbed my jacket from the coat hanger and gave it a curious once over before handing it to me. "It is a good day."

***

Every step down to the lobby was agony. Not just because of the pain in my foot, but the dread that came with eventually trying to leave without having done anything in return for their kindness.

Antoinette had slipped behind the front desk, looking for something. Louis was still in the same spot as I had left him the night before.

"Antoinette," I hesitated. The rollercoaster in my stomach hit every corkscrew as I got closer to the desk. "I need to get to the *Palais Garnier*. Can you help me?

The small bag she held fell from her hand to the countertop. She shot Louis a shocked glare. His eyes cut to me, then averted quickly, grumbling something under his breath. To which Antoinette quickly replied, "*Sh! Il a fait du bien pour une fois.*"

Shaking her head, she came around the counter and took my hands. "No, no. You do not need," she answered. "Stay here. Help. Stay safe."

Her reaction was a little surprising. We'd only known each other a few hours, but she seemed to care so much already about my well being. That's something I couldn't remember feeling for a long time.

"Right. But I need to go there," I replied, a twinge of guilt in my tone as I picked at my thumb.

"*Je sais que tu ne comprends pas, mais tu ne peux pas y aller. Il est là.*"

Whatever she said was behind a worried smile. However, before I could really attempt to ask again, Antoinette had her arm laced in mine, and was dragging me out the door.

"*Goodbye, my love*," she called back to Louis in French I actually understood. *Thank you, TV.*

And we were gone.

***

It smelled as bad as Times Square. Maybe even worse than last night. Everything looked so different in the day. Vendors back-to-back on the streets, trying to peddle whatever goods they had. Carriages galore. People everywhere.

It was also easier to notice the curious looks I tried to avoid before. I was still wearing my jacket, which I kept zipped up, and my dress which, was still pretty revealing when it came to my legs.

I must have looked like something out of a science fiction novel to them. An alien. I felt like one.

The only person who didn't seem bothered by my appearance spent the whole time talking, and I was grateful for it. Even if she wouldn't help me get to the opera house.

Most of what Antoinette was saying was in French, but that was alright. I enjoyed seeing her face light up. It wasn't until she pointed to a church and said "me and Louis" did I realize she was sharing memories with me. Probably ones she hadn't been able to talk about in a long time.

I regret taking Spanish instead of French in high school. Which I didn't speak either, by the way.

Whiplash was the name of the game on this day. Without warning, Antoinette pulled me into a small boutique packed to the brim with all kinds of dresses, hats, suits and really nice shoes.

The lady at the counter greeted us. But not before raking her eyes over me like I was Quasimodo or something.

Antoinette chatted with her for a bit until someone shoved me into a fitting area off to the side. The clerk removed my jacket and took my measurements.

I avoided the four large mirrors. It was clear the woman I was the night before was gone, and I was back to "broken" me.

"I can't pay," I said, trying to stop the woman. "Antoinette."

Antoinette ran her hand through my hair, then pinched my cheek gently. "*One minute.*"

The two women left me standing there as they thumbed through crowded racks of garments.

Being in a store full of strange and beautiful dresses was something I never really thought I'd do. Though I do have the "hourglass" figure from the front. The side is all gut and butt. So, things fit differently, and I avoided it. Jeans and hoodies every time for the win.

I missed my jeans.

The women returned rather quickly with about twenty dresses. Each a different color, cut, and style.

Three layers of weird underwear and one corset later, it was time to

Chapter IV

try on the dresses.

I admit, the corset wasn't as bad as I thought it'd be. I had worn them for costumes before, but was relieved when they didn't crush me in it.

Their reactions to my tattoos were kind of funny. They immediately removed two short-sleeved dresses from the pile.

When it came to the dresses, I nixed about seven more of them just because of the collar. I hated anything touching my neck. It's like being choked constantly, even if it's loose.

One after another, I slipped in and out of various garments. Some were gorgeous. Some were so hideous.

At one point, I thought I was kind of having fun. Until I saw myself and remembered where I wasn't... Home.

No matter what style they put on me, I was still an alien trying to fit in, and it showed. But I just needed to look the part to get into the opera house.

"What?" I asked.

It was clear something was off. Their faces twisted up in thought after the seventh dress.

"Ah!" the clerk said and scurried away.

Antoinette winked at me, and I began to worry.

The clerk came back with an excited grin on her face, holding out a long, curly styled light brown wig. A bit darker than my current color. The overall look was subtle and nice, though.

I half expected the five story high ones you saw in the movies.

Their application was a little rough, but eventually we got it attached properly.

"Yes!" they shouted.

It reminded me of how excited Mom got last night. I wished she were with me. Something I didn't think I'd say, at least recently anyway.

The stupid hair changed my entire look. And I hated that I liked it. I was a beautiful, proper woman in this fake hair and gorgeous blue dress with black trim.

I'm always beautiful when I'm someone else.

"*Beautiful! Beautiful!*" Antoinette yelled, clapping.

I guess this was the new me.

To appease my kind new friend, I smiled and curtsied. Now I'd be able to get through town safely. In theory.

I left with a matching blue hat and a few "work" dresses that I insisted weren't necessary, as well as a lot of extra underwear.

The looks I received were noticeably different from my arrival. Men tipped their hats and women smiled. No one tried to distance themselves.

Great. Fit right in.

***

Lunch was delicious. No wonder all the famous chefs were European. Eating in the corset wasn't that bad. Took a little getting used to, sitting up straighter than usual, but that's alright. At least I could breathe.

During our meal, Antoinette hinted over to a man sitting nearby who'd been eying us since he sat down. There was no mistaking her thoughts. I knew that look.

"Husband," she said.

Relationships of any kind weren't even on my radar. In fact, the radar was left at home, where it belonged. In any case, I couldn't even remember the last time I enjoyed myself with a man.

I mean, maybe if I was stuck here and one day I got lonely enough…

NO! Jesus, no.

The man smiled and nodded. I averted my eyes back to my seared chicken and tomato rice stuff, and shoveled it in.

I felt like a teenager and my parent was delighting in the embarrassment it brought me.

Our last stop for the day was a candy shop. Tasty chocolates and hard candies. We munched on them on the way back towards the hotel. I wanted to enjoy this moment because I had a feeling it wouldn't be like this later.

And I was right.

My body trembled and stiffened when a random cop rounded the corner we were walking towards. Every little hair stood on end. I hadn't felt this fear since I woke up. Today almost had me forgetting about my current reality.

Antoinette grabbed my hands and hugged me with a fierceness that crippled the anxiety and panic. He passed us by without a glance. Then she wiped my face dry.

Chapter IV

I hadn't noticed the tears.

"I really need to go to the *Garnier. Please*," I pleaded.

"*Il vous y trouvera si vous y allez. Vous ne voulez pas ça.*" The worry in her tone was real. But this was my only chance.

"*Please.*"

My French must have been so pitiful, because Antoinette sighed and finally nodded in agreement. "Yes. Okay," she said.

Chapter V

Melody

It took all night, but after a little convincing, Antoinette taught me a few verses to get me through the door. Just something to the point like "I need a job," etc.

She gave me some money to get there and back. Part of me felt like she was just worried because of how she found me.

"Work here," she said, pointing to the area around us as we waited for the taxi.

Taxi was said the same in French. Despite slight differences in the way some of the shared words were said, I've managed to pick out a few here and there. *Win.*

I wished I could just tell her it wasn't work I was looking for, but how do you tell someone that you're actually trying to find a magic bathroom that might send you home?

The sun was out, and I should have been enjoying the ride to the opera house. The place I have wanted to go since 8th grade history. But my insides were having a jump off, and the irritation the wig was giving me had my mind elsewhere. It itched like hell.

Cold sweats and chills riddled me worse when the cab came to a stop. There was no way this was going to be easy. What were the chances

Chapter V

I could just walk right in there?

The building was bigger than I remembered. And now that the light shone down on it, every detail was visible. Pegasi and the angels. Busts of famous composers, and so much more.

What I wouldn't give to have done this another way.

There was a man in blue at the door to the building, stopping people from entering. My mind tried to freak me out, get me to turn back around as I hid behind a pillar, just out of sight.

Those acting classes were finally going to come in handy. Except this was live. Me and live performances did not do so well together.

No. No. You got this... There's no audience.

"*Excuse me. Vous ne pouvez pas y entrer,*" he said, stopping me just as I reached the door.

There was a plus to this. Regardless of what I thought of myself, old men loved the fuck outta me. And the doorman fell into that category. Even as I got older, my chubby face still received unwanted attention. I just hoped it worked this time too.

Please. Please. Don't piss yourself.

"Hello *Monsh~*ieur" I stumbled. Fail one. "*Oh! Excuse me.* Um." *Come on. You practiced this...* I cleared my throat. "I... I have an appointment."

"*Avec qui?*" he said, somewhat smugly.

What did he say?

My stage smile stayed locked, and I took a chance. "Managers?"

"*Gestionnaires?*" he asked with suspicion in his tone. "*êtes-vous un interprète?*"

Interprète? Interprète? I knew that word... What was it? Performer!

"*Yes!*" I twirled, then bowed.

He shrugged and opened the door, gesturing inside.

As soon as my foot hit the tile floor and the door closed behind me, the sweet façade dropped.

There were so many people in the large foyer. Some wiping down statues and railings along the staircase. Mostly a bunch of men carrying construction equipment in and out through doors next to it. No one was even going to notice me for how busy it was.

Casually, I sped across the room to the stairway and ascended like a wasp was after me, all while trying to remember which way to go.

There couldn't have been that many restrooms in this place, right? Wrong.

When I reached the top, I wasn't assured. All the doors looked the same and I couldn't remember where the one I came from was.

Shit. Shit. Shit.

The first door I tried opened into a small private box overlooking the theater. That's when I saw it, the source of a million glasses shattering last night. The chandelier *had* fallen.

Shivers rippled through me as I stared at the dismantled fixture.

"*Hé!*" A young man with bright eyes stood in the doorway, holding a broom. More curious than angry. "*Qu'est ce que tu fais ici?*"

"Uh…Uh…" I glanced back and forth between him and the shattered chandelier, "Uh… no *French. Employ?*"

He smirked. "Ah! *Come,*" he said, waving at me to follow behind.

With clenched teeth I nodded and followed him out.

Shit.

As we passed by door after door, I started to think that I wasn't even sure I'd know the bathroom if I saw it.

It could have been any of them. I was so fucked.

We stopped in front of a door off to the side in the giant foyer, where a few male voices bled through from the other side. It sounded like they were arguing.

I could wait for the dude to walk off and then go back down the way we came, but the young man knocked on the door before I could stop him.

He nodded and left me standing there. Within seconds the door swung open and a tall, lanky, curly haired man was eyeing me with the most annoyed expression.

"*Yes?! Que veux-tu?*" If voices could cut, this one would for sure do it. "*Bien?*"

Another man's voice yelled out from behind him. "Fournier, *Qu'est-ce?*"

"*Employ?*" I asked.

Fournier spoke over his shoulder, "It's a cute, plump girl. I think she's looking for work."

"I am looking for work," I retorted, "Sir."

Chapter V

Fournier's face fell.

The other man jumped up with a big, toothy grin. He was much larger, but roughly the same height as Fournier. Probably had the thickest mustache I'd ever seen, too. For sure, would have given Tom Selleck a run for his money.

"It seems the ole boy put his foot in his mouth, as you Americans say. *Hello*, Elias LeBlanc. And this buffoon is my partner, Jean Fournier."

"Melody Reilly," I said.

"Well, Ms. Reilly. What's an American doing in Paris?" LeBlanc asked.

"That's complicated."

"Yes. This is all nice. We need to get back to important things, Elias…" Fournier interjected.

"Ah. Yes," he answered.

"Well, what can you do, girl?" Fournier spit.

"Oh, uh, I'm a pretty decent actor," I said before thinking.

"Can you sing?" he asked.

"I… No. I can paint though! Practically fabricate anything. I saw that you're having some work done downstairs." The two men grimaced at the mention of the repairs. "I worked construction for a time… I, uh, can do whatever's needed."

"You've done men's work?" LeBlanc asked, raising his brows in surprise? Disbelief?

It was unimportant.

"I wouldn't put it that way Monsieur, but yes? Mostly as a fabricator. Costumes, props, etc," I said. "Firefighter at one point. But I think that means something different here."

Fournier pursed his lips, obviously annoyed by the conversation between us. "We have no use for more in the arts department. Can you clean? Cook?"

"If that's what you need." I knew I shouldn't be picky but there were some things that weren't worth it. "I… I would really, really prefer not to do shit rags. Please."

It was easy to see LeBlanc was on my side, probably just to get at Fournier for his attitude. He chuckled and pulled Fournier aside, where they spoke amongst themselves for a few minutes in French so I couldn't understand. Or at least they hoped.

"Do you have no husband or children?" LeBlanc asked.

"No, nothing. Why?"

"Are you in need of lodging? Or must we provide that too?" Fournier snipped.

The hotel was a way away from the opera house. I could make it work if I had to, but the idea of being in the opera house to get home anytime was hard to pass up. And I was sure Antoinette would understand.

"Uh. Is there somewhere nearby that I can afford with what you pay?"

"A few of the service workers stay on site. You may as well," Fournier said matter of fact, "After a salary cut of course."

I was drawing a royal flush in Hell.

"You start tomorrow, move in today if you need," he said, ending the conversation. Probably itching to get back to current issues.

None of it mattered. I didn't plan on being there long, anyway.

"AH! Comte De Chagny!" The men greeted.

I froze mid signature on the contract for employment. *Did they just say De Chagny? As in Raoul?*

Ignoring the pit in my stomach growing, I turned slowly.

My jaw hit the floor, and my heart fell out of my ass. It never occurred to me at any point in time that this could happen.

In the doorway, dressed to the nines, stood a very handsome man with dark eyes and longer, dark hair. He was almost every character Colin Firth ever played. Arrogance radiated from him as he made no attempt to acknowledge me.

Behind him, an equally tall, handsome younger man with shorter light brown hair smiled with a sweet air about him.

The situation I was in was already ludicrous. But this? The stories of the Phantom were fiction... right? There's no way the people were real. I researched it. It was fiction.

Just a coincidence. There's no way Raoul and his older brother Philippe were standing in front of me.

Completely involuntary, I gasped, "Did you say De Chagny?"

Chapter V

It couldn't be you. How pathetic I was, straining to see through the cracks in the floor above, the second her voice brushed my ears. The girl with the crimson-coated face which had hid in my arms, clinging to me as if I were her protector. Was she truly here? In my opera?

And, of course, her lovely name would be Melody.

At great risk to myself, I rushed the ladder just to peer through the concealed hatch next to M. Fournier's desk, where I collected my monthly salary.

Turn back so that I might confirm...

Life vacated my chest at confirmation of the face I had seen in dreams and again in the night.

"Excuse me," she said nervously and whipped around. Her French was like that of a child learning to speak. How it delighted my ears.

"How are you here?" My words fell into the stale darkness that surrounded me. *Hôtel des Anges* was in the perfect district for work, and she was safe with the old woman. Why venture this far?

Rehearsals were to begin for the new production of *Danser Avec Le Diable* and my tolerance had worn thin for the untalented Spaniard and her tantrums. More so, Christine was ready to shine brightly on my stage and awe the world with the voice I'd given her.

On this morning, I was to urge Monsieur's Fournier and LeBlanc to move Christine from understudy to lead at present. But, stumbled upon their conversation regarding last night's events brought a smile to my lips. Such despair at having to repair the most extravagant chandelier.

Enjoyment fell as soon as they mentioned the girl who had been discarded in a room of the salon the same night. Murdered by hands so vile.

These men were keen on sweeping it under the stage with all the other forgotten things. They would have no justice? Pity. I loved a good chase.

Another would take up the case, that was certain. They always did.

"The Opera Ghost had struck again." So, they would believe.

"Miss Reilly, Marcus will take you to your room," M. LeBlanc said, ushering her out.

"Please go," M. Fournier urged in a tone I found myself disliking.

"No problem. Thank you," she said and disappeared behind the men huddled in the doorway.

To keep upright as my heart beat in triple time, I braced myself against the wall at the base of the ladder.

Clenched hands tingled with the memory as I endeavored to recreate the sensation. Failing like every attempt before.

'It matters not that she is here,' the *Ghost* said. *'Do not forget yourself. While you try to recreate a moment of pleasure. Remember, you were the lesser of two evils, Erique. A means to an end.'*

I scorned his voice with its cold reminder. God continued to taunt relentlessly. Furthering this inhumane existence.

'Dismiss her and don't forget our muse.'

Yes. Christine. Who would bring my voice to the world. Give me a name—and more.

Love me.

Yes. Her career must progress. She would love me. The world would love me because she would love me. Only with her grace, she alone has the power to bring me out of this hell.

Shadows above moved without reason as voices intertwined with meaningless chatter. Imbeciles strived to woo over the Peacocks that abruptly entered, forcing her out.

'No. Do not put thought to her.'

Christine's the key. The beautiful, young soprano, Christine. That believed me an angel…

Pushing from the foundation which leant itself to my need, I hurried through the tight space within the walls.

In and out of passages, empty corridors, and stale rooms, I weaved effortlessly to find my destination. Meanwhile, the memory I both loathed and loved, a memory and dream I had convinced myself was a fabrication until now, consumed my mind. I am the monster that would delight in another's hell because her heaven tasted so sweet. She was terrified while I stood there filled with beautiful thoughts as each moment passed. Uncaring for the men I would have killed had they found us.

I told myself this would be it. She was safe within my walls, and I

Chapter V

would think of her no longer. That I would never entertain fantasies involving her again.

'Foolish boy. What makes you think you will rid your mind of her now that she's here? You have failed to obey.'

"My mind rests certain of her safety."

'Is she safe?'

Insinuation ate at me as I emerged from a panel near the dorms and managed to catch her and her escort as they turned the corner.

The world was as much monster as I. Murder the night the chandelier came down was evident of that.

"Thank you," she said. Her French still transparent. Yet, I wished to hear it in that wonderful low, soft and raw tone once more before I took my leave.

The mask she wore for the fools disappeared as soon as the boy was out of sight. In its place, the face of worry as she opened the door and peeked inside of her new room.

The quarters lacked any comfort or personality. However, better than any refuge behind waste bins.

Crossing her arms around herself, sweet Melody took in her surroundings once more.

For a moment, I swore she looked at me. Why did this mind wish she had?

Fantasy was moot at best and squashed before *he* could intervene.

As if a thought came to fruition, the little mouse glanced around curiously, and crept towards the adjacent hallway. *What is it you search for?*

The compulsion to follow as she disappeared around the corner evoked stillness within me. Only curiosity waited down that corridor, and it was near time for Christine's lessons. Yet, contemplation lingered on the empty space for a moment longer, as if she were still in sight.

"Welcome to my Opera, Melody," I said. "And now I will be free of you."

'Is that what you think?'

Chapter VI
Melody

It was all still so unnerving. Since I'd left Antoinette and the hotel almost a month ago, my room was the only place I felt safe and like there weren't eyes on me all the time.

Everywhere, statues stood, and paintings hung. There weren't many places I didn't feel as if I wasn't being watched. Some days more than others.

Like now.

Once in a while, it felt like the air shifted and the little hairs on the back of your neck stood up, alerting you that you weren't alone.

Good thing it was almost time to walk through another couple of doorways.

I had lost count of how many thresholds I'd stepped through, hoping it would be the one to send me home. How many times hope had shattered into tinier pieces with each failure.

I had found and tried all the restrooms around the theater but figured that any doorway was worth trying at this point. Even retrying, just in case.

Shit, I hadn't even left this place in the time I'd been here, scared I would miss any chance of getting back to my time. Nevertheless, I

Chapter VI

started to question whether I would even be going back home.

I looked down both ends of the hallway, absentmindedly fidgeting with the rag I had used for cleaning. Just as devoid of life as when I started. Though, the feeling intensified down the end I hadn't made it to yet.

The weight of loneliness had gotten a bit worse since I've been alone so much. Truly the loneliest I'd ever been.

The tears were eager to escape. I have wanted to cry since I got here. Yet, nothing happened. Just utter disbelief. Maybe I was still in denial or something.

I buried my face in my hands, exhaling in frustration, and muffling the scream that wouldn't come, either. I just needed to get home.

Forgetting about the little cherub statue that I'd been buffing for the past while, I dropped the rag into the bin at my feet. Nervously, I smoothed out the skirt of my dress. God, I hated wearing the thing, especially for work. The wig made it worse. I was hot all the time. At least the itching had finally subsided. Mostly.

I checked down the hallway again, both ways. Still empty.

Everything in me warned against investigating what was surely just paranoia. Like some dumb horror movie shit. Yet, there I was, creeping towards it.

My heart sped up as I inched down the corridor, scanning nooks between columns and statues.

Just because no one talked to me didn't mean I didn't listen to those speaking around me. There couldn't really be someone running around in the walls. There were way too many people not to have noticed. With all the accidents and things that went on around the theater, there was not one mention of a ghost.

I would know it if they mentioned it, right?

The immense number of lights in this building made it nearly impossible to hide. I was at least 87% sure no one was around. This wasn't an area many traveled through. Not even employees.

My pulse quickened as I neared the entrance to the servant's corridor just before the hallway split off. It was used to get through the building quicker during events. The lights were always on. Except today, it was pitch black.

What if there was someone running around?

My ears burned and my palms clammed up. "You know what, no. Not doing this," I said and turned back.

"Holy shit! Pierre!" I shouted at my boss, who appeared out of nowhere.

His hands flew into the air. "Melody!" he said, just as startled.

"You scared the fuck out of me. You can't just sneak up on people. Jesus Christ," I said, knowing he wouldn't understand.

"*Sorry*," he said, and handed me a small piece of paper.

While my heart tried to find a normal pace, my limbs shook as I reached out for the note from the managers. This was the only way Pierre and I had been able to communicate effectively.

Usually, he'd just drag me somewhere. Probably upset that I was in the restroom a lot.

A twinge of excitement overran the anxious knot inside my stomach as I read. I was being moved to the theater!

It had not only been lonely, but unbearably quiet. I had only listened to a few songs on my phone, trying to preserve the battery, which was at 32% the last time I turned it on over a week ago.

After all that had happened, being able to work while they rehearsed seemed like a dream come true.

Pierre started towards the main hall, giving me no acknowledgment whatsoever.

With my heart rate finally at a normal level, I looked over my shoulder into the dark hallway that tried to draw me in.

It was just that, an empty corridor.

"*Come with me, strange one*," Pierre said, over his shoulder.

My feet picked up fast behind him and the feeling of eyes disappeared the further away we got.

***

I'd nearly forgotten where I was when we stepped into the brightly lit room.

Private boxes and seats wrapped all the way around from one side of the stage to the other. The overwhelming warmth of red and gold in the room had me smiling for the first time since that night.

One of the biggest tragedies of this whole fucking situation was

Chapter VI

that I'd been so focused on getting home, that I hadn't allowed myself to take in the beauty around me.

I was surrounded by history and some of the most stunning art I'd ever seen, and it was impossible to appreciate it. But I was appreciating it now. For a moment, I was a tourist.

Pierre had left me standing in the middle of the theater to talk with someone nearby. So, like a child in awe, I stared at the mural on the ceiling. Giddy at the sight of the famous chandelier I'd seen online so many times at the center of it, currently receiving repairs as it hung.

The theater was nothing like how I'd first seen it after the massive fixture fell onto the chairs below.

Last, but not least, performing on the stage, the company reset for another run through of whatever scene they were working on. Actors, and whom I assumed were the directors, chatted very loudly over something while the orchestra practiced runs and tuned their instruments.

"*Réinitialiser!*" the director yelled.

Everyone fell back into place, readying for the go ahead. It wasn't a dress rehearsal, so it was hard to tell who the characters were supposed to be. Either way, as soon as the music started up, my heart filled with life.

Musicals were my thing. Phantom was technically a musical with operatic aspects, so I'd never heard real opera before. Not live, anyway. This was amazing.

So exciting, in fact, my body moved towards the stage without consent. I couldn't stop myself if I wanted to. The male lead, a very thin man, sang and sang as he paraded around the stage with a book in hand.

"*Stop!*" the director said. "Lorenzo!"

Like I had any right to do so, I clapped, shouting, "Bravo. Bravo," with the dumbest smile on my face. "That was amazing."

Lorenzo's brows raised and gestured at me while he and the director argued. "Dah!" as if to prove a point.

Some actors snickered in my direction, others stared confused. And I was suddenly aware of my surroundings again.

Startled by the sound of clapping that wasn't mine, I glanced to find Raoul de Chagny standing beside me. Raoul… Thee fucking Raoul de Chagny. The golden retriever without ears for listening. Christine's childhood boyfriend.

I wondered if that was the case here too?

He looked as he did when I first saw him in the manager's office. A kindness and sincerity in his eyes.

"That was really wonderful, wasn't it?" he said.

The sound of English words danced in my ears as the heat of embarrassment graced my face for staring too long.

"Yeah. Yes," I replied.

"We have met before, haven't we?"

"Well, not officially. Melody Reilly."

"Raoul de Chagny," he replied, and dipped his head. "That pleasant looking man over my shoulder is my brother, Philippe."

Philippe looked so "delighted" to be there. He eyed me up and down as if I'd stolen something from him, then cleared his throat with intention.

"Excuse me. *Comte* de Chagny," Raoul corrected.

"Pleasure to meet you both, officially." *What in the strangeness is this?*

"Well, Miss Reilly. Have you seen the ghost yet?" Raoul asked with a soft sarcasm in his tone.

"Oh. Not yet, Monsieur," I said, mirroring his playfulness. "Have you? I mean, it's just a metaphor, right? Because things happen during production all the time."

"Ah, no, but I have only recently started my visits to this wonderful place. My brother, however, frequents this lovely establishment. Still, no sight of floating skulls with fire for eyes. So, I think you might be right. A metaphor."

"Floating skulls and fire eyes?" I laughed. In the book version of Phantom, there was something like that. It was just tricks and people just making up stories as they went on.

The director yelled and the cast reset differently this time.

Raoul and I turned our attention back to Lorenzo, who was floating to a woman walking into view off stage as he sang to her.

Oh…

The moment the woman opened her wide mouth to sing, I suddenly wished I didn't have ears. I may not be able to carry a tune, but I knew what tone was, and this woman didn't have it. In fact, she murdered it

Chapter VI

and didn't bother trying to hide it.

Raoul and I grimaced at the sound assaulting the space.

"*Stop*," the director yelled again. "Carlotta, *please, beautiful prima donna*…"

I heard no more as the world began spinning.

Carlotta? The lead soprano in all the stories. The one who couldn't sing but somehow held her title and place in the spotlight, was real too?

That had to mean Christine was somewhere, right?

Maybe even…

"Are you alright?" Raoul asked, grasping my arm, trying to keep me upright.

"I'm so sorry. I just suddenly felt a little dizzy," I laughed.

"No apologies necessary, miss. She is awful, isn't she?"

A hand gripped my other arm roughly. "*Que fais-tu?*" Pierre snapped and yanked me beside him like I was a child as he spoke with Raoul. I think he was apologizing?

I yanked my arm back and rubbed the sore spot. "Asshole," I muttered.

While I attempted to keep the war in my stomach at bay, I stared in shock at the small woman with dark hair and ego that suffocated the room.

"He's anxious, isn't he?" Raoul said, referring to Pierre.

"Every day."

"I must be going. Good day to you, miss. And watch out for the ghosts," he said, winking at me.

Sweet boy. I hoped he was the listening version.

Pierre spewed a very long line of what I'd assume were insults as he jabbed a finger into my shoulder, until someone called out to him from nearby. The man said a few things and pointed to the back of the stage.

The low groan in Pierre's throat and clenched jaw told me he didn't have the availability to chastise me anymore as he urged me along with him.

There were even more people behind the giant curtains. Dancers stretched in groups. Stagehands moved unfinished set pieces around. There was even a prop master off to the side working on pieces.

"*Stay*," he said, pointing to the ground where we stood.

If I worked back here, I would be closer to the restroom that brought me here. I could slip out and no one would know.

As he walked away, my eyes wandered around a little, landing on the set of stairs we'd stopped next to.

Maybe just a minor detour. Just in case I get home this time… Who's square now, Sarah?

With my lip between my teeth, I climbed the stairs with haste. To my surprise, the unexpected exhilaration kept me going to the top without wheezing.

Though I questioned my courage as soon as I stepped onto the catwalk and it moved. Heights weren't an issue for me, but the swinging of the fucking catwalk was. The fact the railings were just ropes bolted into bigger ropes, which were knotted into the boards under my feet, made this super sketchy.

I made it about halfway over the stage until I felt comfortable enough to sit and watch the world pass by below.

As my legs dangled over the wooden edge, Carlotta yelled at some poor random ensemble member while the director begged her for something. Maybe if she stopped yelling at people, her voice wouldn't sound so bad. It's like someone opened up a blender and dropped a vibrator inside. Then put both things on full speed.

Fuck. I missed my vibrator. Not that the urge had come up at all, but it would be nice to take the edge off.

Just another reason to get home. And to get out of this freakin' wig.

Carlotta's voice pulled me out of any daydreaming I was about to do. Even though she was terrible. I couldn't turn away from all of this. It was Phantom in real time. Minus the Phantom.

Mom and Sarah would have loved this. Even though no one was going to believe it, I still didn't.

Ok. Just a few minutes more then I'll go.

A creaking from the catwalk above cut through the glass-shattering vocals and my busy mind. If it were possible to snap my own neck just with a turn, it would have happened as I tried to see into the darkness above.

Chapter VI

Chapter VII

Do you see me, little mouse? Impulse urged me to look upon her, not once, but twice on this day. Luck would have my hand in the end. I continued unseen. Unknown.

Still, the disdain I held for myself rotted within.

I have declared no care for this woman, circumventing any area of her. And here this creature hid within the shadows above, straining once again to glimpse her cherub face.

As the music bled in, she turned back to watch the story play.

My eyes widened as she reached beneath the hem of her skirt and slid it up. Stilled in my breath at such a sight, I gripped the rope tighter.

Dark ink branded the skin of her sturdy legs. Was she in a traveling show as I was?

Who are you?

From her unusually tight black underthings, a small flat rectangular item was pulled from her pocket. She held it up, and just as hastily, returned it to her pocket.

Very odd.

While I found myself wishing my feet dangled next to this stranger,

Chapter VII

who meant nothing, she laid back onto the board and sighed a breath of relief.

Torn between goals and desire, I continued to peer over the ledge. The state of pleasure on her face warmed my own. A feeling I had not known in decades, or perhaps ever. The memory of it eluded me.

Melodies engulfed this angel. Wrapped itself around her and ran its fingers over her as a lover would do. As I had dreamt of doing.

Wishful thoughts of a condemned man that would further delight in another's hell.

Would it be so terrible if she knew me?

'Most definitely,' the *Ghost* said.

The ache of life returned, eroding the fantasy flowering inside.

"Excuse me. Excuse me," M. Fournier called over the stage, M. LeBlanc following behind like a prancing canine per usual. "Everyone stop rehearsals please."

A snarl escaped these revolting lips as I was ripped from my broken promise. The great bore seemed to gush with excitement. Or panic. Impossible to tell with the human embodiment of a flea.

No matter the minor delay. Either way, Carlotta was not going anywhere. Not yet. Though, this could turn even more a savory moment with their unexpected presence.

I grinned with every step the Banshee took closer to her surprise for her unending reign as resident diva.

So close. Just another few steps Madame d'Espagne.

The itch for rehearsals to continue with Christine in Carlotta's place dug deeper than it ever had. The maneuver would be executed without a hitch, no doubt.

She was ready. The young soprano was everything this grand place wished they had and everything I needed to perfect it.

Ah. The Pompous Playboy and Witless Puppy had come along with my managers. Hence M. Fournier's current state.

The younger one, with his fair hair and tailored, modern fashions I seldom saw until recently. However, the older one, Comte Philippe de Changy, that was a face I knew. One that frequented the salon at the back of the opera. Often preferring the company of the head ballerina when available and running through as many chorus girls when she was not.

The Changys were pinnacle society. Not a hardship to be had. Born perfect and given everything simply just for that.

Foul.

The hate boiling, softened as a familiar voice crept back through M. Fournier's babbling.

"I am the best manager in the world! My skinny mustache doesn't look like I used a weed whacker in the dark! And I love the electric stick in my ass..." she said in the worst accent I had ever heard.

So playful and lively. How easily I was distracted. Her presence unnerved me.

Full of surprises, are you not?

The hollering baboon started up again at M. Fournier's request. Relieved, I redirected my focus properly. My ears longed for the days that her voice was silenced once and for all.

The new patrons winced uncomfortably as they listened. Most definitely the only thing we had in common.

M. Fournier watched on, forcing a smile through worried lines. Meanwhile, M. LeBlanc was nothing but reassuring grins. With how much drink he ingested regularly, it was a wonder the man functioned at all. One would need to be intoxicated to tolerate anything that came out of that Banshee's mouth.

Nearly salivating as she slowly took her steps towards her mark, I gripped the rigging eagerly. "Keep going, just a few centimeters more," I urged in quiet breath. "3...2..."

A scream filled my great hall and the snake disappeared through the floor of the stage, a plume of white flour taking her place.

"Holy fuck!" the little mouse said.

Was she disgusted? Or perhaps enjoyment blessed her face? It was difficult to tell as she gawked.

"Long live the Diva!" I laughed, watching as they scattered like cockroaches below.

"The ghost! The ghost!" they shouted, looking around aimlessly. What ecstasy flowed through these veins.

My favorite trick of ventriloquism. "Never was the Ghost to be found, for he was everywhere."

Chapter VII

There's a fucking Phantom.

Covered in what I hoped was flour, Carlotta emerged from the hatch that had opened beneath her feet in the stage. She screamed and cried as the people helped pull her out.

And I couldn't fucking care less.

There was actually a man running around this place doing fucking Phantom shit. The moment was so fucking over.

The creaking above was more erratic, urging my feet faster towards the stairs at the end of the catwalk. Only five long, slightly swaying platforms from where I was...

He's real. She's real. They're all real. And I'm fucking losing my mind.

Screams continued as more of his laughter rang out. Sandbags from the rigging had fallen onto the stage, knocking at least one person over that I'd seen.

"...Christine Daae'..." M. Fournier said, pulling a tiny woman with dark hair from the crowd.

Finally, at the end of the catwalk, I stepped from the last platform onto the stable wooden rise leading to the stairway.

Without warning, a force stronger than surprise yanked me so hard that it left my breath behind, as the breeze of the sandbag grazed me, and landed in the spot I was going to step into.

My heart pounded in my ears as I stood frozen, staring at the bag that could have killed me.

Amongst the chaos and short heavy breaths, my wide eyes sliced to the black sleeve, white cuff and black leather glove that vice gripped around my waist. With his other hand, he clasped my wrist against his chest. Neither showed no signs of letting up as I clenched onto them.

I swallowed hard before stealing a look at my rescuer.

Reminiscent of a dream I once had. I stared wordlessly into extraordinary, blazing eyes, one emerald green, the other stone gray.

Mischief or malice? They were unreadable.

This was him. I should have been terrified. Screaming even. Pulling away. But I stood motionless. My mind raced with every awful possibility of what could happen if he changed his mind. Every one of them ending with me dead on the stage below. Or locked in a dungeon somewhere.

This man had just saved my life. "Thank you," I said meekly. Granted, he was the reason it needed saving.

Hot breath brushed against the heel of my palm as he glanced it over. A glint of softness crept around the fire in his eyes when he locked in with mine again.

Prickles of fear and confusion stirred inside, and the air swirled. Familiar and comfortable. Laced in… safety?

"*Fantôme d'opéra! le voilà!*" a man's hoarse voice yelled out in the distance.

Those eyes flicked over my head.

Several platforms away and coming fast; a gruff, gray-haired man with a wild beard and baggy, dirty clothing rushed towards us.

The grip on my hand and around my waist vanished. Empty was the space when I turned back, like he'd never been there.

Déjà vu.

The grizzled man shoved me aside, searching around frantically. His rough hands grabbed me yelling, and shook. I fought the urge to vomit when his foul, booze-laced breath assaulted my nostrils.

Even if I wanted to get at my knife, I couldn't reach it.

I wriggled against his bruising grip, only freezing when glowing eyes peered over his shoulder.

They really were glowing. Like a jack-o-lantern at Halloween.

"*Bonsoir, Monsieur*," the Phantom said.

It was enough to halt the man in place and flush the color from his face. He yelped, meeting the eyes behind him and let go of me.

I tore away and descended the stairs as fast as I could, ignoring the rustling behind me. I was running and bouncing so fast, I'd thought this stupid wig would fly off.

A sea of bodies had gathered at the bottom of the stairs, staring curiously. They opened enough to let me through, and directly into M. LeBlanc, Fournier and Philippe de Changy.

"Ms. Reilly?" M. LeBlanc asked.

Too frightened to say anything, I hurried around behind them and hoped for the best.

Chapter VII

The stagehand stomped towards us, fuming, and wiping blood from his nose. This moment terrified me more than the thought of being pushed to my death.

"Que se passe-t-il, Buquet?" M. LeBlanc demanded of the man.

Joseph Buquet... The stagehand from the stories. Sure, why not. As if this all wasn't crazy already.

Anyone else?

The men yelled back and forth while I stayed cowering, looking for an exit.

I could run back to my room, hide there for the rest of the day. Maybe Antoinette would have me back and this wouldn't happen again.

A dark-haired man standing back from the chaos caught my attention in my search. Seeming unconcerned for the event at hand, his eyes bored curiously into me.

"Ms. Reilly, was there someone up there with you?" M. LeBlanc asked. His words calmer than the situation at hand, snapping me back.

"No. No one." *Why did I just lie?*

Fixed on me through the crowd of onlookers, the man's gaze flicked up the stairway and back with suspicion. Like he knew I was lying.

M. Fournier's chin quivered as he bit back a nervous smile, hoping I told the truth. Or at least kept it to myself if I had another one.

The last thing I assumed he wanted was everyone telling the new patrons there's a menacing ghost in the opera. Even though they already knew.

Buquet sneered some more spiteful words. Spitting as he spoke.

"He's calling you a liar, Ms.," Philippe said. "He seems to think you were talking to the Ghost."

Oddly enough, it sounded playful. Like he was enjoying the show. At least one of us was.

"Are you sure you were alone?" M. Fournier asked.

"I was almost killed by one of those sandbags." I pointed at Buquet. "The only other thing I saw was him running after me and shouting."

Why was I lying? There's no reason for me to lie, but I found myself doing it anyway.

If this was the past, things would have to play out as closely as they would have, as if I hadn't been here. Right? Otherwise, I could change the course of history or something?

Right?

But what if all this wasn't real?

"Buquet, assez!" M. LeBlanc yelled.

"Alright. That settles it! It's obvious Buquet let the drink get the best of him today," M. Fournier said.

"Yes. Yes. That's enough excitement for one day," M. LeBlanc added. "Comte de Chagny. Vicomte. Would you please forgive us this excitement, and rendezvous in the parlor, gentlemen?"

Philippe nodded. "Of course, Monsieur's." His eyes floated to mine, a glimmer of interest in them that made me uneasy. "Madame."

They disappeared into the crowd along with the managers who were trying to break it up.

The back of my mind tingled with that feeling you got when you think you're being watched, like in the hallway earlier. From where I was, I swear the faintest glow of eyes stared from the dark at the top of the stairs. A twisted feeling in the core of my body came back.

I swallowed hard, and hurried feet took me the other way.

I would run in and out of the doorways all day if I had to, not caring if Pierre or anyone else got upset.

Something's got to give and I think now was that time. They couldn't fire me if I was gone.

Chapter VIII

Notes needed written. Sound created. Words found. Shrouded within the space no soul dared venture, I descended through stale air toward my hell, my solitude.

My chest pounded with song, and mind danced with images so sweet, both fantasy and memory. Only made more sublime by murmurs of the Ghost as I passed through.

To frighten. To evade. Always a thrill. Disrupt the goings on of all who take their freedoms for granted. Who submit so willingly to the normalcy of society.

Or not.

Cold steel slid smoothly beneath my hands whilst I descended ladders between floors.

The hour was early enough to work. Rehearsals resumed as I departed, without Carlotta, and Christine's lessons weren't until the evening.

Oh. The way the Banshee shrieked when the floor swallowed her. If she had not broken a thing, blessed would I be that she at least bruised.

My Christine. Voice so ethereal, entranced them all, proved her worthiness, her spot in the light. A fine step towards the perfecting of my stage. My vision. My feat.

'I fear what invigorating rush courses through your veins is not of Carlotta's screaming nor Christine's doing.'

The *Ghost* missed no opportunities to humble this mind.

These events would please me to no end on any day. Sate me for a short time to make this all worthwhile.

Except, he was right. My victories as of late have been dampened.

Why did *she* have to be there, distracting me with her nonsense. I had nearly missed my mark because of her.

Intention on giving her a fright, ruined, but by my own hand. A miscalculation on my part.

Blasted sandbag.

Soft brown irises, which were now scarred into memory unwelcome, immobilized me yet again as I held her.

Why would she thank a ghost, a monster? A walking corpse.

I'd breached one of the many panels which led to one of the sub cellars beneath the stage. The scent of cold earth laced my nostrils and filled my lungs as I stepped into the darkness of forgotten things.

The quickest way home: I would know it in my sleep.

A table from *Hamlet*. Bedroom set from *La Traviata*. One particular item, however, always held my gaze a bit longer than it should have.

Encapsulated in a sheer netting, was Susanna's wedding gown from *Marriage of Figaro* several seasons past. I had thought of taking it many times. Holding it until the moment was right and it would be filled with a soul for me.

Imaginations were a fickle and cruel thing.

A faint glow near my destination slowed my pace. The chaos of not too long ago was over and the area was clear of crew. *Who would be down here now? Had they come to their foolish senses and posted guards once again?*

Hunched over near the base of the original entrance to the lake beneath the opera, a man examined the caved-in passageway.

The possibilities were endless when it came to what could be done at this moment.

There were no distractions to save. If I killed him, recent events may be overshadowed.

I rocked my jaw in thought.

Chapter VIII

"That entrance has been blocked for several years by now, dear Ardashir," I said. "Something about keeping ghosts out."

My dear Daroga, perhaps the only person in this world I would consider a friend. Even when he would see me in chains if he could. He pulled the pistol from the holster on his hip, whipping the lantern in his hand around, pointing in uncertain directions.

"Erique! You horse's ass," he said.

"How strange it is to be referred to by my chosen name after all these silent years."

"I can think of a few other names to call you," Ardashir said.

Once upon a time, this man was given duty to keep a watchful eye on the deformed prodigy and architect while in the employ of the King of Persia.

So long ago. So many misjudgments.

"Oh, come now, Daroga. You have no need of that. We are the oldest of friends, you and I."

Ardashir's focus flicked to the gun in his hand and back into the dark around him. Looking for the man in the shadows, one would guess.

"Unless you plan to use it this time? In that case." I stepped into the radiance of his lantern. "Here I am."

My bearded friend groaned and clenched his jaw as he holstered his weapon.

"What a shame. I was quite hoping for a rumble," I said, wishing to unleash this energy stowed within me.

"Nearly killing a woman wasn't enough for you?"

"Ha. I am uncertain Carlotta deserves such a title. And, if I wanted her removed from this earth permanently, she would have been long ago."

As a leper within my world, she has done nothing to deserve such an end. A broken femur perhaps, but not the afterlife.

"Give it time. You simply can't help yourself. It's in your nature."

"Why are you down here? I thought you were after the killer of that poor girl? It's been a month now, and still nothing?"

"Ah. Yes. Well, you're making my investigation quite difficult. Especially for someone who claims to be innocent of such a crime."

"Oh?" With careless air, I took comfort in an old chair from this season's Faust. "Perhaps you should have come sooner."

"Alas. Word did not reach me soon enough. Does not matter, my search leads to you every time. Every interview is the same. 'The opera ghost did it'. God, these people. Are all French naive?"

It was a wonder how they believed so quickly that a ghost haunted such a place, even when it was new.

"If you truly believed me guilty, we wouldn't have these lovely conversations, would we? You would have shot me dead. Believing me more abomination than I am."

The thought of lead through my chest was almost pleasant, though fleeting.

"Perhaps next time, Erique." He leaned against a wooden beam and his scorned exterior shed only enough. "How am I to believe you had nothing to do with it if you're causing chaos all the time? You dropped the chandelier to hide what you did, I know it."

"Must we do this?" I sighed and picked at the arm of the chair. "The chandelier would have come down eventually. The rigging was set poorly in the original construction. I only aided in the timeline. No one was hurt." *Unfortunately.* "The vermin need their worlds rattled every now and again. Remind them that they're not untouchable. Now, the girl's death. Of all people, you should know the innocent do not find themselves at the end of my lasso."

"You're a good man now? How your memory fails you, old *friend*."

The jab was sharp. Understandable that he would find it hard to believe. I was no stranger to death. Nor being the cause of it.

Dust danced its way into the distorted nostrils beneath my false face as I inhaled deeply. "You know the very circumstances in which that was." A memory I wished never to replay. "In any case, Carlotta still lives. My hands are clean in this matter. That should tell you something of my innocence."

"Your *innocence*…" He scoffed. "Arrogance is more like it. Though, I suppose you do have a point. Admittedly, that is one accident I could look the other way on."

"Daroga... have you a bit of darkness in you after all?"

"Perhaps too much time with you over the years."

"And I cherish every moment."

Chapter VIII

"Do you now?"

The air was light. Reminiscent of days long past.

To be that young man again.

"Instead of trying to find a way into my home, which I would gladly take you to. There's an unopened twenty-five-year-old brandy that I do believe you would enjoy. Perhaps you should continue your search elsewhere."

"Brandy?" He pursed his lips in thought. "Another time, my friend. Unfortunately, you are right. I must travel to Toulouse in the morning. There's a woman there with information about this girl."

It had been many years since we shared a drink. I'd hoped one day we would delight in such a friendly manner once more.

"Of course," I replied.

"Ah! Before I leave, I do have a question for you." Moving towards me curiously, trying to read the face he couldn't see. "Who's the American to you?"

She was no one. It mattered not the moment I caught her wrist, I wished my hand were bare so I could feel the warmth of her skin in mine. Or how my lips nearly placed a kiss upon the quickened pulse. Had it not been for the singing baboon, I may have been heedless enough to do it.

"Merely a new face in the Opera," I said.

"The people in this place can't wait to tell tales of glowing eyes and magical lassos. Floating skulls and walking skeletons. But not this one. She lies for you instead. Interesting, isn't it?" Ardashir asked, leaning onto the arm of my chair.

"That is curious." I stood, avoiding his probing stare. He was always too good at getting information and there was nothing to find where he searched.

A chuckle escaped his mouth as he shook his head, "In any case, is it strange that I hope you didn't do it?"

"I have the utmost faith you will uncover the truth. And when the time comes, a brandy will be shared."

"You wouldn't happen to know who did it? So we may end this cat and mouse game?"

A smirk tugged at the corner of my lips. "If I knew, you and everyone else would most definitely know. No one kills in my opera and goes unpunished for it."

"Erique, I loathe your very existence. And yet, I don't."

"That may be so. You are a good man, my friend. And perhaps discovery of truth will make you see, I'm not as bad as you think me to be."

"That is a day I wait for." His smile was sincere for the first time. Perhaps there was hope of that shared bottle after all.

"Good night, Daroga," I said and blew out the lantern, leaving him in darkness.

"You are indeed a horse's ass, Erique."

I slipped into the passage near where he had searched and descended for hell once more.

Chapter IX

Melody

"God fucking damn it!" Another failed attempt through the stupid doorways. How many more would it take to break me completely before I'd finally accept the truth?

I wasn't going home.

Frustration was at the forefront of my mind. Anger mixed in with all of it. Fear sprinkled on top. The worst kind of sundae.

Hope was getting harder to hold onto the longer this went on. My muscles ached and weakened like they hadn't in so long. Eating was something I forced myself to do.

Not only had I spent the rest of the day and all of last night walking in and out of doorways, but today was my day off and I spent all of it in this hallway. Failing. I didn't even care that the other keepers and crew gawked at me and laughed as I did it, something I was used to now.

My body wasn't the only thing that had been revolting against me since I'd landed here, but the past twenty-four hours have probably been the worst. Because it wasn't just home filling my mind.

Emerald green and stone-gray eyes plagued my stupid thoughts as well.

The nausea worsened each time they crept in. Yet, it's all I thought about.

When he grabbed me, stopping me from becoming a human pancake. He stared into my fucking soul with a softness I'd never seen before. Oh God, when his breath crept down my wrist…

Even now my heart quickened, and goosebumps blemished my skin as the replay lurked unwanted.

It was only a minute, if that!

Oh god.

I ran back into the restroom and released what little was inside my stomach. Trying not to think about the fact they didn't have *409* in 1880.

After washing up in the sink, I envisioned home again just before stepping through the door.

Damn.

The air in the hall was thick, almost suffocating when I inhaled it. I cupped my hands around my nose and mouth to muffle the sobs trying to escape.

I guess I'd be seeing Antoinette tomorrow for lunch after all. My first time away from here. Maybe she would let me come back.

It was later than I thought it was, and it'd been a while since anyone snickered at me. Sleep was probably the best thing for me at the moment.

I rounded the corner, heading back to my room in defeat.

"*Je suis désolé,*" a small woman said as we bumped into each other.

I'd been so lost in my own mind that I hadn't noticed anyone else.

"I'm sorry. I mean, uh. *So…sor…sorry. Excuse me,*" I said. At least my French was getting a tad better. The single words anyway.

My eyes landed upon the woman. It was her. The Phantom's obsession in every story was staring me right in the face. Christine Daae'.

My ears heated and perked up. If she was here, there was a chance he was too.

"Wait, you're the American? Melody, yes?" she asked.

"Yes, that's me." Ready to run at any moment, hoping it wasn't obvious my eyes were darting around, scanning the surrounding area, as if he'd just be standing somewhere, waving.

Just me and the main character standing in the hall.

It was unreal to see her up close. Straight dark hair. Petite. If I

Chapter IX

hugged her, I'd be afraid to break her.

Christine's blue eyes were puffy, cheeks reddened and rubbed raw.

"Um. Are you alright?" I asked.

Embarrassment crossed her face. "Yes. Of course." Christine turned her head quickly to wipe away the remnant of a tear. "I'm Christine. Are you alright?"

I paused, not sure how to answer. The simplest way would have been just to say yes.

"I mean, with Joseph. He's an unkind man. The stories about him are something I don't wish to repeat either, if that's alright," she continued.

The concern in her sweet voice grounded me a little. It'd been ages since I'd actually talked with someone. Used my voice at all.

"Oh. That. Yes. Guess I was lucky that everyone was there." *And him.*

What were the odds of two shadow men saving me when I needed it the most?

Wow, I'd almost forgotten about my Basement Angel.

Time…

Christine's hands fidgeted as she chewed on her bottom lip. She looked over her shoulder then turned back.

"Are you sure you're alright? I know it's none of my business, but you seem –" I started.

"Everything's very overwhelming at the moment."

"I understand that feeling all too well these days. Unfortunately." I sighed and surveyed the space around us again. For such a large and busy building, there weren't many places to rest.

"Do you want to sit down?" I asked.

"Here? On the floor?"

"Yeah? Why not?"

She looked me up and down, like she was gauging my trustworthiness.

"You will sit with me?" she asked.

"Totally."

The floor wasn't that terrible. Cold, but at least we weren't awkwardly standing anymore.

"This is a bit odd. In the middle of the corridor," Christine said as we settled against the wall.

"Everyone already thinks I'm weird."

"They call you *étrange*. Strange one."

I chuckled. "I know. M. Leblanc told me."

Christine smiled, a hint of laughter under her sad eyes.

I was willing to sit here with her for no reason. Ok, maybe a little reason. Anything to get my mind off everything.

Also, I wanted to know. I wanted to pry, but I was a stranger to her. I wanted to tell her to run away with Raoul and never return just to save her from everything that was probably going to come. But one couldn't just offer up that information without questions. She would straight up think I was cuckoo for Cocoa Puffs.

Finally, she broke the silence. "Someone I care for deeply is here and I have to tell him to stay away. And he doesn't understand. And it hurts."

"Oh." *Shit.*

"We knew each other as children, before my father died and grandmother brought me here. I guess we're…" her face radiated.

"Sweethearts?"

She blushed, hiding a small smile only a fond memory could bring. I don't think I could muster one memory with a man that made me smile like that.

"I haven't seen him in a few years. He's grown so much and yet still so much the same person I remember… My music teacher has strict rules. If I am to reach my greatest potential, I must only focus on that," she said. Her face falling at the reality of now.

"I see."

How would I respond without possibly signing my own death certificate, if he's listening, and still feel good about myself?

"Why not have both? Love and Career? Many people do that," I said.

She hesitated, like the thought hadn't occurred to her. In this time period, I suppose that would make sense though. Most women were only wives. Rarely was a career even an option.

"You're so young, Christine. Don't let anyone restrict you. Love is rare. Do you still love him?" I asked.

She nodded, still hiding the tiniest smile.

"Not everyone gets to have that. But also, don't jump right into

Chapter IX

something. People change. Often, not for the better. So, take your time together."

"What if my teacher were to find out?"

"Send him to me. I'll deal with him." I swallowed hard and stilled, realizing what I'd just said. *Oh well.* "If he cares for your well-being, he'll let you love and live your life. As should anyone that cares about you."

She grinned and wiped away another escaped tear I pretended not to see.

I rubbed her arm, hoping in a small way it would reassure her. Something I wished someone would do for me. Not gonna lie.

"Just see if Raoul is who you remember. And if you don't end up liking who he's become, then you have nothing to worry about, right? You can just go on singing."

"How did you know it was him?"

I could have broken my fingers with how tightly I clamped them in the skirt of my dress. *Big mouth.* "I…I saw you guys on stage the other day."

She shied away, probably embarrassed at the accusation. "I'm sorry to have unburdened myself to you with this. I didn't mean to. Thank you."

I shrugged. "We all need someone sometimes. I guess I was in the wrong place at the right time."

Suddenly, her demeanor changed—worried again and grinding her teeth.

"What is it?" I asked.

"Are we friends now?"

"Oh, I guess so. Yeah."

She glanced around discreetly. As if ready to tell a secret. "Did you see him?"

"Who?"

"The Ghost." She whispered. "Joseph said you were talking to the Ghost. And everyone's been whispering about it. Saying that things have gotten worse since you got here."

Wonderful. The last thing I wanted was more attention. And now I'm the harbinger of death. Awesome.

"There wasn't anyone up there," I answered.

Why do I keep lying about it?

She seemed almost disappointed by my response. Huffing and twisting up her mouth.

"What do you know of him? The Ghost, I mean," I added. "And what do you mean things have gotten worse?"

Confirming once again that we were alone. That we knew of anyway, she leaned in. "He causes a lot of the 'accidents'. Things go missing. Usually, important props for shows that Carlotta's in. Things like that. It's sometimes worse when things don't go his way. You saw what happened to Carlotta. Not to mention the girl he killed last month."

My chest tightened. It was one of the many thoughts in that moment with him above the stage. That he could just push me off or something. We were only a few feet away from the ledge, it would have been easy.

"What do you mean?" I asked.

"The night the chandelier came down. A few people got hurt. But… one of the ballerinas, Elizabeth, was found in a room in the salon. The Ghost had strangled her." She stared at the floor, wrapping herself in her arms. "I hate that place. I'm lucky I live with my grandmother. I don't have to go through *that*."

She was lucky. The salon was just a brothel. A way for the opera and dancers to make more money and keep the nasty patrons happy. I avoided it when I could. Especially at night, usually walking around the long way or cutting through the stage.

"Someone saw him kill her?" I asked.

"No. But that's what he does when things get bad. Most of us hang incense above our doors and pray, so that he doesn't bother us. It works. Most of the time."

Why save me if he relished in death?

She continued. "And when they put up the new chandelier, the Ghost pushed one of the workers from the rise. He only broke his leg and arm though."

"Do people really think it's a ghost, not just a man?"

"A man?" she giggled. "You heard him. No man can do all that unseen."

You'd be surprised.

"Has anyone actually seen him?"

Chapter IX

"Yes! It's been said he has glowing eyes. And flies like a bird, but not with wings. He wears a black cloak. Like Death. And sometimes, he dresses like he's a special guest of the opera."

The man I touched was for sure no supernatural being as far as I could tell. But he did have a strangeness about him. Maybe it was just the mystery. A man in the dark behind a mask.

Christine went on about the random things people said about him. How he commanded the dead. Had hair of fire. But also wore a hat. And that he tormented Carlotta the most.

I remembered the hat. Sort of. But no fire that I could recall. Just soft, curious eyes.

She went on for a while about her father and the traveling they did. It was very cool to hear about her life. And sad at the same time. She loved her father so much. He sounded like a good man. And when he got sick, he only made sure their last days together were everything.

When my mother got sick, it was hard because she got mean. The relationship was already strained because she went so long undiagnosed, but I was the family-less child. Obligation made me her caregiver just so she didn't feel alone because of all the poor misfortunes of her life.

"Have you enjoyed Paris?" she asked. "When you're not conversing with ghosts?"

The question caught me off guard more than running into her.

"I haven't really been outside the theater. So, I don't have much of an opinion. Not being able to speak the language makes it difficult to enjoy anything as well. I'd kill for a book in English. And a really hot bubble bath!"

If it wasn't for trying to get home, I probably wouldn't leave anyway. I hate doing everything alone all the time. That was basically my entire adult life.

"You don't speak French?" she asked. The most confused expression on her face.

"No."

"Why are you here then?" the faintest hint of laughter behind her words.

"That's... I don't even know the answer."

"Well, what do you like? Maybe I can find one? I like the love stories."

"I prefer darker stories, but I have been known to enjoy the highly inappropriate romance novel now and then."

She blushed and her eyes went wide. "Do you know about that stuff?"

"Well, yes."

"Are you married?"

Ugh. "Oh, God no."

"Why not?" She laughed.

"Just never found a man worth saying yes to."

"None made you happy?" The sincerity in her question stopped the light heartedness in the moment.

Not once had anyone ever asked me that. My smile stalled. It was always on me to compromise my happiness. The "love didn't always mean you were happy" people would tell me after confiding in them. At some point, I think I believed them.

Before I could answer, Christine took a quick breath and waved her hands. "I'm sorry again."

"It's alright. The answer to your question is no. As much as it hurts to admit. I don't remember ever feeling happy for more than a short time."

Hearing it out loud made me realize how used and pathetic I was.

"Then why…"

"Because in the beginning they're amazing, actively trying to make you want them. Until you're hooked. Then they stop. And you're sitting there hoping the man they were when you met them comes back. But they never do. So, you try harder. Which makes it worse, for you. And they will use you until there's nothing left. No one should have to beg someone to love them."

Suddenly I was the one wiping away a rogue tear at remembrance of my last relationship. I batted my eyes, forcing any other rogues back in their ducts. This wasn't about me.

Christine looked as if she was in deep thought. Taking in my unintentional warning.

"Have you thought about trying again?" the sweet girl asked.

"I'm too wise to the ways of men to try again. Which," I swallowed the ache in my throat, "Is also unfortunate because who doesn't want to

Chapter IX

be loved, right? Who doesn't want to love?"

"Raoul has an older brother."

"Oh, that's alright," I chuckled. "But you, on the other hand, just take things a little slow. Get to know Raoul before making any decisions. Ok? I mean, if you wanted advice. That's what I would tell my younger self."

Christine surprised me when her arms flew around me. It was nice to feel like a person again.

Well, shit.

"Thank you. I think I will. I think this helped. I think," she said. more sure of herself now than she was an hour ago. "I'm so sorry, I must be going. I have to get to my lessons."

"Oh. Of course. Sure thing."

My knees snapped, crackled, and popped as we got up from the floor. Maybe we sat there a little longer than we should have.

Worth it.

"It was lovely to meet you. I hope that we see each other again soon. We can go to the shops. Maybe find some books or a new dress?" she said as she scampered down the hall.

"That would be nice," I answered. Though I'd hoped I would never have to take her up on her offer. Especially now that I basically just gave an open invitation to the "Phantom" to come find me.

What am I going to do if he does?

Chapter X

Melody

The theater was too quiet tonight. It would have almost been bearable if Carlotta was singing, because even that was better than the silence that had me tossing and turning.

Sleep had been hard to find since I'd arrived, but even worse now with the whole "Phantom" thing being real and running into Christine like that. Literally.

I hadn't been able to sleep longer than a few minutes before jolting awake, straining to see within the dark areas of my room. It wasn't even big enough for someone to hide. Barely enough space for the bed and closet it had. But it still kept me awake more so now.

Oh, and the whole not getting home thing no matter how much or how hard I've tried. That's been pretty stressful too.

"Fuck." I groaned and kicked back the blanket.

Silence wasn't the only thing killing me.

Not being able to create anything was driving me insane. Paper and pencil sat on my nightstand, for when I got the urge to write home, but barely sated the creativity.

I'd started writing letters to Mom and Sarah, just in case. Keeping

Chapter X

them hidden within a broken floorboard underneath the small dresser, so no one would see them and have me committed or something.

I know that *Back to the Future* was fiction, but maybe I could find a way to send them to Mom if I don't… If I never saw them again. Maybe even try to warn myself about the bathroom. Even though that probably wouldn't work.

Bleh.

Dear Mama. Sarah too, I guess.
Can't sleep again tonight…

The last letter trailed off a bit and turned from what started as a recap, into a short story about a woman lost in unfamiliar territory, fighting tentacle beasts, only to end up with one who fucked her into oblivion whenever she wanted. Oh, and also could turn into a man, so they can make out.

A very short, erotic story, but enough to sate the need to create for a moment.

Of course, it ended up under the loose floorboard.

The silence made everything unbearable. I couldn't even finish this letter. Worse, it left my mind free to wander. And that was when trouble slithered in.

I set the pencil down and ran my fingers through my short hair. It was always such a relief to be out of that stupid wig.

I thought wearing the damn thing would at the very least keep me mostly invisible and passible.

It's done one of those things.

Sometimes I feel like I'm wearing a neon sign that says "I'm different. Notice me".

Hoping that a walk would do me in, I pulled on my trousers. My socks and shoes were on before I knew it and I was out the door without that damn itchy thing. It was late enough. No one was around. If anyone saw me, they'd probably assume I was someone else anyway and leave me be.

With everything I know now, I shouldn't be walking alone. Those eyes could be somewhere watching. But I figured if he wanted to hurt me, he would have already.

I hoped.

Ironic, that's all I could remember physically. Eyes. I knew I saw a mask, but I couldn't remember the shape or what it covered. I'm sure it was white though.

The hallways were empty. Except for a few voices off in the distance, it was just as quiet as my room. Even those drifted away fairly quickly when I entered the stage door to the theater.

The lights were dim but never off. It kind of gave a completely different mood, like you were in a dream.

Sets and props stood about, left in place after rehearsal for the following day. A lovely mess.

I strolled through the courtyard scene, fingers gliding over the fake bushes that stretched across the faux stone fencing. Details on the stone and wooden benches could have been better. But they were sturdy.

Some of the animals were taxidermy, a little surprising, while others were paper mâché or some other material, stuck with actual fur.

It was like another little world within my new one. And I couldn't help but smile.

My imagination was always so vivid, so real. This felt like one of those times, lost in a daydream or fantasy just before bed.

From the beautifully varnished stage adorned with rich red velvet curtains and gold trim, I looked out over the empty auditorium. I remembered times on stage with the school band. How I was so nervous, like everyone could hear me play within the mix of fifty other students and hear my every mistake thanks to my shaking hands.

Sometimes I still wonder what it would have felt like had I made it up onto the stage for my first and last acting audition.

So stupid.

Severe stage fright always kept me from things like this. If you messed up, everyone knew.

Acting for the camera was way different than on stage. And being the center of attention was a hard thing for someone like me as it was.

I wasn't a good, or even a fair, singer by any means. Actually, I sang a lot for someone who shouldn't. But I loved it and always fantasized about being a vocalist and performing on Broadway.

As if.

Chapter X

"Maybe if I'd taken choir instead of band." I rolled my eyes while my insides rattled just thinking about it.

But there wasn't actually anyone in the audience. No directors or auditions to pass out before. Anyone to see the flaws.

It was just me.

Peeking around one last time to confirm that I was alone, my lips quirked wickedly, and silly thoughts ensued.

Meandering towards center stage, I went through every possible song I could sing, or at least remember all the lyrics too.

Show tunes. Records. Whatever. All jumbling my mind at once.

I could do an ALW. *Memory* from *CATS*?

No.

Every theater kid in school sang that song to death. I still love it though.

No, I don't want to be sad right now.

"Fuck it." I opened my mouth and the words from The Phantom of the Opera's *Think of Me* fell out like Legos.

Kind of fitting in a way.

It felt so good to use my voice. I should have used it on Buquet and that cop. Shouted. Screamed. So that everyone would hear. Even with *him*.

What was wrong with me? I'd always been quiet. Never able to get any louder than normal speech, even then I was quiet, often having to be told to "speak up" when it felt like I was practically yelling.

Sarah had the voice. She could get loud, shout, and even sing. Lessons would have been easy for her.

I'm thinking of them now. For sure. They'd fall out of their chairs seeing me on this stage, moving through made up choreography and singing.

Except they wouldn't, because I wouldn't do this even for them.

Avoiding the trap door, and anything that looked like it could open, I continued, and pushed the somber thoughts away. Instead, focused on imaginary people sitting out in the brass trimmed chairs, awe struck as my voice tickled their ears like angel's whispers.

I even found myself looking up into the famous box five and imagined those glowing eyes staring back, cheering me on.

All the silly thoughts from a full-grown woman pretending on an empty stage, in an imaginary gown. Pretending to be the best version of myself. The self that people loved and wanted to be around. The one that sang like an angel and was beautiful. And loved.

The one that didn't give every part of herself for men that didn't want her. Jobs that didn't drain her.

Pretended I was strong.

Now the hardest part of the song; the highest note in the piece that required a lot more than I could give.

My range wasn't good as it was, but I was going to pretend that it was. Even if it hurt. And it was going too.

I dropped to my knees and stretched my hands towards the sky, trying to hold it.

It strained. It burned. But it was my moment.

The world may have been a bit dizzy, and my head light. But I did it.

Throat aching and chest heaving, I finished the song. The tensions I'd felt for a while seemed numbed. And a relief filled my whole being.

Laughter hit me after a moment as I fell onto my back, staring up into the twinkling crystals of the mid-repair chandelier.

I was both delusional and delirious. Perfect.

"You were horrendous." His thunderous voice rang throughout the auditorium. Rich and clear, as if he were right next to me.

Recognizing it immediately, my breath stopped in my throat. I hadn't forgotten about him. However, I didn't think…

The embarrassment took over, even though I couldn't stop laughing. Was it me? Or the situation? Both.

"I know," I said, caught in a laughing fit.

"You were both flat and sharp, nearly the entire piece. Which I may not know, but can assure you, was not meant to sound like that. I'm certain your vocals were damaged beyond repair after that beating."

Shocked, my jaw dropped at his infliction, and I laughed harder.

After a few moments, attempting to tame the laughter fit still roaring inside, I rolled over and pushed myself to my feet. "And now, if you'll excuse me, Monsieur. I'm going to go die of embarrassment. Good night."

I bowed and rushed to the stage door and into the hallway and back

Chapter X

to my room.

'Flat and sharp nearly the entire song' he said.... *'The entire song'*

Had he been watching the whole time?

There were so many stories, variations of the Phantom. Was his name even Erique in this one? Is he a serial killer? Anti-hero? Disfigured from birth? Or acid? Jerk off or just different? Psychopath?

This was dangerous and this wasn't for me to have. I needed to be a roach in the dark, not the flower in the vase to be seen.

Still, even fear was only part of what I'd felt. The novelty of the Phantom; the thought that he'd been watching me at all and not attacked, reignited the confusion that trickled when thoughts of him slipped in.

It was unclear whether this was good or bad.

It was bad. So bad.

Chapter XI
Melody

The events over the past few days were still fresh in my memory as the carriage bounced along the road.

I told her to disobey him. What the hell was I thinking?

The stories were very clear on the Ghost's determination for Christine. Music and her alone was his obsession, his only reason for living. He'd kill anyone that got in the way of that.

Dread ran through me. And yet, soul piercing eyes tortured my mind more than before.

It'd been days since the catwalk incident, but I could still recall exactly how they managed to show so many emotions within such a short time. More than any eyes I'd ever seen into.

Last night, embarrassment may have told me to run, but I wanted to stay and talk. Maybe the high from speaking with Christine earlier in the night felt so good that I was willing to risk it. So desperate for connection.

I sighed and rubbed my temples, needing the invasive thoughts to go away.

It had to be a normal thing for him to be going around doing what

Chapter XI

he's doing. He wasn't zeroing in on me. Right?

Desperate to turn my mind, I pulled my phone from my shorts, which had seen better days before the constant washing and wearing.

I'm scared of the day that will come when it will no longer boot up. 16% battery life left.

Every time I turned the thing on, hope sat in my stomach. *Please be a message or a missed call.*

Wishful.

I thumbed through the photo gallery, catching a glimpse of home for a few seconds. Then snapped a quick photo of some of Paris from the carriage. Might as well. Just in case I got back home or if someone found my phone in 130 years.

130 years.

"Melody! My sweet." Antoinette's friendly smile beamed from the sidewalk. She rushed to the carriage door, opening it quickly before I or the driver could think.

I hadn't even noticed we stopped.

The café she called me to stood on the corner of two moderately busy streets. Just to get inside was a task as we weaved through people.

It smelled good though. Almost strong enough to mask the Paris odor.

It was still jarring to see all these people in period clothing. Knowing I am where I am. Where I think I am, anyway. How they interacted with each other. Mostly not that kind, but also kind at the same time?

The sun was warm on my face as we sat outside. Like sinking into a hot bath. What I wouldn't give for a hot bath.

The guilt was a little heavy now that I was sitting with her.

I hadn't visited since I'd left the hotel. They did this thing for me that I can never repay, and I couldn't bring myself to leave, "just in case".

She'd come to the opera a few times to check on me and bring food. But she never stayed long and was only willing to sit outside while eating and conversing. Like the *Garnier* scared her.

During our visits, she did most of the talking, which worked for me. I've been able to catch a few things here and there. But it was still difficult when she spoke more than single words.

Did I mention I failed Spanish after taking it for a year?

Today she's teaching me the menu. Pointing to the words and speaking slowly, like teaching a little kid. Patience is a virtue, and she has it. And I appreciated it more than her kindness.

Antoinette insisted I try something other than the chicken and rice she usually brought me. Pushing the chicken and cabbage pie, *tarte au poulet et au chou*.

That didn't sound appetizing in the slightest. But, I couldn't eat chicken and rice forever, I supposed.

I crossed my fingers after we ordered and hoped for the best. Anything but oysters. Which was half of the menu.

"How is the job?" Antoinette asked, sipping on her wine.

"Boring. Long. Completely soul crushing."

"*Oh come on*. Not bad?" Her tone was light and silly. It was nice to be out and with a friend.

"Oh! Carlotta fell through the stage," I said.

"Oh?" Her eyes lit up as she leaned in. The woman loved gossip. Ate it up.

One time while we were eating outside the theater, she listened in on a group of women chatting about something scandalous. At least that's what I got by the look on her face.

"Yes! Um. *Le fantôme*," I teased, wiggling my fingers at her.

As if the ghost himself appeared, the color drained from her face.

She caught her breath and wiped the spittle from her mouth after choking. "Oh... that's interesting."

The rumors really did reach far and wide.

"You see him?" she asked.

My knuckles suddenly felt itchier than the wig, and no amount of scratching would ease them. "Well…"

"You stay with me, okay." Her worried smile hadn't wavered nor her insistent eyes as she squeezed my hand. Behind aged eyes was more than just worry. She really believed I was in danger. Or at least there was danger. "Stay away, with me. Help me again."

Yesterday I wanted to see about going back with her. Now that the opportunity had risen, I found myself hesitant.

"It's alright," I said, putting on a smile. "There's no ghost."

Worried eyes trailed away and glanced up quickly at something. Or

Chapter XI

someone.

"Are you certain of that?" a man's voice said from beside us.

Confused as hell, I turned and looked up to find Raoul, sweet and doughy eyed as always. And then there was Philippe.

"Pardon ladies," Raoul said.

Philippes face was slightly softer than the few times I'd seen him before. But he still looked bored. Very Colin Firth.

"Comte de Chagny. And Vicomte." I stumbled through, like a bumbling idiot.

"Raoul, please. And I didn't mean to interrupt your day. I only wanted to see how you were faring after the ordeal with the drunkard," he said.

It was hard not to smile when he spoke to you. He had such a sweet sincerity to him. Probably a genuinely good man.

"Oh, do you mean the fly King, Buquet?"

"There did seem to be a cloud about him, didn't there?" Philippe chimed in. Also realizing it was he who questioned about the ghost.

"Thank you, sirs. I'm alright," I said. "I will admit, I was very relieved to have you all there."

"I'm sure it would have been awful for him otherwise," Raoul jested.

"You'd be surprised what I'm capable of."

"I have no doubt of it, Miss."

Antoinette chomped at the bit with intrigue. This was probably the juiciest thing she'd seen in ages.

"Forgive me! This is Antoinette Descoteaux."

"Your mother?" Philippe asked.

"Friend."

The men each bowed as they introduced themselves. Antoinette fell in love immediately.

Both were very handsome; I'll give them that. This was a big deal for her. It wasn't often the wealthy conversed with the "peasants", I guessed.

"Well, again, forgive the intrusion, ladies. Enjoy your day," Raoul said. "*Bonne journée à vous ladies.*"

Raoul joined a group of men near a stagecoach. Philippe turned to follow suit.

"Miss Reilly," he said, halting and turned back. "May I speak with you a moment?"

"Uh… sure."

Antoinette's eyes widened and a wicked smile sat on her lips as I stood up hesitantly and stepped away.

Philippe hesitated to speak. Like he was constipated or in pain. Clearing his throat, as if it was the most unhinged thing he was about to say, "Would you be interested in joining me for dinner? I am unavailable this evening, however, tomorrow would have to suffice before I leave town for a short time."

I lied before.

This was the worst thing to happen.

Like a deer staring down the barrel of a shotgun, I froze. It hadn't occurred to me that something like this would happen. How would that even go?

No. The answer was no. Just tell him no.

On the flipside I might be able to have a conversation with someone. Use my voice. And he is pretty handsome.

"Thank you, but I…"

"*Yes, Monsieur. Elle adorerait,*" Antoinette said.

"What did you just say?" I glared at her. "What did she just say?" I asked Philippe.

"Perfect!" he smirked. It was an unsettling sight. "My carriage will be around at five thirty tomorrow evening. We will be going to dinner, so wear something very nice. Good day."

"What? No. I can't… No. ugh." *He's gone.*

Left standing dumbfounded, Philippe left to join the group of men piling into the carriage.

"A rich man." Antoinette stared with glimmering eyes, like she just did me a favor. "Handsome."

"Oh! No! Oh God no." I stumbled back into my chair and sunk down. "He's a patron at the Opera. And I don't want to do this, not really. Oh no."

"If I were young. *Je chevaucherais ce garçon toute la journée!*"

"I'm so mad at you right now."

Antoinette winked and sipped more wine. "*Ah! Yes! Thank you.*" She said as the food finally arrived.

Please let me go home tonight.

Chapter XII

Melody

How does one get out of a date in 1880 without possibility of severe consequences?

The queasiness lingered as time counted down. Since lunch yesterday, I'd spent the rest of my day off trying to figure out how to decline the invite, that really wasn't an invite. There was probably a canal in the floor between the hall and the restroom for how many times I'd walked in and out.

I should have just said no. I was almost there. *Damn, Antoinette.* I could have still said no though.

My shoulders slumped and my mind weighed heavy.

Along with everything else, I was delivered a note moving me from the theater. From the music. From any bit of reprieve.

"Lucky number seven," I muttered and unlocked the dressing room door.

Dust filled the air in a room I was certain hadn't seen anyone in years. Through the coughing, I fanned away the particles as I searched the wall for a switch.

Cobwebs decorated the high corners of the room, stretching across nearly everything. Crates, mannequins and other random things were covered in at least an inch of dust.

How the fuck was I supposed to clean this without a vacuum? I suppose they couldn't wait another 20 years, could they?

It'd be easier to just set it on fire and rebuild.

"I hate this place," I groaned into my hands.

I tied a rag around my head covering my mouth and nose, trying to figure out where to start.

Feather dusters were useless. All the thing did was kick up the dust and move it somewhere else.

Without blinding myself I continued through the chaos of forgotten things.

Who uses a dressing room for storage?

Eventually, I got toward the back of the room, clearing some small boxes. The tail of a heavy sheet hanging over something against the wall got caught up around my foot and tugged, almost tripping me.

After my near-death experience, I gripped the fabric to the sheet and slid it off gently.

A large vanity mirror and matching table appeared. Dark brown with gold leafed embellishments from the tip of the center mirror to the tip toes of the claw feet. The intricate metal details were cool beneath my touch. Elegant, high craftsmanship. Attention to detail and made to last. Nothing better. Or at least more beautiful.

Victorian era furniture was my favorite aesthetic. Especially Gothic-Romantic. Something I always wanted but could never afford.

The smile on my face was short lived when I caught sight of my reflection. Dirt covered me head to fingertips. The dingy woman hiding beneath a wig and long-sleeved dress, staring back wasn't someone I recognized.

I pulled the matching bench seat out from beneath the table and sat down. Tired of hiding beneath a costume made to appease, I tore the wig and bandana off, tossing them aside.

My nails dug against my scalp, relieving the itching I nearly always felt while I wore the damn thing. Another thing I could say no to but don't.

Apparently, I could kill a man, but that was the extent of my bravery.

When I was done scratching, I attempted to unflatten my hair trying

Chapter XII

to maybe find a little of myself again.

The sides were longer. I hated it. But where would a woman get a cut like this here?

I brought my filthy apron to my face to remove some of the smudges on it. It wouldn't budge.

Humming anything to quiet my busy mind usually helped, but not this time. The noise was too loud. I groaned and threw my face into my hands again.

"Just write to him and say no. That you're not interested like you wanted to when he asked," I said loud enough for the dust bunnies to hear.

It's not that I didn't find Philippe attractive. I do. He's honestly a very good-looking guy. It's super flattering in a normal situation. But, there's just something about him I didn't like. Not to mention the out of nowhere interest.

Why would he ask me out? We've never really even spoken.

I know Mom would want me to go. Sarah too. They think it'd be so good for me. Literally just because he asked me out. And he's hot.

Maybe if I just stayed hidden in here, I wouldn't have to go.

I looked at the tired face in the mirror again. She was begging for a hot bath.

What I wouldn't give for a scalding hot bath surrounded by candles. Bubbles piled high in a tub where the water could cover all of me. Maybe a pair of beautiful eyes staring from the dark end of the tub would be a nice addition.

I smiled faintly at the daydream I was suddenly lost in.

Yeah. A hot bath, my vibrator and a pair of beautiful eyes.

That.

What I wouldn't give for that.

Why does she haunt me so? The face I both know and do not.

Lost in her mind, she pushed back the hair that hung in her face as she stared into the mirror I was concealed behind. An unusual style for a woman, different. A lovely oddity to be seen.

It maddened me. Without a word spoken from foreign lips, curiosity called to me.

I had broken my own vow. Again.

Tortured were my ears at the silence. She had spoken her inner mind so well moments ago and now smiled. What made her cheeks pigmented?

Was a lover on her mind?

To my surprise, I grimaced, and my insides twisted at the thought.

No, she has no lover. From her own lips she said this.

Lashes fluttered, and with a shake of her head the soft smile that once beamed, faltered and whatever sweet thoughts, fled.

Why on earth I had her moved to this room was lost on me. There was no plan. Only action after our last encounter.

She lifted a small crate and piled it onto another nearby, butchering whatever odd song it was she sang.

Apparently, her vocals could manage the beating.

'Say something. Here she is,' the *Ghost* mocked.

She was as bad as the Banshee, however, it was her movements which kept me stationary.

This little mouse could act, this I knew.

"I see you are still alive, Mademoiselle," I said.

Mid-lift she halted, her head slowly moving about. "Were your ears bleeding, Monsieur?" she asked, scratching her knuckles.

Relief left my lungs. "I came to see who was torturing an innocent cat, only to find it was you once again."

The smallest chuckle trickled through her nervousness. *She knows who I am, yet does not run this time?*

"Your heroism is impressive," she said. The sarcasm in her voice tickled my ears and delighted my mind.

"I am not known for such acts of kindness. I was prepared to fight off anyone for that animal, cruelty is not something I savor. And now I know not what to do."

"I am sorry to disappoint."

She smiles for me? My body trembled at the sight of her attempt to hide upturned lips.

"I shall forgive you this time, Miss."

Chapter XII

I could not help but smirk as she roamed, searching the walls somewhat inconspicuously.

"I wouldn't mind being saved from this room though," she said. Obviously trying to figure my point of origin.

Clever little thing. *You are close. Be careful.*

"Ah yes. It is less than desirable. Decommissioned many years ago."

"All of the others are in use, why isn't this one? Did someone die in here?"

"Once Madame d'Espagne clawed her way up to diva, it was deemed unnecessary. Perhaps she thought it haunted with all the things that had gone missing and the voices she claimed to have heard."

Waiting for another quick retort, almost salivating for it, I found myself leaning into the mirror, straining once again to see her face.

Why was I always straining?

The lightness of her face fell and the air shifted. Where she seemed almost joyful to hear my voice again, was now a distant memory.

Turn back, please.

The next few moments might as well have been hours of nerve-wrecking silence. Like the silence she often had while she worked.

Sadness radiated from her as busying hands smoothed out the wrinkles in her apron. "You shouldn't talk to me. We shouldn't be talking." Every word that escaped her mouth sounded of regret as they fell.

Often people ran from me or cursed my name when I spoke to them. Then there was Christine who only spoke to me because she believed me an angel sent from heaven.

But this sad, lonely woman spoke to me as if I were any other man and warned me away with the same breath.

"Why do you say that, dear?"

Tears hid within her throat. "I'm not a part of this story. I shouldn't even be here. *You* shouldn't know me."

A curious analogy at best. "Then which story is it that you belong to?"

"Well. Um... That's actually a good question. I'm not sure I even know." She said it as if to herself.

Tossing a pillow onto the old chaise, Melody moved slowly toward the vanity. Toward me. "I watch others live their lives, progressing or whatever the case. Never really getting to be a part of it, you know?"

"I do." More than she could truly know.

I have roamed this world as an observer for years, witnessing the stories of its many changing inhabitants. Stories in which I have only played voyeur and villain to.

Lovers. Liars. Abusers and drunks. Good people. Bad. All of them. I watched from the shadows into their world and hated them for it.

Carlotta had been a main target for nearly nine years now, and recently, I live to further Christine's career. Her story. One I once hoped to be part of someday, though I feared that fantasy less likely as days went on as of late.

As if we shared the same space, a table, Melody sat across from me, swimming in her mind once again.

"What has your mind spinning, my dear Melody?" I asked.

"Of course, you know my name," she said looking into the mirror as if there were no barrier.

Gnawing on the lip I had dreamt of tasting once, she inhaled deeply. "If you were given the opportunity to… direct your favorite opera. Knowing every aspect of it, would you keep it as original as possible? Let it play out as it's supposed to? Or, would you be selfish and tempted to change it. Rewrite it. Even if it could be a complete disaster?"

It made me chuckle. Her sincerity was precious and her fidgety hands endearing.

However, if she wanted the righteous answer, she should talk to a priest. Or any other man that was not me. I was no saint. I have stolen. Lied and betrayed. Invaded the privacy of bedrooms. Done things that would make the devil blush.

And now, there was this nobody asking if I would do the right thing or the fun thing?

"The opera is my life. The idea of changing works from their original context is obscene."

She ran her hands over her face, a low growl rumbling in her throat. "Well. Yeah. Fuck."

"However." Her eyes hit the mirror deliberately again. "Chaos is embedded within me," I said.

Chapter XII

A sudden spark of life entered her face as I continued. "The director makes the rules, do they not? What would you do if you were the director of this story, Melody? Would you rewrite it to be more exciting? Melancholy? Would you add sun bright days or sword fights? Perhaps Romance. Love?"

As if the turmoil she had been feeling were on the precipice of relief, with bright inquisitive eyes, she opened her beautiful mouth.

Just then, the clock on the wall which had held onto life after all these years, chimed. She jumped as if time itself had made a threat.

As quickly as her face lit up, it dulled again when her eyes left me to look upon it. "Sometimes, we don't have the luxury of writing our own stories." Defeated eyes fell to the false identity she wore and balled it in her fists. "I have to go," she said in the smallest voice.

As long as time would allow, I would have her sit with me.

"Why, if whatever it is displeases you?"

Time was not on my side either so it had appeared. She pushed the bench beneath the vanity, and as she furthered away, I pressed against the mirror. I should stop her. Keep her from telling anyone about this.

She paused, looking back over her shoulder towards the mirror. "I... um…" she stumbled. "What's your name?"

My mouth opened to say the words "I am Erique", but they would not come.

A name held power. It was personal. Christine didn't even know my true identity, let alone my name. I stilled, choking on my fear.

Whatever battle it was which warred within her mind, seized and she was gone. Disappeared behind the door.

'Coward,' the *Ghost* laughed.

"What would you do if you were the director of this story, Melody?"

I'd send me the fuck home. That's what I'd do.

The walk from the employee quarters at the back of the theater to the foyer dragged on for miles. Every step threatened to send me vomiting with what little food I could stomach throughout the day.

I still only had one nice dress; the blue one Antoinette bought for me. I hated it and these shoes. This stupid wig. The fact that I'd have to pretend all night. And I knew I would.

If Phantom dude was gonna kidnap me, this was the time to do it. I would actually let him too.

Maybe if I just go hide in "lucky number seven", I wouldn't have to go.

Get it together. It's only a date.

Really though, when would I ever get the chance to go out with a conventionally handsome, rich guy?

My stomach dropped when I rounded the corner and saw Philippe standing in wait.

"Miss Reilly," he said. "Thank you for joining me."

Philippe's driver opened the door for us, and we stepped out into the beautiful night.

As we bounced along the road I thought about *his* question, coming back to it over and over when I already knew the answer.

He wouldn't even tell me his name, and the problem was and will always be, the Phantom was dangerous.

To befriend him was stupid. To think about it was worse. The fact that I even stayed and talked to him this time - as if he couldn't have just come out and murdered me, kidnapped me, or whatever - was still shocking.

Yet, I think the most dangerous thing about him was his voice.

Alluring to no end. The way he said my name unnerved me. I swear my soul danced as he spoke. Like I had known it all my life.

I didn't know him though. I knew nothing about him other than the things Christine had told me. A few true I was sure, especially the murders.

Still, it was all I thought about during dinner too. Not that Philippe noticed.

He had commandeered the entire date, talking about his newfound love for the world of politics and how he was making his way into it. Yeah, ok. Guess a little bit about his family was thrown somewhere in there too.

The thing about politicians, it didn't matter where or when, you needed a shower after they spoke.

Chapter XII

It was the longest two hours of my life. Only saved by the lamb, which I didn't order, because he ordered for us. However, it was prepared so perfectly, I couldn't taste the farm it'd come from.

I was surprised I could even eat at all, and was able to keep my vomiting level down to a minimum. Something I was getting better at. Even if you could literally cut through the cigarette smoke with a knife.

The carriage ride back was filled with the same idle chat. To my minds relief, it was a short to ride.

"Please allow me to walk you to your room," Philippe said. "I want to make sure you get there safely. There's ghosts running about."

I slipped from his grip, forcing my customer service smile. "The things that haunt me are far worse than any ghost. Good night, Philippe. Thank you for dinner. It was… an experience."

Not a bad experience. Just the same old one. Never asked me anything about myself. Nor did he really allow me to speak much on the rare occasion that I did - just to be polite. I bet he thought this was the greatest date because he was having such a great time talking.

A shiver slithered along my flesh as his jaw clenched. "All right then. Good night, Miss Reilly," he said.

Even though his face did everything right, there was nothing behind his eyes. The smile refused to touch them. I'd noticed it during the night, his perfect politician's smile. I didn't like it.

My own faux smile I held all night dropped the moment I turned away and a sigh of relief overtook as soon as I disappeared around the corner.

I laughed at how ridiculous this all was.

A world where Phantoms exist. Counts take me to dinner. I'm a murderer.

The new norm.

"Finally." The solace I felt when my door came into sight was unparalleled. I would never have thought I'd be so excited to crawl into my well-used bed.

The tension rolled off and true relief began when I stepped inside and locked it behind me.

A short lived feeling when the light switched on and something on my nightstand caught my attention.

My heart sped up a little and the hairs on my arms stood. I glanced around before landing back on the package bound with red ribbon.

Curiosity won, and with trembling hands, I picked it up. Hesitant fingers slid over the paper, finding the tail to the ribbon, which slid off without resistance. I entwined the ribbon around my fingers, then found a flap to open on the back.

Inside the nicely wrapped parchment was Mary Shelly's *Frankenstein*.

Hope told me Christine had left this. She would be the only one who knew.

Logic told me *he* left it.

My eyes flicked up from the book. I was certain I locked the door when I left. Was there a panel somewhere in the room? The wardrobe wasn't fixed to the wall, so it couldn't have been through there.

He was in my room. He could come into my room at any time. This should be the most frightening thing. And yes, my heart was pounding.

I cut back to the book and ran my fingers over the worn cover. The spine had for sure been opened at least a million times. When I opened the well loved book to a random page and saw that it was an English edition, suddenly, I didn't care where it came from. I'd never been so excited to read a book without sex in it.

Chapter XIII

The one thing I knew better than any—was music.

The harrowing aches that sounded from my cherished organ were the one thing that kept the awfulness of my mind together.

Like breathing, how the music came to me. No effort, though it drained me of every energy when I composed.

The moment I touched skin to ivory as a boy, God had gifted me in exchange for the injustice of my existence.

Nights upon days, weeks upon years, I had spent perfecting the one thing I could. Allowing me the freedom to escape within imagination brought on by my own practiced fingers.

A gifted freak which made Queens cry and Kings delight.

These gifts were supposed to have been my key to the world. It had granted me employment for a King, and in that position, new found talents in architecture. Which I utilized to aid in building that King his Palace of Illusions.

The end of the beginning.

Notes came flawlessly, as sweat gathered on my brow. Fingers ached while I beat the ivory as if they had wronged me somehow. Words I had but cannot relay onto paper with the same ease.

With all this, I was stunted.

I forced fantasies of Christine as I played, hoping she would be enough to push me beyond this. Remind me to which my purpose was. And that I may continue on with this opera that must be finished.

I replayed her lovely, soft face emoting every meaning of the staggering aria she had rehearsed, written solely for her voice.

Soft brown eyes and a smile that could melt ice on a cold day looked upon me with care.

No… Christine's eyes were blue.

My fingers slowed and the strikes against innocent keys softened as Christine faded away and that of another took her place.

With closed eyes I gave in and continued with the surprising light sound.

The dream from that night.

Where I ran around in darkness for eternity. Until I saw a light in the distance. I raced for it as if it was God's hand, finally, come to take me.

Only it was her. Staring into a mirror at the center of the void.

The girl seen in many dreams. Always from a distance.

Vanilla and something I could not place scented her bare shoulder. When I glanced up into the mirror, she stared back at me. Unafraid. Then the stranger was gone.

The memory was not enough. I needed more.

When I reached the light this time, I stepped into some place different. A light breeze flickered amongst the trees as I stared out over a lake. I could almost smell the nature.

The one I knew the name of now, Melody, stared at the calm waters. Black dress flowing in the breeze. Sun kissing her bare shoulders. Hair whipping softly about.

My fingers ran along wildflowers and hanging leaves as I walked towards her.

The second my foot left the tree line and planted onto the sand; she turned with opened arms, beckoning with a smile. The sun was made for her, sparkling in her eyes as she stared adoringly at me, begging to be kissed.

Something I could only imagine.

"Erique." She smiled with *love*…

Chapter XIII

I twirled her and watched her adoration for me grow.

"My Melody," I said, caressing her face.

Both music and fantasy stopped abruptly, and silence filled my hell, as the dream rolled down my rotting flesh.

Not my Melody. And never with love.

I could not even give her my name.

It was a cruel thing, what I had just done to myself. Imagined an embrace, a kiss in which I could never know the feeling of.

Clenched fists came down onto innocent keys, and a terrible sound echoed throughout the underworld around.

A trembling sigh fell from my lips while the *Ghost* egged me on to take for myself. To force what I want. Make her mine. Bring her here since I refused to quiet my thoughts of her. The girl. The woman who meant nothing.

The damned woman was ruining everything. Consuming my thoughts. Changing my determinations.

Worse yet, I was giving into it.

"You shouldn't talk to me. You shouldn't know me." Melody had made it clear that she wanted nothing to do with me.

No longer would I entertain her.

A ride beneath the stars should rid my mind of her.

Of it all.

***

The beautiful thing about midnight was the illusion of peace. Especially when the rain fell.

The theater was quiet, and anyone left behind was in their room or the salon, no one around to notice a missing horse.

My hands found the levers to the unknown entrance of the stables.

There was only ever one stableman on duty overnights and they were easily persuaded to look the other way when the Ghost called. This night was no different.

Hidden beneath the brim of my felt hat, I passed each stall, heading for that last one. Cesar, the Opera's favored stallion, was certain to be up for a moonlight ride.

Upon hearing a voice, I halted.

I inched closer; my wicked mind had to have been playing tricks on me. What on earth would she be doing out here this late?

"He composed heroic songs and began to write many a tale of enchantment and knightly adventure," she read out loud in a half decent English accent.

Every thought of banishing her from memory vanquished the moment her voice laced around my ears. Not just with any words, but the words of my gift.

I slipped into Cesar's stall, where the beautiful white and gray peppered Holsteiner greeted me with the nudge of his soft muzzle. I returned in kind a few strokes between his nostrils and released him.

Sweet Melody was nestled in a large stack of hay, wrapped in a blanket. Short, light colored hair laid on the side of her face. The thought of pushing it back behind her ear to see her face better crossed my mind again.

"He tried to make us act plays and to enter into masquerades, in which the characters were drawn from the heroes of Ronces…Ron.. Roncess…" she stumbled.

"Roncesvalles, of the Round table of King Arthur, and the chivalrous train who shed their blood to redeem the holy sepulcher from the hands of the infidels," I finished.

I had not intended on speaking. Just to look upon her for a second while she read would have sufficed. For now.

Her head snapped up, eyes darting around.

"Forgive me," I said. "I did not mean to startle. I will leave you be." My feet did not waver, despite what my mouth promised.

The sound of rain beating atop the tin roof and the grounds around drowned out any silence between us.

She gnawed on her lip, deep in thought.

I wished she would not do that. It only made me wonder what a kiss would feel like. What it would taste like.

A little sigh escaped those lips. "Hi," she said.

"*Enchanté,* Melody."

Her eyes closed and a faint flutter in her breathing caught my ear. I was aware of the power in my voice when used. The effect it could have on whomever I spoke depended on what I wanted.

Except, with no intent, I used my own voice.

She picked at her nail beds and twisted her mouth to the side. "I know you're not a ghost," she said.

"Does it frighten you? Knowing that I am just a man in the walls?"

"I'm not sure yet," she said. "It should… but I… Are you following me?"

"We do keep finding each other, do we not?"

"Well, it's only an accident if you're not looking."

Her defenses were understandably high. I never thought I would ever be in such a position, reassuring another of their safety. This was uncharted territory.

"I have not followed you tonight," I said.

I found myself wanting to be truthful with her. She could have told anyone about our encounters. Yet, no one has hunted for the Ghost.

She scratched her knuckles like she was digging a hole. "That didn't make me feel better. Nor did it answer my question."

The little mouse was nervous. That would make two of us.

"I have looked in on you."

She swallowed hard. "I see." Her chest rose as she inhaled deeply and ran the back of her nails across her lips. "Why? Do you want to hurt me? Not that someone who did want to hurt me would tell me that."

The things I was capable of. The fact that I did not want to let her be. That I could not keep myself from her. The things I have imagined between us. Things I had not entertained, not even with Christine. She should be scared. I would ruin her.

How had the little mouse dug her claws into me?

"I was curious. Only that," I answered.

Her brows twisted in confusion. "How many times have you been in my room?" she asked.

"Once."

"For the book?"

"Yes."

It was true. I'd only entered once.

"How did you get in?" she asked.

"Locks are merely an inconvenience here."

"I see."

My tongue ran along the back of my teeth while my mind jumped around. If I was to feed into this curiosity of mine, I would need her to want to speak with me.

With trembling breath, I exhaled, "Erique."

"What?"

"You asked me for my name, and I failed to give it. I am Erique."

The tension in her shoulders dropped slightly and an air of alleviation slipped from her. She chuckled and ended with a sigh. The kind that was laced in irony. Something I had not anticipated.

"Is there something amusing about my name?" I asked. The edge in my voice a little more apparent than intended.

"Oh, no. Not at all. I like it."

"Then why do you snicker, Ms. Reilly?"

"I suppose… I didn't know what I was expecting?" she said looking baffled by her response.

"I could change it if you would like," I said. "How does Frankenstein sound? Or perhaps I could try something more exotic like Cheshire."

"Would that make me Alice?"

"Or the Mad Hatter."

"That would be close to how I feel anymore. But I think M. Leblanc wins the hat."

"Oh no, he is the Walrus for certain. Do not let him fool you."

"And M. Fournier, the White Rabbit."

"Very much on the nose, my dear."

My soul soothes with the soft giggles pulled from her. A foreign feeling that I would do anything to keep.

I should witness her smile as she opened Lewis Carroll's *Alice's Adventures in Wonderland.* That will be my next gift to her.

The imagery ignited a long forgotten sensation within my chest that traveled further to a much more disregarded place. Not even by my own hand, a part of me that had not seen life in many years sparked with a twitch and sudden want.

"Yes. I am Alice," she whispered to herself. Fingers fidgeting against each other.

I wished my own could touch them, maybe soothe whatever had her mind in chaos. Soothe each other.

Who do I kid but myself. She would recoil in disgust. My presence

Chapter XIII

sets her on edge, and I would only make things worse by touching her.

"I called out for you yesterday," she said, trepidation in her voice. "But because I didn't know your name, it was kind of silly."

My heart needed reminding of its purpose when it ceased at her confession.

She called out for *me*?

A surge of rage burned within. Not with her, but myself for having hid away, afraid of her rejection.

"'Hey you… are you there?' Yeah. Kind of like that," she said, scrunching her face. "I wanted to thank you for this," she added, lifting my book. "And also, you shouldn't be eavesdropping, however, I'm grateful. You don't know what it means to me."

"You are more than welcome. It is my favorite story."

"I can tell," she said, glancing at the worn cover once again. "Thank you for trusting it with me. I'll return it when I'm done. Promise."

"It is yours."

"No. That's ok I…"

"It would mean a great deal that you would have it."

"Thank you."

The warmth from a small bit of joy that she would accept my gift truly, brought a warm smile to me. A true innocent smile. Another thing forgotten.

"Have you read *Frankenstein* before?" I asked.

"Yes. It's one of my favorites as well, but it's been a while."

"How does it make you feel? When you read it."

"Sad. I feel sorry for him."

"Victor?"

"No. The creature. Created out of sheer hubris. Then discarded almost immediately and hunted for not being what Victor had planned. Expected. Every hand that touched him was cruel. All he learned was that he was bad. A monster. You're either made a monster, or you're Victor…"

She sympathized with a monster, yet her words bit. Did she think herself a monster? Something to do with the blood on her the night we first met?

"…Mary Shelley was so good at the story telling in this. You can almost read her own hurt. Her own views of how she saw life. Birth even. How it wasn't a thing of beauty, but awful for everyone involved. I could have never written anything this profound. It's so good."

My brows lifted and new intrigue wiggled its way in. "Are you a writer?"

"Yes. No. I was. I tried my hand at screen...plays and stories. But it just never went anywhere. Sometimes you just have to accept that you're just not good at something you love. No matter how much you wanted it."

She chuckled, but the hurt in her voice voided the attempted masking.

"What kind of stories were they? Dark like our favorite books?" I asked.

"Yes, actually. There's something about them that I've always liked. Maybe it's because there's more truth to them or they're outlandishly outrageous that no one would believe it'd happen. Whereas light hearted, love stories for example, are full of shit and give false hope to people who desperately want it."

Lightened hair danced in her face as she shook her head about. "Anyway," she said, pushing the hair back behind her ear. "Enough of that. The subject gets me riled up. Sorry."

Writing or Love?

The passion she had for the written word was beautiful. With such fire, how could she not be good at it?

"Why are you in the stables reading to horses, Alice? I can tell you that Cesar nor Norah, enjoy dark stories—unlike you and I. It gives them awful nightmares," I said.

Her eyes lifted, slowly passing from one point to another. It was hard to concentrate on anything other than the glow from the lantern in her eyes. It sparkled, emulating the light in which my recent fantasies yearned for.

The warm glow caressed the skin of her face. I could stare at her for hours in the glow of fire. If she would let me.

Or not.

"It's peaceful out here. When I can't sleep it helps. Also, this is one of the few places outside that masks the odor of the city," she said.

Many of the city's inhabitants still lived in the old ways, emptying

Chapter XIII

chamber pots and buckets into the streets, though indoor plumbing had been around for a time. Gong unbathed for weeks. That, paired with years of untreated water and sewage yards.

Even my home below the opera had indoor plumbing.

"It is something one gets used to I suppose," I replied.

"You're either very lucky or not. Where I'm from, it smells like Satan's anus all day. The Aroma of Tacoma. You would think that I would be used to a smell by now. No. Not at all. In fact I'm angry. Home smelled awful. New York City smelled awful. And now this place. I couldn't have ended up anywhere that smelled even remotely better? Among all the other shitty things that have happened, it had to be somewhere with the constant stench of an outhouse on fire."

I fought back the amusement climbing within my chest.

God, her passion was unrivaled. So alive as she spouted. Hands flailing about, animating her frustrations. I almost felt bad enjoying it.

She was not a little mouse, but a life force that only needed pushing.

"Then I take it you do not like it here then, in my Opera?"

"*Your* Opera? Last I checked, M. Fournier and Leblanc owned this place?"

"Those two idiots know nothing of Opera," I snapped. "And they do not own it. It belongs to Paris."

"Hm. That's interesting."

"Now. Answer me, Melody," I demanded, lowering my voice.

"Answer what?"

"Do you not like it here?"

A part of me hoped she would say yes. It would make things easier with our relationship. Maybe she would come with me willingly when the time came. No illusions, only a yes.

"Uh, that is the question, isn't it?" she sighed and scratched her head. "Under other circumstances, I would have loved this. Being here."

"What circumstances were those?"

Her sudden playful tone slipped to melancholy. "I don't want to talk about it if that's alright," she said. "I want to talk. Just not about that. It's complicated."

I needed to know about her. What made her tick. She would tell me in time. I would draw it out of her one way or another. But the fact that she said with her own words, she wanted to talk with me. This angel was dangerously close to never being rid of this demon.

"Would you care to learn to sing properly?" I asked, surprised by my own offer.

I was already teaching another. Yes, I could take on more, but as much as she draws me to her, it would take a miracle to form a voice worthy of stage.

Yet, I would not retract.

If time with her is what was needed to prove this only mere curiosity, then so be it. I knew in my mind that Christine was my chosen. My future. Even when there were doubts.

"What?" she asked, just as surprised.

"Would you like lessons? Learn to sing properly and not damage that throat of yours any further?"

Her sweet face lit up, no remnants of whatever bothered her remained. "*You* want to teach *me* to sing?"

When I thought the jolt of life in my cock was a foreign feeling, this was other worldly. To bring true joy to another fascinated me. Even if my offer was not selfless in reason, I found her reaction pleasant.

"That is what lessons consist of, yes," I answered.

Divots decorated her full cheeks. The giant grin on her face begged to have a thumb run across it. I imagine they were soft, just as her cheeks looked.

I waited in anticipation for whatever came next.

A moment passed and as if reminded of something, her joy faded.

My jaw clenched and I swallowed. "Why do you hesitate? Would you not like that?"

"I would love that! Please, don't think that I don't."

"Then why decline such an offer?"

"I don't want to waste your time. And I don't want to disappoint you," she said.

Such sweet words.

"If you follow instruction and take it seriously, there can be no disappointment."

"It's not that. Well, it is that too," she stammered. "I just don't know how long I'll be here for. I'm trying to get home."

Chapter XIII

Why did the thought of her leaving upset me?

"To the place that smells like the devil's anus?"

Cesar bumped into me, startled by the laughter that erupted from the haystack.

What sweet intoxication laughter was.

"I know. I know," she said, trying to rein herself in. The tears in the corners of her eyes were a spectacular site to behold. "It's not perfect, but it's home. I guess." Then she sighed. "I have to get back."

Did she have a lover? I swore she spoke of none with Christine. A child perhaps? Who could need her so badly that she would have to leave?

"There is someone that awaits you? A husband?"

"No. No," she was quick to say. "My mom. She's uh… really sick. And I'm the only one that helps her."

"She has no other to care for her?"

"My sister has her own family. So, it's kind of up to me. To be honest though, I've been gone so long now, I don't even know what I'd be going back to. Whether she's even alive or not."

My heart beat with relief at confirmation of her marital status, but hurt for the utter pain in her face.

I could send her home. I had the means. It would take but a day to acquire such a ticket.

"Have you not called on her?" I asked.

"It's complicated," she said, gripping the blanket and tugging it tighter around her.

"I am starting to dislike that word."

"Me too."

It stirred something unpleasant within to see her in such a state. I only wanted to see her smile again. For me.

"Allow me to teach you until then?" I said. "Perhaps it could bring you joy amongst all that ails your mind."

"You would do that? Knowing that one day I could just be gone?"

She would stay here with me for eternity if I had my way.

"No one is promised tomorrow, dear."

This angel's face lit up again. "Alright. Yes. I'd love to."

"Then it is done."

I had broken my own promise again. I did not wish to banish any thoughts of her. Instead, I had made sure she would never leave them.

She settled back into a state of ease, picking up the book and looking it over. Bottom lip between her teeth.

I wished she wouldn't do that.

"Do you want to read with me?" she asked.

Startled by her invitation, my eyes snapped up to hers. "Would you like that?" I hoped she had not noticed the break in my voice.

A hesitant smile graced her face. "You can come sit with me. We can share the book."

As I am, I was not unsightly. The false face covered all the shame I held. My wardrobe chosen specifically with my frame in mind. Done up, I did not think me terrible. Still, it could make her uneasy enough to run away.

I could not fathom the rejection in her eyes at sight of me.

Why would I do that when I had just won?

"I know it by heart. We can alternate chapters if you would like."

"Yeah. That's perfect," she said.

Disappointment hid behind a smile. My rejection had stung her.

How odd.

We read out loud for a short while, until her eyes were too heavy to keep open and she had succumbed to sleep, gripping my book like it was something precious.

With caution, I turned down the lamp above her head. My eyes roamed over her sleeping face. Sweetness radiated even while she slept. I wanted a taste. Just a little taste.

I removed the glove on my hand and pocketed it, bringing my bare skin to her cheek, hovering just above it. The pulse in her neck and breathing said she was in deep rest. Slow and soft.

Just a little more and we would be skin on skin. I would know what it felt like to touch a warm body.

The length of my knuckle ran gently over her flesh, to the corner of her lips, just under her jaw and down her neck.

Her breathing changed. Chest rising with heavy breath. A small moan escaped, which nearly buckled me over.

I had taken too much, and pulled my hand away, staring just a

Chapter XIII

moment longer.

Never have I looked forward to a meeting so much in my life than the one I had with her tomorrow evening.

I had damned myself with my curiosity.

'Are you certain you wish to go through with this? You said yourself, she was a lost cause for the stage. That was the only way to bring you everything you wanted. Christine has that and more,' the *Ghost* said.

"Christine does not know my name," I answered.

Chapter XIV
Melody

I have got to be fucking stupid. I fell asleep in the stables. How unsafe was that? How did that even happen? He—or anyone could have just done stuff to me.

My heart rattled around my chest as I stood outside one of the practice rooms of the opera house, strangling the strap of the messenger bag I wore.

This had been the only thing I'd thought about since waking up in my bed. Which still was a little fuzzy on how I got there.

Though I looked forward to the possibility that I would actually get to learn something I had always wanted to learn, something else was on my mind.

Surprisingly, it wasn't home…

He was going to teach me.

It was like being in a dream but not a dream. A nightmare with a dream element. Sometimes I still ponder whether this was real or if this was that place between life and death.

What a weird fucking place if it was.

Part of me hoped he'd come to me sometime during the day while

Chapter XIV

I was cleaning the dressing room, but he didn't.

I mean, I still didn't think I should be doing it. Any of this. Interacting with him or anyone else really, but… I was here.

It had to be the loneliness thing. I had gone a month without talking to anyone really.

Even now, Christine was off with Raoul and stayed at her grandmother's most days, so if I wanted to see her, it'd be rare. Antoinette was amazing, but the language barrier still made it feel lonely.

Then there's Erique.

It's like trying to avoid someone, but then the universe is like "uh no" and forces you into a small room together.

Speaking of small rooms…

I stared at the closed door. The one I had failed to open yet.

It still made me a little nervous. He's unstable, obviously. But talking to him was so easy. Relieving even.

His voice. Oh my God, his voice. It was hard to describe. Smooth and soft. But there was command in it. Power even when he was gentle. No wonder Christine believed he's an angel. He sounded like one.

Then there's the "what if I displeased him?" thing I kept thinking about. That my inability to be more than mediocre turned him against me.

A certain way to never get back home, that's for sure.

God. I hated knowing what I did. It almost seemed that this would've been better without my Phantom knowledge. At least maybe I wouldn't be as erratic.

"It's unlocked," he said from the other side of the door.

My heart jumped. Of course, he knew I was here.

Once inside, I scanned the room.

The back half was dark, not really sure how since there was a light at the center.

"I was afraid you changed your mind," he said.

"Me? Come to my senses and not meet a random man in a small room somewhere no one knows? Nope. Couldn't be me."

On a music stand at the center of the room, beneath that light, lay a stack of papers. Sheet music, I discovered as I got closer.

I fingered through the pages, curiously. The hairs on my arms stood and the back of my neck tingled when I glanced into the dark. "Where are you?"

"I'm here," he said. "What do you know of music?"

"I can read it." I stepped towards the dark half of the room slowly, peering into it, just hoping to catch a glimpse of him.

"Do not go any further. I would hate for this to end."

I sighed. "You know that only makes one more curious, right? And I don't care what you look like. It's just weird to talk to nothing."

"You will be used to it soon enough," he said calmly. "Before we begin, there are some rules you must abide by."

"I'm listening…" I said, still staring into the void.

"You will dedicate yourself solely to this. Lessons are just the first step. You will need to be practicing whenever possible. And you will not come into the dark to find me."

"Fine." I reluctantly agreed. "And?"

"You will have no outside distractions."

My ears perked up. "Elaborate."

"This must be the only thing on your mind at all times. You will not distract yourself with personal relationships."

"Are you trying to say that I am not allowed friends?" *Oh, fuck no.* This is what the Phantom does to Christine.

"They will distract you from our goal."

"I see." My skin crawled at his comment. "Well. Thanks for the opportunity anyway." I gripped the strap to my bag again and backed toward the door, hoping not to activate attack mode in him. "I'm going to go."

"No." His voice was quick and low.

"Look. With everything going on with me, I'm not ok all the time. But I'm also not going to let someone tell me I can't talk to my friends or do whatever. So. Again, thank you for the opportunity but I must decline." My heart raced, threatening to jump through my back. This man would be the first to kill me for rejection. There wasn't a doubt about it. Would anyone hear me scream? Probably not. I don't have the voice for it.

"Forget what I've said," he said.

I paused with my hand on the doorknob. "What? So easily?"

Chapter XIV

"I only want you to take this seriously, Melody. People would dissuade you from this. Do not throw away a chance to find your happiness, peace, your voice. Your place in this world. Not for anyone. Nor some unworthy, self-titled viper."

Nearly speechless, I blinked hard and looked off in the distance. "Are you talking about Philippe de Chagny?"

"Snakes spill lies while they crush their prey, Melody. I know his kind. He would take you from here and chain you to a life of servitude. No matter the dreams rolling down your face at such an empty life. All while your friends would support such matters because it is what is done."

Was he jealous? No... Oh no. I was not dealing with this shit. I won't. This was already a gamble at best, but this was going to end badly.

Jealousy is a terrible thing if not checked. And no way Erique's going to do that.

Didn't matter that he was right.

"Ok. That was really random. Philippe's not even a friend. So that's not an issue. And I already told you, I'm trying to go home. That's the most important thing. But also," my hands trembled, "You nor anyone else is going to tell me who I can't and can see. or befriend. So, I'm just going to leave. Because…"

"Alright," he said quick, yet stern. "I have heard you. I have no right to demand these things of you."

My mind told me to run. To get the fuck out of there. That it was only going to get worse.

But he sounded so sincere. Words that have only ever brought me misery in the past.

Go. Go, dumbass.

"Come. Please." His voice soft as it had been the night before. I hated that I trusted it already. "Now, we will warm up."

I hesitated only a few moments until I inched towards the stand, removing my bag and setting it at the base.

It'd been so long since I'd seen sheet music. Scales and simple songs were stacked neatly one in front of the other.

Memories of school band trips and goofing around in class came to mind. Faces I hadn't seen since graduation. All those years.

"I will strike a key and I want you to match the note as best you can. Do not strain yourself. Stop when you can no longer reach them. Do you understand?" he asked.

"Yes," I said, focusing a little too hard on the first note and trying to figure out what was happening inside me.

"Relax, dear. Breathe."

I took a deep breath and off we went.

It felt good to even do scales. I followed every note he struck, praying that it was even close to what I heard in my head.

Several minutes passed until he stopped.

"You can find notes," he said, almost surprised. "So, you're not a complete loss after all." My jaw dropped. The audacity that he spoke the truth. "You're too much in your throat. Bring it up and out. Almost as if you are trying to sing through your nose. For now," he finished.

"That's a very odd…How?" I stopped and blew through my nose as well as trying to make a sound. "Ok, I'll try."

We went on for a while as I tried to replicate the notes he played. I relaxed the further we got into the lesson. It was nice to have a teacher that was both critical and praising.

It didn't stop me from trying to see into the dark. I knew where he sat. I could hear the pings from the keys. I just wanted to see his eyes.

"Melody…" he scorned at my not so sneaky attempt. "Now, again."

The lesson went on for a while longer. More scales and direction from Erique on how to move my jaw and where to redirect sound and breathing.

"You need much work still, but you will get there in time," he said. "How do you feel?"

"A little sore. But, really good actually."

"Good. Now, behind the sheets and folder, there is something for you."

At the back of the stack of papers, wrapped in red ribbon was a folder.

I took the ribbon off and opened it up.

Blank pages.

"So that you may write when you're feeling down. Or joyful or what have you."

Chapter XIV

He had to have known I was on my last sheets of paper. I was really going to need a new lock on my door or something.

It still moved me in an unexpected way though. Twice he'd given me a gift, something I needed. I couldn't remember the last time someone gave me something other than depression. "Thank you. I was in need. But I'm sure you already knew that."

"Now, open the folder that was in front of that," he said, ignoring my accusation.

After placing the papers in my bag, I returned to the stand. Behind the stack of sheets there was a yellowed folder with a leather strip wound around a button with calligraphy styled writing inked on the front.

"Oh! I know this one. *Marriage of Figaro* by Mozart. I mean I don't know the whole thing. Or words. But I know of it, I guess."

In an attempt to hide the reddening in my cheeks, I dropped my head. Every time I opened my mouth, I felt stupid. For someone that knew so much, only because of the time I grew up in, I knew nothing that mattered.

I sifted through the pages, noticing it was too thin to be a full opera. The show was like four hours long. This was only one of the scenes from it.

"*Vio che Sapete*," he said.

"This is in Italian. I'm struggling with French as it is."

"You will do well," he reassured me.

I set the folder down a little roughly. "That's extremely presumptuous of you, Erique. I don't know this piece, but I can already tell this is too big for me."

"Would you like to hear it?" he asked.

I tried to hide the sudden excitement I felt at his offer. "You want to sing for me?" There's no way I was going to be able to sing this ever, but I'll be damned if I was going to turn down a man singing for me. This was one fantasy I was going to actually experience. "Yes. Please!"

The piano came to life once again. This time with music instead of tired scales.

The piece was light, almost bubbly. The last thing I expected.

My soul froze in place as he sang. Within the first few measures, I couldn't stop my eyes from welling up or my hands clenching the stand to keep me upright.

The voice that I'd imagined so many times, failed in comparison to what he projected. Erique was a siren.

Even in lightness, it was devastating. The power of it wrapped itself around me, encapsulating my body like a cocoon and snaked its way through every bit of me that it could find.

Heat filled my cheeks and pulsing aches called out from between my thighs. I may have been smart enough to understand what was happening, but even I was having a hard time fighting it.

Then it stopped, and I nearly whimpered at the silence.

I wiped the trail left by a tear and giggled a bit on edge. "I had no idea you would sing like *that*. What a dirty rotten trick."

"How did you think I would sound?"

"Not like that. Maybe more like Lorenzo."

"He is good." There was a smugness to his response. He knew he was better.

A moment passed long enough for me to collect myself.

I wanted to stay as long as I could, get him to sing again. What if this was the last night I was here? This could be something I carried with me always. That and his book.

"I must leave. We will meet again tomorrow after your work has ended for the day," he said.

"Oh. Uh. Yes. Sure. It's late."

I grabbed my bag and turned to go, hesitating. "You wouldn't want to read again with me, would you?" I pulled the book from my bag. "We're almost done."

"I would like nothing more, but unfortunately I must go this evening."

"Ok. Yeah. No problem," I said.

"Good night, dear Melody. You did well."

"Goodnight, Erique."

Chapter XV

A devil I will be until the end. It was a trick. To see if I could achieve what the music on stage had over her.

What I had not anticipated was the effect at the sight of her befalling into a moment of ecstasy at my command would have on my own decrepit body.

As soon as the door latched behind her, I caught myself on the piano with one hand and gripped my cock with the other, trying to ease the relentless throbbing.

Christine listened to me with innocence, like a child with her teacher. Not once had this happened with her.

Melody. Sweet Melody listened with yearning.

Desire. That was what this was. It had not dawned on me that this kind of emotion played a factor in what urged me towards her.

'Nearly brought to her knees. Breasts heaving. Tears stained her cheeks with the overwhelming sensations you brought her. You excited her, Erique,' the *Ghost* in my mind said. *'How interesting.'*

How much I wanted to keep her in that state. To read with her. God, the look in her eyes when I denied her. I loathed myself even more than the average day. But the ache in my own body was stronger than it had been, even when I was a younger man. If she had stayed, I may have…

No, I would not go to her unless she asked. Even then.

Suppressing the urge for release, for her, I let go and grabbed my cloak. Frustrated, my hat came next as I departed from that room for a much needed distraction.

Home or to inconvenience someone?

Passageways slipped by without thought, having trekked them more times than one could count, they slipped by as the *Ghost's* voice taunted.

He wanted to play.

The dancers had not been startled in a while. Perhaps it was time to muck about there.

The cramped space between the walls of the dorms were built with my slender frame in mind, not my broad shoulders. A small oversight on my part when building the damned place. I despised moving through them.

I had come to a stop, perfect placing to see within the room.

On the other side of the wood and plaster, a shaky humming bled through.

With slight trepidation, I peered into the cracked knothole.

What was left of my soul was gone upon the sight of her.

It was not humming. My angel was moaning, only this time she was awake.

Moonlight caressed her small naked breasts as she laid out on her bed. Soft stomach beckoning to have hands lain upon it. A focused palm circled a hardened nipple and massaged a pert breast while the other hand tended between her thighs.

A vision of true beauty. I would fall at the feet of this goddess if it would not frighten her.

What fantasies twirled within her mind? Did she imagine vile counts or monsters that hid within the dark?

'*Perhaps she imagines that her hand is your own,*' the *Ghost* suggested.

She would never. No living soul would.

This should not have been witnessed by me.

'*Since when does the Opera Ghost care about such things as privacy?*'

I had sworn to keep myself from here. Yet, God's army could not

Chapter XV

pull me away.

Wood slats pressed into my side as I strained to get closer.

Just this once.

"I am sorry, beautiful Melody." Gritting my teeth, I yanked at the clasp of my trousers and sighed in relief as I pulled myself from behind its cell.

Braced against the wall, I matched the rhythm of her hand.

Every stroke brought me pleasure I had long suppressed. Behind my eyes, scattered lights threatened to blind me as bliss spread.

I saw myself with her. She accepted me, begged for me even. To give her this kind of gratification. To smell her, taste her…

I was ready to collapse at any moment on the verge of zenith.

At the apex of her thighs, fingers continued to move. Never had I coveted a hand until now.

Slide inside. Make believe it is me that gives you such delight.

Her pace picked up. My body shook violently as I matched it. Her thick thighs clasped together as she convulsed. "Erique," she gasped.

Did my ears deceive? Had my name fallen from her lips during a moment of pleasure?

Stars blinded me, and bliss leaked from my eyes as I spilled onto the wall that enclosed her room.

"Mine," I muffled into the fabrics of my sleeve.

Lightheaded and weakened, I found the knothole through the fading stars. She rolled over and covered herself.

Left with a sense of disgust by my actions, I jammed myself back into my trousers.

The *Ghost* was right.

I had looked in on many as I wandered the opera. However, never had I done this.

***

The claws of guilt only tore into me one other time. When a friend heard of a King's plan to execute all who built his Palace of Illusions. For acts of treason, that friend lost his family as well as title of Police Chief for aiding a young deformed composer in escape.

The door closed behind me as I breached the roof.

Empty as usual. Made perfect for outdoor getaways on the rare occasion I would treat myself to the night air.

Not far in the distance stood the weathered pegasi and golden angels.

After descending a ladder, and many heavy steps later, I settled in at the base of the golden angel that stood watch over the busy streets.

The tranquility of night soothed like nothing else.

Almost nothing else.

When the world was dark, I could suspend myself from reality just a little more. My favorite time of day.

I was the Ghost. Or I was Erique, a man looking down into a world I longed to belong to and hated with every fiber of my being.

The glow from the moon in the starry, black sky touched all around. The night was so clear, it was like daylight. And I wished she were sitting with me, reading.

I sighed and removed the hard molded false face I wore. The Paris air roamed over the tortured thing that was my face, drying the sweat that accumulated inside when I shared a beautiful one sided moment that should never have happened.

The cool air flowed through my nostrils and filled my lungs. To breathe the air in without obstruction was a glimpse into the disgusting normalcy others felt.

When I exhaled, my body felt little relief from the effort.

Below, very few souls walked about. Men on their way home from the brothels. Late shift workers. Police. Women of the night.

Faint laughter drew my attention.

Leaning forward, I gripped the lip of the roof. A young couple had rounded the corner holding hands, seeming to enjoy the others' company.

My heart ached as I watched the man steal a kiss from his companion. How she accepted it with open lips and a smile.

Longed have I to kiss another. A soul that would not recoil and run away.

An impossible ask. A treacherous desire.

She may call my name, but even Melody would run at the sight of this… *thing*.

No. Christine. She will. No. Yes. Perhaps?

I growled into my palm.

Chapter XV

Upon hearing a familiar voice, my wallowing paused as I leaned over the edge again.

Ah. The little Count. Satisfying your rotten cock on this eve as well?

The thought of the rope in my pocket crossed my mind. Instead, I scanned the surrounding area of the roof, finding a small piece of the concrete ledge which had broken off at some point.

I scooped it up quickly and searched for my target again. He was with another patron near the street.

"What are the odds I could hit a moving target from here?"

'Good enough.'

"Who was that?" Philippe de *Vermin* yelled after the rubble ricocheted from his shoulder. "Who was that!"

"Lucky bastard. I was aiming for your head," I said, loud enough for only the angel to hear.

The couple that had been passing by hurried away as his rage grew. The man with him tried to ease the situation.

I chuckled, but the joy failed to alleviate the wretched twisting inside. This was *her* fault. This stranger. This accidental angel…

My eyes lifted to the stars again, searching for the brightest one.

"Have you brought her here to torture me further or save me? Please. I yearn for something I have never tasted. I dream of life I can only read about. Deliver me from this anguish. My soul has faded to nothing. With every day I grow that much more of a monster. Something I have never wanted. I beg you every night, yet you still answer no, why? Is there nothing for me beyond this?

Am I only to be the devil you made me?"

Of course, there would be only one answer. It was foolish to have asked once again.

Chapter XVI

*G*uilt. *What a fascinating and repulsive feeling.* It took nearly a week for the savage fantasies, which relentlessly replayed, to finally subside enough for me to function adequately. So that I could look upon her, teach her, speak with her without every thought being consumed with beautiful memories of pale skin beneath the moonlight.

No matter my desires, our time together was precious. I deserved the discomfort, the masochism that came with such suppression.

In the few months since my intrusion, the many conversations we have had - some which spanned all day - were the most marvelous and aided in restraint.

Per her request, I recounted my many travels across the eastern world. A very diluted version of my time as a performer in traveling shows. The wonders of Persia and the Palace of Illusions, where I met Ardashir. Even how I had come to Paris and partnered in the *Garnier's* erection.

Sweet Melody saw the world with curiosity. What this desolate man would not give to show it to her. To experience it as she did. Wide eyed and at my side.

Chapter XVI

It was difficult to pull stories from her in turn. Surprised when I inquired about it. She seldom spoke in detail of home, or of herself much. Short evasive answers seemed to be her favorite, except when she spoke of her mother and sister.

"Again. You are too tense," I said, as she worked on her scales.

"Yeah. No problem. Give me a second?" she asked.

A hint of nervousness hung in the air around her as she hummed looking over the sheet music once more before our last stretch in the night's lessons. She was progressing faster than initially expected. There was much work to be done yet, but she was surprising. The nerves should have subsided by this point.

"Alright. I'm ready," she said, settling back in at the music stand. "I can do this," she whispered to herself.

Though she was far from stage ready, as she ran through once again, I started to believe there was real promise there. That someday, the stage may be made for her as well as Christine.

"How do you feel?" I asked, when she finished.

"I can't believe I just made that sound with my own voice. *MY* voice! Erique!" she said.

"Less tortured cat."

Brown eyes rolled. "Gee, thanks," she said.

What wonderful friendship.

She pulled our copy of *Alice's Adventures in Wonderland* by Lewis Carroll from her bag.

"Shall we pick up where we left off yesterday?" I asked.

"Oh, uh, yes. Ok," she said, and dropped into the blue chaise I had moved here for her.

I joined her, settling in behind the backrest where I could still be well hidden. As long as she didn't turn around.

"I believe it was my turn to read," I said.

She held out the book over her shoulder.

I reached for the symbol of our mutual love and stilled. Incandescence shot through my fingertips and spread through me like electricity the moment my hand settled upon hers.

Such carelessness.

Yet, this angel did not recoil, nor made any attempt to move.

Not to waste such a moment, I pulled the book from her hand slowly, running my fingers as far along her skin as I could go. To keep contact before she finally dropped her hand, and fingers fidgeted against her lips again.

Difficult as it was to concentrate with what had just transpired, I could not shake the fact that something riddled her mind still.

"What is it, my angel?" I asked.

"Just a little preoccupied. I'm sorry."

"You need never apologize to me."

My heart fell as her lovely legs swung over the side of the chaise as she sat up. I pushed back further into the darkness without thought.

Her eyes landed in my general direction as she chewed her lip.

I wish she would not do that. Despite the inappropriate setting, my cock threatened life at such a sight.

"Antoinette would like me to come for dinner this evening," she said. "That's why I asked for an earlier lesson."

To know that I would not get to spend the night with her unsettled me, but selfishness would not stop her either. That mistake was already made once and would not be repeated.

'You could take her home…'

"Then you should go. We will take the night off," I said.

As if the answer did not suffice, words attempted from her mouth, but nothing formed.

"Melody," I said, trying to coax whatever it was from her.

Finally, she shot up from the lounger. "Why don't you come with me?" she asked.

"Melody…" I sighed.

"I mean, I can tell her whatever story you want. It just might be nice for you to get out too. And Antoinette is so kind. I told you how she took me in."

Her sweetness never ceased to take hold. To have dinner with her and her friends. "Yes" was on the tip of my tongue.

Antoinette, though indeed kind, was terrified of me. Even with the financial help over the years in reparation for my deeds while in her care, that would never change.

Imagine *this*, casually dining? Like I was not a creature. A monster. A

Chapter XVI

spectacle; for just a night.

"Perhaps one day, my angel," I said, hoping the mask in my voice was enough to content her. Assure her that there would be a "one day". Even when I did not believe it.

Her arms crossed her midsection, and she cocked her head to the side. "You know you don't have to hide from me anymore, Erique."

My name rolling off her lips made me want to give her everything. She always said it was such care. Even when flustered with my existence.

"It just feels silly to have you hiding all the time. I mean, I have seen you. Sort of. I know that you're… different. That's ok. They're not going to care either. And if they do, fuck 'em," she added. "We'll leave."

We…

I believed that she believed she could take the man in the mask. Accept me as that.

Perhaps if I hid beneath it?

No. The risk was too great. If she were to snatch the thing from me - I had killed the one person that removed it before because I was foolish to believe…

Only I knew the horror of what lies behind and further below. Every mirror that caught my reflection was in pieces because I could not even stand what was behind it.

Yet, why do I know she would never do such an act?

She would never wrong me, and I would still be the end of her.

I never wanted to give myself a reason to hurt her. I was a monster and that was never going to change. I would crush this angel's mended wings if we got too close.

"You know what, never mind. It was a stupid ask," she said.

The pain of her disappointment stabbed through the bones of my chest and twisted. "No, it is now I who should apologize," I said. "I would love to dine with you. It would bring me great pleasure to share in such a thing."

"Then why won't you? You should know by now I don't give a shit about what you look like. We're friends. And to be honest, I'm starting to question my sanity a little more than when I got here."

"What is me, will haunt you until you no longer breathe. I do not wish to bestow that upon you, my Melody."

This was not the first time and probably would not be the last for this conversation.

"There's no way you're that bad. Or scary. Or however you want to put it." Her voice grew with frustration, certainly on the brink of screaming. "You're just scared."

"Please understand," I said, raising my voice.

"I just…" Defeat crossed her face, and her hands flew into the air. "Ok."

She turned away, glancing around as if looking for something.

"Shall we continue?" I asked, adjusting my tone to calm and ease.

The strap of her bag flew over her head, landing on her shoulder. "I think I'm going to leave earlier," she said, and pinched the bridge of her nose. "Good night, Erique."

My blood boiled as I gnashed my teeth. "Yes. Of course. Good night, my dear."

'You damned waste of flesh,' the *Ghost* spat.

The shutting of the door jolted my nerves. A cold reminder of the world granted upon me.

She had invited me to dine with her. To come near her. As if we were truly friends of the same flesh. Of the same world.

The book hit the cushion of the lounger. Disappointment fueled the storm building within my core. Words of the past haunted, evoking memories which forced navigation of even simple, innocent desires such as dinner.

I buried my face within shaking hands, gripping hard at the mix of flesh and *shame*. I had denied an offering from an angel. I had denied myself.

From my throat, fury filled the room. Parchment flew. The chaise rebounded from the parallel wall, falling into pieces. The book fell to the floor, and I was left with the aftermath of my decisions.

'This never would have happened with Christine.'

"Silence! No more!"

Chapter XVII

Melody

I was mad at him, and it wasn't his fault. This world wasn't supposed to bleed in. I'd forgotten where I was in the time space continuum. Happens every time. Curiosity finally bit me in the ass. Still, I'd asked him to dinner and ended up hurting my own feelings.

It was easy to forget when we spent time together. When he spoke, it was effortless to gloss over who he was and the things he'd done and still does.

Erique was well spoken. Tender. Attentive. It was impossible not to feel things. He surprised you when you'd least expect it.

The times he was unintentionally playful, and how absolutely, embarrassingly it affected me, were worse.

Well shit.

I had a crush on Erique. A bonafide crush.

Stupidly, I even thought when he brushed his hand over mine, the gifts, the time, he might have had one too.

When will I fucking learn.

We needed a break. He was clouding my judgment. Making me feel and forget, which I couldn't have happening.

It was good he said no to dinner. Knocked me right back into reality. Which was—I don't belong here.

How do you avoid someone who's everywhere?

I groaned at the memory trying not to bring attention to myself during the morning meeting.

"Did you hear me?" Christine asked. Breaking the spiraling rabbit hole of thoughts.

I frantically glanced around, like a kid who fell asleep in class.

"Oh, sorry. No. What did you say?" I asked.

"Carlotta's coming back."

I winced; Erique was going to love this.

M. Fournier had gathered the cast and crew to make an announcement. Christine was kind enough to offer to translate for me during these rare meetings. It was really helpful, even though I didn't care. Nor did anyone else for that matter.

It was mostly just him sweeping everything under the rug and reminding everyone the show was only a week away and that everything was going to be fine.

Wow. I'd been here for almost three months. My attempts to get home had waned. My stomach flipped and mind fuzzied. It'd been a while since I felt like vomiting.

Yeah. We needed a break.

"Does that mean you're not debuting then?" I asked her.

Christine shook her head. "Unless she has another 'accident', no."

I felt terrible for my friend. Despite Erique's help, she'd worked so hard and was more than worthy to open the show at the very least.

"You lose money on bad talent. Carlotta is basically walking horse shit in a pretty dress," I said. "Eventually, they'll see that she's not worth it and finally just drop her all together."

"They're stupid," Christine's friend, Chloe, whispered.

The three of us shared a little giggle.

The managers were either scared or they were actually stupid as Chloe said. Either way, something was going to happen. Erique wasn't going to take this lying down. And to be honest, I hoped he didn't.

"I don't get how she's even allowed here. Didn't she spit on you last rehearsal you worked together?" I asked Chloe.

Chapter XVII

Christine translated for me; Chloe nodded.

"She *knows* everyone," Christine said. "That's why she always gets what she wants."

I guess if she's fucking everyone, or did and knew their dirty little secrets, that held a lot of weight.

Erique's "pranks" made more sense now. There would be room for growth within the theater. Have an amazing cast. If she quit, they'd have no reason to hunt him. There could be no backlash against the theater either.

Christine stared at me with knitted brows. "Are you alright?" she asked.

"Yeah. Just… Yeah. Thank you."

"Are you sure? You look… troubled."

"No. I'm fine. Just a little frustrated with life."

"You do work a lot. You can come stay with my grandmother and I for a few days? We can go shopping!" she said, very excited with the last option.

The thought of staying away from the theater wasn't a pleasant one. It gave me a lot of anxiety, actually. But staying was giving me that too.

I didn't want to be away, but a short time would be nice. I'd also been here longer than I thought I'd be. "Shopping may be good. I do need a few things."

I zoned out the rest of the meeting, thinking on Erique, even though I didn't want too, and how I was going to deal with it.

Then there was the touch I couldn't stop reliving. My cheeks burned at the recollection. How igniting it was. Gentle. How much I hated when I pulled away, but I would have just sat there to touch him longer.

"Understudies are rehearsing first. I'll see you later?" Christine said. She hugged me, then both her and Chloe ran off.

I made my way towards the very back of the stage.

Last week I was offered temporary duties repairing a few props and set pieces. Someone had misplaced or damaged them and the usual prop guy was temporarily working in another theater.

I was a little mad Erique did that. However, it's nice not to be cleaning dusty rooms or statues for the time being. If I was lucky, I wouldn't have to go back to cleaning.

The stone wall set was fabricated in sections. Having a separate piece made it easier to wheel around for repair.

Yesterday I'd tacked on the corner stone that had broken off. It was badly scratched up and a few sections had pulled from the wood.

Though Erique swore the damage wasn't him, I had my suspicions. Erique.

What was I going to do about that?

Worse yet, I hated that during dinner all I thought of was him. And how I wished he was there.

The bristles from the paintbrush ran over the uneven textures of the plastered rock. It was nice to get to be a bit creative. Even if it was just a rock.

The more I thought about it, the more I was glad Erique didn't come out with me.

It'd probably make things worse. More real. And I don't think I could handle it. It wouldn't be fair to either of us.

Ugh. Fuck him and this place.

Without fail, a strange change in the atmosphere alerted my senses. I didn't need to say a word to know that he was suddenly with me.

I always knew when he was near. At least when he wanted me to know.

Go away.

"How was your evening?" His voice caressed my ears. Calming as always. My stupid body betrayed me as if it longed for his sound. Because it did.

I need to go.

"Fine." I did my best to cover the desire in my voice, instead replacing it with indifference.

"Are you ready for your lessons?" he asked.

"Yeah." *Though I'll stay my distance and be quiet.*

I dipped the brush into the paint bucket and slapped it onto the plaster again.

"We will be meeting in another lesson room," he said. "Our usual is currently unavailable."

"Okay…" I said.

"Would you like to do something with me?"

Chapter XVII

The way he asked it made my brows furrow.

"Together?" I asked, suspicious.

Without hesitation, he answered, "Yes."

"Erique…"

"Carlotta has returned."

"I'm aware."

"Do you not think Mademoiselle E'spanga deserves a welcome home gift?" His tone was too playful. It worried me.

"Damn it," I sighed under my breath. "What are you planning?"

A panel in the wall a few feet away slid open.

"Come with me, *mon cœur.*"

My skin rippled over my body at his call. I wish I could say the rising in my pulse was from fear.

No one seemed to notice the panel opening. Or me, for that matter. I chewed my lip while my core turned and danced at the thought of what was on the other side.

Surprisingly, not a negative thought in sight. *Suspicious.*

The opening was narrow, maybe a bit too narrow for these hips. It did make me wonder about Erique's size. If he was running around in the walls, slipping in and out of these panels, he had to be a smaller person?

"It's safe. Nothing will happen while I am around. Ever," he said.

Why did I want to believe him?

Against my better judgment, as always, I slipped into the dark, which opened up to a much wider space. Not much bigger though.

Bits of light peeked through cracks in the wall. Mostly on the stage side where the wall was unfinished. Not enough to illuminate my surroundings, but enough to see a few inches in front of me.

"Turn around," he said. "Then walk until I tell you otherwise."

"It's a bit dark."

"I will be your eyes. Trust me."

My heart quickened. Obviously, I did trust him, but the dark and the unknown were still terrifying. "I swear to God, Erique, I will kill you if I get hurt in here. If a spider bites me…"

"You don't believe in God, my angel," he cooed.

"I'll make an exception."

"I will keep the spiders at bay."

My heart beat only in my ears while my body went into panic mode. I didn't have to stretch my arms out far to touch the walls.

I hated the dark. I knew there were no demons or actual monsters that could get me, it didn't stop my mind from trying to form faces within it though. A lifetime of horror movies coming to fruition.

"I upset you," he said as we walked on.

We were going to talk about this now? I was not in a great place to talk about what happened last night. Mostly physically. I'd be happy to forget the whole thing actually.

"No, you didn't. Not the way you may think anyway," I answered.

"But I did upset you."

"It's my own thing. Don't worry about it."

Hands that weren't mine slid around the sides of my waist gently, stopping me in my tracks.

Afraid to move, I left my hands on the walls as his body pressed to mine. I had to remind myself how to breathe.

In. Out. In. Out.

How cliché.

"Please know I never wish to displease you." His breath caressed my ear and rolled down my neck, like a light breeze on a summer day. Goosebumps avalanched over my flesh. "I would love nothing more than to join you in all things your heart desires to experience."

My eyes watered at the overwhelming sensations within the small space. "Erique," my voice fluttered. The grip on my waist tightened as I said his name.

It sent me spiraling. My head dizzied as I focused on the pressure of his body.

"Melody…" he said with a slight hum.

My will wanted me to lean into him. Touch him. Let him fuck me right then. Lord knows I needed a good railing.

I fought through my animal brain and found the words to keep us going. "Erique, I understand the boundaries of our friendship. And I respect it."

He fell silent as I pulled away and continued moving without direction, hoping I didn't turn around and say, "just kidding. Come here

Chapter XVII

stalker boy".

"Left," he said.

Finding a corner with my fingers, I turned down another corridor. Erique close behind. If I stopped, he'd walk right into me. The temptation was strong to feel him again.

"If you could go anywhere, where would you go?" he asked. "Home is not an option."

"I don't know."

"Would you prefer silence?"

I sighed and thought for a moment. Where would I go? He already knew that I'd love to travel, but what about something not so grand? A quick fix.

"The carnival," I said.

"Why would you want to go to such a place?"

"I don't know. I just love the food. The games and rides. I know everything's rigged and the rides can kill you, but there's something about it only happening once in a while that gives it some sort of magic. Especially at night, when the lights are up, it's like a whole other experience."

"I wish I could have seen it as you do," he said.

A stab into my heart forced a flinch. When he'd mentioned his time in the show during our talks, it was obvious he glossed over some things. Saying that he enjoyed performing, mask free and making people uncomfortable. But that was also the darkest time in his life.

Something happened that not even the Phantom was comfortable talking about.

I could be so dense sometimes. "I'm sorry. I didn't mean to…"

"No, I love hearing the world through your eyes," he said. "We're almost there."

Through one of the cracks, I saw we were near the dressing rooms. What could he possibly have in mind?

"What would you do?" I asked, pulling back from the wall.

"I would take you to a carnival."

I blinked away the tears that had welled in my eyes again. It's too bad I couldn't blink away the urge to punch him in the face for whatever that was. This man was going to gut me if he didn't shut up.

"Turn right," he said.

It's a terrible game we're playing. One where both of us would get hurt in the end.

"We have arrived," he said. "There's a latch and notch in front of you. Twist and pull the latch. Then push the notch."

"Is that how all these panels are set up?"

"Now you know."

I thought I'd done it correctly, but when the panel didn't budge, I heard a chuckle from behind.

"You're here too, you could just do it," I said.

"You need to know this. Do it again."

Lucky try number two. The panel popped open and swung to the side.

"Step out, but do not leave," he said.

"You're coming with me, right?"

"Trust me, *mon cœur*."

Sighing, I did as told and stepped inside, immediately getting smacked in the face by some hanging fabric.

It was a freaking closet.

Light peeked around the edges of the curtain where the door would be. I pulled it open just enough to see Carlotta's dressing room and the door to the dressing room next to it.

We were in one of the hallway closets.

Admittedly, this was kind of exciting. As long as it was just a prank, and he wasn't about to hang someone in front of me.

"Ok, now what?"

When he didn't answer, and the air felt different, I realized I was alone.

"Erique?"

I rushed to the wall where I had just stepped through. It was closed. I felt around, trying to find anything that would open it back up. *Someone* forgot to show me how to get back in.

"Erique, you fucking asshole!" I growled, mauling the wall.

Irritated and a little freaked out, I turned back to the curtain that separated me from the hallway. From anyone seeing me.

Just as I was about to step out from behind it, a very distinct voice

Chapter XVII

faded in.

Carlotta was nearby.

Coming into sight from around the corner, the managers, her hand maid, and Lorenzo were with the entitled diva.

Of course, they weren't speaking English, so I assumed they were kissing her ass by the looks of it.

M. Fournier rushed to the door to the dressing room and fiddled with the keyhole, trying to unlock it.

Carlotta huffed, stomping her foot, like he was inconveniencing her.

"Ah ha!" she said, when he finally got the door open. M. Fournier bowed and gestured into the room.

The second her foot hit the other side of the threshold, she let out a blood curdling scream. Horse shit and hay had fallen from the ceiling just inside the door.

Carlotta stood there crying and shouting. Tears streaming down her shit covered face. Lorenzo was helpless, lightly trying to dust it from her shoulders.

Erique's thunderous laughter echoed throughout the area. As always, unable to be pinpointed.

My jaw dropped and my hand raced to my mouth to keep the surprise and laughter at bay.

I must have moved the curtain or something, Carlotta pointed out towards me, yelling.

"Run," he commanded.

Wide eyed, I threw the curtain open and ran away from the scene.

"*Stop! Come back!*" someone called out from behind me. Like hell I was going to stop and find out who!

"Left." Erique's devilish voice sounded again, so full of life.

I rounded the corner, nearly colliding into a solid black mass of fabric.

He grabbed my hand and pulled me along.

The rush of everything blinded me as we ran. Stars formed at the loss of breath and lightheadedness. The fabric of his cloak wrapped around my arm and billowed as we went on.

I was losing my wind while voices still called out behind us.

We stopped abruptly. Erique swung a closet door open and yanked me inside with him closing it behind us.

My back pressed against the wall and my chest heaved chaotically, trying to catch my breath.

Voices grew nearer as my anxiety level went through the roof.

Then, a finger pressed on the underside of my chin lifting it upwards. A gloveless thumb ran over my bottom lip. Shivers, lightning bolts and everything else zapped through me at once.

"Shh. Dear," he whispered. Warm breath skimming across my lips.

I covered my mouth, trying to muffle the sounds of dying. It was the catacombs all over again. Only this time I'd be fired and lose my way home for certain. I think that was almost worse.

Curious, I bent over and peeped through the keyhole in the door. M. Fournier and Lorenzo, who was still covered in shit, had stopped just outside, a few feet away. Hunched over, trying to catch his breath, M. Fournier, white as a sheet, waved Lorenzo onward.

I backed away quickly, squeezing Erique's hand, pulling him with me.

My back hit the wall that I hoped to shrink into. Why wasn't he popping open a panel or something?

"Do you think she liked our gift?" he chuckled softly against my temple.

I should hate him for this. For putting me in this position. It was hilarious though, even if we did get caught.

"I think she wore it well," I said breathlessly.

I glanced around him at the light coming in through the keyhole, focusing on the voices that were still outside.

"*Je serai là. Continue*," M. Fournier's voice muddled through.

A cool, gentle hand pressed against my cheek, guiding my focus away from the happenings outside.

My eyes closed against their will at his touch as prickles of heat cascaded through my being.

Was my heart still hammering against my ribs from the run or was it something else now?

Through foggy eyes, I tried to adjust to the darkness. Maybe see a glimpse of the man I'd been talking to for months now. Even just his eyes would do, to confirm the memory from that day on the catwalk. One emerald green. The other stone-gray.

Chapter XVII

The heat that filled me shifted. The ache between my thighs returned with a savage want at his proximity, and the sudden realization that our fingers were interlocked.

What was happening? Was this on purpose? How could he know we'd end up here? Wait, he was the one that didn't want to be close… What if he kissed me? What if I kissed him?

No. That's just the adrenaline talking.

This was so dangerous.

Be closer.

"Are you alright?" His voice was soft and low against my cheek. The brush of skin was surprising.

"Yes," I barely got out.

With him here, in this closet, I would stay forever. Lost in this moment.

Because only heartache waited for us when we left it.

"I am going to lure them away, so that you may go back," he said.

I panicked and grabbed at him absentmindedly. "No." He stepped closer, pressing his body harder against mine, cementing me to the wall. "Not yet… They're still nearby. I can hear them." *I lied.*

The heat from his cheek found mine again. "That's the point, *mon cœur*," he whispered. His uneven breathing rolled over my skin.

Amongst the haze of bliss, my focus drifted to the pressure against my stomach. His own pulsing arousal pressed into me.

This was becoming a problem. The lightheadedness nearly had me on the verge of fainting. It was too much, and I never wanted it to stop.

"Oh, right… yeah," I said. But my grip on his jacket and hand wouldn't loosen. If I could pull him closer, I would.

I inhaled deeply to calm my breathing and control my mind before I did actually pass out.

A familiar scent tickled my senses and pulled an almost forgotten memory.

No. It can't be. The scent of a campfire in the rain.

I stilled. It couldn't be him. That would mean… He knew me. More so, was this some sick twisted trick? Disgusting act of "fate"?

So many thoughts hit me at once. Things I couldn't make sense of even if I thought outside reality. Which I was never really certain this was.

The hand that comforted my face ran along my jaw and under my chin softly, tilting my head upward slightly.

The prolonged anticipation was torture.

Kiss me. Please. Or we'll miss out. We won't get this chance again. Please.

My heart skipped. Or had it stopped altogether? I couldn't tell.

"After you hear me, wait a few minutes. It will be safe to leave." His whisper entered my mouth and flowed through my veins.

If I pulled him into a kiss, would he forgive me? My blood surged from head to toe at the thought.

I nodded helplessly. Again, not going after something I wanted because of whatever bullshit reason.

Be brave.

His hand left the comfort of my face, leaving behind reality.

"Erique…" I said, fragile and shaking. "Don't go… please…" I squeezed his hand harder, trying to keep him in place.

"I will find you later. We have lessons, *mon cœur*." There was a gentle softness to his voice. Almost hopeful in its tone.

"You don't understand," I said, on the verge of bursting into tears.

He kissed my hand. "Shh."

Frozen in place, my arm stretched as far as it would go with him. He slipped into a panel next to us. Our fingers unlocked and slid against the other as he furthered away into the dark within the walls.

Come back.

A slight curl in the tips of those fingers halted his departure for a few moments longer. Until he was gone.

The Phantom of the opera had found his way in, and I needed to expel him.

No matter how much it hurt.

Chapter XVIII

Alas, a soul lives within this body, and it dances with life. Ivory bounced beneath delighted flesh. Sounds filled my loathsome home with foreign feelings of joy and fantasy.

Though I fumbled with words onto parchment, notes came as flawlessly as they ever did.

Not even my dear Daroga would recognize what radiated from this living cadaver. It would terrify him more than any misdeed I had done. To tell him of what had flourished since his departure, he would truly think me mad.

To feel such things within the true meaning of the word innocent. *What wonder.*

'These delusions will only destroy you. We have come too far to lose sight of our ambitions, boy.'

"You will not provoke me today," unbothered by the monster of my thoughts.

Recollections of heavy breaths. Laced fingers. A closeness that could never be close enough, furthered these measures.

Keys, which had never seen the likes of my music, continued to blend effortlessly within my technique.

Fantasy intertwined within the strands of memory, and a new opera entered the world as I entertained visions of her toes in the sand. Our hands grazing long grass in open fields. Stealing a kiss from sweet lips under the *Arc de Triomphe.*

No, she hated the way the city smelled.

I would kiss her at sunset on a balcony in Spain that overlooked the Balearic Sea.

'You could not even kiss her in a closet, Erique. She was right there. Bosoms heaving, hand gripped tight in yours, begging you to stay, and you could not do it.'

"I did kiss her."

'Anyone could kiss a wrist. I am sure the count placed vile lips upon the same spot.'

For the first time, these fingers blundered over keys not intended as a quake of discomfort took over momentarily.

The *Ghost's* laugh ricocheted in the spaces of my mind.

"You know nothing," I bit, and continued on with the new lovely sounds. "She makes me believe…"

'Believe what? Believe that you could walk in the world above like any man? Free. Unburdened. Without fear? Frolicking through fields towards a woman waiting for you with open arms? Who would let you kiss her, fuck her freely?'

Fantasies of lifting her skirt and dropping to my knees before her dissolved away. "She calls me friend," I said.

'Bring her here then if she loves you. Bring her here and see how joyed she would be at never seeing the sun again. At sight of you.'

Now I wondered if she would in fact accept me as I am after our moment together. All our moments.

Or was the *Ghost* right?

My hands fell from the keyboard and I sat back, staring at the newly inked music.

"The changes I have begun within these walls would please her," I said.

'Christine is moldable in her age. She would have no choice but to accept her fate. She has voice and grace. Melody could not and will never. Why fight so hard against destiny, suddenly? You are well past curiosity. This woman does not love you.'

Chapter XVIII

"Love…" A word I have known but never experienced.

The moment I left her, my chest ached in her absence. Could it be possible that she could love me?

'No Erique! The moment she sees you, learns the truth of you, she will run like everyone else.'

One thing she can never know. But the other? If I were to reveal myself, in mask, would she still read with me? Sing with me? Let me close? Maybe closer?

She had asked several times, perhaps it was finally that time?

And speaking of time, it was near time for our lessons.

"You will see."

***

Upon finding the practice room was empty, I searched every corner she could be hiding. Her room. Stables. Even the manager's office.

Had she forgotten our lessons? Or perhaps had gone to the hotel after the event with Carlotta?

No. Communication was something she held to high standard. Melody would not leave without mention of it.

Her unannounced absence should be the least of what ailed this mind, yet I found myself bothered.

'You see. She ran from you,' the *Ghost* gloated. *'Disgusted by your touch.'*

The muscles in my shoulders ached at thoughts of her leaving. I strangled the railing of the catwalk, and ground my teeth together as I rocked my jaw. "She will be back," I sneered.

'You are so certain of this woman's care for you. You have lost yourself.'

He was wrong. She would never wound me.

A familiar voice caught my ear. "Over there." My eyes flicked down to find Joseph Buquet, that the vile stagehand that dared to violently touch my angel, had returned to work. There were many things that could be done to ensure his permanent departure from this place. Some I would delight in.

"Soon," I whispered with warning. Not that he would hear.

The glare I had on the beast faltered when another stepped into view with him. Christine.

Christine with the brightest of smiles upon her face. More brightly than any I had witnessed of her. I had almost forgotten how lovely her smile was.

But, there was a reason for this smile. The silly little Viscount, Raoul, strode alongside her. Her excitement during our lessons recently made more sense now.

I filled my lungs; eyes locked on the young couple hiding in the shadows. Rehearsals had ended for the day. They were hiding from view. From me.

A smirk rested on my mouth. "I see you," I said.

She pushed him away, yet still looked on with adoration and melted under stolen kisses. My heart ached at such a sight.

'She betrays you. Look how she dances around with him. She knows your rules and breaks them. There is still time to fix all of this. She can still be your future. Without her, no one will hear your music. No one will care!'

This should send me into a fury, but there were more important matters at present. I straightened up and pushed back my fallen hair.

I would find her and all would be right.

But first, a pair of ropes tied off near the end of the catwalk just above their heads called out for a bit of play.

"Courtesy of the Ghost!" I said and pulled the tails of the ropes.

The two small sandbags missed the young lovers as they scurried off.

It was not like the Ghost to warn, though I suspected had my Melody learned I may have hurt someone, she would not be too pleased. Our courtship had come too far.

Nor would I ever hurt Christine, even as she betrayed her angel.

The dressing room!

Why it had not occurred to me to check the very place we first spoke delicious banter, was beyond me. She liked to read in there sometimes. It was more comfortable than the practice room or her bed.

The back of the mirror came into sight as I closed in on the room. Erratic were the beats in my chest at anticipation of our soon to be union.

And there she was, curled up on the lounger, face buried in the cushions.

Filled with the bliss of earlier, I took a deep breath, grasping hold of my courage. This would be my proof.

I had started for the latches, until foreign sound stopped me.

Chapter XVIII

Back to the mirror, I pressed my hands against the wall, trying to understand better what I had heard.

Her shoulders shook as she sniffled. "Go away!" her sad voice called out. She always knew when I was around. Sweetest thing.

"What ails you my dear? Are you hurt?"

The worry and rage mixed within. Buquet was back, perhaps this was somehow his doing.

"No," she answered. "Just leave me alone, Erique. You need to leave me alone."

My heart wrenched in the walls of my chest at her command. "Please tell me what has happened. Have you been weeping all day, *mon cœur*?"

"It doesn't matter. None of it does. I'm not even supposed to be here. You're not even supposed to know me. And you wouldn't—"

"It matters," I pleaded. This was an issue I thought long gone. "You matter. To me. Please. What has prompted this?"

Her silent sobs grew heavier, as her shoulders shook harder. "You can't understand."

"Allow me the opportunity."

Melody rolled onto her side and pushed herself upright. Red puffy eyes and swollen cheeks screamed to be cradled. Heavy with whatever weighed her down, she glanced around absentmindedly.

'Go to her now. What do you wait for?' the *Ghost* taunted. *'Show her how you care for her.'*

"Why didn't you tell me it was you that night?" she said through a broken voice. "In the catacombs."

How did she know? Antoinette? That would be dealt with later.

"It did not matter, my angel. What mattered…"

"Stop! Don't call me that," she said in a low, tormented voice. She stood, throwing a pillow at the mirror. "I'm not your angel. That's Christine. That's what this whole fucking story's about. I'm nothing to you."

"That is untrue in every word of it."

"Don't lie to me, Erique. Stop lying!" The glazed look of despair spread over her face.

"I have never given her such a name. Other than Ardashir, you are the only one who knows me."

"Your whole life here is based on a lie. And I'm just another one. I don't know you," she said. "And it does matter. The only reason you ever even spoke to me was because of that night. You never would have noticed me, let alone befriended me otherwise. I would probably have been just as dead as that girl everyone was talking about months ago." She glared directly into the mirror, at me, with burning, reproachful eyes.

Her accurate words brought on physical pain. My chest tightened as my heart threatened to explode.

"I would have never hurt you," I said pathetically.

She gave a choked, desperate laugh, then turned her back to me.

'You see. It was you that knew nothing. She is just like them. Melody does not love you.'

"Do you regret our meeting? Our relationship?" I asked, catching the pain in my throat.

She brought her hand to her face and shrunk between her shoulders. I waited with bated breath for her answer. Praying to a God that does not listen, that he would return her to me just this once.

A sniffle and rapid hands wiped at her face before turning back.

Hurt and longing lay naked in her eyes. "In the worst moments of my life, you've saved me twice. I will be eternally grateful. I wish I could explain better. That everything, this," she said, gesturing to the area around her. "You. Nothing is my own. Everything is something else. I…ugh."

She muffled a scream into her hands.

"I made no mention because I…" I hesitated. Why had I not told her? Could I even tell her the truth? That it was one of the most amazing moments of this pathetic existence? That because of that horrific moment in her life, I now saw a different future? "I don't know. But it was not to deceive you, my Melody."

"Would you have killed me? Had they not come?"

"At first, I thought you were there for me. To lure me out. I had just shattered the chandelier. But the fear in your eyes and life splattered across your face, told another story."

"You didn't answer me. Erique, would you have killed me had they not come? Or would you have done worse?"

"No."

Chapter XVIII

A sigh of relief left her.

Not all trust was gone.

Melody paced around the room biting her lip, worried. "I didn't want any of this."

The pain in my throat was worse the longer I held it there. My guts wrenched and my heart ached.

'She did not want you,' the *Ghost* said. *'Can we be free of her now?'*

"I don't belong here. I miss my mom. And sister. God only knows what they're going through." She sniffled and wiped her face again. "This place is terrifying. I was trying so hard to get home and even trying to make this work while I was here. It's the only reason I'm here. In this beautiful building. I thought it would send me home. But everyday…" she choked. "And then you. You fog my mind, make me forget to try for home."

She wanted to leave still. Of course, she did. This wasn't her home. I'd forgotten that. If anyone knew what it was like to feel like you didn't belong, it was me.

"…Every day I lose hope of ever seeing them again. And being stuck here. Alone. Terrifies me," she finished.

"I'll buy you a voyage home, dear," I said as my heart fell. "Tomorrow. I'll go with you if you wish."

She muffled the heavy sob that came on at my words. "I wish it was that easy," she said with a half-hearted smile.

"How could it not be?"

Heartbreak streamed down her face again no matter how she tried to squash it. Mirroring my own attempts. "Just stop. You're making everything worse. I'm just so out of place. And so alone--"

I've been with her every day now; how could she possibly feel this way? "You're not alone. I'm here with you. Whenever you need of me. Always."

"You're not though," she shouted. The insult was barbed and hurtful. "You might as well be my imaginary friend. Someone that just fucks with my mind. Messing everything up."

We've held each other. Given gifts. How could she think I was in her mind?

She continued in a defeated tone. "For all I know, that's what you are. I'm doing this to myself because of how terrified and sad I am. I needed something to keep me from going insane. So, I made up an imaginary boyfriend. Who makes me insane."

"Do not say that," I barely got out.

Melody broke down into her hands again sobbing as tears stung my own eyes.

'Well? This is your chance, run to her. Hold her. Make her feel safe. Make her know she's not alone as you say. That you are real. That you care for her as you claim to.'

With haste, I rushed at the door. Metal latches within my hands. I gritted teeth, forcing myself to pull them open.

But the courage had evaporated.

Coward's hands retreated from the door and hung at my worthless sides. Fingers fidgeted fiercely, yearning to try again.

Gnashing my teeth, I turned back to the mirror and pressed my hand upon it.

"Just go," she cried. Finally, completely defeated.

"What of your lessons?" I asked, attempting for any reprieve of this.

"I won't be taking them anymore," she replied, her face vacant. "You should be happy. You won't have to hear this drowning cat any longer."

My throat seemed to close as the final blow of life had been knocked from me. Deep sobs wracked my insides as I strained to keep upright.

She did not want me. The *Ghost* was right. He was always right.

As the door closed behind her, I slid to the ground tearing at my chest, attempting to get at the source of this pain. To numb it. Stop it in any way I knew how.

If she wanted no more Ghost, no more Erique, there would be none.

Chapter XIX

Melody

Well. It'd been the quietest thirty-six hours, and time wasn't done.

"What do you think of this one?" Christine asked, holding up a pink dress trimmed in burgundy frills.

After being "asked" to work the opera tomorrow night, Christine agreed to go with me to make sure I found something appropriate. Something to appease the managers with the money they'd given me.

"Oh, uh. Very pretty," I said, trying to hide the disgust on my face. "But I don't think it's quite me." *Not that anything here was.*

She sighed and put it back on the rack, continuing to thumb through the other garments.

I found it hard to be present while we shopped. It'd been years since my mind had been this fucked up. About another human that was.

When I left him in the dressing room, I just left. I couldn't stay in my room at the opera for now. Not because there was a chance he'd somehow come in and kidnap or murder me. But because of the small bookshelf of gifts my Shadowman had given me over the past few months. It was painful to look at.

Antoinette greeted me with open arms when I had arrived. I spent the night crying in my temporary room at *Hôtel des Anges*.

It'd been so long since I cried that hard. I think she suspected a man was involved but just this once, I was glad for the language barrier, so she didn't pry.

Sleep eluded me even though I was exhausted. It replayed the whole night relentlessly. Trying to make sense of why I did what I did to Erique. To myself.

I needed my focus back. That's all it was. If I cared for someone, truly cared like I do for him, then it'd make it harder to go home.

Worse, I've been so worried about what the consequences of it would be.

"You've been really off since we arrived. What's the matter?" Christine asked.

"I'm fine. I've just been really missing home. I'm sorry," I lied. Sort of.

"I can understand that. Really," Christine said. "I'm here if you'd like to talk about it."

Her kind face was inviting. However, it just seemed different to talk about with her.

I shook my head. "I don't really want to right now, if that's alright."

"It's perfectly fine," Christine said, squeezing my arm. "What was wrong with the pink one? I think it would flatter you rather well."

Many beautiful dresses and not so beautiful dresses hung on the rack I fingered through. I was never one for dresses, but I did say this was the year I was gonna try new things. I just didn't think it'd be the year 1880.

"The neckline was a bit too high for me. I don't like anything near my neck. And the arms are too short." Because they'd show the tattoos on them. "And pink is nice, but I think that I would like something darker. Maybe red? Or maroon?"

"Oh! Alright," Christine said. "What about this?" Christine pulled a gorgeous dark red garment with matching trim and flared ruffles at the cuff of the arms. "You should try it on!"

It fit my requirements. Low neckline, longer sleeves. A whole lot of layering that added to the dress. Very beautiful.

"How do you tell the sizing on these?" I asked, taking it from her.

Chapter XIX

"Oh, this should be alright. But you won't know until you try it on."

It was obvious that Christine was more excited about the dress, or shopping in general, than I was.

"Okay," I said reluctantly.

I still hated shopping. If I was honest, it was the shopping that made the outing unenjoyable. The sizes in this time still catered to the petite.

"Are you nervous?" I asked, trying to find anything to talk about other than home or thinking about a certain wall dweller.

Christine's eyes turned gleeful. "Yes! I feel like I'm going to explode. This is something I've only ever dreamt of and now it's finally here."

I hung the dress inside the fitting room. I struggled to get the last of the buttons undone on my dress, Christine and her little hands helped the rest of the way.

"You're going to be amazing. I just have a feeling," I said.

"My angel said it's going to be a life changing night for me."

It wasn't just Erique I felt bad for. I'd also still been lying to Christine. Not intentionally. But knowing that Erique was her "angel" and teacher and not telling her was a lie too. I was no better than him.

Just a bunch of deceivers running around.

I also found myself not liking it when she called him that either. It was hard to listen to her talk about him sometimes. Especially today…

Oh my God, emotions go away.

"Has there been any accidents the past day or so?" I asked, nervous about the answer.

"No. I don't think so."

Maybe he was waiting until tomorrow's opening show to do something drastic. I hoped she couldn't see the color drain from my already pale face at the thought.

"Christine…" I started, thinking I was going to finally tell her about him. "About your angel…"

"Yes?"

Selfishness overturned the truth. "He… um… Has your… angel, ever called you Angel? Made any attempts to take you anywhere? Or anything…" I asked. The twisting in my stomach threatened to push the little bit of food Antoinette had forced me to eat, up and out.

She laughed. "Like to heaven?

"Like anywhere."

"No!" she laughed. "And he either calls my name or says "child". Sometimes "my dear". I call him Angel though, because he is."

"He's never hinted you may go somewhere together?"

"One day. When I'm done here and ready to go."

The nausea subsided almost immediately, but the guilt worsened.

"Right," I replied. It hurt my heart to think that Erique would harm her or force her into something. That the Phantom could be as devilish as the stories made him to be. Especially after I'd hurt him. Which I know I had. I cleared my throat. "How about *mon cœur*?"

She laughed even louder. "Why would an angel say that?" *Because that's what Erique calls me and I'm afraid to know what it means.* "It's reserved for someone you lo-"

"No reason. Ha," I said, cutting her off. "Anyway. As far as the night changing your life, I don't doubt that it's going to catapult you somewhere you wanna be."

Christine smiled wide, undoing the last button. "There!"

"I hate that these things have so many buttons."

"Laces are just as awful," she said.

"Let's just be naked."

Her face reddened as she giggled at my suggestion.

Mom would have loved to be in a store like this. She loved pretty things. Also, she would have gotten a kick out of watching me suffer through it. They'd always wanted me to be more "girly".

BARF.

I slid the dress off and laid it across a nearby chair. The weird underwear was less weird now. I still wore my black shorts underneath for comfort though. Shockingly, they hadn't fallen apart yet.

"Raoul will be there," Christine said like she was fishing for approval.

"Have you been seeing him much? I know we really haven't really talked about it."

"No. I've told him that he needs to stay away. But it hasn't really worked…" she hesitated.

"Is he who you remember?"

"Yes. He may even be…" she said. "What is that?"

I'd completely spaced when taking off my dress. Christine's mouth

Chapter XIX

was agape staring at the ink on my body.

"Oh. Um. These are tattoos," I answered.

"The permanent ink that sailors get?"

"Yeah. I guess."

"I see why you wear long sleeves. How do you have them?" she asked, grabbing my forearm and running a finger over it.

"Well, where I'm from a lot of people have them actually."

She stared fascinated at the artwork on my arm and leg. A smile tugged on my mouth at her curiosity.

Erique was just as curious. It was hilarious when he thought I was in the circus at one point, having come to the conclusion that I was not a sailor. Though my mouth suggested otherwise.

The smile turned painful at the unwanted memory.

"Did it hurt?" she asked.

Less than the pain I feel now. "It wasn't pleasant, but fine to sit through."

"You're a very different lady, Melody. I am very excited to know you."

"Well, thank you. Could you do me a favor though?" I asked, picking up the red dress.

"Yes, anything."

"Don't tell anyone about them if you can. People aren't really as accepting with this stuff."

She motioned to her lips and closed them, twisting her hand over it as if to lock it shut.

I stepped into the dress and shimmied it up over my hips.

"Since you shared a secret with me, can I tell you something?" she asked.

"Yes, anything."

"We've been writing. Me and Raoul. He wants to take me to a celebration after the show tomorrow."

"You should go!"

Her bubbly face fell. "I can't. My teacher…"

"I told you before. Your *teacher* will be fine. Or he won't. Now help button me up," I said, getting my arms into the sleeves, which were a little snug.

"What do you mean?" Christine asked, working her way up the row of buttons.

"I just mean that life is more than just following one pathway. Remember what I told you forever ago. You can have love and a career. Many journeys can lead us to the same ending. I mean, I haven't had it. But you can."

"I don't think I'm as brave as you are," she said.

"I'm not brave. Believe me," I sighed. I caught a glimpse of my grim reflection, made worse by the stupid wig that reminded me of how brave I was. *So brave*. "I'm just tired of all the fucking bullshit. People hiding instead of just being who the fuck they are. Or that bullshit of having to always choose between this or that. Why can't you have both things sometimes?"

Christine's face widened in shock.

"I'm sorry. I'm ranting," I huffed.

"No. I've never heard a woman say such things. I like it," she said. "Well, actually my grandmother likes to curse too."

I chuckled.

"Finished," she said and stepped back.

The dress was a nice fit. I just wish I could focus more on it to see whether it was actually a nice fit.

"Well, in any case, I think you should go with Raoul tomorrow night. Have some fun. Dance with him. Forget life for a while," I said. "Because sometimes you don't get any more than that."

I wanted Erique to kiss me so much in that stupid closet. Why didn't I just do it?

"Would you come with? I know that Philippe will be in attendance as well."

That was a name I hadn't thought about in a long while. Nor someone I wanted to see again.

"Oh. No," I replied. "I don't think so. Thanks though."

"Why not? It would be fun. You should have fun too! And Philippe is available." She wiggled her brows and gave a suggestive stare.

The move made me miss Sarah. That was her signature move. Tears almost welled up at the thought. New York was so long ago now.

The emotions were too much today.

"Didn't you have dinner with him?" she added.

Chapter XIX

"Yeah. But we weren't a match. Zero mental stimulation." *Not like with Erique.* "Politicians aren't my favorite either. And he's very uptight."

"Perhaps in time you could build something?" she said.

"I'm going to pass. Philippe is not for me." I smoothed out the skirt of the dress again. "I do think I love this dress though."

"It is so lovely. You could find a husband with that!"

I glared at the poor girl just trying to be a sweet helpful friend. "I would rather drink turpentine."

"Then go with Philippe as friends! For me? Or do you have someone already that could go? Your friend Erique maybe?"

Just then, an obscure image formed in my mind of what Erique could possibly look like next to me at a gathering. If I went to a party, I'd want to go with him. He would be delightfully judgey with me and close, so close.

I tried to hide the hurt forming in my eyes. But it was too late.

"You can tell me what's wrong, Melody," Christine said, tugging me to look her in the eye. "It's him? Why you're sad?"

"I think I messed up," I sighed and slumped into the stool next to the mirrors. The long hair of my invisibility cloak hung over my shoulders. I twisted the long strands in my fingers. "Not intentionally. Or maybe intentionally. I don't know. I do things like this. Seems like me to fuck up something… good."

"So, this is about your Erique?"

"Not my Erique. Just, Erique. My friend." It hurt to say that after what I'd done. There was no way he'd ever forgive me. I wouldn't.

"What happened?" she asked.

"It's complicated. But I think I might have royally fucked up and pushed away the only friend I really had here." I grabbed my face and groaned. "Other friend."

"I know what you meant. It's alright," she smiled reassuringly.

"I was angry about something he kept from me, but it wasn't even that. I just used it as an excuse because I can't tell him the real reason I needed him away from me. It's stupid really. Being with him was starting to make me feel stuff. I said some really hurtful things, and I haven't heard from him since. Part of me is afraid he's gonna do something stupid because of it."

Like set the place on fire. Kidnap you. Kill people. I don't know.

"That doesn't seem like a problem. Many people have arguments. You miss him, right?"

Tears had soaked my face and snot formed. Christine rushed to her small bag and retrieved something. "Here," she said, handing me a handkerchief.

"Erique isn't like many people," I replied, wiping my face dry. "He takes things to heart much deeper than I think I've known. It's for the best. I know it. But I fucking hate it."

"But you like him. He's your friend."

There's not a word in the dictionary that could describe what I felt for him.

"I really enjoy our time together. But one day, I won't be here, I have to go home, and it will have been pointless. And it would hurt him worse. And me, if we continued whatever it was we were doing."

"Just talk to him. If he cares about you, he'll understand."

"I don't know that he'll forgive me. Or if I should just leave him be as I asked him to do for me."

"I think you should talk to him. If I should go to the celebration with Raoul, you should write to Erique."

I chuckled. *If only she knew he was a wall away.* "I'll think about it," I said. *If he doesn't ruin the show or kidnap Christine. I'll find him and apologize.*

A quick and disturbing thought pressed me. *What if he did try to grab her?*

My stomach clenched tighter and icy fear twisted around my heart.

He wouldn't really do that, would he? Not the man I'd come to know... I shook it from my mind for now. I couldn't believe that he would do that.

I hoped.

"Now then. Maybe I can focus," I said, completely lying. I stood up from the stool and returned to the center of the fitting room. "Oh my God. It really is beautiful. Hopefully beautiful enough to help earn me some forgiveness."

"You look like royalty!" she said, clapping her hands with excitement.

"Don't say that. I'd like to keep my head, thank you."

Chapter XIX

We shared a much needed laugh. It wasn't everyday that you were in an era not too long after they were beheading nobility.

"You should write to him and tell him that you were just upset and miss him. And then ask him to go to the celebration with us," Christine said, as I slipped off my new dress.

I knew she was right. I needed to apologize to Erique. Make him understand he didn't do anything wrong. This shit was all me.

Would he even hear me? Or would he go legit Phantom after I'd hurt him? There was a chance that Christine could possibly never be seen again after tomorrow night, so there's that worry now too all of a sudden.

Fuck. I hate this story.

But, just in case…

"Can we go to the bakery after this?" I asked, pulling on my old dress. "I want to order something for tomorrow."

Chapter XX
Melody

An apology shouldn't give me more anxiety than time traveling or possible impending doom. Yet here we are.

The show went off without a hitch. Shockingly.

There may have been some worry that Erique would make a surprise guest appearance or something. We were in his private viewing box after all. But nothing. Which didn't help with being on edge all night.

No matter how amazing Christine was doing, it was hard to focus on the opera. Which also made it hard to pay attention to the managers and the de Changys sitting not too far away, who I was supposed to be serving all night.

The air had shifted where I stood in the small, yet surprisingly spacious private box. My mind was so preoccupied, that I thought I felt Erique nearby. But it was just me.

It was still a very moving and exciting show, when I could pay attention. And it was also really neat to see my patch work and updated painting on the sets as they cycled through scenes.

Something I wished my mom could have seen. She'd be so proud. Despite our problems and how she changed so much over the past years,

Chapter XX

there were still moments when she was my mama again. I'd like to think this would have been one of them. She would have been so proud of me getting to do some sort of art for work.

Even if it was just for a few days.

Raoul grinned ear to ear with excitement watching his lovely Christine perform. He was worried when he arrived that she wouldn't like the two dozen roses he brought for her.

Yeah. Okay.

Still, a total sweetheart. It's always nice to see him.

Philippe on the other hand. Just as uptight and off putting as he was two months ago. I was relieved to see a date had walked in with him.

He stared a little, but mostly let me be. Thank God.

I wished that was the only thing that bothered me tonight. As I ran drinks and food for the occupants of box five, my mind warred with conflicting thoughts.

What was I going to say to Erique? If he didn't do something drastic that was…

Ugh. Stupid brain.

Finally, the curtain fell bringing *Danser Avec Le Diable* to an end. A roar of applause filled the auditorium like I'd never heard for a performance. "Bravo. Bravo," yelled out from every corner of the room. Christine was remarkable. I wiped away the tears that welled in my eyes at the beautiful conclusion.

In the same moment, the shift in the air I thought I'd felt earlier, was gone.

Please don't, Erique.

Raoul leapt from his seat and rushed from the room before anyone had the chance to comprehend what was happening.

Which was a good idea, and one I was about to follow.

"Someone's in quite the hurry to congratulate the young diva," M. LeBlanc jested.

"So, it seems," Philippe said, unamused by his brother's excitement.

M. Fournier hurried over to me as the party trickled out from the room. "Just clean up and then you may go home. Well done tonight," he said.

The curls on his head bounced as he scurried out behind the rest of the visitors before I could stop him.

Raoul was going to her. She should be fine. But what if Erique hurt him in the process?

I decided to just leave when they were gone. Which didn't take long.

"Ok," I said to myself, and headed for the door.

"Excuse me," Philippe said, returning to the room. "I had forgotten my scarf."

I was restless and irritated by his presence. Obviously. I stepped back and let him in.

"Ah. Thank you, Melody," he said. Somehow my name on his lips sounded strange. Something I didn't care for. Maybe just remnants of the uncomfortable date.

I stood waiting, eager for him to leave again so that I could go. *But why? I could just leave now.*

He found it quickly on the chair he had been sitting. I took the opportunity to make my escape.

"It was a good show. Were you able to enjoy it?" he asked.

I stopped and faced him. "It was my first and it was amazing."

"You've never been to a show before?" he asked, stepping closer, toying with the red scarf in his hands.

"Not opera. This was an incredible experience."

"It was," he said. "I can see how my baby brother could be so drawn to such a girl."

"Christine is a wonderful person. And clearly very good at what she does."

"Indeed," he said.

"Now, if you'll excuse me." I nodded and turned to leave.

His hand gripped my bicep, halting me in place. A shadow of annoyance on a face that he attempted to hide beneath the politician's smirk peeked out.

"Ms. Reilly." He cleared his throat and removed his hand. "How have you been faring? That is a handsome dress."

"Thank you. It has pockets." I shoved my hands in the pockets on the skirt and wiggled it around.

"So, it does," he chuckled. It almost seemed genuine. Maybe Christine was a little right about him. Not a bad guy. Everyone gets nervous.

Chapter XX

"Where's your date?" I said, glancing around anxiously.

"Indulging with the managers. I should probably be getting back."

"Yes."

"I must admit to something."

"Ok," I said with tempered impatience.

"I hope you don't think me pathetic when I confess. I am sorry that I had you working tonight. I would have much rather this been another evening together."

"You were the reason I was requested for tonight?"

"Yes. Shameful as it is. When you hadn't responded to my letter, I wasn't sure how else to go about seeing you again."

I flinched in confusion at his comment. "You wrote me?"

"Yes, while I was in Toulouse. I had it sent to the managers addressed to you. When I did not hear back after my return home, I admit I was disappointed."

"I'm sorry. I haven't received any letters." *Though I can guess where it went.*

I turned my attention back to the few people trailing behind. It was getting late. I needed to leave, inching towards the exit.

"Must have been mixed in the post," he said. "It is my understanding that our evening out was not satisfactory, and I would like to apologize. My mind was focused on my trip to England. Which took much longer than it should have."

I scratched my knuckles, nearly drawing blood. I didn't think Christine would tell him. "I thought you were in Toulouse?"

"An emergency which needed my attention had come up, prolonging my absence. Again, my apologies."

"It's alright. All water under the bridge."

He stepped closer again. I stepped back.

"I would much like to make up for the mistake on my part. I should have written several times. As well as called on you when I returned. When I hadn't heard…"

"Oh, no. Philippe. It wouldn't have helped. I just really don't see us going further than we did."

The scarf he'd been wrapping around his hands and toying with pulled tight at my words. Perhaps it was my own anxiousness, but the act left me uneasy.

"I feel like you need someone better suited for you," I added, hoping to calm the tension.

My back hit the edge of the wooden threshold as he moved closer again.

"What if I disregard that comment? That perhaps I know who it is I need for my future?"

Where there was nothing behind the eyes of his smiles before, there was now direct intent.

I swallowed hard.

Something moved just out of sight. My eyes cut over to the balcony. A second glance confirmed my first thoughts.

"Excuse me," I said, pushing past him.

I gripped the banister as I looked out to find Christine and Raoul hand in hand glancing up at the stage. Joy on their faces.

"He didn't do it…" I muttered.

The Vicomte stole a kiss from the young debutante who blushed and graciously took it.

Every worried thought that riddled me since the other night, melted away. The shame of thinking the worst still lingered, but there she was, proof of the man I'd been getting to know.

"Pardon?" Philippe asked, joining me. "Ah. Yes. I will have you know; I've given Raoul permission to court her proper now. It will never last though. Their worlds are of two very different experiences."

His words contradicted his actions towards me. Which further solidified my rejection of his odd advances.

"Yes. But that could be beautiful too. Love can be magic sometimes. I have to go now. Like right now!" I backed away. My feet carried me fast to the exit.

Philippe's hand found my arm again. "Please, Ms. Reilly," he said through a gritted smile. His chin quivered as he searched for the words. "May we share another evening? I would like that chance."

"There's somewhere I need to be. Have a good night, Philippe. I'm sure your date is waiting."

I yanked my arm back and hurried through the open door.

My room wasn't that far. It took only a few minutes for me to get in

Chapter XX

and out. Everyone loves cake, right?

"Erique!" I called as the door to dressing room seven closed behind me. I rushed to the vanity and placed the little box in my hands down.

"Erique!" I called again, wandering around the room. Jitters are terrible. No matter how many times I took a breath, trying to calm myself, it didn't help. They only seemed to get worse.

I hurried to the mirror, checking my face and "hair". I didn't even know why. Shit, I was still confused as to why I was there. I literally blew off Philippe who was apologizing to me, to come search for my Phantom so that I can apologize to him. Because he deserved it.

I stepped back, looking over my dress, making sure nothing was out of place. Like if I wasn't presentable, an apology wouldn't matter.

When no shift in the air nor words alerted me to his presence, I started to worry. Could he really be done with me? Or worse, was he ok?

I called out his name again, more laced in concern this time. He had to be somewhere. Erique was too high on himself to commit suicide.

When minutes passed and still no answer, I worried I had my answer.

I walked to the small box on the table and picked it up. Humming to ease my disappointment. I did this to myself.

In a last stitch of desperation, I called out again, fighting the ache that threatened. Then the air shifted.

"I should kill them all for taking my box," he said in an odd, yet gentle tone.

A slight smile lifted at the corner of my mouth. It was so comforting to hear his voice. The anxiety in my soul soothed and relief prevailed.

"You could have. But then I'd be the one left to clean up the mess," I replied.

The silence that followed was deafening. A drumline played in my ears masking as heart beats.

"I'm so sorry," I said, choking on the lump in my throat. "There's no excuse for what I did. How I treated you the other night. I just…" I scratched my scalp through the wefts in my wig. "I freaked out. Not about you. Just…erg…" My face dove into my hands as I groaned.

Two days to come up with an apology and I still didn't have one.

As if to put me out of my misery, he spoke. "Did you enjoy it?" he finally asked. "The opera?"

The flutter of life in my heart sent relief through me. "Yes. Though I could have thought of better ways to enjoy it."

I ran the tip of my tongue over the back of my teeth, then clicked my tongue. "I wanted to say congratulations. Christine was superb, sublime and all the words that can describe such an amazing accomplishment. You should be so proud."

"She was everything I could have wanted on that stage."

"She was."

My mouth twitched around as I contemplated my next move. "Are we still friends?" I asked.

"*Mon cœur*. Only God could take you from my heart," he said. "What's left of it anyway."

A soft, thankful chuckle left my chest and the tension in my shoulders seized. I wiped away a rogue tear. "You're ridiculous," I said

"Only for you."

I rolled my eyes and sighed, fiddling with the box in my hands.

"Crimson is your color, Angel."

"Thank you." I smiled like a fool, blushing so hard it burned my skin. "Anyway. I have something for you."

I set the box on the vanity again. Excited, I opened the top and dug out the small cake within. "You know how hard it was to find a small, skinny candle?" I asked. With the strike of a match, I lit the little candle after setting it at the center of the cake. "Congratulations… and happy birthday, my dear Erique."

Chapter XXI

"*My dear Erique." She speaks my name, and it is a peace I have never known.* A remembrance of my day of birth mattered to me not. My age was unknown, even to me. Though she estimated early forties by recollections of my stories.

Sometimes this life seemed to span centuries when solitude was your only companion.

Flabbergasted, I stared at the bakery item. Never in my years have I been given a gift. At least not one without consequence. Then she appears and showers me with them.

"Ok, you're probably thinking 'what is she talking about, right?'" she said.

Nervous or excited? This particular moment was hard to tell which her quick speech was incited by. Both perhaps. Stumbling over words and spouting nonsense, I adored her for it.

"Curiosity holds me," I said.

Divots in her cheeks appeared as she smiled. Enthusiasm sparkled in her eyes. "Well, I figured, since you didn't know your birthday, that I would give you one. And what better way to celebrate a birthday than with a triumph of Christine on opening night, in the opera house that you love so much…"

Her words circled my ears yet did not truly enter. For shame, I stare at her loveliness. So full of life. Mouth moving with sweet words for me. An apology so welcomed and accepted.

"…But I'm also a terrible friend. I don't think I ever asked your favorite cake, so I had them make my favorite, with a recipe I know vaguely, so that I can share with you something new. They don't have it over here yet. It's chocolate cake, filled and topped with a coconut-pecan frosting."

Staggered in thought, I was at a loss for words. She desired to share something dear with me. Only because it comes from her, I would treat it as if given by Gods.

"But there is one stipulation," she added.

"What is that, dear?"

She closed her eyes, grazing her bottom lip with her teeth. Pulses beat rapidly through these veins at sight of it. I hated when she did that.

"In order for you to have this oh *so devilishly divine* German's Chocolate cake, you have to come share it with me," she finished.

Speaking with her on a daily basis was enough. For now. Even the ache of her words the other night had vanished. Here, with her was where I wanted to be on this triumphant evening. I could only ruin it.

On the other hand, what if time had come? Someday had been promised, fate would have it be now?

"And don't worry. I have a compromise." Her voice stopped my erratic mind and refocused my attention on her cherubic face.

She walked away from the mirror, pulling something from her pocket. A long strip of fabric dangled from her hand. "I'll stay blind folded and you can come in," she said, tying it around her head and over her eyes.

I deserved no care like this. To say the least, her gesture overwhelmed. I had thought of nothing the past few days except Christine's debut. *That was a lie.*

Even as I lay unconscious encircled by empty wine bottles, and twenty-five-year-old brandy meant to be shared with an old friend, she haunted my every dream and lucid thought. Not even my opera would

Chapter XXI

play from shaking fingers.

'The woman you dote on so much breaks your heart, yet you entertain her. You gave up the one thing that could give us everything, for continued torture,' the *Ghost* said.

His words bit like a mouse. There, but only a nuisance.

More than anything I wanted this offer to be real. But in part, I was reserved. What if she ordered me away again? It was unbearable the first time.

"And if this is a trick to get me out of the shadows just for you to whip the blindfold off and see the monster?" I asked.

"I can see how you might think that *Le Fantome*," she said, waving a hand in the air then resting it on her lips. Always so playful, and I craved to play with her.

"I would never do anything to hurt you. Not like that. Guess you just have to trust me enough. And if I take this off, then you can kill me or whatever, I don't know. It's up to you."

'She will hurt you like the others. She has hurt you worse. You would risk that again, boy?'

To risk sweetens the reward.

"Better hurry, birthday boy, I'm hungry and the only thing in here is this really delicious cake, which is now getting covered in melted wax..." she teased.

Every disgusting part of me ached for affection. But none screamed louder than the suppression in my trousers. Which I ignored, per usual.

This was about trust, something also never given to me. Such fascinating feelings with it. Very limiting yet refreshing.

I hung my cloak from a hook next to the mirror. Hands ran over my hair to ensure it was in place. Fingers wrapped underneath the hem of my jacket, and I tugged, straightening any dishevelment.

My hands found the mechanism that held the panel in place and I released it.

Her head turned slightly in the direction the door sounded as it slid open. "I knew that'd get you out here," she smirked.

"You had me at chocolate, madam. Though pecan was a close second."

Shadows attempted to keep hold as I stepped hesitantly out into the soft light of the forgotten room.

The flickering of the candle on the vanity held no interest for me. How could it when its flame paled in comparison to the beacon in red.

The highlights of her face as she watched from behind the darkness of the blindfold, the curve in her waist, and her fidgety hands screamed to be touched by my own equally unsteady fingers.

"Ok, so, now you make a wish and blow out the candle," she said.

"I thought you couldn't see me, my dear."

"You know how it is when one sense is shut off, the others explode in order to make up for the loss."

If I were a worse man, I would take her now just for her intellect.

"Must I?" I asked.

"I don't make the rules. I just follow them." She shrugged and leaned against the chaise casually.

"I thought you decided you were the director of this story?"

"Just make the wish already!" she urged.

"What if this is my wish?"

Her false brown curls coiled over her shoulders as she rolled her head back. "Your wish is to ruin the best cake in existence with wax because of your innate need to torture me?"

"Yes."

"That is a sad wish, Erique, even for you. You could do that any day. Wish for something else."

"Wishes are for people without hope. Do you think the wealthy, the fortunate, make wishes?"

Her lips rolled inward as she stood up straight, hands fidgeting in front of her. "Well…"

"I wish…"

Her hands lurched forward suddenly. "You're not supposed to say it out loud! Or it won't come true!"

"What sense is that?"

"Yeah, I know. I mean, yeah… To be honest, I don't think any wish I've ever made came true or at least the ones I kept to myself anyway… ok do what you want, just blow out the candle before it ruins the cake."

And in a quick moment, the flickering glow from the small candle went out and a poof of smoke took its place.

Chapter XXI

"Is this too much?" I asked.

The prolonged silence was killing me. Being blindfolded was just as bad.

The air shifted yet again. I was certain if I reached out, I'd find him right there. Within arm's reach.

My heart quickened and my breath grew heavy. I tried to calm it, but it wasn't working. He was too close.

What have I done?

"Never has a moment been more perfect. You are exquisite. Never doubt that," he said. His voice, though soft and low, was certain and clear.

An ironic and apprehensive soft laugh bounced around my chest as I tried to hide the bashful smile.

"Are you ready to share this with me," he asked. There was an underlying sensuality in his tone that captured me.

I nodded absentmindedly. "Mmhhmm."

"Don't do that." The rich timbre of his voice shook slightly with warning. A familiar shiver of awareness coursed through me, pooling lower and lower with each passing second.

"Do what?" I said with breathy voice.

"If you bite your lip again, Melody. Mmm. We may regret it."

My cheeks weren't the only thing heating up. The aching and pulsing between my legs was suddenly very awake and set to Mount Saint Helen mode.

It wasn't right. I didn't want to feel this. We were friends. Among other complications. Sure, the idea of the Phantom was hot, at least before. But it was different now. I knew him.

Don't laugh uncontrollably. We want closeness. Please, don't say something stupid.

It was my trademark to fuck this kind of stuff up, because intimacy made me uncomfortable. Terrified me. Even when I yearned for it the most.

I truly hadn't thought this far. Honestly, I thought I'd be leaving a cake on a table for him to come get after I was gone.

"Open your mouth," he commanded softly.

Without thought, my lips parted, eagerly awaiting whatever he was planning.

The sweet smell of coconut-pecan filled my senses just before a small bit of fluffy, chocolate hit my tongue.

The flavors danced in my mouth. It was better than I remembered.

The faintest touch of a finger ran over my bottom lip. "How is it?" he asked. A hint of desperation in his voice deepened the thirst building inside me.

"Perfect," I said almost inaudibly.

"Good."

"You're supposed to try it first. I forgot to tell you that," I said, managing a full sentence to my shock.

"I will try it."

"That's not fair. It's your birthday."

"And it is the best birthday I've ever had."

I raised my hands in search of the cake. Knowing, I looked silly fumbling around.

"Oops..." I said, finding the cake with my thumb. "Sorry."

"It will not go wasted."

Cool, bare fingers wrapped around my hand. Tender, warm lips rested on the side of my thumb, forcing the smallest of gasps from me. He took me further into his mouth and sucked gently, running his tongue over it. Lightly grazing with his teeth as he pulled me out.

Suddenly, I was thankful for the blindfold. My eyes would have given me away as they rolled back. So away.

To continue standing was a feat in itself. My mind swirled with crazy, delicious thoughts. All of them ending with this man bottoming out inside of me on this chaise lounge. Maybe over the back of it. The vanity. Everywhere.

The desire for him was disgustingly strong. It screamed— SCREAMED—to be given attention by the masked man that spends his time teasing me. I'd even stay blindfolded if that was what he wanted.

An image began to form as he hummed into the palm of my hand which now rested against a partially exposed cheek and smooth mask.

Chapter XXI

He shifted slightly, careful not to lose contact with his skin, and stepped forward. With his free hand, he tilted my head up. "That is the best German Chocolate Cake I have had. Thank you." His hot, sweet breath hit my mouth.

Was I giving into my need for physical touch over getting home?

No, I'd still try to get home. That was the most important thing. Right? Right.

It didn't mean I couldn't indulge a little before then. And I care about him. More than I think I want to.

At least now I could leave with a clear conscience, right?

Could a kiss heal a fractured soul? This was my childish wish.

Time seized as pink glistening lips begged for tender attention.

My trembling hand hovered her unblemished, perfect face, attempting courage to cradle her as she did me.

Terror held back this act in fearfulness that it may go through her. Everything about her was pure. How could anyone like this exist?

All we have done until now, fantasy. Friends who stole moments in the night and shared secrets. Who fell asleep together after a night's reading. Played games that could be the end of us.

To lose such heaven because I scared her would be my undoing.

Demon's lips waited in ache to press to her. My cock raged to be set free. To bury myself within this woman who stands so freely with thee, and never leave. To make her mine and take her with me into the night.

My trembling hand froze above her shoulder as she made contact with my ribcage. Nimble fingers that could easily dance across a keyboard if taught, crept upwards to my chest.

Dearest God. You stop me with a word, and you kill me with your touch. Do not bite your lip... oh god, please don't look at me that way.

Allegro was my heart beneath her hand, could she feel such a tempo?

I weighed with nothing but want and leaned into her.

'Take her now!'

She needs to want me. That would be the only way. I said, shutting up the *Ghost*.

Thawed fingertips pressed against the roundness of her soft cheek. A moan and lean of her head had me weak. I traveled down to the crook of her bare neck. The pulse beneath her flesh mirrored the beat in mine.

Courage closed my eyes as I reluctantly took my hand from hers and slid both of them around to the back of her head. Desperate lips hovered hers as I contemplated stealing the kiss she begged for, before this would end as it was meant to.

I had thought letting Christine go was the most terrifying choice I had made. This *thing* had never been more wrong.

The fabric that was once a barrier to keep me from sight fell as startled brown eyes dropped to the floor. Slowly, they moved upward. Closely, I watched for the moment angelic eyes would land on mine. Search for a wince or hint of lie to hide her own fear. Confirm everything I have ever known to be true.

Cautious brown eyes caught and held mine. I was stone as she searched the falsity I wore upon my face. Curiosity turned soft quickly, and a charming little smile crossed her face.

"Hi," she said, in the sweetest tone. Her eyes told me everything.

The world ceased to exist, and we were lost in the void. My hand found the nape of her neck as I stepped forward, closing any space left between us.

Lightning surged through this living dead man as my inexperienced lips collided with hers. I was Frankenstein's monster brought to life. This time by the kindest hand creation ever made.

Decades of desolation were incinerated within the explosions of my mind. Hope rose and wove around strands of unaltered, pure bliss.

The warmth of her hand on my face both calmed and excited. Lips were made of heaven, far more than any fantasy. And she was warm. So warm.

Emotions I had never known mixed within the euphoric chaos. My cock both pleased and disgruntled with the friction as we pressed together.

Hesitantly, we pulled apart only to take breath.

"I'm sorry it took me so long," I said, against the softness of her mouth.

Eyes that saw me stared back with a foreign hunger. I fell into her offering hand, clenching joyous weeps back. This woman, this kindness was too precious. Too much.

Her stare implored me, and the hot ache in my throat grew. My heart would never have a chance to run.

Fearing this experience would be a long gone memory, I crushed her into me, and reclaimed her lips for another soul mending kiss.

∞ℳ∞

This man's kiss tasted of sugared pecans and coconut, baked in desire.

His cool touch was like ice on my heated skin. The perfect mix of sensations had me wishing the barriers of society were gone.

On the verge of orgasm and/or fainting I wasn't sure which, I forced myself to stay in this beautiful moment.

Fantasy had nothing on this. We were here. And we were real.

Every part of me yearned for this man. I ran my fingers through his dark hair, entwining them within the soft keratin strands. I gripped tighter, forcing a moan from the Ghost that rumbled into my mouth.

The already firm hold he had on me tightened, forcing my head to loll back. Eager lips moved along my jaw and left a blazing trail of desire along the skin of my neck.

How did it get to this point? It was just talking...

Oh, I needed this masked man's cock inside me so badly. Craved for him to crush me with his body. Above me. Behind me. Beside me. Any which way we pleased, until dawn's early light, and then some.

He planted a heavy kiss in the crook of my neck. "Melody. My Melody. My Angel. *Mon cœur...*" he whimpered.

Moan inducing tingles spread from the vibration of his voice and hot breath on my already sensitive flesh.

I laid my head upon his as I stroked through his hair. He hummed a familiar tune in which I joined and we swayed.

The bare skin of his cheek ran up my neck and to my jaw. The innate need for him grew with every inch he moved. Skin on skin was intense and all consuming, furthering my indecent desires.

I'd hoped that he was going in for another kiss. Or I was going to be the attacker this time. Yes. I would take his tongue and allow my hands to wander. Maybe a bit south.

Thud.

My head snapped down to where the sound had come from.

On the floor at our feet, laid a white mask.

"No!" Erique screamed. His arms swung up quickly.

Startled at his quick movement, I stepped back, catching myself on the hem of my dress and fell to the floor.

I found horrified, tear filled eyes staring through stretched fingers trying cover a face. Hope seeping over his pale skin.

Then he was gone. And the secret door closed.

A wail made of sheer pain and heartbreak, bled through the vents in the walls a moment later, as I tried to gather myself.

Anyone within earshot of a vent would have just heard the Ghost's shattered dreams.

Tears leaked from my own eyes, and I dropped my head. "Oh, Erique."

Chapter XXII

Melody

"*His kiss tasted of sugared pecans and coconut, baked in desire.*" Sarah would have loved to hear about how I made out with the Phantom. How his touch was so strong, yet almost unbearable in its tenderness.

I wanted to live in that moment forever. The perfect kiss. Simple. Unexpected and overdue.

I didn't expect it to go as far as it had. When the blindfold came off, I wasn't sure what I was going to be met with. Gerard Butler was totally wishful thinking. With my luck he was going to be some variation of the Lon Chaney version or the fucking Crypt Keeper.

For a second, I even questioned whether he'd be human. Everything else was still unbelievable, so why not that?

He was none of it. He was just Erique. And fuck, he was beautiful.

The soft light on his mask only intensified his stunning eyes. The suit he wore, surprisingly clean and in pristine condition, hugged his slender frame and broad shoulders.

He really did look like he was going to the opera. What a weirdo. Every day he dressed like that.

The thought made me chuckle a little. But the moment was fleeting. The terror in his beautiful eyes as he hid behind his hands overshadowed the memory. It was like we were always taking one step forward and two steps back.

Oh, Erique.

The theater was usually empty on Sundays. This Sunday was no different.

I hadn't stopped searching for him since I woke up. Which was pretty early, since I couldn't sleep. My voice was already hoarse with how much I'd called out for him. But he never showed me how to open the damn panels from the outside. Searching had been a bit difficult to say the least.

"Ms. Reilly!" M. Fournier called out.

Before I could slink off as if I hadn't heard my name, M. Fournier hurried down the grand stairway toward me, curls bouncing like kids on a trampoline.

"Might I borrow you a moment!" he asked. He seemed in better spirits as of late. He must have had a wonderful night. That made one of us.

I was supposed to meet with Antoinette for lunch today, but I sent word that I was sick. Now I wish I had gone to see her.

But I needed to find him. Tell him whatever happened was alright. That I really didn't care. I just needed him back.

Needed him.

No. I just needed to know that he was alright. So I could keep trying to get home.

"Yes, Monsieur?" I asked, reluctantly.

He reached the bottom of the stairs, his curls somehow still bouncing. "I have been asked to give you this," he said, pulling a letter from his pocket.

Since when did the managers deliver notes?

My stomach dropped when I saw it. Was Erique not even going to talk to me? He would really have the manager relay a message?

"It seems Comte de Changy has taken a liking to you."

Oh. Great.

I thought I dealt with this. How many times did he need to be

Chapter XXII

rejected?

"Did you read it?"

His eyes widened as if I had the audacity to ask. "No, of course not! It came only twenty minutes ago from his personal messenger. I was just glad to catch you when I did."

Though my heart was lighter knowing it wasn't from Erique, this was another problem I sure as fuck didn't want.

"You seem displeased," he said.

"He's asked me to dinner again… well, more like demanded that I join him tonight. I don't want to. I have plans." *That is if Erique shows up.* "And I'm not interested in him. I've told him…"

"You would be so lucky. He's an infamous bachelor and for him to be interested in…" he paused, looking me up and down. "Wouldn't you like to be out of here someday? A family of your own perhaps?"

I hadn't planned on leaving this place with him at the very least. As for family… "uh, that's not…"

"You may have a lovely time. Please go. It would be a favor to M. Leblanc and myself."

"Will I lose my job if I don't?"

He hesitated a moment, glancing around as if he were about to get caught doing something. He cleared his throat, "You have secure employment."

Bless you, Erique.

"Thank you. Have a wonderful day," I said.

"Then you'll go?"

"Nope. And you can tell him that."

***

The twisting in my stomach was cruel as I got closer to the practice room. It was dark and cold, even with the light on. Usually, it felt like this until he arrived, unless he was already there, then it was a cozy spot by the fireplace on a winter day.

Not this time.

"Please come out," I said. Even though I couldn't feel him, I still hoped.

When there was no answer, no sign that he was there, I wandered into the dark part of the room, and sat at the piano.

I pulled the mask from my bag and stared at it.

There was nothing really special about it. Not like the movies or stage or anything.

Plain white and beautifully hand crafted. It covered two-thirds of his face, leaving open his mouth and a cheek, and was held on by two leather straps. I didn't know the material of the mask itself, but it was sturdy enough to crash to the floor and not crack.

Yes, I tried it on.

A bit big. Even with my round face.

I had noticed a partial distortion of his mouth. Like he'd been burned or something. Same with his hand. But they felt no different while they touched me.

Erique was punctual, if he was going to be here, he would have been. I still waited a while longer.

I knew I was going to leave the mask for him. That was the plan when I came in. But I couldn't do it just yet. I didn't want to risk someone finding it.

At least that's what I told myself when I packed it back into my bag and left for my room.

Normally getting ghosted wouldn't bother me to the point of tears. I was used to it, no matter how much it sucked. But once I hit the mattress, the overwhelming reality took over, and I cried silently for a while. I hoped that tomorrow would be better.

It wasn't.

Work was undisturbed for the next few days.

No ghost sightings to be heard about. And I was still sad.

There was a moment that I swear I saw him while I forced myself to that restroom. My throat dried and my chest pounded.

Nothing came of it.

I showed up to the practice room for the fourth night in a row. Ready to either see him or leave him behind.

The room was empty. Just like the days before.

I pulled the mask from my bag and held it to my chest. Every step to the piano was like walking the plank. I was either going to jump off or get pushed.

I set it down on the lid of the piano hesitantly.

Chapter XXII

It hurt to know that he was here somewhere and chose not to see me.

I took a seat and ran my fingers lightly over the ebony and ivory keys. I wasn't much of a pianist, really at all, I knew very little and hadn't touched one since high school.

My unpracticed fingers found middle C anyway and settled into the first notes.

It'd been so long since I played this piece. It was really the only one I knew. *Moonlight Sonata* always soothed me. In my current mental state, it felt appropriate.

I fumbled through the piece. Not sure what I was even doing it for. I guess in some weird way, I hoped it'd coax him out if he was nearby.

The moment I'd fantasized about with Erique had come and gone, just like him. And now I had nothing here.

I'd become too attached.

The music stopped abruptly. Even playing held no joy for me. I stared at the keys he'd played many times before. It was clear he wasn't coming.

My eyes raked over the mask one more time. Memorizing every detail.

It didn't matter that he was Erique, the Phantom of *Palais Garnier*. I couldn't waste any more time being a pathetic sack like I had over the past few days.

I was never meant for any of this.

If he wasn't going to come to me, after I'd clearly shown that I was here for him, then it didn't matter anymore, and I was done.

Maybe I should have gone out with Philippe again.

My stomach turned at the thought of it and I instantly regretted it.

It didn't matter what century I was in, it felt like all the men were cowards and I was over it.

Tomorrow, not one thought will be for him. Every attempt home would be without remorse.

I left the mask where I sat it down and closed the door to us.

It was late when I started back toward my room. I needed to sleep the sadness away one more night.

When I rounded the corner, ice stilled my veins. Exiting from the salon down the hallway, was Philippe. He seemed agitated.

"Ope!" I gasped and jumped back before he could see me.

Usually, I would just avoid this part of the building at this time of night because of the stumbling, handsy patrons.

It reminded me of the times I'd pick up Mom and whatever shitty boyfriend at the bar when they were too wasted to drive, only to have to listen to her be treated like she was a waste of life the rest of the night. All while being accosted by the nasty old drunk dudes.

I didn't want to deal with that or Philippe tonight. I already felt like shit and didn't need someone to make it worse.

The door to the backstage was always unlocked. Too many needed in and out at any given time, it was also the second quickest way back to my room from the practice room.

A small part of me hoped Erique was hanging around back there. Maybe under the stage, waiting. I don't know.

"Stop it! Stop!!" A woman's muffled shout echoed over the stage. *"Stop! Stupid, vulgar pig!"*

At the bottom of the stairs to the catwalk, Joseph Buquet, the dirty stagehand that shook me the day Erique saved me from the sandbag, had one of the chorus girls pinned against the wall. Forcibly groping and kissing on her.

"Hey!" I shouted. No one came to help me when I was attacked. That wasn't going to happen again.

Buquet ignored me and continued with his assault. The woman was obviously distraught, swatting at him best she could, trying to get away.

Without any thought, I pulled the knife from my pocket and flipped it open. With all force I jammed the little pig sticker into Buquet's hip and twisted. He squealed and fell onto the stairs, moving enough for the small, terrified brunette to get free and dash off.

I yelped when a hand gripped my shoulder tightly and yanked me back. As the sharp edges of the stairs stabbed into my back, I gasped at the pain.

He towered over me. A crazed look in his eye. This was going to be revenge for humiliating him.

I crawled up backwards frantically, as he lurched forward.

"Ghost whore!" he yelled, just missing me.

Chapter XXII

I reached the top, not sure of where to go except over the hanging catwalk. The thought of running away from someone on them was almost as terrifying. The unstable rope railings and the swaying… Still a better option.

Pain shot through my arm as it twisted. It felt like it was going to rip from my socket. I didn't even know what hit me before I was on the ground. The ringing in my ears was deafening as my head spun. It was like I was slapped by a thousand bees.

It was hard to focus as my head pulsed. He was flashing in and out of sight. Like an old moving picture machine.

"The Ghost!" he shouted.

I found my bloodied knife on the floor and managed to my feet. If I couldn't get away, I was going to fight the losing battle.

In all the dizzy darkness, Buquet's terrified face came in clear. So did the white of a mask and eyes that were full of wild darkness.

"Vous voulais the Ghost! Me voici!" Erique sneered. His menacing laugh and wicked smile chilled me.

This is who the Phantom was. Who he was.

I still worried for him. Buquet was much larger than Erique. Even if he was enjoying the fight, he could still lose.

"Bâtard du devil," Buquet yelled, as Erique whipped a rope over his head.

Erique's hands pulled it tighter around the stagehand's throat. His glowing eyes cut to mine. Pain was alive and bright in them. "Do not watch this, my angel."

The Phantom dragged the kicking and gurgling beast out onto the swaying catwalk. Buquet's face turned purple and his swinging arms slowed.

Focused on the struggle he was winning, Erique hadn't noticed the rope running across the surface of the platform. His grip on Buquet loosened when he tripped over it, and the pig broke free just enough to swing at him.

"Erique!" I screamed, running to the ledge.

I wanted to run out to help him, but my feet were concrete. All the courage I once had was gone.

I was going to watch my… I was going to watch Erique die because

I was scared.

The wretched man grabbed at Erique. Had him nearly off his feet, pushing against the railing. It was astonishing they didn't both just fall.

Glowing eyes burned with hatred. Gritted teeth bared beneath a grin. There was no mistaking it. Erique loved this. The fight. The chance to kill.

A sinister laugh escaped the Phantom's throat, and in a burst of energy he broke free.

Erique grabbed hold of the noose that still hung around Buquet's neck, and yanked him toward the ledge. The stagehand's eyes locked onto me as if to ask for help. The same fear I saw in the officer's eyes.

It was like slow motion for a moment. I almost didn't believe it happened.

The rope pulled taut and the sound of a twig snapping jolted me. The creaking from the rope under the weight of Buquet's lifeless body and Erique's exhilarated heavy breathing filled the stage.

"Erique..." I said through quivering lips as I stared at the swinging body.

Pulled from his frenzied ecstasy, Erique was by my side in an instant. He looked me over, finding the bloody knife in my hand. Taking it from me, he closed it and put it in his pocket.

A large, thin hand took my face and held it gently. "Are you alright, my brave girl?" he asked. His tone was fragile and tender, unlike what had just happened.

I couldn't take my eyes off Buquet. I just witnessed the man I care about kill and enjoy it. After saving me again.

"Melody," he called gently.

My eyes walked back to find him. The pain and concern were heavier now that I could really see them.

He was also disheveled from head to toe. Hair all over the place. An untucked white shirt and black slacks. By the way he smelled, it was obvious the disarray wasn't from the fight. Alcohol and sweat emanated from him, like he hadn't bathed in days.

"Come," he commanded, low and pleading.

Voices crept in nearby, probably coming to check on what the commotion was.

Chapter XXII

"No. I can't…" my voice shakier than I would have liked.

"Don't force my hand, *mon cœur.*"

The voices grew nearer and fear along with them.

Without further hesitation but still shaken, I took his hand and followed the Phantom of the Opera into the unknown.

Chapter XXIII

Down into the darkened depths of my mind I would take her. She had seen the worst of her almost lover.

Coward.

Killer.

All my doing. All my failures.

Not one word had been spoken since she had taken my hand. With vacant eyes, she stared into the distance ahead, disregarding the present as we floated along one of the many tunnels of my underground lake.

Never in dreams nor imaginations was this how I would bring my angel home.

As I tied the boat off to the dock and led her from it, she was still lost to another universe, unfazed by the wonder of my domain. Not even my forest drew her attention as we neared our home.

'How could she be in awe when a monster leads her?'
the *Ghost* reminded.

My mind forgets it is I who put her in this trance. This creature's nature had affected another in such a detestable way, not even I could see beyond it.

Thus was life when kindness was bestowed upon me. And yet, I

Chapter XXIII

would continue to delight in her hell as always until she ended me.

The disarray and shame of these past four days laid about my parlor in the form of shattered bottles and torn stories. It was only hope that her mind was elsewhere as I continued to hold her hand, guiding her quickly through it.

"You may rest here," I said, opening a doorway to my barren room. Time, nor fate, had been charitable. It was intended that this room be renovated for her arrival. The cruelty of life always had other plans.

Still, she did not run.

Vacant eyes scanned my quarters slowly.

I forced myself to release her hand and visit the dresser. "For comfort," I said, and set down a nightshirt on the bed.

Absent-mindedly, she met me at the bedside and stared at the pile of linen on the mattress. "You'll take me back in the morning?" she asked, her voice distant and tired.

I clenched my jaw and swallowed the despair in my throat at her request.

"Right?" she asked, glancing up at me.

'She does not have to leave,' the *Ghost* suggested. *'There is a second room. She could stay there until she changed her mind.'*

Tempting as his proposal may have been, the growing concern in her eyes at my silence suggested fear would not turn to love.

Against my will, I nodded. "If that is what you wish."

Slight relief filled her eyes and they dropped back to the linen, where she fiddled with it again.

Poisoned were these hands that longed to hold her. Just once more. To recreate a moment that seemed fiction now. Yet I refrained. These hands had done enough damage.

The silence between us was just as unbearable as her fear. To find reprieve from this constant pain, misery carried me towards the door, to leave her in peace.

At least with her nearness, the music of my mind played again.

As I reached the threshold of the door, I hesitated departure. "I regret you have witnessed…" I started.

"How many people have you killed?"

She continued fiddling with the fabrics on the bed. Her question stirred. Not for shame, but curiosity.

"Thirty-one," I replied, matter of fact. "Perhaps more."

It was not something kept in my mind. Nor did it elicit shame. When it was done, more than not, would never be thought of again.

"I see," she said. brown eyes hesitated to find mine as she faced me. "Do you feel guilty for it?"

"No. I feel no guilt for *them*." Restless were the fingers at my sides as my eyes clung to hers, analyzing her reaction. Her eyes fell away as if it were not what she had hoped to hear.

'Say something!' the *Ghost* urged.

"If it would ease your mind to know, when it were not for hire by the King, the lives ended by my lasso, were all very deserving of it. No tears were shed nor did any mourn their death. Nor did I seek them out," I said.

Every refined word from my mouth sounded like a snake trying to convince a mouse he was not going to eat it.

My body inclined, half in anticipation, half in dread, for words that would not come. She looked up, a change in her stare. Had my confession been wrong, that she would look upon me with confusion?

She swallowed the words of something which rolled within her throat. Her gaze roamed to the vanity near the foot of my bed.

"My first night here, I was so terrified. Actually, I don't think that word even comes close to what I was feeling," she said with a small ironic chuckle. She stepped closer to the vanity, slowly glancing at the masks which hung on the wall around the shattered mirror. "I didn't know where I was. It wasn't my world. Someone helped me, at least I thought he did. Until he tried to rape me in an alley."

My mood veered sharply to anger and my blood turned acidic. I was near her within a second, restraining what little composure I had left. "Some *thing* dared to violate you?" I said through gnashed teeth.

"Tried."

Her careful hand reached out to find a decorative mask made from a moment of sheer vanity. Bone white with black cracking and small horns. One never intended to be worn after its fabrication, yet still too beautiful to toss out. "I like this one," she said. A faint smile on her mouth. "You should wear it sometime. Really add to that ghost thing."

Chapter XXIII

Her voice strained and cracked.

Ache intertwined with the rage ruminating within my chest at her attempt to mask her pain.

"I didn't even remember getting the knife from my pocket or driving it into his neck. The blood gurgled when he blew into his whistle for help. I watched him die then ran away." The words came casually, as if someone else told the story, like Melody Reilly hadn't personally experienced it. Her deepest, darkest secret—at least one of them—was finally out. Yet, her demeanor was unusually calm for such a recounting.

"I assume it normal to feel guilt for taking a life."

"I don't," she said quickly. Subsided was my rage when curiosity overshadowed. My brows lifted, not that she could see, but her admission had taken me by surprise. "That's what has me so fucked up, Erique. I feel bad for not feeling bad. Not because I killed someone or watched you kill Joseph, but because I didn't care afterwards."

A glazed look of horror and despair spread over her face at her admission and her eyes ripped away back to my wall of illusions.

'Go to her, what is it you wait for?' the *Ghost* asked.

"Where did you find this?" she asked, pulling down a black and silver mask from the wall. The tremble in her voice left me further unsure of our situation.

"I was curious about you," I said. "Covered in blood, wearing a face like mine."

A moment of clarity changed her face. A wide glistening stare turned up to mine. "You were in the bar too? The reason the men stopped pounding?"

I nodded.

"Did you follow me to the hotel then?" she asked.

"I've known Antoinette and Louis for many years."

"Why did you…"

"I do not know."

Her eyes fell back to the mask she never thought she'd see again. "I told you I was at a show with my mom and sister," she said.

"Yes."

"We were dressing up. I'd made one of these for each of us. I was the only one who wore one though. It was special to the show. I like to do that. Dress up and be someone else for a while," she said, running her fingers over its surface, falling into a memory. "There's some things you can't escape. Even when you're… away." Tears bit at the corners of her eyes. Thumbs wanted desperately to wipe them away for her as they slipped out. She cleared her throat and hung her mask back up in its place, suppressing another secret. "I need to clean up."

The lack of outburst. Tears. Emotions I had seen in many others over years of observation, evaded her and unsettled even me.

"Yes. Of course," I said, staring a moment too long, contemplating if she would allow the taking of her hand. "This way."

A silent walk through a dim hallway made this *creature* light, knowing the heaviness of what would come.

I opened the door to a dark room and flipped on the lights. Fresh paint of the dark green that decorated the walls still filled the air. The first of many planned changes.

Feeling eyes roamed around her bathroom, then landed on the latest victim of my self-loathing. A mirror which hung above the basin.

"I will replace it for you," I said.

I sat her in a chair next to the new claw foot bathtub, which had only been delivered recently, and turned on the faucet. Water fell into the porcelain, splashing around. This was something she wanted long ago. Hope would have it be enough to heal.

"This should only take a few minutes," I said. It was probably apparent that I would need a wash as well, that would wait until after she had gone to bed.

Steam rose from the tub as I left her staring into the rising water.

The door closed behind me, and I glared at my hand on the knob. She would leave after this. The light within the darkness would be gone. She thought herself a monster, same as this diseased man and would need away from him.

My one wish for her in all this world was that she lived in beauty and wonder. This precious tormented soul ached with guilt she did not deserve. To feel guilt for not feeling it. What torture that must be.

Strained shoulders hit the wall, and I slid to the ground weakened by my own weight.

When she was rested, what then? What we have built together, would that cease? What I and others have done, would every glance at this *monster* be a constant reminder of pain?

Fingers ripped through my hair as I gritted teeth, howling in silence. *I am made to destroy.*

The sound of heavy sobs replaced running water. It pulled me from loathing and closer to the door. The purest soul in existence cried on the other side.

She believed herself a monster. The same as I.

A coward I was once when it mattered. Not this time. She would know sunlight again.

Thought dissipated as I sprung to my feet and opened the door without hesitation. As the steam rolled over me, I marched to the porcelain basin that should have eased, and slid in behind her.

The water stung my flesh, continuing the retribution earned. Soaked arms wrapped around my broken Angel, who latched on immediately, clinging as if she were dangling over the edge of a cliff into oblivion and I was her only salvation.

"You are good. You are so good, baby," I said. A look of surprise I have not seen before touched her pale face as she looked up. I ran a hand through her natural hair and kissed her temple. "Believe me, my heart, please."

"I shouldn't be ok with this. Any of this," she cried.

Desperate hands grabbed her cherubic face once more. "Hear me," I said, staring as far into her eyes as I could probe. "The world is filled with monsters. Ghouls. Men who would see it crumble for the excitement of it. I should know. You. You are nothing but beauty. Your soul is the sweetest. You are no spring fawn, Melody Reilly. Some men are unredeemable, you know this. Be free of these chains you have shackled yourself with."

Tears came again as she fell into my chest.

Hades would lose in battle to pry me away. Even as my limbs numbed, I would refuse to undo myself.

Demons had dragged her to hell the moment she arrived in this godforsaken place and had since been attempting to claw her way out. Only to find the devil himself delighting to be her last refuge.

Chapter XXIV
Melody

A campfire in the forest after rainfall. The bed smelled of him. I thought it would smell awful like he had tonight until our bath. But no. Damp sulfur and a hint of wood. Just like the rest of the home smelled.

I laid there for a while, tossing and turning. Unable to find comfort or ease. Even with Erique playing softly just around the corner, I couldn't sleep. My mind was too fucking busy.

All my thoughts jumbled together. Murder. Comfort. Care. Home. What tomorrow morning would bring. What this all meant for us. Even though there shouldn't be any form of "us". Because I still had to go home…

Not to mention that he saw me completely buck ass naked.

When I imagined a bath with him once upon a silly thought, it would have been sensual and fun. I didn't think it'd be out of necessity for both my nose and mental state.

We hadn't talked about us. It was best we didn't. Just act like it didn't happen. And go back to the way it was. Just friends.

I wonder if I'd ever be able to tell him the whole truth? And if I did, would he even believe me? Would it even help how I feel about

Chapter XXIV

everything?

I hated this.

Unable to take the traffic jam in my head anymore, and the conflicting feelings with it all, I tossed back the blankets and swung my legs over the side. Bare feet hit the cold wooden floor and carried me out towards the living room.

I watched from around the corner as he played. The melody was familiar. I couldn't place it, but it was nice, and it was calming.

The minor chords were harsh and dramatic. Anguish saturated the air. Yet, it was a beautiful type of pain.

I'd fantasized about seeing him like this. In the mellow glow of candles and the fireplace. He was for sure the epitome of beauty. The dream of every dark romance. Even with how drained I knew he was; he was still an enchanting sight.

Lost in the music and madness of everything, I closed my eyes and rested my head against the wall.

The organ had a completely different feel to it when he played. It was something that wove itself through you. Its haunting sound could carry you or drown you. Both welcoming to the spirit, if you were open minded. The beauty that came from pain was often the worst. What kind of pain do you have to endure to create something so soul stirring?

The music faded into a softness and then finally ended. I opened my eyes to find him standing, staring at me.

"Please don't stop," I said.

Without a word, he retook his seat. Fingers settled onto the keys and danced away. Something different, more melancholy. A slow waltz of some kind.

Practiced moves caressed the keys perfectly in time. Its melody forced images to my mind. A gifted book. Caress of hands in the dark. A kiss so perfect it could never be duplicated with another.

The white shirt he wore, which matched the one he lent me, hung on his shoulders, the loose fabric flowing with expression as dozens of silver pipes towered over him while he played.

I forced myself to look away. To avoid any further fantasies or delusions of what could have been. It didn't matter that he called me baby. A term I didn't know he knew. Nor that he'd been referring to me as *my Heart* this whole time.

What a wicked man.

Now that I could focus better, I roamed the space instead. Sparse would be the word I would use to describe it. There wasn't much to look at. Simple wood furniture, though nice, nothing resembling the work done in the bathroom.

He'd cleaned up. No more empty bottles or torn sheet music cluttered the floors or tables everywhere. Though a new graveyard of crumpled papers had started building up around his organ.

The only thing that really had any life and finesse to it was the tall dark brown pipe organ Erique played.

However, there was one thing that really stood out. Several hats from different countries hung around the walls or rested on globes, busts and shelves. One sat on a skull—gonna ignore that last one for now.

He liked hats. The Phantom's hobby was hats.

The faintest smile hit my lips. It was all I could muster up with everything going on.

A brown settee sat not too far from where I stood. I took a seat on the small couch that paralleled the fireplace and pulled my knees up as far as my borrowed shirt would allow me without exposing everything. Not that he would care. We'd just taken a bath together.

The mix between Erique's beautiful playing and warmth from the fireplace soothed me like I needed so desperately.

The notes slowed into something else. I recognized it. *Voi Che Sapete*. The song we'd been trying to get me to sing.

He'd told me once that it was about a young man figuring out what love was and that he was excited about it. A very cheeky, fun song. Pretty sure he meant sex. The thought of Erique trying to talk about sex. It would hurt to laugh if I did. For as sassy and smooth as he seemed sometimes, he was also very reserved in some ways. Shy.

Erique was so good. He'd slowed down the bubbly piece to a soft, almost sad tempo. The way he played the piece now seemed to give it a different meaning.

Entranced anytime he sang, I sat there unmoving, staring at the back of his stiff and yet swaying body. The powerful voice I'd come to know, rumbled softly along with the new version of the melody he played.

Chapter XXIV

*"Voi che sapete Che cosa è amor, Donne vedete S'io l'ho nel cor.
Quello ch'io provo Vi rudirò; è per me nuovo, Capir nol so."*

Something in the anguish of his words filled my eyes against their will. Like I was being forced to see into his hurt.

What was he doing? I didn't want to feel anything more.

"Sento un affetto pien di desir, ch'ora è diletto, ch'ora è martir."

The organ stilled and only his voice remained. Erique rose to his feet, turning slowly to find my eyes.

"Gelo, e poi sento l'alma avvampar, non so cos'è."

His steps slowed and his voice weakened the closer he came.

*"Sospiro e gemo senza voler, palpitl e tremo senza saper.
Che cosa è amor?"*

At arm's length away, he fell to his knees and hung his head low. Palms rested on the floor, as beautiful dark, wavy hair hung freely around repentant eyes as they looked up from beneath the white of a different mask.

If you were to look up "unbearable" in the dictionary, this would it.

The urge to reach out for him, comfort him, and hide him away was so strong as I watched on.

"Je l'ai dans my heart for you."

The last sentence barely fell from his lips. It was different from the ending I'd heard many times before, and it was in French.

No man had ever gone so far as to even say sorry and mean it, and the shit thing was I didn't know whether I was mad, sad, hurt, or not.

Until he jumped into the tub with me, I wasn't sure what his emotions were. His demeanor had been so cool. Or was it? I was kind of lost during that time.

Even before I came to the practice room with the intention of leaving him behind, I didn't know my own feelings on it.

"I... I..." His voice was hardly audible as he tried to speak.

Unable to take it anymore, I extended my hand to the groveling man before me.

Within a moment, the commanding, intimidating presence that the great Paris Opera house had known and feared, crawled desperately to take my offering.

Lips covered it in kisses as tears leaked out from beneath his mask. His face pressed against my hand like I was some sort of deity. "I'm so sorry, my angel. Sweet Melody. So sorry."

Erique crawled closer, sobbing into the folds of the borrowed shirt that barely covered my thighs. Gripping at it tightly, as if the floor was going to fall away beneath him. It was hard to listen to him cry. It tore my heart into pieces to hear it.

I ran my fingers through his hair, trying to calm him? Reassure him? Or soothe myself?

"What are you sorry for?" I asked.

"Like all the monsters you've met in the dark, I hurt you. How you could stand to let this *thing* near you at this moment, baffles me..." The disdain for himself rang in his voice with venom.

It was different to see him without the façade of the Phantom to keep him strong. Begging on his knees, groveling and sobbing was a man, not a mask. Not a character. But a man who desperately wanted to right a wrong.

"The terror in your glittering eyes at the sight of this diseased face. Despicable were these hands when they landed against you and you fell, I..."

"Erique, I tripped on my stupid dress. You didn't touch me."

"No. You saw..." he said pathetically, gesturing to his face. "You fell. With my own eyes I saw you..."

"I think you saw what you wanted to see. I only saw you run away after you freaked me out." His mouth hung open at my words, and realization sparked in his eyes. "You didn't hurt me. You didn't do anything to me. It only hurt when you left."

He buried his face into my lap again, digging his fingertips into my

Chapter XXIV

hips. Any other time I would have loved his head in my lap, touching my skin. But not like this. I never wanted to see him like this. It hurt so much.

"Truly, from my heart I am sorry. I swear by the stars I wanted to come to you. Even when you attempted to play your lullaby, *Moonlight Sonata*, I warred with myself to come to you," he said. "I couldn't bear the rejection of your friendship for what I'd done. Thought I had done. And now what you've seen."

"You were there?"

He nodded vigorously against my stomach.

What hurt worse? Knowing that he'd left me, or didn't?

I sighed. It was a losing battle to think about it.

In this light I could finally see the extent of his birthmark creeping out from beneath the edges of his form fitted mask, especially at his hairline. One side of his head had the brunt force of it as it crept down his neck, and below his shirt. The distorted skin of his right hand suggested it at least reached that far.

Modern dating and history have told me to move on from this. From him. He's unstable. A serial killer, if I were honest. And he'd only be someone I'd have to train. The idea of training another man how to be an adult already drained me.

"If you showed me your face right now," I said, lifting his chin. "This... that has you trapped in your own hell; I wouldn't care. It wouldn't change anything. Just as you said nothing could change how you feel for me."

"I will give you everything, my Melody. Anything you desire. But I do not know that I could ever give you that. Nor would I want to. Not even my own mother could bear it," he said, and gripped the hem of the shirt tighter. It was obvious he was trying to regain some composure. Until finally a neutral face that tried to hide pleading eyes appeared. "If you would permit me to be your teacher once more, your friend, I will never do that again unless you command it. I will never leave you."

I somehow believed him.

I pressed my lips onto the little exposed flesh at the top of his forehead. The Phantom's body melted under the touch and he sighed.

Erique righted high on his knees, hands flying to meet my face. His eyes were misty, yet intent. "I am so truly sorry to have done that to you." He kissed my forehead and wrapped his arms around me. The feeling of safety and care cradled me like I'd never known.

Erique was my angel. My demon. My friend. And now branded on my heart.

Shit.

"There are things I need to share with you, *my heart*," he said.

Chapter XXV

Hungry lions circle me as she waits for my truth. Why do I wish the beasts would take me now?

"It wasn't as bad when I was a child. Even the beatings my father *gifted* me before he left never changed it."

Bewitched I was when she befriended me before she knew I was the reason for her survival. That was the reason I never gave mention of our first encounter.

It was astonishing how many firsts there had been with this stranger. A story only told once before, vaguely, was about to come to light in its unedited wholeness, just for her.

Hate would burn in me with her pity. Her love for me, for who she's made me, is all I wanted. Not for who I was made into before her.

"It was contained to my face after birth. Catholic guilt and stigma led my mother to keep me. From what I can recollect, maybe tried to love me. I wore a makeshift mask cut from my father's old jacket. But it may have only made things worse. The constant ridicule from children and adults paired with the inability to find a new husband, weighed on her. It was hard to care for a child and herself when she wasn't able to work much more. And despite having tried, I was too young or hideous to aid in that."

Fire danced in brown eyes, filled with worried anticipation. To stop had crossed my mind, though this had been her wish for some time.

"The circus had come to town. I remember the excitement when my mother mentioned taking me for the first time. She dressed us up in our best. I can't see her face anymore, but I remember thinking how beautiful she looked, and yet so sad. I was in awe when we arrived. Never had I thought such a place could exist. Lights. Food. Animals like I had never seen. I would like to think I saw it as you do."

It was hard to focus on the unwanted memories, when the soft glow kissed this angel's skin the way I would prefer to do right now. Kiss away the tears she blinked back as I spoke, in dread for what was to come.

"When the show ended, she was quiet as she took me outside. A man met us there, Radu Laurentiu, the Ringmaster. The Flea. The Gollum. Unfeeling was my mother's face when she handed me off to him, taking the coin purse he offered." I choked on the memory. Not only to be unwanted, but sold. What hurt. "She did say goodbye. And called me by a name that fails me. I couldn't have been more than ten years of age."

I did know the name. But it belonged to a boy no one wanted. Someone that died the day the world proved no love for him.

"For the next several years, I traveled with the show as I told you. Found out quickly that I had a gift for music. Who knew the little rotting corpse could play in such likenesses as Mozart. Wagner." I set my finger under her tortured face, running my thumb across her chin and winked. "And Beethoven."

I fight unseen restraints to kiss away the sad smile which now graced her sweet face. Would time be so kind once more that we would have that chance again?

Perhaps that time had gone.

I dropped my hand and stared at the crackling, dancing flames.

"No matter how well I did, the heavy hands never stopped. But I preferred the unprovoked whippings over what it became. Something no one should ever endure. Until one day when the Flea came to visit my cell after everyone had drowned themselves in the bottle. Much to my surprise, a bit of rope I'd taken from the tack tent before the matinee earlier that day, and some pressure was all it took. I thought the guilt

Chapter XXV

would eat me. It never came. I bathed in the hate as it imbedded within me, and I enjoyed it."

The lift at the corner of my lips surprised me at the retelling. Not in joy of the memory, but remembrance of pride.

"Things were a bit better after that. With my face and talents it wasn't hard to find another show. I was still roughed around for a while, but nothing like before. And I had even made a few friends. There was a time I was proud of this face," I said, holding my chin up, falling into the memory of it. "The crowd would recoil as I came out and sat at my piano. I delighted in the terror and disgust it brought the patrons that frequented our shows. I hated them. I hated their perfect faces. Normal lives. I pitied them all the same. In my mind it was a small bit of revenge to be proud of it. For years it was like that."

The glow of the fire had begun to dim. More or less procrastinating, I added another log. Pity would follow soon enough and the moment, over.

"In 1857 we came to Paris. It was like any other place. Except, during a performance one night, a lovely young heiress, Josephine Dubois, spoke to *me*. Told me how amazing I was and that she would like to hear me play again. Privately. The following night, I did just that. Trying to wow her with everything in my arsenal. After her private show, she had invited me to join her at her home later that night. Being a silly child and never having…"

I halted, averting my eyes. It was not shame that turned me. Perhaps embarrassment of which I had forgotten. Pleasures of the flesh had remained a suppressed memory since my youth. That was, until this angel graced my world.

"I was over the moon. Not only was she beautiful, but she wanted to spend an evening with *me*. No woman had ever spoken to me before then, not like that. A mentor of mine, The Amazing Raphael, lent me his best suit once I told him. He warned me to be careful, but the headstrong fool I was, paid him no mind and ran off. I stood at the back of the door to this giant building wearing a borrowed suit that was a tad big and holding stolen flowers I had snatched from a garden. Not for a moment did I think it odd she lived in a hotel. I lived in a wagon. She had snuck me around through the kitchen and into a large suite off the main floor. I should have worried then, particularly when she wouldn't let me touch her after she'd ripped her hand away. But adolescence."

"And hormones," my sweet Melody jested with a hint of sadness.

"Yes," I answered. "She teased me. It was sweet. Dared me to get undressed first, since it was her first time as well, and she was scared. Eager, like any young man, I did as told." I paused, trying to gather my thoughts. Would this be too much for her to hear?

As if reading my mind, she placed her gentle hand on my arm. "You don't have to keep going," her sweet lips whispered. "I know this isn't going anywhere good."

"You shared your secret with me, my Heart. I will hide nothing from you. You wanted to know me. I want you to know me."

She nodded, but there was a sense of guilt in her eyes. There was something else she hadn't told me and that was alright. She would, in time. This was enough for now.

"My trousers had just hit my ankles when I heard the faintest snickering from outside the door behind me. Josephine told me to pay it no mind and continue, that she was very excited, even taking off her indoor coat.

"The last thing I remember was a crowd of young faces, including Josephine's, staring down and laughing as flames seared the flesh from my body. As if what they had done was a game."

At the moment of realization, glistening irises stared horrified. Despite having been next to the fire for some time, her lovely face was flushed of its color. Her head swung away as she tried to stifle the sobbing that threatened to come forth.

I moved closer to her, taking her hand in mine. "Shh. Dear. It is alright," I cooed. Tears blinded her eyes as she found mine. A small bit of glee filled me as I wiped an escaped bit of sadness away.

"I woke up several days later in a bed at *le Hôtel des Anges*. Antoinette tended my wounds. It was her hotel the girl was staying at for a time. That large rug when you walk into the main foyer hides the past."

She fiddled with our hands and laid her head on my shoulder.

"The show had left without me once they got word. I was with Antoinette and Louis for several months. They told me what had happened. That nothing could be done because of who the girl's father

Chapter XXV

was," I said, then cleared my throat. "I should warn you, the rest of this is more unpleasant than what you have heard."

"I will hear whatever it is you want me to know," she said.

"When I was able to move without what was left of my flesh attempting to peel itself from my bones, I snuck out one night. I had found Josephine alone in the giant tenement her father owned in the city.

"Gratification was the fear in her eyes when she realized it was me that played with her mind the entire evening. Her fear awakened something within me that I had not let sleep since.

"She pleaded for her life. Apologized. Begged. Offered money. Offered herself. Even offered up her friends.

"I was too ravaged by the red. Hands that played beautiful melodies, wrapped around her neck and squeezed until she changed color. A few times. And then she was gone. That was the only time I had ever used my hands.

"Revenge was the sweetest thing I'd ever tasted.

"Then I cried.

"When Antoinette heard of Josephine's death, I had already slipped into the night. I knew what it would do to her. I couldn't bear it nor did I care at the time.

"Amongst all of this, the *Ghost* was born. Within my mind he lives, guiding me. I have never been caught off guard again."

'You lie,' the *Ghost* growled. *'Evidence sits in your arms now.'*

I ignored the voice that spit the truth, though this time I did it with a light heart. "Eventually, I found a new traveling show and the rest you know. The King of Persia eventually brought me on as a means of entertainment. I built his palace. Became his prized assassin."

"I'm sorry, what?" she asked.

"Yes. Another talent of mine." I smiled smugly. "I came back to Paris in 1861 to help Charles Garnier build this palace. Then again, a few years later to call it home after the King put out a death command on all who aided in erecting his Palace. I ran from him with Ardashir's help."

The crackling from the fireplace was the only sound for several moments.

"Did you find the rest of them?" she asked.

"That I know of."

"And Antoinette knows this? That you killed the people who did this to you?"

I nodded. "Until the night you arrived, I hadn't seen her since my departure. For her kindness, I had sent money over the years to help in some way. I had done some terrible things in her care and for that I deserved her silence.

"When asked to take you in, stories of the Ghost had reached her. Though she was scared, surprised even, she would never turn down the opportunity to help someone in need."

Tired eyes avoided my stare for a time. Looking everywhere but at the monster that sat with her.

Everything aside, it was nice to sit with her. Even in silence.

The few times Ardashir had come, it wasn't like this. Nothing could compare to the feeling this moment held.

"So, you really didn't kill that girl in the *salon* room?" she asked.

"I may not be a good man, Melody, but no one murders within my walls and escapes consequence. I had written Ardashir the day after you arrived. My dear Daroga is the best at what he does. Even now, as I know, he is still trying to solve it. I hope you are given the chance to meet him one day."

With gentle fingers, she grazed my jaw.

Desperate to focus on the touch, my lids grew heavy, and I leaned into it. She trailed down my neck, to the collar of the shirt, pushing it to the side.

Unstable was my breathing at such an action, though frozen was my body. The faintest of tingles trailed behind her fingertips as she traveled along the reminder of the world's cruelty.

Sadness oozed from her. I never wanted this. Her soul should only ever know happiness.

Yet I did nothing to stop her.

"Does it still hurt?" she asked.

My hand found hers and locked it in place against my chest. "Not for many years."

She crawled closer, tucking herself beneath my arm, wrapping her free one around me.

Chapter XXV

Glad to be rid of that dead rodent she wore, my hand went immediately to her hair, snaking through to cradle her head. I pressed my cheek against her and sighed.

'It could always be like this,' the *Ghost* said.

She would leave in the morning.

'She does not have to.'

Chapter XXVI

Melody

Somehow the dark, cold passageways felt warmer as Erique led me back to the opera. He was safe and comfortable now that there was this new kind of trust between us.

I wanted to call my mom. Tell her I slept with a man who didn't try to have sex with me even though I was only wearing his shirt in his bed, holding him all night after a very horrific, vulnerable exchange. Tell her that Erique was stronger than me. That it took everything in me not to lead him into sex as his breath was between my breasts all night while I held him. Or that his leg between mine almost did me in.

I'm pretty sure I would have had sex with him too. I'm glad we didn't. There was too much going on. But still. *Oh my God.*

She wouldn't believe any of it. A vulnerable man? A man that didn't try to have sex with you? Who took care of you?

Unicorn.

Oh, the bar was low.

We approached the vanity mirror to dressing room seven. The room was dark when I peeked through, making sure the coast was clear. Also, I'd never seen a two-way mirror before.

Chapter XXVI

"Do you watch everyone?" I asked.

Erique shifted uncomfortably, like a child who just got caught. "It's an unfortunate side effect to my condition."

He set the lantern down and unlatched the door before retaking my hand.

The glow from the lantern faded as we went farther into the room. Erique stopped us just shy of the door. "You will be alright. I will see you for your lesson tonight," he said, but didn't release my hand.

Even though I nodded, I wanted to say I didn't want to go back today. That staying with him, lounging about sounded like a dream.

The wounds were still a little raw though and neither of us knew where we were going next.

I'd hoped he wouldn't kiss me. I don't know if we were ready for that. Or that it was something that should happen again.

My blood warmed thinking about a kiss, but the pit in my stomach grew when my hand found the door handle and opened it enough, just to close it.

I threw my arms around Erique's neck, squeezing tightly. His hands locked into my spine and held me like he hadn't seen me in years.

"Mmm. My Melody," he hummed.

I forced myself to pull away. If I didn't, I would have made him take me back. "Here goes nothing," I said.

Reluctantly I grabbed the door handle once again and I opened it.

"Where have you been?" Christine yelled, rushing up to me. Erique's grip on my hand tightened as he hid behind the door, taking half of me with him. "I've been looking for you. Where's your hair?"

My heart raced. "Uh. I lost my wig. This is my hair."

In all the clouded thoughts surrounding everything, I'd forgotten to grab the damn thing somewhere in Erique's home.

"I like it. It's different."

"Thanks. Um. I'm just finishing up. Are you alright?" I asked.

"I wanted to see how you're doing after last night."

My blood froze. Did the girl I helped tell?

It was hard to focus between my heart's erratic behavior and Erique moving my hand to his chest, forcing me to feel his heart beating beneath it.

"What do you mean?"

"Joseph Buquet, the smelly stagehand is dead. They found him hanging above the stage last night."

His soft kiss pressed against the back of my hand, then my wrist. I thought I was going to drop.

Everything was so confusing, and my heart rate was so high.

"What?" I nearly squeaked.

"Everyone thinks the Opera Ghost did it. I was surprised not to see you this morning."

"I was staying with a friend. I just got back."

She gasped and a wicked little smile spread across her face. "Were you with your Erique?"

"Um. We should go," I said, swatting my hand away from the pesky demon behind the door.

***

After a few days, no one seemed to care about Joseph's death. The managers tried to convince everyone that it was an accident because it looked like he was drunk and merely tripped into the rope.

No one even mentioned the stab wound in his leg. It was finally time to breathe.

Well, almost.

The managers had me working the private box, despite my reluctance. I agreed to one more. Which meant the nice dress again and an evening without a certain someone in the lesson room.

I don't know why they're so hell bent on this fucking box. They couldn't just go to another one? This is the second weekend in a row they had commandeered it against the "Ghost's" wishes. I'd love it if Erique fucked with them, just a little.

We still hadn't talked about us. Nor had there been any more kisses. It didn't stop me from thinking about him constantly nor my stupid desire for him either.

Lessons had been going on like nothing had happened. Except now, I got to see my teacher while he teaches. Which was hard, because I could never take my eyes off him. Also, kind of scary when I can't quite get something right. The stare he gives could stop a charging bull.

We'd finished *Alice's Adventures in Wonderland*. I'm very glad our

Chapter XXVI

reading had resumed. I think that might be my favorite time together. When we sit close and recite words from our current read.

As I readied for the night, I smiled thinking about the next few chapters we'll share together. Maybe talk him into taking me to his home again and reading by the fireplace together.

Maybe not. That could be dangerous.

M. Fournier hurried over to me. "Miss Reilly, what happened to your hair?" I'd forgotten it was M. LeBlanc who had asked me to work.

His eyes cut to the door where Philippe and Raoul followed in behind, surprisingly unaccompanied.

"You don't like it?" I asked, facetiously.

He huffed and returned his attention to the guests. I hated the sound of kiss ass. M. Fournier's forced laughter was enough to make me want to vomit.

I didn't understand. They were already patrons and it's not like the managers lost money if they left. What was the need to continuously nose into their asshole?

The group migrated to their seats. Well, most of them. Philippe seemed to hesitate, staying behind.

"Can I get you something before the curtain pulls?" I asked.

"Actually. Would you care to join me for the performance?" Philippe asked. "Since my letters keep getting lost in the post."

"Oh. Thank you. I'm working. You understand, I'm sure."

"Nonsense! Miss Reilly, you may have a seat with us and enjoy the performance," M. Fournier screeched.

I bit my tongue. I'm not even sure why. "I would be delighted, Monsieur. Thank you."

If I were any other girl, I'd be happy just to be here.

My sister would eat this up. Man, it'd be nice to talk to someone about everything.

The lights dimmed and the curtain lifted. Once the performance started, I'd forgotten all about the men I was with and this uneasy feeling, and just focused on Christine.

Unfortunately, it would be her last weekend. Rumor was Carlotta was coming back with security this week. That woman was a masochist for real.

Erique was gonna have a heyday, and I couldn't wait.

"Miss Reilly, would you mind so terribly grabbing a round of drinks?" M. Fournier asked.

"Nonsense," Philippe said coldly.

"No, really. It's fine. I'll be back quickly," I said. Any excuse to get away.

Philippe gritted his teeth and nodded.

I was back with the drinks quickly as I said, only instead of retaking my seat by Philippe, I took my place in the dark near the column.

I could see it bothered him. I didn't care. I felt much better away from him. And a part of me hoped Erique was nearby.

It'd been a whole new world being able to see him while actually getting to do stuff together.

And as if he were reading my thoughts, like always. "Does it still move you?" his soft, demanding voice whispered into my hair.

It was like a drug, something I needed, wanted, had to have more of. My breath hitched and my eyes darted to the guests, hoping Philippe would stop looking in my direction.

"I could see this a hundred times and it would still move me," I said.

His breath warmed my ear. "Do you really want to sing?" Then his hand slid around my hip, pulling me further into the dark against him. Shivers rippled through my limbs as another hand caressed my arm.

I relaxed, sinking into his warm embrace. Lolling my head against him.

"Do you want to sing like that?" His breath trickled from my ear to my neck. My knees weakened. The only thing keeping me up at this point was luck.

His scent engulfed me, and his touch ensnared me. I thought I'd burst into flames as his hand trailed down my arm to find my fingers eagerly waiting to intertwine.

He pressed his lips to my ear. "You will continue to blossom. One day you will shine."

"I can't."

"You will." Unique eyes beneath the silhouette of the Phantom's false face stared back at me as I found them, always soft. Always adoring. Even when he was upset that I may have missed a note or two.

Chapter XXVI

Parted lips rested close to mine. "You will sing for me." His words fell into my mouth, as if they were my own.

It was brutal. Being this close. Erique's face was millimeters away, I could kiss him. What was he doing?

The man in the darkness pulled away slowly. Hoping to prolong our proximity, I squeezed his hand as the applause roared ending the first act.

He gave one final squeeze and slipped away. The ghost was gone, but left behind in my palm was a folded piece of paper.

My heart fluttered as I unfolded it. He'd never written to me before.

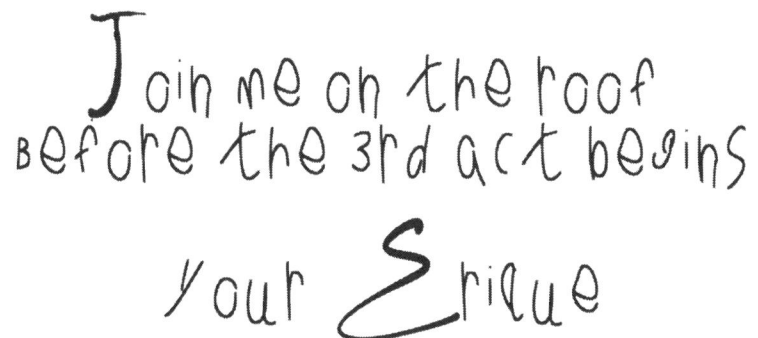

> Join me on the roof
> before the 3rd act begins
> your Erique

His handwriting really was atrocious, and I loved it.

"Melody?" Philippe's voice pulled me from the note.

I hadn't noticed the booth emptied and we were the only two left.

"Yes? What can I do for you?"

His eyes flicked to the note in my hand, then overlooked the evacuating theater. "Would you join me for dinner? After the show?" he asked.

Jesus, can't you take a hint?

Madame Giry, the head keeper and one who usually tended to Erique in his box or arranged things delivered to his home, had stepped into the room and stood in wait.

She glanced down at the note in my hand and gave me a knowing look.

"I'm sorry, Philippe. As nice as that sounds. I am otherwise engaged. Actually, I need to leave now."

"Wait," he said, grabbing my arm. "My apologies, Madame." He let go, drawing his hand back. "You really have no desire to accompany me?"

It was like the air was sucked from the room. How did he not understand that I wasn't interested?

"I don't think we're a compatible pair," I said. "And I'm not really interested." *Oh my God, I finally said it!*

"I see."

"I can just tell we are two very different people, Philippe."

"How do you know? We have spent very little time together." There was an edge to his comment. He was right, but I didn't owe him anything.

"There is another," he said, looking at the note in my hand again.

I shoved it into my pocket. "I need to go," I said, and spun around, leaving his dumbfounded face standing there.

The audacity.

My nerves pulled jump rope while I walked the hallway. Why was I so nervous? I'm just meeting with a friend.

A friend that I wanna do things with, and care about… *Ugh. Chill out.*

The access door to the roof was not far past my room, as long as it was the one I was thinking of.

The door creaked open slowly and the cool spring air flowed in as I stepped out into an overwhelming glow of candles and moonlight.

My jaw dropped. Tall brass candelabras stood about holding long white candles that danced in the surrounding darkness.

The only thing more beautiful than the layout of candles, was the dark figure that stood at the center of them.

Move over Gerard Butler, there's no more room for you in my mind anymore.

A slow smile spread across my face when our eyes met. "Erique, what is this?"

He stared with a longing then stalked towards me. My eyes raked over his frame as he grew closer. I hated him. I was a deer caught in the headlights, waiting for the impending collision.

Firm hands slid along my arms and took mine in his. He put one over his shoulder and kept the other. I was almost disappointed that he didn't kiss me.

We moved along with the sounds that crept in around us. "How are we hearing music?" I asked.

He moved us close to a vent that had been propped open. There

Chapter XXVI

were several around the roof. It was like our own surround sound.

My heart couldn't take it. It was surreal. How was I going to fight against wanting this?

"Why...?" I asked.

"I wanted to dance with you."

I felt so stupid for the immediate tearing in my eyes. It was so beautiful, but still, I couldn't believe this was just because. Have I fallen so far in my life that candles and music would bring me to my knees?

"How are you such a good dancer?" I asked.

"Not every moment of my life was agony, dear."

We danced all the way through Lorenzo's song and the one that came afterwards. I didn't even know I could dance anymore, that's how long it'd been, and I sure as heck didn't want to stop.

"You told me that you were a writer. That you tried and failed." His voice vibrated against my cheek as it crept into my ear.

"Mmhmm," I answered through intoxication forgetting everything else. He pushed me into a twirl, catching me on the recoil, I didn't know I was capable of.

I was indulging so hard.

"With the passion you have, there is no part of me that believes you were less than adequate," he said.

"Shhh. Don't ruin this moment," I whispered. "I don't want to talk about it."

"We will talk about it," he said. "You are going to write with me."

"What?"

I stepped away, breaking our connection. Erique closed in on me quickly. As if I had no choice in the matter.

"I have many operas in need of physical words, Melody. Ink to parchment. I have the words, but..." he said. "As you saw, I was not taught to write, and conveying such things needs a practiced hand."

"You want me to transcribe for you?"

"More than that. I want collaboration. Partnership. I want you to tell me what my stories need. I want to tell your stories. You've told me of them and I hear nothing but promise. Just like in your voice, dear."

"I don't know. That can get complicated. I'm not the easiest person to work with. And remember, I can't speak any other languages."

"You are quite stubborn, that is true," he said, smirking. "However, you're a storyteller, like me."

"That doesn't change that I can't speak the language."

"We will write in English."

"They would never be played," I said.

"Let that worry be mine."

Stars sparkled all around. How could it be such a perfect, clear night? Even the smell was dull. I chewed my lip as we continued moving around the rooftop, thinking about his offer.

A mischievous look grew in his eyes. "Enough of that…" he said.

As much as I wanted to tempt him, AND turn away from this topic, I responded, "You can't think just because I'm passionate means I'm good."

"I've seen your writing."

"Erique… You swore…"

"Shhh… *My Heart.*"

It was nearly impossible not to believe him. He always sounded so sincere and confident. Hopeful. For someone so tormented, his outlook on this was confusing at best.

A chance to write again. A connection with another. Everything I've been missing and wanted was right here offering himself to me.

Exactly what I was afraid of.

I loved that he showed this side of himself though. And I hated it at the same time.

My eyes cut away from his gaze. I slowed us to a halt again. "What if something happens?" *Like I go home. Or you don't want me anymore.*

"There is nothing in this life that could stop this if you accept," he said. His eyes glimmered with tenderness and passion, as the light danced in them. "And if there is something, we will meet it together."

Why did I think he was talking about something other than operas?

He moved us into a dance again while I searched my mind. It was always my dream to write. But two dozen failed screenplays slapped me like phantom pains.

Come on, musicals and operas? What did I know about writing that?

"I would be lying if I said the thought of writing with you didn't excite me." My insides shivered, warning me against the unknown.

Chapter XXVI

"Remember, I may not even be here tomorrow."

He nodded slowly.

I bit my lip going over one last thought. "Ok. We can see how…"

His mouth covered mine with a great hunger. I returned his kiss with reckless abandon.

A part of me thought we'd have to start over after what happened and how we'd been since. I even tried to convince myself what happened in the booth earlier was just, I don't know. I'm just out here lying to myself all the time.

Reluctantly, we pulled apart. Chests heaving with surprise and something more. My body screamed at the disconnect as we stood there.

"I needed to make sure you were real," he said.

"Beautiful Erique," I whispered, gliding my fingers over his lips.

His lids closed as if the words branded him, and a boyish grin spread across his mouth. He moved us faster around the rooftop. We were almost floating at one point. Laughing, and gazing in adoration as he spoke excitedly of the stories we'd start on.

"Aren't you tired yet?" I asked. "I'm starting to see stars that aren't there!"

He laughed a true, light laugh. "I could do this for a hundred years, my angel."

We'd covered every bit of space within the confines of the candelabra. Even nearing the edge of the rooftop by one of the golden angels. Dancing behind me, kissing my neck like the devil I wanted him to be.

There was a dreamy ecstasy to our kiss now. He was a quick study. Swiftly, he flipped me around and pressed me against the base of the statue, reclaiming my mouth.

We fought the buttons to his jacket, tossing it aside as soon as it was undone.

The pleasure and the teasing was all so delectable. I matched his energy with my own lust filled need. Squeezing him and entwining my fingers in his hair, I parted my legs and forced him tighter against me.

My tongue flicked his, and like a switch had been flipped, Erique dug his fingers into my hips. It almost hurt how harshly he held us together. I groaned into his mouth at the devilish new pressure against my stomach.

This was about to happen with someone I really cared about.

Abruptly he stopped and stepped back, taking my breath with him. "Forgive me," he said. Astonishment and confusion plagued his widened eyes.

"What's wrong?" I asked, panting like I'd just run a mile. I tried not to gawk at the erection I'd felt against my stomach, which I desperately wanted rocking into me.

His eyes cut around frantically, like he was trying to figure something out. "I haven't... I'm not..." he stammered, as he paced. "I should take you back. It's late."

No. No. This couldn't be happening again. I was dumb to think it'd be different this time.

"I don't care," I practically yelled.

His gaze cut back to me with a hunger that I knew all too well.

He prowled towards me. Expression dark and primal. Fiery filled lips caught mine before I knew it. Everything gave out immediately. My instinctive response to him was so powerful. I pulled him onto me as I laid back.

Every brush of his tongue against mine had broken another dam below. His movements were better with every passing moment.

"What do you want, my angel? I'll give it to you. Anything.... Everything," he said breathlessly, nipping at the spot below my earlobe.

I tugged at my skirt, desperate to feel him on my skin. "I just want you to touch me, Erique," I whimpered.

"Where?"

"Everywhere."

Like a man in the desert being offered water, Erique left my swollen lips. Kissing, licking, and nipping down my neck to my covered breasts that begged to be taken into his mouth. To have a tongue roll around them.

This stupid dress had no freedom to do so, and it was torture.

He rocked onto his knees. It was like he was afraid to touch me. "Do not let me hurt you," he demanded.

Awe and wonder burned in his eyes as trembling hands pressed against the outer part of my exposed thighs. The pressure from his fingers seared my tingling flesh as he moved up slowly.

"Is this ok? It is not too late..." His voice was shaky, like he wanted

Chapter XXVI

me to want to stop him.

I wanted this badly, but it sure didn't mean I wasn't anxious either.

Eager hands moved around my hips and hooked over the brim of my underwear.

"You're fucking killing me, Erique. Do it."

A smirk formed on his lips. He was toying with me.

"You *are* the devil," I said.

With haste, he yanked them down as far as he could. I wiggled to aid in getting them off.

He found my thighs again and ran his fingers along my tender skin. It tickled in a deliciously agonizing way.

"Interesting composition," he said, circling the tattoo on my leg.

"Uh huh," I panted. Any other time I would have loved the irony in his attention to it. The Phantom finding interest in the *Phantom* score.

"From your favorite show?"

I nodded quickly, trying to move it along. My hand found the underside of his chin and brought his attention back up. One heated kiss later he was traveling up my thighs again.

The breath left my lungs and my heart stopped as he neared the more sensitive area of my body.

His finger lightly traced the soaking wet fuzzy crevasse at the center of flesh that hid the joy we both desperately craved. Each slow pass of his fingers was like a thousand little tickles flowing into my core. The need to have him grew painful.

I gasped as he slid a finger in between and ran across the little button that made me twitch.

"Yes. There!" I took his hand and moved him to the spot again.

My eyes rolled against their will, as I moaned when he moved with me.

"Is this alright?" he asked. The need in his voice only heightened my own.

My body jolted against him; I didn't even know which way was up at this point. He leaned down, hovering over my body. I couldn't wait to have the full weight of him on me.

Intent lips met my neck, kissing and grazing his teeth against it.

If it were possible, I would burst into stars and no one would question it if they knew why.

"Answer me, Melody. Or I'll stop," he commanded.

With watery eyes, I nodded feverishly. "Yes. Yes."

"That is my good, sweet, angel," he said.

No matter what kind of imagination I had, nothing could have prepared me for this. For him.

His own arousal pressed against my leg. "Let me touch you," I whined, trying to unbutton him. Free him. Hold his cock in my hand. I wanted the man in the darkness. To complete our connection.

And I was horny as hell.

Erique smirked as his fingers migrated. Greedily, I scooted, trying to find them again.

In a slow and forceful motion, Erique entered me with a finger. The coldness of his gold ring pressed against my thigh as he held my sex.

A very audible groan escaped both of us. Erique fell into my chest as my back arched.

My eyes felt like they were going to pop from my head at the overwhelming pressure from just a finger. Cheeks burned like the summer sun, and I sighed in relief.

His name fell from my quivering lips as he moved slowly in and out. I gasped again when he added a second.

The skilled composer's palm rubbed against my happy little button as he rocked against me.

Here I was without a second thought, my legs spread apart, skirt pushed above my knees, beneath a starry sky. Surrounded by candlelight, on the roof of a building in 1880 Paris. While the man that filled my most vivid dreams, pleasured me with just his fingers and I was lost to him for it.

The pressure that had been building within was reaching its peak. "Please… don't stop. I'm there. I'm…" I cried out.

Determined eyes locked on mine as he maintained his tempo.

"We will write beautiful music together," he demanded.

I couldn't answer. I was there.

"Melody…" he strained.

"Yes! We will!"

"Sing."

Chapter XXVI

My eyes closed and tears of bliss leaked while my body jolted and bucked against him as I sang out his name.

He didn't waver in his duty no matter how much I knew he achingly throbbed until I stopped him.

Through aftershocks and hazy sight, I found beautiful, overjoyed eyes staring. Tears rested in the corners of them.

We fell into a kiss so deep our souls sparked. He pulled his fingers from my body and wrapped his arm around me, pulling me tighter into our scorching kiss.

"Please," he begged through panting breath.

"Please."

He pushed back onto his knees again between my open, waiting thighs as he slipped off his suspenders. Our hands flew to the clasp of his trousers undoing them as quickly as humanly possible.

Erique stilled and lifted my face to meet his penetrating stare. "No sonnet, nor poem, nor composition can compare to the beauty that you are. Close as they may come, nothing could ever reach such a plane," he said. "I love you, Melody."

Chapter XXVII

Melody

Fuck.

Chapter XXVIII

Melody

Nothing like the shattering of reality to ruin a moment. My hands flew to his mouth. "No. No. No. Please don't," I whispered, staring into the most confused, panic-stricken emerald green and stone-gray eyes. "Shit."

A thousand miles an hour my heart beat. If I didn't get somewhere safe fast, I was going to pass out.

I slid out from beneath him quickly, trying to scurry away like the scared little mouse I really was.

Erique stayed frozen in place, staring at the spot I had just laid in wait for him. "I do not understand," he said.

The hurt in his voice was a vice grip on my heart. Something I pretended to ignore as I forced myself across the rooftop to my escape.

Before I could get close enough, Erique grabbed my bicep and swung around me, grabbing the other. "Why?" he asked, searching my face trying to find an answer.

I took his face in my hands. "You did nothing wrong." My lips pressed to his. The weight of him leaning into it broke me. "It's me. And this fucked up situation I'm in."

I stepped out from his grip and continued my course. "And those

Chapter XXVIII

words… Those words only make people suffer." *Look at us now. Look what will happen when I leave.*

Love. What a wonderful fantasy.

The many times I was told how "loved" I was after an ex got caught cheating. After they were called out for how badly they treated me. All the lies. Nothing but "love".

My mother was told over and over how loved she was when she was held down or thrown through a door as we had no choice but to watch.

When has love done anyone any good? Even if you think you feel it.

Even when you believe *him* when he says it.

"But you want me?" he asked. His voice deep and dusty, as if he could choke on his next words.

In so many ways.

I stopped as my shoulders slumped and spun around. "Yes. Of course I do," I said. Erique hurried the next few steps to me, capturing my elbows in his hands as I gripped on to his forearms, trying to stand on courage. "Please, try to understand. All this takes time. And I don't know if I have that. And…" *There are things I can never admit, like how I feel for you.*

"What does that mean? You always speak of time. That you would be gone from me one day. That it should stop me from giving this wretched heart to you," he said. A flicker of candlelight reflected in his emotional eyes, highlighting the watery glistening across them. "I have loved you, Melody, for so long now."

The words continued to burn. Ache. It's what I've wanted—but I don't. It'll mean nothing in a few months. Weeks maybe. And what will be left of me after, will be a pile of broken sadness again.

"You can't understand. And that's the point. And I should have known better. But you were just so…" *Good.* "What about Christine? I…"

Lips pressed against my wrist, easing my mind. *What a trick.*

"What I thought I felt for her once upon a time was not love. Nor anything that compares to what my being screams for you. I have dreamt of you, Melody. You are here, with me. We will write stories for my music and whatever else you desire. I have told you, I would give you everything. Inexperienced as I am with matters of the heart and body, I knew, though I denied it, the first time I held you that you would be my undoing."

I let go and turned my back on him. To let him go. To hide the tears from falling. Hide any other stupid truths or lies.

The music that still played through the vents changed as they were just getting to the third act. The Priest's Confession.

Ironic.

Flames danced on top of melting candles. The beautiful glow made my lip quiver and my eyes water more. The sight of the city around us. The golden angels. Bronze pegasi. And at the center of it all—him.

Reality was harsh.

I would be fine. Like always. In time.

Time.

"I forgot where I was," I said, my voice cracking through the pain. "I don't know what I was thinking. I can't write with you. I can't sing as you want me to. I can never give you what you need. What you deserve. Because I'm…" *Broken.*

Flames still flickered in melancholy eyes. Light glinted off his ring as his hands fidgeted at his sides.

"You're so beautiful, Erique." My arms crossed my midsection. "It's not fair."

I stared at the paneling of the roof and followed it the rest of the way. Every step was agony, but this was for sure the right thing to do. I had played in fantasy land for too long now.

Then why did it hurt like this?

The knob was cold in my shaking hand. I wanted to look back at him again. Just to cement the image of him surrounded by the glow of light. But I know me, if I looked at him again, I wouldn't be able to go through with it.

We were having the perfect night and I fucked it all up again.

A firm arm wrapped around me before I could twist the knob.

"Don't." His voice was soft.

"I have to. I can't want this."

"Don't," he said again, managing no more than a hoarse, desperate whisper as he crossed another arm around me, latching onto my shoulder.

My human safety belt.

Chapter XXVIII

"I can't..." I said.

"Do you want me to let you go?"

"I should."

"Why?"

Was this the time for the truth? All the truth? I was going to be sick, it hurt so much. "It terrifies me," I said. "And there's a lot you don't know."

"I want to."

"I can't tell you."

My heart beat mercilessly against my ribs harder than when we were in the throes of passion. I wanted to be in those moments again. Not here.

Suddenly the savage beating eased slightly as his hands found mine. With a gentle tug, he turned me to meet him. "Though you do not love me, do you still wish to have me?" he asked.

"Don't say it like that."

There was something inviting in the calm warmth of his eyes as he awaited an answer.

"There are so many unknowns, Erique," I said.

"Seas part and flowers bloom when you say my name." He kissed my hands. Then my forehead. It was like submerging into a hot spring after a long day.

"I can't promise anything," I answered.

"I'm a patient man."

My brows raised in surprise.

"When it matters," he added.

"But what if you aren't? What if I can't...?"

He tilted my head upward. "Shhh," he said and kissed my lips. "Time is fleeting and all we can do is watch, love."

My hands found his face. Then slid into his dark hair. He squeezed me tightly. Why did he feel like home every time we touched?

No. He's not. This place isn't. I can't forget again.

Erique lifted me and twirled us around.

"Stop. You're going to hurt yourself," I cried out.

"You're a feather," he said as my feet touched down again.

My hands trailed from his face, down his chest to his stomach, stopping at the rim of his trousers. Since his suspenders were still off, we could just pick up where I stopped us.

His hands caught mine. "Not until you love me."

"But… That's not fair to you. Or me," I whined.

"It is not my favorite idea. But I will not lay with you until you are fully mine."

I nodded rapidly. "Yeah. I totally respect that," I said. "What exactly does that entail?"

"Simply that. Until you love me, *my Heart*," he said. Then his eyes darkened as he pushed me back against the door and pressed himself to me. I loved when he pressed himself against me. "And until then…" His hand traveled up beneath the skirt of my dress, finding the soft, wanting area between my thighs. "…I want to make you do *that* around my fingers again."

Chapter XXIX

Melody

Beautiful is the night sky, but an underground forest? How cool is that? We'd fallen into a rhythm. Nearly a month of endless conversations walking through Erique's juvenile sycamores. Reading by the fireplace, which usually didn't last long before one of us attacked the other. Harmless little stunts, like releasing feathers from the highest catwalk during Carlotta's rehearsals. Stolen kisses in dark spaces where eyes couldn't see. Borrowing Cesar and Nora from the stables for a moonlight ride.

You know, normal couple stuff.

Not a couple. Just two people who cared for each other and did things together and were a bit obsessed with the other. Who also got frisky every now and then.

I would say it was all too good to be true, which it probably was, however, it turns out we were hard to work with.

When it came to music, which was a lot of our free time, we disagreed a bit.

Minor suggestions from either of us usually escalated quickly for some reason. Eventually after a few minutes apart, we'd give it actual thought and then come together again. It was complicated, but still functional and getting better.

"Contract and breathe," he commanded. "Do it again. I must hear it, Melody."

We'd been working on one of his operas *Ailes en Métal* – Metal Wings. A demon hell bent on avenging the death of his best friend finds out that the woman he'd fallen in love with on his journey was the one that killed the friend, leaving him with a choice to make.

A really great story.

The problem was, I couldn't sing it.

"Take this to Christine. She can do it. I told you Erique, I'm not even close to ready and I am not going to be able to get to these notes," I barked. I scowled, trying to cut him with my stare.

He returned the cold glare. "Do it again."

I just wanted this over tonight, there was something I couldn't wait to talk about.

Maybe that was part of the problem.

I took a breath and tried again. The sound was coming out, but it wasn't right, and it hurt.

"No!" His frustration was not hidden by any means. He clenched a pile of paper in his fist, crumpling several. "You advanced beyond initial cogitation. Why have you stopped growing?"

My eyes shifted away embarrassed. I warned him I would only ever get so far with this. Mediocre was my middle name.

I tried again.

"You're screeching. Enough," he said, gritting his teeth.

"I'm guessing that's the end of today's lesson?" I asked with a sarcastic tone in my voice. "Better now than later."

Maybe I wouldn't bring up the dance. We just weren't on the same page.

I searched around for my jacket, the draft in the tunnels nipped when we journeyed back up. And since I knew how to get here and out, I wasn't worried about getting lost.

Just irritated.

An audible growl from his throat hit my ears as he huffed. "If you do not take this seriously…"

"I take this very seriously actually. I'm trying so hard for something that I know I can't do. I told you I didn't want to do this because I knew

Chapter XXIX

this would happen," I said, pointing back and forth between us. "I'm never going to be 'stage' ready."

I whipped around, grabbed my jacket from a nearby chair and pulled the front door open.

Erique prowled towards me and slammed the door shut. "You will do it again."

His hand flew just below my ribs and pressed in.

It still made me uncomfortable to be touched there. No matter the situation. It was infuriating more so during sex. He loved holding my stomach. Laying on it. Whatever.

"I push because I know you can do it," he said.

I opened my mouth to try again or fight, I didn't know exactly which.

"No," he said, before I could say anything. His tone slightly less edged than before.

He stepped behind me, his hand still in place, and pressed harder. "Do you feel that?" he asked.

Even though I was irritated with him, my face reddened under the pressure from his body. The nerves that wrecked me, including the ones ignited by him, started to subside. "I do feel *something*." I said wiggling against him.

"Melody," he growled.

"Alright. Alright. I feel it."

"Calm and breathe. Reach far within. Up and out. Up and out."

With a deep breath, my body eradicated the remaining nerves on the exhale.

When I opened my mouth, a sound came out that I didn't recognize as me. A real operatic sound. Powerful and surprising.

My skin turned to goosebumps immediately.

Were the shivers from him or the resonating sound of my voice?

"There you are," he said, his voice deep and sensual, proud, as it rolled over the bareness of my neck. "Keep going."

I continued through his aria, hitting most of the notes I couldn't even come close to earlier. If I could sprout wings, I'd be flying above the clouds.

"Yes," he said into my neck. "Sing for me."

I fought the intense rising feelings. I needed him now, but I needed this even more. Finally prove that maybe I could do it.

If I could do this. Perhaps I could make it past the first step onto the stage and not pass out?

His other hand trailed up between my breasts. "Brilliant," he said, and slipped into the top of my dress, teasing and lightly pinching my nipple. "Don't tense."

There was no way he could keep up this pace much longer. He was going to fizzle out, right?

I hoped not.

Every day was a fight not to look for signs of that. Pulling away. Losing interest. Change for the worse. Like men always did.

Not even when we fought did I see it. Just a man obsessed in love with me.

I couldn't wait to get Erique out. The thought of seeing him in the world with people? There was no way he was capable of freeform dancing, something I wanted to see badly.

A giggle escaped at the thought of him letting loose. Moving around like a newborn foal. Just like me, having the time of our lives.

"What amuses you, love?" he asked, grazing his lips from my jaw to my temple, leaving fiery tingles in its wake.

My head fell against his chest. Mischievous eyes stared down into mine. "Nothing. Just happy…"

"I knew you had it buried within you," he said. "Stop fighting me."

Passionate, determined eyes simmered with a different kind of passion. I was glad we were never stubborn for too long.

Caring hands took my face and lips pressed to mine. It was the kind of kiss that knocked you off your feet and put you in a coma. It's still shocking that it had turned into this with us.

"So, my dear maestro," I said, running my hands up his chest, wishing his shirt was gone. "Do you have plans for us?"

"There are a few things," he said, pulling me tightly to him. "Why is it that you ask?" His lips grazed mine as I tried to remember why I asked what I did.

The thought of staying in, kissing and touching, running my hands through the silky hair on his chest, having his hands and tongue all over, sounded like heaven, but we needed to go out. I needed to get out. With

Chapter XXIX

him.

"Well…" I playfully hesitated, moving my hands down and around his hips. "I was invited to a party tonight… and I want you to come with me."

His loving gaze grew sad. "We have spoken about this." He kissed my forehead. "Let's work on our opera," he said, his adoring gaze attempting to return to its previous expression.

His dedication was his best quality. He never went into anything with half a mind. With the passion he held, he could burn this world down without fire.

"You did so well, my love," he cooed.

"I have the greatest teacher. Without him, I'd be just another dying cat."

Hot lips found my neck as he slowly rocked me back towards the little couch.

I knew what he was doing. And it was extremely hard to fight it as electricity sparked with every touch of his lips. But I couldn't give up just yet.

"Hold on. I'll be right back," I said, regrettably pulling myself from him. "Just stay as you are."

I disappeared around the corner and slipped into Erique's room.

Or "our" room as he liked to say every night.

The guilt of knowing he wanted a life with me weighed a bit. It's gotta be a shit thing to keep this going just because I've never been happier.

It was obvious he already had great taste, but the bedroom update was something else. A large black four-poster bed, matching side tables, dressers and an updated vanity. I loved the red and black bedding. But it must have cost a fortune.

It still baffled me how he got everything delivered without issue.

I pushed the returning guilty thought to the side and rushed to the vanity, pulling a few masks from the wall display. Including the white crackled one with horns that I really want him to wear while he fucked me. Or while I sucked his cock, which he still wouldn't let me do.

It's so hard, he's so good to me. I wanted to do the things for him too!

Erique's organ started up, working on the same movement, perfecting it as much as possible. Always working. My passionate Erique.

It warmed my heart to have witnessed his small transformation from completely tortured soul to only slightly less tormented with a sprinkle of love.

I don't think he's ever smiled so much in his life. At least without mischief of some kind behind it.

Having ransacked his closet, I rushed out to the living room carrying everything I found. "Ok. Hear me out," I said, approaching him.

"What is this?" he asked, eyeing me curiously while he continued to play.

"I didn't tell you the best part about the party."

The music stopped. "Melody..." he said.

"Erique." I inched playfully closer, running my finger over the top of the keyboard. "I forgot to mention…" I held up one of his masks over my face. "…it's a masquerade. Kind of."

Fingers caressed the mask I wore and the most unbelievable eyes fell sad again. "Push this from your mind, dear," he said.

"It's a poor man's masquerade. Nothing fancy. No one will even notice you, unless you want them to," I said, taking his hand. "Come with me? Please. I want you with me."

"The world has no opening for me, Melody. Nor do I want one." He pushed away and stood up, obviously upset. "This is my world. A world without care for society. You need to understand that. This is the life you choose when you choose me. You know this."

"This is a party that supports anti-society," I said, then stood up. "It's for us poor outcasts. No directed dances. No 'elites'. No rules. And I don't care what anyone thinks of you. I would walk with you, as you are. With or without this," I said, running a finger over his mask.

He scoffed and walked around me, grabbing a bottle of wine from the table.

I rubbed my temple. "Why do you have to be this way," I grumbled.

"I never thought you to be this naïve."

"Don't be a dick."

He turned back and towered over me. I wasn't scared for a moment, more irritated than anything. Ok, maybe a tad on guard.

Chapter XXIX

"You can't even tell me you love me yet say you would walk with me on the streets above, proudly? As if I were some dashing count?" he laughed. It was cold and deep, like being impaled by icicles.

He'd been hiding too long, what made me think for a moment that he'd leave the confines of his safe haven to an environment he couldn't control.

Especially when I was still on my own guard apparently.

"Ok. You win," I said, throwing my hands up in defeat.

Maybe it was something I had to think about. It didn't matter that I was completely in... that I really cared about him. There were real restrictions to our relationship.

Grabbing my mask and one of his loose-fitting shirts from the pile of stuff I'd brought out, I went to one of the lesser shattered mirrors and changed.

It'd been so long since I'd dressed up. For fun anyway. My wig hadn't even left Erique's vanity since my first visit. It'd been freeing not to have to wear the costume.

He threw back a glass of wine as he stared me down. "What is it you are doing?" he asked.

I removed the top of my black work dress and threw on his shirt, letting it slip off my shoulders. "Getting ready to go have some mindless fun," I said, tucking part of the hem of my skirt into the band, just to show off my tattooed leg.

It was almost Phantom night in New York City. I smiled at the memory for a moment then sighed. I really wished I could at least talk to Mom and Sarah. Let them know that I was ok.

Suddenly my heart ached for home.

With the mask settled on my face and costume in place, "There," I said and set sails for the door, doing my best to avoid the stare down I could feel from across the room. And I could *feel* that stare.

It was a good thing he showed me how to get out of here safely. Yellow dots were direction. Red was a trap. If you fell into a trap, he'd find you later. Alive or dead. He didn't check them often.

It's still easy to forget who he was sometimes.

I gripped the handle of the front door and pulled. His large, pale hand landed on the door and pushed it closed. His stare was intense; it sent shivers of both pleasure and unease through my body.

I hated that his mere presence soaked me. Even when I was pissed.

"Move. I'm going," I said.

"No."

"Like hell." I tried to pull it open again, but he shifted slightly enough to keep it shut.

"When will you be back?" he asked. There was a possessive tone in his voice. For a split second, I saw myself locked in a room against my will.

"Don't know. I may stay in my room tonight. Like you said, I should probably think some things through. Now move out of my way. I'm going to go have some fun."

His gaze went dark as he stepped forward and wrapped a hand around to the back of my neck, pulling me to him. My back hit the door while his lips pressed harshly against mine. My hands found his hair and pulled him closer. God, my body wanted him. No matter how mad I was.

Erique's hand ran up my thigh to the place that made me crazy under his touch. He slid his fingers inside me and my eyes rolled. But this wasn't what I wanted.

Fighting my desire, I turned my head, breaking the kiss. "Stop." I barely got out.

He just pushed harder, forcing me to kiss him again, like a punishment.

"No!" I said and pushed him away. Erique stumbled back. "You can't just fuck me into submission!" I said, ignoring the confused, embarrassed look in his eyes. I swung the door open. "Just stay here. You and the darkness are perfect for each other."

Chapter XXX

Melody

I just wanted him with me. Was it too much to ask? Probably. Past the stables, music played from the barn. It was a welcome sound to numb my stupid mind.

The many employees of the Opera hung about the simple, yet quite large building. Smoking, drinking and laughing.

I wished I felt like laughing.

I passed through the large sliding doors and into the sea of wiggling, thrusting bodies. It like was a scene out of *Dirty Dancing*.

The music that played was very different from what I'd been hearing for the past few months. I loved the Celtic, upbeat sound. A little surprising to hear in the middle of France.

Erique played pops here and there—mostly for me. He was very "highbrow" and specific in his taste. Which was also a little odd, because when he did play pops, he seemed to enjoy it. I'd catch the hint of a smile as his eyes glimmered my way. Or maybe it was that I enjoyed it that made him so keen to play.

Fucking Erique. Fucking men. Fucking time.

Now, to find Christine. She swore she'd be there, and I hoped it was sooner rather than later.

"*Strange one!*" Pierre called out, stumbling up to meet me. He bowed. "Melody."

"*Hello*," I said, a bit surprised by his friendly demeanor toward me. Nine out of ten times he was irritated by my presence. Now, I was starting to think it was just a French thing.

He snatched my hand and dragged me out to the makeshift dance floor. I didn't know how I felt about it, but I also wanted to have fun.

Smiling ear to ear, I danced with my supervisor, hoping that was all he was trying to do. But just in case, I had my knife on me.

He held my hands and tried to show me how to dance to the music. At least his version. I watched his feet move and picked it up quickly. It was a simple hop and kick. Alternating feet.

I threw a hand in the air and hopped around some more, kicking a foot in and out.

A few more people joined in with Pierre and I, forming a circle. We danced in and out and turned about. Clapping along to the beat.

"Hello, Melody!" someone called out.

Just then, Christine and her friend Chloe, joined the circle. Relief washed over me. I wasn't alone.

Their masks were simple domino style, matching their pretty dresses. They looked like they were ready to party.

The music ended, which I kind of needed. I'd been really physical a lot the past month for sure, but I was still a little winded.

We pulled off to the side as the music started up again, leaving Pierre on his own.

Christine hugged me. "You look so beautiful."

"Do you recognize me?" I asked. The ladies stared confused. I hunched over and brought my arm to cover the lower half of my face. "*Le fantôme de l'Opéra*," I said, moving around like a ghost at them.

They laughed, swatting at me. "Raoul is going to meet us soon. Where is your Erique?" she asked, looking around.

So much for trying to get into a fun mindset.

"Oh, he's... We got into a fight," I said, and shrugged. Thinking about it hurt a little. Was I really going to go back to my room in the opera tonight?

Chapter XXX

Christine's face fell. "Are you ok?"

"Yeah, just a little argument before I left. It's nothing." I hoped.

Facing Christine now, it was probably best he hadn't come. If she recognized his voice, that'd be a hard one to explain away.

"Well, that's all right. We will have fun anyway. I see Pierre was trying to show you how to dance?" she said, wriggling her brows.

My skin crawled at her joke, and I shook my head. "Oh god, I know. Is he still looking this way?"

The two women glanced over my shoulder and nodded.

"Ugh. Let's dance, maybe he'll go away," I said.

The music started up again just in time. The song was another upbeat, bass and fiddle, heavy sound.

Christine grabbed our hands to form our own circle. A minute or so in, there was a tug at my arm. In a moment of excitement, I turned around hoping to see those heterochromic eyes. Unfortunately, it was Pierre again.

Christine shooed him away. "*Just girls tonight*."

He almost looked sad. It was that fake sad though. "*Ah come on. It's just a dance*," he said, taking my hand.

Suddenly Pierre's face dropped, and he let go.

I groaned at the sight of Philippe when I turned to see what Peirre was looking at. As if my night couldn't get any worse, Raoul and Philippe had joined us while I was distracted.

Philippe was dressed as normal, how boring, yet not surprising. Raoul on the other hand wore a mask and very colorful outfit similar to Christine's.

I know Christine mentioned they were coming. I just hadn't expected to see them. Especially Philippe.

"Looks like you all have been having a bit of fun," Raoul said. He took Christine's hand and twirled her. She giggled insanely. Chloe stared at Philippe, probably hoping he'd ask her to dance.

"Well. I'm really surprised to see you at something like this," I finally said.

"It is somewhat unbecoming of me, isn't it?" he said, looking down his nose at the people around. "You look," his eyes raked over me, landing on my tattoos.

"Oh, yeah. Surprise. I told you we wouldn't be a good match, didn't I?"

"Yes. Thank you for saving me."

I laughed. It was funny.

Don't get me wrong, Erique could be quite stuffy too. But it felt different. Erique lived with so many different kinds of people. Whereas Philippe just saw us as pests.

"Speaking of, where is your companion?" he said looking around. "The one that stole you from me?"

"No one stole anyone," I sighed, and rolled my eyes.

A smirk snuck onto his face. Was he joking around?

I gave him a little nudge. "That's not ok."

"Ah. Can you blame me? You're an interesting woman. Dance with me."

"What? No," I said. "Dance with Chloe. She seems to actually like you."

He glanced at her indifferently. "Your gentleman is not here," he said, returning his grumpy gaze to me. "Dance with me."

His presence usually irritated me, but what would it hurt? He's obviously okay after I "broke" his heart. And it would keep Pierre away.

"You see. I can be surprising," Philippe said. I shook my head and took his hand. As we hopped around, I think I found myself having a little fun.

He pulled me closer, wrapping his arm around my waist. As long as he didn't kiss me, I was good. It was nice to see this side of Philippe. Maybe he wasn't as stuck up as I thought.

The song ended and I stepped back quickly. We bowed to each other and clapped for the band.

When the music started back up, Philippe's hand was wrapped around mine again, ready for another go round.

"May I have this dance?" *his* voice caressed my ears.

Familiar, captivating emerald green and stone-gray eyes stared out from under a mask with white crackled paint and horns. It was like the music went silent and it was just us. He wore the same shirt as me, matched with riding pants that had a cape or something tucked into it, flowing off to the side, sort of like a Matador.

Chapter XXX

We were almost twins.

I half expected him to choose the red outfit.

"I would suggest you leave us be, *friend*," Philippe said, stepping in front of me.

"No. It's alright!" I said, trying to keep the situation under control. As much as I wanted Erique here, I didn't want a fight to break out. Or murder…

Erique's eyes sliced to Philippe as he took a step forward. Philippe may have been a bit taller than him, but Erique would kill him before he knew what happened.

I had a belief that Erique could be civil. But Philippe was someone he hated.

I weaved around Philippe in between the two. "It was good to see you, I hope you enjoy the rest of the night," I said.

Understandably so, he was irritated, looking around, most likely hoping no one saw him get rejected, again.

"You're not going to introduce me to your… *friend?*" Philippe's voice had a snide edge to it. This night could literally not get worse.

I didn't need to see Erique's face to know that he was staring daggers at the count. And probably plotting his death. Dread shot through me and suddenly I'd forgotten how to speak.

"Of course. Where are my manners?" I said, forcing myself to say words. "Comte Philippe De Changy, up and coming politician. This is Erique. *Leroux*. Composer and Architect."

"Leroux? I'm afraid I don't know that name. Is your family local?" Philippe asked. The arrogance in the room was so thick, I was trying not to choke on it.

I couldn't believe I just gave him *The Phantom Of The Opera* author's name…

Erique straightened up, somehow suddenly much taller than I remembered him being. "I reside nearby, yes."

"Architect? And composer?" Philippe asked, in a condescending matter.

Erique tilted his head, "Guilty again, Monsieur."

"Is there a living in that? Would I know any of your work? Either musically or structurally?" Philippe asked.

Though I smiled, my jaw was clenched hard. I swore I could hear my teeth cracking.

"Ok. Well, that's enough for tonight," I tried to interject.

"You know my work," Erique said matter of fact. "However, I have been a silent partner for many years. Because of this, I am afforded the luxury to care for not only myself, but another as well, very comfortably." Erique looped his arm around my waist and pressed his hand against my stomach. "More if we like."

I hoped it was just banter to get under Philippe's skin and not something more as he was insinuating. Knowing Erique it was both. Great, another "fun" conversation I "wanted" to have…

"Good night, Miss Reilly," Philippe said with a tight-lipped smile. Then shot Erique the dirtiest look I'd ever seen.

Erique's grip tightened around me. "I should kill him for touching you," he muttered.

"Stop."

The dim lights of the barn touched his face gently but accentuated the hate in his eyes. The mask didn't cover as much as his regular ones. Scarring crept out around the edges a lot, revealing more of his jaw. Shocking he would have so much uncovered. I loved it.

"You're here," I said in the most pathetic voice.

The intense stare he had for Philippe melted away. Long fingers cupped my face then he pressed his forehead to mine. "Forgive my stupidity," he said. "I don't want to be that kind of man for you."

This was what it was like to have someone who wanted to be in your life.

This is what Sarah's had all her adult life. This is what Mom always wanted for herself and never found.

"Are you ok?" I asked.

"I will be."

A gentle kiss was all it took before my arms went lifeless and I saw stars. God, he was overwhelming. And he was there for me.

"Come home tonight…" he said, rubbing his cheek against mine.

With what will I had; I whispered, "I had every intention of coming back."

Christine and Chloe glanced at each other with suggestive and

Chapter XXX

approving smiles.

It was weird introducing him to the women he already knew. But, like the man he was, greeted with a gentlemen's bow and acted as if it were the first time.

"Do you want a drink?" Christine asked me.

I nodded, "Wine please."

"You loathe wine, Love," Erique said quickly.

"We're having fun, right?"

"One bottle of wine then," he smirked. "Would you allow me to fetch your drink?" he asked the two young women.

They nodded, and he was on his way.

Christine grabbed my arm. "Oh my, he is so in love with you."

"Yeah, I know," I sighed. "He's a bit obsessed."

"Where can I get one?" Chloe asked.

Just accidentally fall back in time. "He's one of a kind. I'm afraid."

"I don't think Raoul even looks at me that way," Christine said.

"Don't compare. Also, where is he anyway?"

"Philippe was a bit upset when your Erique showed up. He stormed off and took Raoul with him. Raoul should be back sometime soon though," she said.

"So, you and Philippe are not…?" Chloe asked.

"Oh. No."

She smiled like she'd been caught. It was obvious she found him very attractive. Too bad he showed no interest in her.

Erique bulldozed through the crowd holding a bottle of wine, passing a few women that tried to dance on him. His eyes were set on me, and only me. I felt like the luckiest girl in the whole world.

This man could probably filet a person in front of me, and I'd still be wet as fuck and completely love him against my will.

Shit.

***

After some very interesting dancing, without a word, he took my hand and led me from the barn.

Sneaking past Cesar and Nora, Erique took me to the hidden door in the stables. "Here," he said, showing me how to get in.

Just inside, he pinned me against the wall. I moaned his name.

Rubbing my hands up his body, gripping everywhere I could. I loved when he pressed himself against me.

My hand migrated south to the raging, hardened thing hidden in the prison of his trousers.

"Erique, please let me," I begged. "It's gotta be killing you too."

He groaned into my mouth. "Not yet," he quivered and pulled me back to the journey.

"Where are we going?"

"You are so curious, my love. Trust me." The way he spoke to me, teased... I was boneless most of the time.

I tried not to let him know that though.

The journey took forever with how often we stopped. No way was I going to complain.

"Come," he said.

"I'm trying to."

He eyed me like he did when he thought I was ridiculous, then ascended up a ladder. He reached down for me and I followed blindly, because I didn't care.

I couldn't believe that a couple sips of wine had me so tipsy.

We emerged into the darkness of box five.

"What are we...?" I started.

He took my mouth and walked me into the dim light of the theater. He turned us around and lifted me onto the wide banister and built-in table.

"Don't, I'm too heavy," I said.

He wasn't listening. Hungry eyes only saw what he wanted. His love, his obsession, laid out like a feast before him.

And I wanted to be devoured.

"Open your legs," he commanded.

I did as told, and he stepped in between, pressing his hand against my naked sex.

Oops. Someone had forgotten underwear. Again.

Kissing me with unbridled fury, he ripped my shirt open exposing my breasts to the warm air of the theater, so desperate to have his mouth on them.

Never in my life had I ever done something like this. I was suddenly aware that we were in a public place, a place anyone could come and go.

What if someone saw us?

All was forgotten when Erique took my nipple into his mouth, moaning as he circled the tip with his tongue. Nibbling and sucking on it as he held onto me tightly, staring up from beneath his white Devil's mask. The one I wanted him to fuck me in.

I was a broken sieve for him. Every time he moaned, it was more wood added to the fire.

"Oh fuck!" I gasped as his fingers entered me.

Forced sighs and grunts escaped me with each thrust. My head rolled back and the sex-tasy elevated. He had come so far since our first time.

His other hand held me down, keeping me balanced on the railing and table. I was terrified I was going to fall, but I trusted Erique so much. I knew he wouldn't let anything happen to me.

Is that the dumbest thing I could do?

"What is a boyfriend?" he asked.

The Ghost's presence around the opera had diminished somewhat since our union. Hardly did the *Ghost's* voice visit anymore either. However, there would be no complaints found about how that time had been used.

"What?" Her breathy voice matched the foggy, satiated look in those warm, brown eyes. Powerless she was as the tips of these pianist's fingers massaged the spot inside, straining her focus.

"What is a boyfriend?" I asked again, enjoying the squirming of her body under my touch. Closer she would be in her admission of love.

"Where did you hear that?" she asked.

"Once upon a time, you referred to me as your imaginary boyfriend."

"No, I didn't."

I massaged again, admiring her hungry gasps as her blushing cherubic face lolled back.

Torturing her during our most vulnerable moments was a divine elixir in which she bathed beautifully.

"When you hurt me and told me I wasn't real," I said. I gathered the tattered remains of the shirt she wore in my grasp and pulled her to meet me. As I hovered, her sweet, reddened face, I continued my torturing of her physical state. "What. Is. It?"

"Ugh. Why are you doing this now?" she whined, upset that I wouldn't close the gap between our lips. "It's just a stupid title before engagement."

"Am I your boyfriend, Melody?" She bit her lip and averted her eyes. "Don't do that," I warned her. "Look at me. Am I your boyfriend?" I asked, moving my hand again.

As if confessing a deep dark secret, she nodded.

I relieved her of her suffering and closed the distance between our starving mouths and then dropped to my knees before her.

Already laid open and exposed for *me*. Always smelled ready for me. Every bit of this woman was celestial.

Eager hands found my head, and fingers entwined in my hair.

With the fabrics of her skirt barricading the *monster's* face that would please her, I removed my mask and set it aside.

To feel her fuzzy, soft womanhood against my flesh was a blessing. One she never asked to give but had turned grateful for my involvement.

I pressed my wretched face to her and closed my eyes in the comfort it gave me. Gently, I moved along the crevasse to what hid beneath, sighing as the aroma took over.

Under my newly practiced fingers, my willing partner moaned and whimpered. Jolting and rocking against me.

Willing partner.

This demon had gone an eternity without a kindred soul, and now it had the most precious of them all. Willingly she adores. Willingly she stays. The stubborn woman must be delighted in my torment. I was certain she loved me.

Unable to abstain any longer, I parted the flesh hiding the wonder of her pleasure and buried my face farther within.

I moaned as my tongue joined in the tempo my hand created and the sounds of her whimpers heightened.

Pain was not foreign to this creature. My cock's aching for freedom and used deep within this angel who begged for it, should have been a distant memory. Yet it leaked and raged in wait as if it were the first time it became aware.

Chapter XXX

She would be thrilled to take this rotten thing. Happy. Grateful even. But to bedevil her. To make her beg for me, pleased me just as much.

My hand flew to the clasp of my trousers, attempting the quickest undoing. Relief was only partial as I pulled the frustrated, throbbing flesh from its prison.

She whined as my fingers pulled from her to grip myself, covering it with the natural secretion of her arousal. Wrapping my arm around her leg, I held her in place so this monster could stay nestled within the crook of her.

"No," I commanded, as she pushed at the hand on her belly. This angel should know I adored every part of her by now.

My tongue ran along her hot sex, trembling as I moved. I pushed into her wanting, waiting desire. A surrogate action to what my body wished of my cock.

Magma traveled through my veins as I neared closer to precipice.

I dug my fingers into her belly as I bucked against my own hand. With a fierceness, I sputtered and jolted as I spilled onto the floor of my box.

Aftershocks forced convulsions as I held onto her, catching my breath. One day I would spill into her, and we would both rejoice in bliss.

A moment passed, until undeserving fingers reentered her, and this snake's tongue licked at needy flesh again.

My name rang off her lips like a goddess's blessing as she clenched around me with convulsions of her own. Her legs clamped my head, and she was done.

I returned the mask to my face, locking her scent inside. After years of unrelenting darkness and utter despair, how this had become my life would baffle the greatest scholars.

Weak arms and a blushing face searched for me. "Erique, please," she said, breathless.

My love was insatiable for me. What an unthinkable experience to be had. I pressed myself to her, furthering my need to torture. Surprised at a new sensation with the action. Amidst the chaos, I had forgotten to re-holster myself.

Her wet heat slickened and radiated against my semi-hard cock, as it readied again. Not something which happened often.

It was in me to give it to her. One slight movement was all it would take. She wanted me, how could I be so terrible to even myself?

Intoxicated as this man was, this mind knew there was something I needed more.

Her sated, round face grew desperate and hungry again, pulling me into a feverish kiss. A month now since our first shared moment, this continued to be a surprise every time after. A reminder this was not a dream and that I am wanted by another.

Greedy hands traveled to my hips and around to the brim of my opened trousers.

We were both taken over by the need. Her ravenous kisses burned and her body begged to be filled.

Perhaps if I just teased her a little bit.

I grasped myself, pushing her back onto the table, and ran the tip of my readied cock along her beckoning wonder.

"Erique! Please... yes," she cried.

Hell. Blood ran hotter than a steam engine when she begged.

Pride held my every urge to plunge into her as I rocked back and forth against that little button. Ravage her like I'd always wanted. Take her. Make her mine in every way.

Though if I were honest, it would only ensure I was hers for eternity.

'As if she could be rid of you,' the *Ghost* said.

Welcoming was the passage to her core as I circled it, and her eyes rolled. I caught her lovely, pale hand as she reached for me. Which would now be adorned with signs of forever.

Many times had she tried for permission to relieve me. Never have I given it, nor let her touch me bare. I would be afraid of my own control.

These experiences were a gift that I would not blemish. My heart could only take so much.

"You know what I need," I said into her mouth. "I know you love me." Whether she cared to admit it or not. She would, soon.

Glazed eyes barely focused on mine. My angel was another world away flying above the stars with me.

It was going to kill me to have to put myself away.

"Erique..." she smiled groggily, sitting up to meet me.

Sneaky little girl. A wanting hand traveled down my stomach toward my opened trousers, while the other pushed beneath the opening of my shirt and through the hair of my chest. The firm caress of my sheathed cock commanded me, close to giving in.

"What's that?" she asked.

My eyes open slowly to find her pulling away, staring at my ring on her finger. Wide eyed and confused.

"Everyone should know that you are mine," I said, caressing her arms.

She groaned. Claws slashed at my heart as she tugged at the ring on her bridal finger that seemed to be stuck because we were meant to be.

"I can handle myself. Everyone already knows that I'm with you, Erique. Especially now."

"Are you?"

"Why do you always have to ask me?"

"Good. Then wearing my ring to solidify it should not be an issue."

A heavy huff in her chest, she finally yanked the gold medal off. "I believe you lost this," and slid it back onto my smallest finger.

Before I could open my mouth, she placed a kiss on the inside of my hand and rested her cheek within it.

The drink may have gotten the best of both of us tonight. An excuse I would use. Or not.

"Can we go home now?" she asked, then kissed what I'm sure were my pouting lips.

Home. She called it home.

That would do. For now.

Chapter XXXI

Melody

I'm a thirty-five-year-old woman and I'm scared of a door. Butterflies filled my stomach as I stared at the threshold to that bathroom. No. Not butterflies. Wolverines. Slashing and ripping at my insides as I attempted to find the courage to step through.

My gaze cut down to the mask in my hand. The one I wore when I walked through it to get here in the first place.

I figured that maybe the reason it hadn't worked before was because of my clothing. But if that were the case, it'd never work. I didn't have my beautiful Michael Kors shoes anymore.

Maybe it was simpler than that. Just the mask. It was why this world existed, right? Or whatever it was. The power of the mask.

Oh my god. That is so stupid.

If it was stupid, then why was I hesitating to put the thing on and step through?

I exhaled nervously as I turned it over and gripped the elastic.

I'm going to throw up.

"Are you ready?" Christine asked.

I nearly jumped out of my skin at her voice. I thought I was still

Chapter XXXI

alone.

And then suddenly I was relieved that she found me.

"Why do you have that?" she asked.

I shook my head and shoved the mask into my bag. "No reason. Yes, I'm ready."

We were meeting with Antoinette for lunch. It had been a minute since I'd seen her. With Christine coming along, I could finally thank her for everything she'd done for me.

"What an absolutely beautiful day," Christine said as the carriage bounced away.

It was beautiful actually. There has been nothing but beauty in my life for the past month. Even with the downs.

It'd been two days since the *Masq*. Since Erique had come to me, something had shifted between us into something a little deeper, a little more profound. More real.

Yesterday we laid around all day. Writing on and off. Snuggling. Other things.

This sunny day made me wish he was with me. Which always led to other thoughts, like could I ever get him this far?

I could be crazy, and probably was. He's such a complicated, emotional man. I shouldn't think about things like that. A future wasn't possible. I was still obligated to get home.

I mean if I never got home... Even then, it was complicated. Just like him.

Last night, as I watched him sleep, I wished my phone had been charged. I wanted a photo of him. And I missed seeing the faces of the people at home.

And God what I wouldn't give to hear some Evanescence or Ghost. Fuck, I'd even take Justin Bieber.

Ok, no, I wouldn't take Bieber. But that's how much I missed my music.

"I really appreciate you coming with me today. I've been wanting to do this for a while, but we both seem to be really busy these days," I said, scratching my neck. *Guilty as charged*.

"I know. It's wonderful, isn't it?" she said. "And of course. I am very excited to meet the woman that saved you. I just don't understand why

Erique hasn't translated for you?"

I would have loved to have him come with me. But after learning of her fears about him, I didn't try to push it. Ever.

"Yeah, about that," I said, with hesitation. "Please don't mention him."

Christine's brows wormed together in confusion.

"It's just that Antoinette doesn't like him much. And I don't want to upset her. I want this to be a good meeting."

"How can it be bad? I've seen how he loves you. And you've said nothing to give doubt of that," she said. "She should know you have found happiness."

"She knew him from a long time ago, and it didn't go as one would hope. Just please don't say anything."

Just more deceiving on Erique's behalf. The only thing I felt bad about anymore.

She sighed in defeat. "Promise. But I think you should tell her how happy you are."

"Maybe one day. I'd like that." *Or not at all if I was gone. Then I wouldn't have to see the disappointment on her face.*

We arrived at the café on time where a very cheery Antoinette stood outside to greet us.

Not long after introductions were made, we were seated inside. Before I knew it, Christine and Antoinette were lost in conversation about her career and Raoul.

I learned things about Antoinette I never knew. When she was younger, before she met Louis, she was a ballet dancer and worked many of the operas. One of the best times in her life, she said.

"I owe you the biggest 'whatever you want for this'," I said to Christine.

"Yes, you do," she said. "She's lovely though. So, thank you for bringing me."

My rabbit and puréed veggies were amazing. Not surprising. It was wonderful to be able to eat food that didn't make me sick immediately. The one thing I did like about this time and place.

Erique had introduced me to different foods just as much as Antoinette. He loved to make sure I was fed. The best part was that I

Chapter XXXI

hadn't gained weight from all of the eating. Especially when Erique was in charge of it.

We'd cooked together a few times. The kitchens were kind of weird. Every room had a door, very claustrophobic. He said that would be his next update for me. An open kitchen.

Maybe I could get something on the way home to cook for dinner.
Ew. What am I thinking? Bleh. No.

"Composer and Architect?" Antoinette said. "That is very nice for a nobleman."

My attention left the delicious plate of food and my uncomfortable thoughts, and went to the face that spoke the words that just stopped my heart.

"What? What are you guys talking about?" I asked as my voice squeaked.

"Does she think 'you know who' is Philippe?" Christine whispered.

I sighed and closed my eyes. "Maybe. I've avoided the topic of my dating life. She doesn't know what you do, remember."

"What do you want me to say? I accidently answered her already."

It was wishful thinking that it wouldn't come up. All wasn't lost just yet though. "It's ok. Just don't answer any more about him. Talk about something else. Like your grandma or something."

"Oh, of course. Alright. But she wants to know if you're happy and if he has a nice…" Christine's face reddened, and her eyes widened. "A nice… um."

My eyes mirrored hers at the realization of what she wanted to know.

Antoinette would ask something like that especially right after I told Christine not to answer anything. I felt so bad for Christine now.

"Oh my God. Uh…" I stumbled.

Antoinette sat smugly, staring. Her brows suggesting I answer because she was in dire need of knowing.

I had actually never seen Erique's dick come to think of it. I've felt it a few times through his pants, which made me shudder like no other. Once inside his pants when he was a bit more sloshed than usual and let me, until he didn't. Such a tease.

I'm a terrible person, I know.

"He makes me feel like I'm the only person in the universe that matters. Supports my decisions. Talks through our problems. Which, what man does that? Or at least comes back to talk about them after one of us stormed out. He's a beautiful soul that makes me feel whole and loved. Forces me out of my comfort zone. He believes in me. Especially when I don't. So yeah. I'm happy. And also, he makes my toes curl and stars burst in my eyes like no man has ever even cared to try."

Like a terrified Chihuahua, Christine relayed my answer.

It was nice to finally get to say something about him. All the good stuff. I smiled a bit bashfully.

"Ah! Yes!" Antoinette sighed. "He is a good man and a magic man."

I laughed until I sighed again at the irony. "Yeah. He's pretty great."

"It has been too long, dear," my older friend said, squeezing my hand. "*Thank you.*"

My cheeks burned and I smiled. This was already getting harder than I thought it'd be.

"I'm sorry. I have been so occupied lately," *with the man you hate*. "I hope to see you more soon."

Antoinette smiled sweetly, squeezing tighter. "If you are going somewhere with that handsome young man, I completely understand," Christine translated.

I hated lying to her. At least it felt like a lie. I just wished I could tell her everything and she'd be ok with it. But I knew, just like everyone else, he was what he was in their eyes.

I swallowed hard and changed the subject quickly, hoping we wouldn't end up back on the topic.

"I wanted to bring my friend today to tell you something actually," I said.

Antoinette's features softened as she looked back and forth between Christine and I, waiting on whatever it was I wanted to say.

Even though I knew Erique had a hand in her finding me, it didn't change what she did for me. In some way, it made it more important because she helped someone at the word of a man she hated.

It wasn't long into my poorly executed gratitude that the older woman was crying and telling me that I reminded her of the daughter she wished she had. That my friendship with her made her feel useful again and cared for.

Chapter XXXI

Her own declaration made me tear up, especially thinking of my own mother and how I missed the times she was like this.

Antoinette moved closer, resting her fragile hand on mine. Christine continued to translate for her. "It may have been darkness that brought you here, but you are full of light. I see nothing but love in you. You were worth saving and I would do it again. Even if you did smell terrible."

We wiped our tears and laughed the moment away, though it still lingered.

"Yes. You smelled like the bins we found you behind," Christine translated.

"It was so bad. I know," I said.

"J'espère que tu ne sens pas ça pour ce jeune homme," Antoinette said, laughing.

I glanced at Christine who was also laughing uncontrollably.

"I'm sorry. I'm trying to imagine you in trash," she said.

"Oh yeah, I may have forgotten to mention that part. Not my favorite moment of the night." *Amongst many others.*

"Anyway, she said she hopes you don't smell like that for Erique," Christine said, then covered her mouth as quickly as she said it. "I'm so sorry," she whispered.

"Erique?" His name on Antoinette's lips was sharp.

My heart stopped immediately when my gaze cut to Antoinette who was staring as if she'd seen the devil in a black cloak himself.

"Erique?" Antoinette said again. Her voice was more guttural this time.

My mouth fell open, trying to find the words to rectify whatever was happening, but I found nothing.

Antoinette began spewing words so fast, her eyes full of worry and terror.

"What is she saying?" I begged Christine.

"She's speaking so fast, I almost can't understand. You've seen him? She says he's dangerous. She told you to come back. And keeps saying dangerous over and over… I'm sorry, she's not making much sense."

Shit shit shit shit shit shit.

I grabbed Antoinette's hands, trying to calm her. "Will you translate for me again?" I asked Christine.

"Yes, not to worry," Christine answered.

"It's ok. It's ok," I said, trying to keep my voice calm. I didn't know if it was for her or me, but the anxiety was running high all around. "He's not what you think. You heard me speak of him already."

"He is the demon," she said, with warning in her eyes. Every word she spoke, she believed.

I shook my head and scrunched my brows, frustrated. "His heart is so kind. He has the gentlest hands. He cares so much for me. It's a little overwhelming sometimes. But there is nothing I would trade for it. He is not the same as you knew him. Or maybe he is. But not bad."

I listened to my own words. The truth in them surprising even me.

Antoinette didn't seem any more convinced. In fact, at the mention of his touch, she almost flew off her seat.

"Even the devil is kind until he's not," Christine translated.

"Are you…" Antoinette looked at my stomach. Fear like I'd never seen before flashed in her eyes. "*Es-tu enceinte?*"

"She wants to know if you're pregnant," Christine said. "Are you?"

"Oh! No. He hasn't. We haven't. No. And it's impossible." *Not just because he hasn't had his cock in me.*

"You said he makes you shake!" Christine translated.

"Yes. But he… he uses… It doesn't matter. I can't be pregnant."

Relief replaced fear quickly in my older friend's face. Like that would have somehow been the worst thing to happen. I mean yeah, she was right. I never wanted kids. But damn.

"Christine, can you leave us alone for a few minutes?" I asked.

"I'll go to the powder room," she said, and left us.

I waited until she was out of earshot before finally trying to speak to Antoinette. There were things I couldn't have Christine hear and hoped Antoinette understood.

I sighed, taking her arms in my hands.

"He is bad, *butterfly*," she said. Antoinette's hands cupped my face. She was terrified for me. It was written all over.

"I know everything about how you found him. The fire? How you helped him." Her eyes watered, I knew she understood perfectly well. "I know about what he did afterward. And some other things."

"You cannot be safe," she said.

Chapter XXXI

"I trust him. I do. I trust him so much."

"You come back? He stay away."

"He won't. And I don't want him to…" I said. *I didn't want him to ever leave me. What was I going to do now?*

There was more silence than I cared for. I didn't think either of us knew what to say after that. What could you say? Even without a language barrier.

I was in love with a man everyone deemed dangerous. And he was. And I'm the stupid ass that was ok with it.

Antoinette eventually sighed and squeezed my hand again. "*Sweet girl. May God watch over you.*"

***

The ride home was quiet. Christine didn't say anything. Neither of us did. I understood where Antoinette was coming from. Erique was who he was. We'd been in such a state of bliss basically, that I kept forgetting that.

I didn't know what else to do.

The fucker had done nothing but earn my trust. My body. My fucking heart.

It seemed everyone was against him. That he wasn't worthy of growth and a second chance.

He wasn't the same person anymore. Right? Or was I just too blinded by orgasms, and loving words, and writing, and singing, and all the stuff to really see that he hadn't changed, only simmered down?

I wondered how long it would take Antoinette before she would see me again. The disappointment and terror in her eyes even as she left us was still etched into my memory.

I hoped Erique was home. I really needed a hug.

Chapter XXXII

The cold air of Paris failed to nip, for my heart beamed brighter than the sun. Night kept me shrouded beneath my hat and cloak as I walked the streets amongst its inhabitants. To them, this shadow was just another man in the late hour on his way home. They would be too busy to notice there was no face beneath the brim. Only a void where my black false face sat.

Only venturing out on this eve to collect the small package in my pocket that was too precious for another's delivery of it. Too precious to leave to fate.

I would hurry home had I not another engagement. I wished I were home. That was where she waited for me now. Rewriting the very lyrics I had given her earlier in the day.

It pained me to leave her on this night. The sad little heart of my love, hurt after lunch with friends. To see her so broken twisted my chest. Yet, my heart still danced like pixies amongst flowers that I was her safety. Her *home*.

Every minute apart from my Melody was too long. So, I prayed this meeting with Ardashir moved along quickly.

Chapter XXXII

He'd written of his arrival back to Paris and just so happened to be staying near a shop I had an appointment with.

Getting into his room was rather easy. Locks were never an obstacle, only a minor delay.

My friend slept peacefully in the small bed. His clothing and pistol laid out on a chair across the room. Not very smart on his part.

Curiosity called me to the notepad on his nightstand. His lovely hat—which he has refused to part with, beside it. My feet carried me as though I walked on clouds across the small room.

My Persian was a bit out of use, but parts of his notes made sense. Working different cases, as he should. One here in Paris. A missing wife.

Paris would burn if Melody were to go missing. Sanity would play no part. More than my fractured mind could comprehend anyway.

Even now I calm myself at the thought.

My curious fingers halted within the pages when the snoring in the room broke. Ardashir rustled in his sleep. In wait, I watched for him to still again.

"I'm going to kill you, fucker!" he shouted, bolting up in his bed.

"I no longer wish to taunt death, dear friend," I said, holding my hands up in surrender.

Ardashir could never win against me, even if he tried. And I adored him for that.

"Erique! You bastard," he said, throwing a pillow, hitting me directly in the chest.

Amused by the reaction, I caught it and tossed it aside. "Forgive the late hour," I said.

"We're supposed to meet tomorrow morning," he groaned, running his hand over his face.

"I had an appointment in the area and thought why not come see my dear friend now."

"You? An appointment? At nine thirty at night? For what?"

"I am… trying new things," I said. "Would you believe that?"

Ardashir groaned. "No," then rubbed the back of his neck. "Alright. Sit."

I continued to stand, keeping a watchful eye on my friend. He had been gone some time. It was uncertain what he saw as my fate.

"I would have simply written you my findings, but I have another case here and thought I'd check in on you," he said.

"Ah. The missing woman?"

"Of course, you know," he glanced at the notepad. "Anyway. I did visit the chorus girl's friend in. The deceased had written her telling of a proposed marriage with an unnamed patron, because she was with child. They were going to run away together…"

The only patron that came to mind was one that could threaten my union with Melody. She may think in her mind he was nothing, the fact remained he was an interference.

Though chances were slim as to his involvement, since it was before he and his charming little shadow slinked into the halls of my opera more often.

Even so. It would be delicious to disembowel the vermin. An act never having crossed my mind until as of late.

"…The reason it took so long to get back from Toulouse was that someone had murdered the poor girl after we spoke. The local police and I investigated for several weeks. Nothing came up unfortunately. I am sorry my friend. This will probably go unsolved. Though I will not give up."

There would be no punishment for a wrongful death and that disgusted me. "The Ghost will continue to take claim of a death not done at his hand," I said, disappointed.

"I'm sorry I couldn't be more help in this," he said. "I am also sorry it took me this long to return. My wife gave birth last month and I wanted to be there."

My waning attention was pulled back again. Age had shown on his face for many years now. Old was he when I was young. It hadn't occurred to me a child would come to him after all these years. What a terribly wonderful thing.

For them.

"A child?" I asked.

"I hadn't wanted to get my hopes up. It has taken many years to be free of the black within my mind at the loss of my family at home…"

My heart recoiled at mention of the past. A past in which I was to blame for the loss of everything in this good man's life.

Chapter XXXII

He continued. "…But Isabella has healed my heart in many ways and now she gifts me with a new family to protect in honor of the one lost to me. I am at peace. I will miss nothing if I can. Which means I will also be departing in a week's time."

A family.

Not until the mock *Masq* had I imagined such a thing. It was out of spite in which it even crossed my mind in the first place. All to shut the cretin up.

After pulling her to me, swearing I'd be able to care for her and more, with my hand on her belly. This creature suddenly wished it were swollen with child. My child. Our child.

My cock twitched in anger at not having penetrated when she begged so often. If my fixation on needing her love had not trumped my desires, she could be glowing more than she already does.

Would I wish this curse on a child? Would I desire a child? Would she?

'We will know soon enough,' the *Ghost* said.

I palmed the small item in the pocket of my trousers, fiddling about with it. "Never apologize for love," I said. "I have learned it to be a precious thing. And I bid you any and all happiness. You are the most deserving of it."

Ardashir stared bewildered. "Right." He squinted, eyes full of suspicion. "What is different? You're less… arrogant than usual."

"Even I doubt that."

"I've known you for over twenty years, my friend. You are different."

A light smile befell my lips. It unsettled him. "I have been kissed by a woman, Ardashir." Surprised at my own quick confession. "She waits for me even now to return to kiss her again."

He jumped from his bed. Eyes widened as if he were seeing the most horrific sights again. "You what? What have you done? Is she the woman I'm looking for?"

"Pardon?"

"Erique? Where is she?"

"Home."

"You did it. I can't believe you finally did it," he said, avoiding my gaze. Chastising himself for not arresting me years ago. "If you return her now. I will not kill you."

"She is not who you seek. I would do no such thing." Would I?

'Christine would have had the fate in which our friend accuses,' the *Ghost* reminded.

"There was a time I may not have been… well. But that time is no more," I said, in an attempt to convince myself. "Would it be so shocking that someone could love me?"

"You can't force someone to love you, Erique!"

Old fears and uncertainties crawled from the depths. With an awkwardness I had not felt since adolescence, I cleared my throat. "I'm certain she does."

"Anyone would make you believe they love you. Do what it takes to survive if they're being held against their will," he spit.

"She kisses me. Whispers words of affirmation. Touches me. Holds me like I matter. My beautiful angel lets me bring her to bliss I'd only ever dreamt of," I said, stepping closer to Ardashir. "A future has opened bright and for once I see myself there."

"You lie to yourself, why?" he asked. The sincerity in his voice almost crossed as worried. Had his mind convinced him I was indeed mad?

Was I?

"It is no lie. She begs for my kiss. My touch. My cock! Does that sound like a prisoner to you? Someone pretending to want me?" I asked. "Why does doubt plague your mind of me? Why do you think me so wicked? You are happy. Why can I not be?"

"Because you don't deserve it, Erique!" he bit.

The past had come full circle, and I was left with truth. I loved her more than I wished for grace. But would never be deserving of her.

Ardashir's shoulders dropped along with the volume of his voice. "You're broken, my friend. I am sorry for the truth of it. But the ailment that twists your face warps your brilliant mind. It always has. Your hands are tainted with death. Your soul is just as black. You would ruin her."

It is something I've always known. I could not pretend the truth of his words did not rip me limb from limb.

What he failed to understand was that this mind had never been more calm. More quiet.

"I wouldn't!" I said. "I love her."

Chapter XXXII

He sighed. "Has she seen you? Know who you really are?"

Hesitation grabbed hold. Did it really matter that she had not seen my face? Every inch of damage to my body? Experience at her care told the story of a woman that did not care what hid behind the mask. Yet I would still not risk it.

"She kisses me. Here." I pointed to my lips as if it would prove something.

"Do not deflect. Has she seen what is beneath that false face of yours?"

Rocking my jaw, I blink back a rogue manifestation of my rising doubt and turn away.

Ardashir slumped onto the bed and hung his head low, exhaling with heavy weight. "You didn't answer. Does she know who you really are?"

I nodded. "Melody knows everything, and she still cares for me."

His brows lifted and demeanor changed. "The American?"

I nodded again, curious now at his quick change.

"Huh. I admit I would have thought it was the little songbird you would pay attention to. All those 'accidents' were for her, right?" he asked.

That little songbird would have been caged until she loved me. Which is how I knew change had grown within me.

"…I had not thought the American would be in your sights. I guess she wasn't 'nothing' after all?"

I shifted, standing tall once again. "I am changed, Daroga. I would like to think for the better."

"This Melody is the reason for this change?"

My chest sank with a sigh. "Anger and hatred have subsided with her friendship. After a lifetime of being loathed for simply a face I was born with. Forced to be the embodiment of fear. Live an existence of loneliness and hollow fantasies. Forgotten so easily by the world that threw me away. I now see beauty in my shattered mind. Where there was delusion, I now see hope. I saw her… Held her," I said, digging the tips of my fingers into my chest. "In that moment, I wanted to be wanted. Do you know what it is like to be wanted? I wanted her. A life. Love. And she has chosen me. Willingly. All I ever wanted was to be loved for myself."

Passion and truth lit my tongue. With hope it burned my friend so that he may see who I had become.

"I know this mind is fractured. Daroga, she is so beautifully broken too. Our broken pieces fit together and made us one. Never have I felt such peace." I dropped my fists and took a ragged breath. "I thought I was dead and she was my heaven. But I live and she is real. Never did I think this path was an option. You were right to fear what I may have done had she not literally fallen into my arms. She has given me the one thing I have always wanted. My Angel wants me for me. For some reason beyond this world, I was given a chance. And now she owns me. Every part of me. I will do nothing to betray. This I swear to you."

The dark eyes of my friend turned soft at my declaration. Free seemed the weight on his shoulders as he neared me. "She loves you then?" he asked.

Muffled shouting from outside the window drew my attention. A low growl rumbled in my chest at what I found. *Le Comte Vermin* stood in wait outside his lavish carriage yelling at some other vermin.

'What a treat on this interesting evening,' the *Ghost* seethed.

And I agreed.

"As always, I enjoy our conversations," I said and meant every word.

"Erique," he said, attempting to rest a hand on my shoulder. "I feel I should…"

With haste, I slipped from his sympathy and rushed to the door. "Good night, dear Ardashir. Go home. Perhaps the next time we meet, it will be on a joyous occasion. You will see."

I held nothing my friend said against him. He had been the only person to speak freely with me all these years, unafraid.

As my feet moved swiftly down the stairway, I found myself looking forward to proving him wrong. The things I would do to end his doubt of me.

After I'd finished my business with *le Comte de Vermin's* carriage, I rushed home only to be greeted with a greedy mouth and arms wrapped so tightly around my neck, breathing was suddenly a memory.

"I missed you," she said between heated kisses. "I want to try something tonight. If you're ok with it."

Always so worried about my comfort. The sweetness of her rotted

Chapter XXXII

me.

My aching cock thrummed with images of her nakedness basking in the glow of candlelight.

I tore my shirt from her wanting body. She moaned and gripped me tighter when I bit into the flesh of her neck as we rocked towards our bedroom.

Our bedroom.

"Come away with me," I said, running my disgusting lips up to her ear.

"What?" she asked.

"Come away with me."

"I can't leave," she tried to protest weakly.

I ran my lips along her jaw, my hand mirroring the act along the other side. "Let me take you away for a short while."

"Really?"

"My Heart. Just say yes."

Brown eyes stared with curious confusion as I hovered swollen lips. "We would go together?" she asked.

"You and me."

"Erique, I'm…"

"Say yes."

She chewed on her lip as a smile grew on her cherub face. "Yes!" she said and pulled me closer. "Do you trust me?" she asked, caressing along the visible part of my distorted soul.

"Unequivocally."

Ardashir was wrong. So very wrong. She loved me willingly. *I know it.*

Chapter XXXIII

Melody

It was getting harder to convince myself that this was temporary. That anything with him was temporary. I wished Antoinette could see Erique as I did. Especially after she confirmed everything he'd told me. I suppose her reaction still stung.

I couldn't tell Erique, it would upset him to know that he inadvertently was the cause of my sadness.

Unrelated, after our sexy time stuff, he asked me to stay home and write with him full time. Endure more lessons. I would never have to go back up to the opera if I didn't want to.

We'd either kill each other or just end up writing, singing, and fucking all day.

Where was I going with this? To fucking la la land, that's right.

I admit, the offer was tempting. But if I quit, I didn't think they'd like me hanging around the opera. Not that I had been walking through restroom doors much lately.

I smiled at the sweet thought as I sanded down the freshly cut edges of the wooden cross I'd been working on, and sang songs that I missed hearing.

Chapter XXXIII

I had really come to like repair work. And lucky for me, something broke almost every performance. And it was easy to sneak away if I needed to.

"Christine!" I called out, jumping from my stool, as the understudies meandered into the backstage area for their rehearsal. I couldn't wait to tell her Erique and I were going away together. Finally.

She averted her eyes immediately, and her head went down as she walked away with haste. Was she avoiding me? Lunch probably upset her. She heard some not so great things. Something I'll have to figure out how to fix.

Fuck. I had put her into a stupid situation. At least she hadn't found out *everything* yet.

I returned to my stool and pushed on singing and working, pretending it didn't bother me. Could it get any worse?

"Miss Reilly," M. LeBlanc called out.

Jesus.

My body tensed. I was not in the mood for bullshit. The managers only talked to me when they wanted something. Usually something to do with Philippe.

I met the mustache first, then his eyes. M. Fournier wasn't far behind. *Did they ever go anywhere without the other? Seriously.*

"Just the woman I wanted to see," M. LeBlanc said. "I didn't know you could sing. Very pretty. Perhaps you should consider ensemble for our next production."

Sweet talk. Great.

"I've been taking lessons, Monsieur. What can I do for you?"

"Would you happen to know where we can find Comte de Chagny? Someone said they saw him around. We thought perhaps he came to see you."

I rubbed my temple and groaned again. "I have no idea. Nor do I care."

"We have to keep him happy, Ms. Reilly. He's the biggest donor we have and he likes you."

"You know. I would like you to stop trying to hook me up with Philippe. We do not like each other. And I have someone. He wouldn't like it either."

M. LeBlanc's eyes shifted away. "Well, if you see him, could you…?"

"Yeah, sure."

Maybe I should have told them exactly who my *someone* was. Might keep them off my back in the future.

I blew the wood dust from the large cross and laid it down for painting. My favorite part of the fabrication process.

"I thought they'd never leave," Philippe said, stepping out from behind a large wardrobe crate.

A literal growl rolled through my chest at his voice.

First Christine won't talk to me. The managers won't leave me alone, and now this. Maybe I should have taken Erique up on his offer to quit.

He scampered over to me as if we were school friends.

"I guess you already know that the managers are looking for you," I said, searching for my bandana. Paint fumes were not going to do me in. Unlike my irritation.

"They always are. It's quite annoying really," he said. "Must be the upcoming campaign. I'm mulling the idea of holding it here, and ever since they caught wind, I haven't been able to get rid of them."

"Really?" *Erique was going to love this. I'm going to enjoy watching it, too.* "Maybe you should."

Paying him no mind, I grabbed my paint brush and dipped it into the white paint.

"What is it that you're doing?" he asked.

Did he not have eyes? I did and I rolled mine. "I'm repairing this set piece. The other one shattered during a rehearsal."

"Hm. That sounds *enjoyable*," he said, his upper lip pulling back like he smelled something awful.

"It is. What do you want, Philippe?"

He stepped closer, fidgeting with some rags on the table, dropping one and rubbing his fingers in disgust. "Would you join me for lunch?"

"Thank you. But, I think it's best you just be on your way. I have work to do," I said, keeping my eyes on my brush strokes.

"Well. I shan't get you into trouble. I promise." His quick change to playfulness lately made me uneasy.

"It's not the managers I'm worried about. And really, I don't want to."

Chapter XXXIII

Just because I couldn't feel Erique, didn't mean he wasn't hanging around somewhere, watching.

"I would like the chance to talk with you. If you are displeased with our meeting, I will never ask you again." Regardless of Philippe's lightness, there was an undertone of displeasure in his words.

I sighed, shrugging. "Sure. Ok." At least this was a chance to finally get rid of him in an adult manner.

We walked down the hallway towards the salon. The only place to get hot and ready food in the *Garnier*.

It was actually my first time in the *salon*. Pretty much as I thought it'd be. Decorated in reds and golds like the front of the house. A stairway that led to what I assumed were the rooms they did their business in, were.

Even a small stage, where the show went on after hours.

The bartender met us at the booth Philippe had led us to.

"I ordered for us. I hope that is alright," he said.

Actually it's not. Part of why I don't like you.

"I really wasn't hungry," I said, scratching my temple, trying to figure out where to start. "Look I--"

"I fear there must be apologies made," he said. "My behavior since our first encounter has seemed to put you off to my friendship."

"Um…"

"Truth be told, it had been a long time since I danced. In many years, I haven't found myself enjoying the company of another, until now. It was bothersome to say the least when you were stolen away once again." There was a realness in his eyes. What a weird thing to see for the first time.

"Well, we all need to let loose sometimes," I said. "I did want to talk to you though."

"As do I," he said, leaning forward. "I am worried for you." The warmth in his eyes was gone again. Or maybe it was just the context of the conversation we were about to have.

"For me?" I said, surprised. It was laughable. He had no idea what to be worried about.

"I've spent the past few days inquiring about this *Erique Leroux*," he said. I cringed hearing the false last name I'd given Erique in a moment of panic. "It seems he's a ghost. Not one contractor, architect, nor the other opera houses have heard of him."

My blood ran cold and the color left my face. "Why did you do that?"

"Because despite my better judgment, I care about you."

I thought he'd just be jealous for a moment and then move on. Apparently not. If I hadn't danced with him, this wouldn't have even been a thing.

I pulled back my hands as Philippe tried taking them from across the table and got out of the booth just as fast. Philippe mirrored my movements. "No one knew the name. I spoke to several people. There is no record of any Erique by any name on any building in Paris. Not in design nor erection," he said.

"There wouldn't be. That's what it means to be a silent partner."

"Convenient, don't you think? For someone to hide their genius is absurd."

I glanced around for a shadow that didn't belong. This day was getting shittier by the moment. I could only hope Erique didn't get involved.

"I'm sorry I didn't just blatantly say it before. I was hoping you'd just get it because you seem smart." I ignored the dismay on his face as I spoke. "I have no interest in you. At all. And I wish you'd stop doing whatever it is you're doing. You can say you rejected me. That I'm so broken. Too old. Whatever. I don't care–"

"Do you not care for your safety?" he said, squeezing my arms.

"What's it matter to you? Really? We're not even friends. We've barely spoken," I said. "Men like you want pretty housewives and children to neglect. I don't want any of that. And if it helps, I can't even have children. Which is great for me, but not for someone who wants them."

"That won't matter," he said. His words were empty compared to before. It was frustrating to say the least.

"You're not hearing me on purpose, Philippe! Just leave me be!"

He yanked my arm as I stepped away to leave, pulling me against him. "What if I love you despite all that?" he said.

"I'd know you were lying."

With no warning, his lips pressed harshly to mine. I may be very angry with him, but he just signed his own death certificate.

Chapter XXXIII

I pushed him away and slapped him across the face, shocking even myself. "Don't come near me again!" I spit.

He stiffened, his eyes burning with resentment and humiliation. A dangerous place for a man's fragile mind.

Divine was my paint splotched angel as she stormed through the door and out of sight.

Where I should rejoice in her claim of me, in the blessing it was with knowledge this curse would not be passed on when we finally joined together internally, I was left with scalding fury. Blood boiled and threatened to eat through this wicked flesh and the fabrics it was wrapped in.

The *Ghost* seethed with hatred beyond any it had felt before. My hands throbbed with stinging as I gripped my lasso tighter watching the swine attempt recovery after such a beautiful rejection.

Now she knows you, vermin.

Shrieks would ring from the bar maiden and others that infested this place when my rope looped around the wounded buffoon's neck if I were to burst from my hiding. He would be off his feet without a second thought as I yanked him around for all to see in punishment for the heinous act he had committed. This soul would enjoy sounds of his attempt for air and relief as the edge of every step dug into him while I dragged his worthless body up the stairway. I would find reprieve in seclusion within one of the many rooms to unleash every vile thought searing in my mind.

Or not.

"What are you all looking at?" *le Comte de Vermin* spit, throwing himself back into the booth. "Come here!" he shouted at the bar maiden.

Attention drawn to the Ghost now would be unwanted in such a way. Difficult to maintain the shroud of mystery and elusiveness if I were to pull such a stunt. Then there was my Melody.

'It is not just the Ghost who wishes retaliation,' the *Ghost* said.

I slid back into the wall and rushed the passage nearest the woman behind the bar. With eyes still on the commotion, not one pair noticed an arm reaching out to place a small purse of coin on the ledge of the bar top.

"Take the Count to room one. Leave him there," I ordered the barmaid so that only she would hear. The girl's frightened eyes landed on the payment. "Lock the door behind your departure."

She took it, jamming it between her breasts and sauntered over to the vile thing.

Stale air rushed over me swiftly as I cut through it, nearing my destination. This moment held my imagination many times. To finally witness light leaving his treacherous eyes at my hand. The thought enamored me.

I nearly flew up the ladder to the second floor. The lasso pulled tighter around my hand as I eagerly closed in on the room.

The snake waited like a sacrifice within the small day room. Lips which dared to touch the flesh of my angel, ravished the woman that would bring him to his death like a pig at a trough, as if rewarded for his sins.

"One moment, Monsieur," she said playfully and opened the door. "Be good."

A signature thing my noose may have been, I slipped the lasso back into the pocket of my trousers and readied my hands. Twice now I would use these killer's hands as intended.

"So good of you to come, Monsieur," I said.

The rat had no time before my hands clamped around his neck. Rejoiced was my heart when his feet lifted from the safety of the floor and kicked about.

One could only hope something had broken when his back hit the door.

"She told you no and you touched her anyway. You touched what was mine," I spit into his *pretty* face.

"You can't… kill me," he said, clawing, trying to reach for my false face. "You can't…"

My grip around his neck tightened. I was almost there. The point of no return. I would never again have this snake slither his way into a space he didn't belong.

"She'll know…" he sputtered as he turned blue.

Chapter XXXIII

My beautiful Melody. The look in her eyes had she found out. For her to look at me as if I were still the monster the world said of me.

My Melody would be my undoing.

Hate rumbled in my chest, wracking against the bones that housed it, tearing through my throat as I roared into his face and loosened my grip.

The cretin grabbed the handle, coughing and gasping for air as he tried to escape.

"Not so fast," I growled, catching him again and slamming his useless body into a nearby chair.

Death may not have intended to visit any longer, but he would instill a fear like the rat had never known.

"Guess it wasn't a costume," Philippe said. A harsh rasp in his voice from the crushed windpipe. "The famous 'Opera Ghost', I presume."

Depraved fingers entwined within the greasy strands of his hair with force as I yanked back. "She refuses you, yet you keep crawling from the sewers. Do you not take warning? The lady does not want you."

"Are you the reason my carriage wheels suddenly came off last night?" he asked.

"Answer me. Why do you want her so much?"

"I would give her life *purpose*," he struggled to say.

"You try my patience, vermin," I said, dragging his head back again.

"Does she know it's you?" The smugness of his face begged to be peeled from the muscle it was attached and fed to him. "It's only a matter of time until she sees who you really are. Killing stagehands and chorus girls."

"You beg to be added to a list longer than you would know," I said. "If you touch her again, I will disembowel you and hang you from Mozart for all to see."

"Then her love for you would die."

"You know nothing of love." The lasso kept in my pocket, found its way into my hands, savoring the moment having been returned to its rightful place.

His frightened hands slapped, and spit spewed as the rope tightened around his noble neck.

"And you will keep your politics and diabolical self from *my* opera!"

I seethed into pulsing ears.

Against my own desires, I would leave him unconscious and go to my Melody. This changed man would drop to his knees, mouth and hands at the ready, and reward her for never needing a reminder of where she belonged.

Chapter XXXIV

Melody

The brisk evening air nipped at my face and it was the best feeling in the world. If you looked up the word "excitement" in the dictionary, you wouldn't find a picture of me. In fact, you probably wouldn't be able to find me anywhere in there. You would think as a writer I could come up with one. There were no words for a moment like this.

His soothing, warm voice caressed my ears as we turned down onto a well-maintained driveway. "We've arrived, love." Decorative stones lined along the gravel drive, but it was giant trees that had me entranced. They went on as far as the eye could see. And suddenly, amongst all the good things, I missed home.

Washington was always green. No matter the time of year. For a short time, I was home, and Erique was with me.

"How far from town are we?" I asked.

"Not far. Why is it that you ask?"

"I'm getting a bit hungry."

"We should have food inside and other supplies as we arrive. However, my dear, if nothing is to your liking, I will have the delivery boy change the order tomorrow."

Why was I not surprised that he'd already thought of it. He has ruined any other man for me. If I ever went home, I'd never recover.

God, I wanted him.

"Maybe sometime this trip we can go get food together…" I said.

He didn't answer, which was surprising, but his expression said it all. I was pushing it.

The moonlight was enough to see the small cottage and matching barn coming into sight. It was something out of those paintings you find at the secondhand store.

We weren't going to be found out here. No managers. No counts. No murder. Nothing.

"Oh Erique. It's perfect!" I said. Before the carriage came to a complete stop, I opened the door and jumped out onto the grass.

"Melody!" Erique shouted, pulling the carriage to a stop.

I wanted to cry and scream and shout and sing as my lungs expanded, taking in the fresh forest air. Not a scent of Paris anywhere.

"You could not have waited a moment longer? You are mad, woman," he said, wrapping his arms around my midsection and placing a heavy kiss on my neck.

Lost in the freedom of our new temporary world. My head rolled back, and my lids closed. "Do you feel that?" I asked.

"I feel you."

"It's so quiet here, Erique. But the good quiet," I said. "The air is clean. And we're safe."

"I will put Ceasar in the stalls and meet you inside," he said, then gave me a kiss as if it were the first time.

The cabin was smaller than our home under the theater. A cold and stagnant studio layout. Perfect for just the two of us. And at the center, against the wall, a beautiful stone fireplace.

Just as I got the fire going, Erique emerged from outside, both suitcases in hand. "I will get the fire, dear," he said, setting the bags near the bed.

"You can't do everything. Plus, it's already done. Now you can come and warm up right away."

"I do not need a fire to warm this body when I have you," he said stalking towards me with the most mischievous look in his eyes.

Chapter XXXIV

Empty was the space where she rested her weary head as I reached for her.

My eyes snapped open to confirm my worst fear. She had taken the opportunity to run from me in the night.

Daylight, though dampened by the surrounding foliage, now beamed through the opened windows.

'She would not do that to us. Not now. Not after everything,' the *Ghost* said as I hurried for a shirt.

Without thought, I ripped the door open but halted before stepping through its threshold.

Clenched fists fidgeted as they hovered above the stream of soft light. A kiss from the sun had long been a memory. Would it burn or merely sting as hot water did?

I pushed into the filtered light glancing every which way. Searching for evidence of her absence.

I ran to the barn. Ribs threatened to burst open while my heart pounded behind them. Cesar still roamed in his stall flicking his tail around without a care in the universe, feeding on freshly lofted hay.

I pushed the hair back from my false face, calming what nerves I could, and stepped out into the shade again.

Perhaps he was right. "Then where have you gone, little mouse?" I whispered into the trees.

Like a siren, her voice called to me. My ears perked in the direction its sweet sound came.

Down a forgotten path I followed, still uncertain if this was wishful thinking or was it truly her I heard.

Sun peeked through swaying branches. Twigs snapped beneath my bare feet. Leaves rustled as the light breeze caressed my exposed flesh, as these fingers brushed along low hanging foliage and wildflowers. It was a dream I had written about once.

From the tree line, I watched. There she was, basking in the sun as she stared from the safety of the shore. The wind flicked her hair and whipped the fabrics of her skirt about, carrying a song I did not know, but lovely on her lips nonetheless. This angel had come far.

Fear disabled me as my eyes cut down to the direct line where the true sun started. Bright and terrifying as any nightmare.

With trembling hands, I extended one slowly into the unknown, retracting it almost immediately as the earth's light stung.

Hesitation held me as I contemplated another try.

"Erique?"

My gaze sliced up at the sound of my name.

Even from where I stood, love glistened in her eyes as the sun kissed every bare part of her. Fear would be no more as my foot pressed into the sandy shore of the lake. These eyes shied away, attempting to adjust to light they had not endured since childhood.

Light in my arms, she was, as I embraced her. Every burning step a forgotten memory. Adoration grew in twinkling eyes as I twirled her about. Just as I envisioned.

My heart swelled with glee and the overwhelmingness that this moment was. Never did I think I would bask as she does. For the light of day caressed my flesh in the same warmth.

"Good morning, my babe," she said, overflowing with dawn's embrace. Warm hands held my cheeks and eyes searched my face. "Are you alright?" she asked.

"I… Everything is… beautiful."

With a gentle swipe of her thumb, she removed the escaped joy resting in the seal of my mask.

After a short while, she accompanied me for our morning meal. Happiness shone on her face after every bite as she gazed outside. I would harness daylight and bring it home with us if only to continue this sight.

"I was thinking that we could work out by the lake. If that was ok."

The light would take some getting used to, but I didn't want this time away to be about work. Even if we enjoyed it.

"Actually," I said, clearing my throat. "I was hoping you would like to go for a walk around the lake?"

Her eyes widened in surprise at the suggestion, and it melted me. A smile spread slowly across her dimple imprinted face.

"Would you like that?" I asked.

A quick happy little nod from her was all I needed.

Chapter XXXIV

"Warm by the fire, my love," Erique whispered, and walked to his bag.

I had brought the basket of random food we had left from the walk with me. Cheese, bread, wine, and salami. Perfect time for snacking.

I never thought this day would come. We had walked the lake and it took forever. It was only because it got cold that we even came back inside.

"I thought we could read tonight," he said, joining me on the rug by the fire. "It has been a while since we've read and I thought on this special evening, it was only appropriate."

I glanced the small worn cover over. *Frankenstein.*

"Are you sure you want to read it? It's so sad."

He nodded. "Nothing would please me more." There was an extra softness to his answer. Like he'd been waiting for this all day.

I pulled a piece of salami and nibbled on it as we settled in.

"I will start," he said. "*You will rejoice to hear that no disaster has accompanied the commencement of an enterprise which you have regarded with such evil forebodings...*"

His reading voice always soothed me. Sent me into a place of fantasy and safety. All while setting me ablaze with unbridled want.

It didn't even have to be a song for his words to sound like music. How could someone be so blessed with such a thing?

Yes, I missed movies and music. But admittedly, over the past few months, I hardly noticed the absence, at least when I had time with Erique.

I just know that I was calm with him.

Soft orange light flickered against his mask, and lips moved smoothly as he read. Tempting as it was to stop him, I tortured myself, and held off. Even though I was a little frustrated.

Believe me when I said the things he did to me were enough. I was the luckiest girl in the world. But my need for him was greedier than logic. And the reaction my body was already having at just mere thoughts of him and I together…

"Are you listening, my angel?" he asked, his voice filled with knowing.

I hoped the fire hid the heat blushing across my cheeks, because they burned hot. "Yes, of course," I answered. "You know how I love to listen to you read."

"By the look in your eyes, I thought perhaps you were lost in some sinful thought," he smirked. "And I would hate to have to put down this book and remind you of what trouble those kinds of thoughts can cause."

My heart raced as I bit my lip. "That would be so horrible, yes. Continue please."

Of course, the delicious thoughts of us together started back up as soon as those captivating eyes returned to the pages.

This time away was going to be it. We were totally going to do this thing. I mean, even Erique's stubborn ass could only wait so long. Right? He'd been pining almost five months already. Before we were even a thing.

"Ok, that's enough for tonight," he said. Erique set the book aside quickly and closed the short distance between us.

"We aren't even through the first chapter," I yelped as his kiss scorched me.

"There's always tomorrow."

His body was on a mission that would not be detoured now. He grabbed me by the nape, massaging as we melted into the other.

"I thought it was going to be you this time. You radiate need, so loudly, my dear. Concentration was impossible. It is I that has lost this time," he said.

Our tongues danced together as he laid me onto the rug beneath us. Was this it? Was he finally going to allow us to connect? This had already been a magical day. With Erique walking in the sun's light and all.

But my wonderful Erique stuck to his conviction and fucked me with his mouth again, forcing me into a soul rocking orgasm. Though, by the look on his face, you would have sworn it was his.

In between feverish kisses, telling me it wasn't near over, he sang sweet words, *"I love you. I love you so much."*

Since we'd left the *Garnier*, he'd been more affectionate than usual. He was already very affectionate. I loved it, but it was a lot.

With strength only desire could wield, I rolled us over, forcing

Chapter XXXIV

Erique onto his back as I straddled his pelvis.

I moaned at the pressure of his hidden, hardened desire as it pressed against my ultra-sensitive clit. Rocking against him, I undid his shirt and kissed his mouth every time he tried to speak. My hand ran through the mix of silky chest hair and scarring, down to his abdomen.

"*My Heart…*" he panted into my mouth.

"I respect your boundaries, you wonderful man. But I *need* to give you something," I said desperately.

"I don't need…" he started.

Ravenous was her mouth on mine again, too quickly to form words or thought. A burst of white light blinded my mind as she mauled the fastenings of my trousers.

My beautiful angel made it harder every day with her insatiable need for me. Only making mine for her worse. Weakly, I tried to raise a hand to stop her, so I told myself. She pressed my wrist to the floor. "Do you want me to stop?" she asked. "I will. I just…"

I shook my head meekly side to side. We would be one soon. Together for all eternity. It did not matter anymore.

A whimper deep within my chest rolled to an escape as my cock sprang free of its blasted cell. I trembled beneath her like newly born fawn learning to walk.

Wide, sparkling, brown eyes stared at the pulsating thing in her hand. Hope begged I was enough. A wet tongue ran across her swollen bottom lip, and I suddenly wished those swollen lips were around this rotten flesh which ached for her.

Gentle fingers ran along the sensitive length of my want as I twitched and shivered under foreign touch. Pleasure pulled my head back, but disbelief forced eyes on her. This cherub's face lowered next to my straining cock. Involuntary were the sounds resonating from within my throat. My eyes slammed shut as she hummed and ran her face along the pillar of flesh, worshiping it like it had given her everything.

My body writhed against my will as stars formed behind my eyes. Lightning bolted and webbed out from the center of my body, begging for release. More intense than any pleasure I'd given myself. "You are… you are more demon than I," I barely managed out.

Never had I enjoyed torture in my life until now. A devilish smirk branded *my heart's* face as she kissed the tip and dug her nails into my chest, then dragged them downward.

"Yes," I cried.

Attempting to prolong climax was proving ineffective. The wetness of her tongue from base to tip had me undone. My back arched and hips rolled against her hands as I grasped the rug to keep me grounded while love stroked me through the body numbing, mind-altering eruption.

The ceiling swirled and my chest heaved, as if breathing for the first time.

Through glazed, sated eyes, I raised myself enough to see over the mess on my abdomen. Glowing light surrounded my Melody as she rested her head on my pelvis. My satiated cock laying across the side of her face.

Divinity was she, as I ran tingling fingers through her soft hair.

Long enough it had waited. It will happen tonight.

Chapter XXXV

Melody

Time, please stand still. Just this once. Not for a second did he take those piercing eyes off me.

"My Love. Come," he said, lacing our fingers and pulling me to him.

I settled into his side as we laid back down in front of the fire. Though I was absolutely dying to get railed by his surprisingly thick, juicy… it meant so much for me to give him that.

Finally, even if it was a little quick.

"Let's go to bed, my babe," I said, stroking his jaw.

"No."

"No? You're so sleepy."

"Let us read some more." He sat up, looking down at me, waiting for my joining.

Dark hair hung around his cheeks. White dress shirt still unbuttoned, showing off his now cleaned body. Silky chest hair glimmered in the flickering light. I was so blinded that I didn't even notice the extent of scarring anymore.

"What are you looking at?" he asked as if he didn't already know how beautiful I found him. He would make me say it. I wouldn't give him the satisfaction.

"Come on" he grinned, patting his hand on his thigh. "It is now your turn to be tortured, my love."

"You're a sadist," I replied and flipped over, laying my head in the lap of the demon that sat at the other end of the rug we'd just defiled.

"And you love it," he said as I settled in. "You love me."

Without warning, Erique's free hand slid up under my skirt and found its rightful place between my thighs.

"You are absolutely soaked," he groaned. "Shall I get you a wash rag? Or should I continue…?" he said, moving his hand slowly against me. "Now, where were we before you so abruptly ended our reading?"

"I…I…you," I stammered.

"Try to pay attention or I'll stop. Do you understand?" he said. His serpents' words slithered into my ears. What a terrible, beautiful man.

He cleared his throat, still running his fingers around all the places that liquefied me. *"These visions faded when I perused, for the first time, those poets whose effusions entranced my soul and lifted it to heaven…"*

***

One amazing, prolonged orgasm later, it was finally my turn to read. I was a bit tired already and a little drained, but Erique was insistent.

"One more. I promise," he said, again.

I was impaled by his steady gaze. Playfulness had left his body and his eyes flicked from mine to the book. It was just starting to get to an intense part of the story. But even he was acting weird. I laughed and took it from him. "You know what happens next, why are you so anxious?"

I opened the book and my smile immediately fell. I short circuited and my limbs went numb. "Erique…" I said, as my stomach clenched tight and panic rioted within.

In the pages of *Frankenstein*, was a hollowed out square that held the bottom half of a circular, red box. Sitting in the center of the box were alternating blue sapphires and white diamonds set in a silver band shimmering in the firelight.

He hadn't been reading. He'd been reciting from memory.

Erique had shifted to his knees before me. Terror and certainty in his warm eyes. I was going to vomit. My heart either was beating too fast

Chapter XXXV

to feel it or it stopped. I was stuck. I couldn't move. "Erique… don't."

Trembling hands took my own shaking hands quickly. Every hope and dream went on for miles in those eyes.

"Peace was a myth. Love, something you had to take. Selflessness was for the weak. This was my mind before you," he said. "In the few moments I held you the night you emerged into my darkness, unbeknownst to me, this fractured mind fell together."

"Erique, stop…" My heartache leaked down my face no matter how hard I tried to hold it back.

This was the cruelest thing possible and it was my fault. I allowed myself to be with this man knowing his feelings for me. In this world I don't belong. It's the most beautiful thing. I think that's the cruelest part of it all. Not once had any proposal before come close to something so simple and perfect. So *wanted*.

"Every note written since that moment has been you. In my denial, I still found you. Your strange, odd ways hold me captivated. I see the world in a new light through your eyes. Certainty holds me knowing I was made for you and you for me. I see you. I have loved you and promise to love you." He pulled the book from my frozen hand and removed the beautiful ring from it. "With that, Melody Amber Reilly, will you do me the greatest honor this creature never thought possible, and allow me to be your husband?"

I was *too* happy. Of course, this would happen. Every millisecond crushed me more. Why did he have to ruin everything? Why did I have to ruin everything?

My shaking hand raised and clamped around his. "I can't. I'm so sorry," I said, choking on my cries.

I couldn't look at him. Never ever had I wanted to hurt him, I loved him.

My lashes were heavy, laced in my own tears, as I finally looked up to find emotion had overtaken his as well.

He lunged at me, catching my arms in his grasp. "Tell me you love me," he cried with desperation, squeezing harder. "Please!"

I held his face as he leaned into my hands, kissing them. "Please tell me you love me, Melody," he begged, and rubbed his cheek against mine.

"Erique, my Erique…" I pleaded through a waterfall of tears. "Do you not see with your own eyes, in your heart, how I feel for you?"

"I need to hear you say it…" he answered. "Why won't you say it?"

Everything inside told me to tell him. To yell it out and take his hand. But it wouldn't come. It couldn't.

His hands dropped from me, and compassion left his eyes.

"You do not love me then?" his voice suddenly low and cold.

"Erique, please don't," I begged, grabbing at him. He shook me free and turned away. "It's not like that at all."

"My patience has run out. No more make believe," he said, then whipped around. "I have stood by as you used my body, mind, and my heart. And yet still you will not love me."

"No… I…" I said, trying to reach out.

His eyes were dull knives as they cut into me and I deserved it. "You what?" he seethed. He stepped forward and grabbed me like he'd never done before. Rough and intent. "You what, Melody?" he growled in my face.

I quaked in his grasp. This was the real him. The first time his anger would be directed towards me. I deserved it, totally, but now I was scared.

It was only a matter of time.

"You really need to see this disease to make your decision? To bear the thought of loving me?" he spit. In a swift movement, he ripped the mask off and threw it aside, shoving the deformity of his face into mine. "Here I am!"

Nothing could have prepared me for what I was looking at. It was horrible. I recoiled but couldn't look away.

The area around his eyes was mostly sunken like he was missing the muscle beneath. A skeleton with skin. What covered most of his face looked as if someone had ripped it off and tried to reattach it blindfolded. I wasn't sure what was from the fire or birth, it was so bad. To my surprise he had a nose, if that was what you wanted to call what was left of it.

"This is the monster you beg to fuck you. Who takes you with this face and these hands, hands that delight in removing life from this world. Look upon this, dear." He laughed. "I am no dashing Count with the wit of a stone, that is for certain. I am a walking, breathing corpse. Decaying

Chapter XXXV

before your eyes. Cold as death's visit. A corpse that loves you more than anything this god forsaken life can offer.

This is what you wanted, needed, to see before you could love me?"

The anguish mixed with rage twisted my heart until it was unrecognizable. This was the cruelest thing I've ever done to someone I cared for.

I tried to look away. Not sure out of fear for his face or the heartbreak we were both enduring.

"Look at me!" he demanded, not giving me a choice. "Do you love me now, Melody? Now that you have seen the real man, the monster beneath the mask? Scream! Fill this cabin, this forest with the voice I have given you!"

Violently shaking within his grip, I stared. What was I going to do?

The rage in those eyes softened and sorrow suddenly took its place. Tears fell, and so did I, when he let go.

From the floor where we read not even minutes ago, I watched as the broken man walked out into the spring night.

Tears stung my cheeks and snot suffocated me. I got caught up in a fantasy and fell in love. I knew it was going to break us and I did it anyway. We were never meant to be.

Without warning I could be gone. Ripped away from the only man I've ever actually loved…

"We are never promised tomorrow," he once said.

Then my sister's words echoed in my mind. *"God himself could literally hand you the man specifically made for you, and tell you 'This is the one' and you would still be like… No thank you. I'll just hide my heart."*

I sniffled back at the memory. "What am I doing?" I said. I was going to be here and have the one person I've always wanted, why the fuck would I throw that away?

I leapt to my feet, searching for his mask. If anyone saw him, it could be trouble and he didn't need any more of that. "AH!" I screamed, finding it underneath the couch.

I rushed through the open door and into the moonlight. It was as bright as daylight.

My head spun trying to pick a direction to go. Maybe out to the water? I would just walk that way until I couldn't anymore. No matter if it was freezing, or that my feet numbed. I was going to find him.

I took a deep breath, hoping to calm everything. I exhaled slowly, trying to keep my head level. That was hard. He was unpredictable.

"...*un giorno Dio mi porterà via e sarò bella e amata...*" I heard his song in the distance.

My chest heaved in a sigh of relief. He was here and alive. I followed the voice through some of the trees towards the lake. It was so faint, but for sure was him.

Breaching the tree line, I listened carefully, honing in on the weak voice that sang.

"...*lei sarà lì ad aspettare e io sarò amato. un giorno sarò amato. fiori e luce del sole. camminare in primavera...*" his voice grew louder as I neared the dying tree.

At the base of the tree, rocking back and forth with his knees to his chest, singing to himself in a language I didn't know, through the most heart wrenching sobs I'd ever heard, was the heartbroken monster of *Le Garnier*.

The sounds he made were devastating. Unbearable. I stepped closer. His hands flew to his face as he recoiled, trying to further hide himself within the tree. "...*mia unica amica. la notte mi amerà solo e i demoni mi abbracceranno. perché non sono degno?...*"

I set the mask in the sand as I kneeled beside him. Gently, I touched his face, trying to get him to look at me. He quieted and looked up through fallen hair. Mournfullest eyes slowly met mine. They told me his whole existence was to see how tortured a soul could be before they broke.

There was so much to say. I didn't know where to start or what should even be said. I froze.

"Go inside" he mumbled, breaking the silence and pulling his head from my hands.

"*We* need to go back inside. It's freezing out here."

Erique let out a low menacing laugh. "What do you care what happens to this creature? Just leave me, Melody."

With a gentle hand and deep breath of courage, I pushed the hair away from the twisted face he hid. "How could you ever think for one moment that I don't love you?"

Chapter XXXV

Erique looked away and clenched his jaw. His eyes seemed uncertain now.

"Of course, I love you, Erique," I said. The words rolled off my tongue as if they were meant to be there and my lungs expanded as though I'd just breached the surface after nearly drowning.

To finally admit it. Wow.

"You love me?" he asked, sitting in wait to hear those words he'd longed to hear his entire life.

"Yeah. More than you could ever know. Every day I am in disbelief that this has happened to me."

"Then why?" he asked, exasperated.

"Because I'm a scared piece of shit that's afraid of what it will mean."

Erique moved quickly, pulling me into his lap. "Say it again," he urged, holding me tightly. Searching my face for a hint of a lie.

"I'm a scared piece of…"

"No. Not that."

"I love you," I repeated, a smile spreading across my face.

This time when he cried, I wasn't sure what it was for.

"I love you. I love you. I love you so much," he declared into my neck. I could hardly breathe with the strength in his hug and overbearing care that radiated from him. "Why could you not tell me, Melody?" he finally asked, cupping my face in his hand. "It could not have simply been fear. There is much you have not said."

This was it. This was the truth time. When I didn't think my chest could ache anymore, it did at the thought of losing him again.

"Please know that it wasn't anything to do with you. I told you once upon a time those words were only used to hurt. It was that and I was afraid that if I admitted, said those words, then it would mean I'll never go home."

The future returned to his eyes once again. It almost stopped me. "I will take you home. I will buy the next tickets to the Americas. I will go with you. You can show me New York. I do not care where I am. You love me. That is all that matters."

"I don't want to go home!" I said, surprised by my own admission. This wasn't the truth I was going to tell him. Nor myself. Just then I realized what I'd actually been lying about.

It wasn't even that I wouldn't be able to go home. It's that I hadn't wanted to. And admitting my feelings would have cemented it.

I glanced around, trying to collect my thoughts as curious eyes filled with longing bore into me.

"I… I'm such a terrible person," I said.

"No, you are the furthest from any variation," he said, and kissed my forehead.

"The truth is, even though everything's been scary as hell since I got here, and it smells awful… at home all I did was work and take care of my mom, because no one else would. It's the only reason I was trying to get home. Not because I had such a great life to go back to, but because I still feel the immense guilt for wishing she was gone. So I didn't have to do it anymore." He ran his fingers through my hair, the glimmer of moonlight danced in his eyes as he caught my glance. "I can breathe here, even though it smells like ass. I don't have to spend every waking moment taking care of someone who's mean and miserable all the time. Who's completely…" *Useless. Oh god I'm shit.* "I haven't had to put my life on hold. And you… I've done things I've only dreamt of. I couldn't have done this with the life I had. I miss her. But I've been so relieved."

"How does wanting for yourself make you a terrible person?"

"I'm her daughter. I should want to help her…"

"You do not think she would want a good life for her child? Where her child's dreams come true? Where she has undying love and career?"

I stared at him dumbfounded. It had never occurred to me for a moment that it was an option for me.

Oh my God, he was right though. I knew telling her that I was miserable would kill her. If she knew I threw away something resembling perfect, she'd beat me.

Any worry I had before of Erique ever leaving me, becoming bored of me, had all vanished as well. I was here right now in this moment.

Like the weight of the universe had been lifted from my shoulders, I exhaled, and I was lighter than a feather.

I'll continue to write home. But I wasn't going to feel the guilt anymore.

"So, this is what you have been holding back from me all this time?" he asked, continuing to stroke my hair.

Chapter XXXV

I nodded like a child finally fessing to something they did. "Mostly."

"Hmm."

"There's more. Not emotionally. But, logistically," I said. "It's super complicated. I don't even know how to tell you about that."

"If I do not understand, make me understand," he said, with pleading eyes.

Taking his cold hands in mine, I kissed them. "I love you. I just wanted to say that. In case I never got to again…" I said. "Ok, I have to stand up for this. I can't be right here or I won't be able to do it."

"My Love?"

Not sure if it was the cold or the nerves making me shake, but it was getting painful. I turned back to the man who'd just returned the mask to his face, and stood up, knocking dirt from his trousers.

"I fell in love with *you*, Erique, without a last name, remember that when I tell you this. It wasn't the *Phantom* or the fantasy of it all. You and your kindness. Friendship. Love. Passion. Weirdness. Everything that you are and have become since I've known you. That's who I love."

I wanted to remember him in this moment. Because even the "crazy" Phantom wasn't going to believe me.

Chapter XXXVI

Melody

Universe, give me strength. The hardest part was already done, right? "You don't have to wear that," I said. "Your face doesn't scare me."

"Do not detour. Will you please say whatever it is that haunts you enough to keep your love from me. Your silence unsettles," he said.

"Do you remember when I told you this wasn't my story?" I asked.

He nodded.

It shouldn't be this hard to tell him this. I groaned, staring into worried eyes that I loved so much. "I tried not to love you, but you've been everything I've ever dreamt about in a partner. Well mostly. I could have lived without the murder and stalking. But everything else… how could I not? The thing is you weren't supposed to be real."

He took my hands, placing a kiss on each. "You saved me from darkness. I owe you my soul," he said.

"No, stop." I pulled my hands from his. I couldn't allow him to lure me into his safety zone. "Please, let me do this or I won't, and it may be worse later."

I shook a bit of the cold off and looked out over the rippling water. It was still so peaceful. But my stupid heartbeat was ruining it. *I can do this.*

"You said it yourself, I'm a bit odd, strange. How I speak. How I was dressed when you first met me. The jobs I've had. Why I won't talk much about myself."

"Yes."

"And that I just randomly woke up here. Which I'm sure you never really believed."

"Yes."

"Wait. If you didn't think I was telling the truth, then why—"

His concerned eyes softened. "Because it was the only thing you were untruthful about."

I sighed. *Damn it.*

"I…" my heart skipped and the breath in my lungs did very little to ease the anxiety. I closed my eyes and forced it out. "I was born in 1988. A little over a hundred years from now." I ignored the dumbfounded look in his eyes and continued. "I went into the restroom of the Majestic theater January 17, 2023. And walked out into the *Palais Garnier* January 17, 1880. I have no idea what happened or exactly how I got here. At first, I thought maybe I was hallucinating and dying somewhere. Or aliens. Or something. Not a time travel thing. Alternative timeline. Nothing like that."

"The cold is setting in; we must get you inside," he said, attempting to usher me back towards the cabin.

"No. Erique, you need to listen," I said, stopping him. "You want to know why I couldn't tell you I loved you. I'm telling you now. I tried to convince myself that if I didn't tell you, then it would hurt less when I was ripped back to my time or whatever. That it wouldn't kill me to live without you--"

"What you are saying does not make sense, love."

"Try being the one living it! None of this makes sense," I said. "I don't know what this is. Maybe I was sent here to find you. I don't know. But the Phantom's not supposed to be real."

"You have said this before. What do you mean I was not supposed to be real?" he asked.

I rubbed my temples and groaned again. Maybe this was the part I didn't want to actually tell him.

"The mask you wore?" he asked, as if the lightbulb went off. "The ink in your leg?"

I shrugged, a little embarrassed. "The Phantom of the Opera is my favorite musical."

"The *monster* in that story, is me?"

"Well. Yeah. He is you, a man. But you're not him. Not really. Or maybe you are."

His eyes shifted, as if searching his mind for something. "Tell me," he said, with deep curiosity.

Against my better judgment, I did.

"...Ah. Leroux. Why does that sound familiar?" he asked, but it wasn't a question. It was accusing in a playful manner.

For someone being told that they're a fable, a warning, and that in most of the stories they're evil, cruel and cold-blooded, he held his composure well. Not to mention that he died at the end of more than half. It was a lot to take in. I couldn't imagine it.

"Knowing these tales, you still love me?" he asked.

"You're not him," I answered. "Do you still love me? Knowing what you know now?"

I didn't have to wait before his cool hands cupped my face. Caring eyes narrowed in on mine, piercing and intent. "I spent a lifetime waiting for you. Thinking you were only a dream cruelly given to torture me. Every moment I'm gifted with you was worth the risk of losing you. With or without the fantastical intervening. I could just as easily be taken from you. Though only death himself could take me from your side."

I melted into his warm hands, as his hot breath heated my face. "I always thought you'd be cold," I said.

"Impossible when my heart beats so wildly in your presence."

"I never needed you, Erique. But I wanted you. I wasn't supposed to want you."

"That is because you are as mad as I," he said. A soft laugh crept out as he wiped my tears away. "Only an unwell person would fall in love with a man in the walls," he added. "I would not have done it."

"Shut up," I said, and playfully backhanded his chest.

"Down the rabbit hole you fell. Into the den of the Chesire you stay. You are Alice, after all," he cooed.

Chapter XXXVI

I laughed. A good, deep, belly-rumbling, soul-relieving, laugh. This was my wonderland and I didn't want to leave. Even if I did miss my music. Or modern medicine. And tampons. And my mother and sister.

I laced my arm around Erique's as we stared out over the water. No breeze. Just the calm life of nature and healing.

"We should go back inside," he said, as I shivered.

I nodded in agreement and took his hand.

"But first. Now there are no more secrets between us?"

I shook my head.

"Good," he said and reached into his pocket.

"Before you say anything. I have to stand my ground on marriage. Even at home, it was never something I wanted. Men change after you say yes. I don't want to feel like that again. I like who you are."

"Well, as you know," he said, pulling the ring from his pocket. "I am not like most men." He slipped the beautiful, glistening metal onto my finger. "This is a promise. A promise from me to you and you to me. We will only grow together if that is what you want."

Shaking, terrified and cold, of even this level of commitment from a man that I truly loved, I nodded. "Ok." I looked at the ring again and only felt joy. "Can we get one for you?"

His eyes lit up, "You would want that?"

"I want anyone that runs into you to know that you are loved, as I am."

Oh my God, I'm so gushy.

"Then tomorrow we will go into town, and it should be so."

"Really?" I said, not believing my ears.

He nodded.

"My mom and sister would shit themselves if they knew I even went this far. Figuratively speaking of course."

He grimaced at my crude analogy. "I would hope so," he said.

The flickering embers may have warmed us, but it was love's unbridled passion which burned us with the power of the sun.

Cold was a distant memory as we fell onto our bed. Protest I did not, as she clawed at the fabrics covering this flesh she craved to touch. Onto my knees I pushed, straddling wanting thighs as she shifted upright.

Glowing was she with fire, passion, and love as glistening brown eyes stared up. Desire hardened intensely at sight of her. This would be the first time I would bare myself completely. Not only has she known my mind and soul, but now she would know me in body whole.

Eager wanting hands pushed apart my unbuttoned shirt, gripping at my anxious flesh. Fragmented were my thoughts when she moved from my hips over the small, rounded stomach that she adored so much, and up through the dark hair of my chest.

"Are you ok?" she asked.

Placing a kiss in the palm of her reaching hand, I nodded against the wedding band she wore. "Yes," I said in a broken whisper. I ran my trembling hand through her hair and entwined the strands within my fingers. "Say it again," I commanded softly, pulling her head back enough to hover above her cherub face.

Fingers dug into the meaty flesh just below my back as she pulled my body closer. Desire strained within the confines of my trousers against her chest. Images of my cock laying against her face made it strain harder.

"I love you, Erique." Warmness filled every syllable and continued to brand upon my reborn soul.

"Good," I hummed and stepped onto the floor. "Now, to your knees and turn around."

With wide, captivated and curious eyes, she did as instructed. I rejoined behind her, pulling her to me. This body fit so well within the contours of her backside. "That's my good wife," I said.

"What—"

Lips ravished her neck, forcing her to forget what would ruin her mind. As my imprisoned cock pressed against her backside, hands explored the curve of her waist. The round of her belly. Down under the skirt of her dress to explore her thighs. Into the bodice of her gown to caress budding nipples.

My heart thumped wildly when her frenzied hand entwined within the thick of my hair and tugged.

I moaned, and bit into the crook of her neck eliciting the same response.

Heaven and Hell had novels long of my begging for her. This woman believed intervention brought her to me across time. If true, then even God answered a monster's prayer once.

With intent, our tongues twisted around the others, and lips became one. The pressure of her. The smell of her. Every moment made real.

Unwilling to let her out of her dress just yet, no matter how I wanted her, I traveled up her thigh as she clamped my hand with hers, urging it to take its rightful place at her warm center.

My Melody gasped when the heat of her core scorched my fingers as I pushed into her. "That is it, my angel," I said.

The tantalizing tension around my fingers while she rode my hand, tightened as she bucked, riding out her climax. Trembling and twitching until she stopped me.

She lay against my chest, catching her breath. Hungry, glazed eyes shifted to mine, wanting. Needing. Craving.

Nearly ripping the gown from her, I tossed it into oblivion. I would buy her a new one if needed. My own desire even stronger and unwavering in the moments between turning and laying her back onto the bed.

Starved mouths found the other as we tore the shirt from my body and tossed it without thought. The wild, primal hunger in her gaze reflected my own as I prepared myself above her.

Like a predator salivating over the lamb. This man took in every curve of her luscious body. Heaving breasts. Hips. Belly. Wanting, strong thighs spread open, resting at my sides.

With unbearable care, she ran a hand along the physical distortion of my soul. I liquefied with every inch she moved, traveling up my chest and to my jaw.

Fingertips hooked beneath the side of my mask, and I was too intoxicated to stop her.

My heart seized. Soul screamed. In terror I stared down at this naked angel below me as she sat my false face to the side. Not to run or shy away. Not one hint in her dazzling eyes that this decayed flesh disgusted her.

'She is ours. Love her. Our Melody. Your Melody only wants this life with you.

Be not afraid anymore,' the *Ghost* said. *'She sees you and beyond.'*

Engulfed were our bodies by the fires of love and passion. Longing ached and throbbed as I lay against her, giving every area the attention that made her mine.

My trousers joined the other discarded clothing, as her moans cemented me to her. Soft and hardened was her nipple in my mouth as my tongue flicked it. Such an act every time nearly sent me into climax.

The room filled with sounds of ecstasy as my cock slid against the source of her pleasure. Both hers and mine. The overwhelming beauty threatened escape of my eyes, yet I would not stop. To see her in such a light, this woman would never be loved in darkness again. Ever.

She clawed at me, trying to guide me into her. Like a fawn, I trembled pressing myself to the path which would bring us together. The heat of her radiated with welcome.

This would be ours. Never to be shared with another. Never to be tainted by cruelty or heartache. Forever ours eternally.

"Within you, I see what life is supposed to be," I said.

A smile which would weaken my knees, only had me wishing those lips were against mine once again. Yet, I halt.

Do I hesitate to prepare her or myself?

'Perhaps three fingers should have been used,' the *Ghost* teased.

To hurt her would be the end. To do it wrong should not scare. Would I deny us because fears teeth still had hold on the tuft of my neck?

Everything else we have done had been easy and beautiful. She guided me in unknown territory and praised me for my achievements.

No. This will be everything we want it to be.

Rubbing myself against her wanting flesh, practicing the motions that seem to come naturally, she gripped my back, beckoning me closer still.

"Please," she whined.

Melded were our lips as I pushed into her. Finally, I had succumbed to the searing need that had been building for my entire consciousness.

In unison, our breaths hitched, catching the other's gasp. Stars collided. Explosions ran down my spine. Collapse threatened these limbs as she molded around me.

Chapter XXXVI

"Oh, my dearest God," I whimpered.

"Oh fuck, Erique," she cried. "You're so thick. I almost can't even…"

I took her mouth again, hoping to stop whatever could potentially end our consummation a little quicker than I liked.

Further into her I moved, worshiping every second. She moaned something guttural as my body pressed against her. Slowly, I dragged my cock back. The precipice dangerously close as her nails dug into my flesh. Which I wished she would tear from my bones.

This was heaven. I had been granted such paradise after all my atrocities and I would not take it for granted.

Our emotions whirled within our kiss. Deep and profound. Connection finally in whole. Lost was I in the depths of our embrace, I had almost forgotten we had joined. Until she moved.

I rocked slowly against her, dragging myself to the tip, exposing the body of my cock that she had so desperately begged for and was now owned by.

But my need. My own insatiable need for her grew impatient, and I quickened my pace.

Sweat glistened over our burning skin. Breathy, loving words sang from us both while I moved, rolling deeper with every thrust.

"You are a home I never knew, my Melody," I said between staggered breaths. "Safe and warm. So safe and warm."

Never would I hold her off again. Deny either of us. Every night. Every day, whenever we wished, this would be us.

"Erique… My beautiful… I'm… going…" she said, dazed out of her mind.

My hand found her bliss filled face, "Look at me," I commanded.

Lids fluttered. Eyes rolled. She tried.

What a feeling to know that the pleasure of my cock overpowered her. The feeling was indeed mutual.

"You are mine?" I asked.

"As… as you are mine."

"Always."

"Always."

Nails dug into my ass, rolling my hips into her as my own climax edged.

Thighs quaked around me. Body convulsed and pulsated beneath me harder than any she had before. The world faded when I crashed against her, sputtering as I held in place, spilling into my angel. Filling this woman. *My* wife.

I collapsed into shaking arms as they embraced me. My own trembling hands found their way around her shoulders and clasped on, to keep me from joining the stars.

Overjoy leaked down my face and onto her perfect breasts. What beauty was that? Such divine power to be shared.

Time was nothing.

A nipple was haloed by the dying embers of the fireplace as oxygen attempted its way back into my lungs. I was further soothed in euphoria by the gentle stroking of fingers within the moistened strands of my hair.

I dug my fingers into her, gripping her harder before I raised my head to look into sated eyes. Heavy eyelids and a soft smile on her lips. She was left with the peace this body had given her.

"We could stay here. Never go back," she said, running a finger along the dips in my cheek. "We'd need a better bathroom though."

I had the means to give her this. Could it be possible? Not one soul would bother us. Could I live without the opera?

To give up the opera, how would the world know my music, our music, if we were away?

"What about your lessons? I want you on my stage, my love," I cooed.

She shrugged. "It was just a thought."

"A wonderful one that I will give you someday. You will be happy until then. I promise."

She caressed my shame a little longer. "So, tomorrow then. How is that going to work? Getting you a ring."

Mention of laying claim to me lit my soul ablaze once again. It would mean to the world that *I* was a husband. That *this* creature in the shadows had a loving wife.

My wife... *I* would get to be a husband. A loving, adoring, doting, faithful husband. All because this woman needed the world to know she loved a monster.

Chapter XXXVI

"We will make it work," I said.

Unfortunately, though my life had changed, there were some things not even the infamous Ghost could overcome.

The fear of day and the people that dwelled within it.

I would have her go in and find one she liked. Perhaps the owner would close for a short while.

Either way, she wanted it and I would have it done.

"Ok… can we, maybe grab some food afterwards?" she asked.

"Of course."

"I mean eat out… In public."

Blessed I was that this flesh shared the same tone as paper, otherwise brown eyes would have seen it flushed further.

"I will try," I said, knowing fear still had hold of me.

Bliss it was to lay there with her as the world stood in darkness of the most beautiful kind. Three more times I would be afforded to make love to her until dawn. Several more over the next few days.

And as we drove this carriage home, back to the *Le Palais Garnier*. I refused gloves so that the moonlight glinted from the matching metal band on my finger.

The future was both written and yet to be. If what my love claimed was true, then truly she was my saving grace, and the chance would not go to waste.

Alone I would never be. For I was now a husband to an angel across time. Love was with me and warmed this fractured soul, melding the pieces back to whole.

Even as the cold of night burned my fingers.

Chapter XXXVII

Melody

I'm full blown willing to risk it all for a man. What the fuck is wrong with me? It'd been forever since I'd been in my room. Dust had a;ready gathered on the little books of my bookshelf. I would have known *Frankenstein* was missing had I stepped even one foot in here in the past month at least.

Goosebumps blemished my skin at the thought of moving in with him officially. Even though I was excited, I was still a little nervous about giving up my room. It's not that I didn't think we wouldn't work, it was more I'd have no place to go when it didn't.

I shook off the creeping, natural fear and moved the little bookshelf near the door to take home.

Home. With a man… I guess this was my home now. What a really weird feeling. Both sad and filled with hope.

The memories of the past absolutely unadulterated bliss filled days and beyond played through my mind like my favorite movie. I stared at the beautiful ring I'd accepted. A ring of promise. One that Erique took time to design. My heart swelled at the thought of how long he'd been wanting this. How I never thought I would.

Still couldn't get over that he had a custom ring made for me. Back

Chapter XXXVII

home, I couldn't even get a candy bar from a guy.

Erique wasn't ever going to leave me. That was a sure thing. What a scary calming feeling.

Guess we were *really* addicted to each other. And it's probably going to blow up in my face.

Did we even eat over the past few days? I'm sure we did…

It's all gone too far. But I couldn't even stop myself if I tried. And it's all because I fucking love him.

Fuck!

I took one more look around the closet sized room just to make sure I had everything ready. I would come for my clothes on the next trip.

I opened the door and nearly lost my balance as I jumped back. If it were actually possible to do so, I would have jumped out of my skin. "Jesus Christ!" I shrieked, staring at who I thought was Christine beneath a pile of fabrics.

"Sorry, didn't mean to scare you," she said snickering. "Can you help me?" She dropped the mound just enough to see her face better.

I pushed my hand into my pocket to hide my ring for whatever reason, hoping my smile would take away any attention from it.

I looked over the fabrics, it seemed to be a dress. The one from the show.

"Can you sew?" she asked.

"Yes. But it's…"

"Great."

Christine turned and hurried away. Still a little confused, I followed behind her, eventually ending up at Carlotta's dressing room.

Before I could even try to speak, she practically shoved the dress in my face. "Look what she did!" she said. This was the first time I'd seen her angry. It was so weird.

Upon closer inspection, it was obvious the dress had been maimed a bit. The seams had been ripped open in the bodice and brim of the skirt slashed.

"Do you think you can fix it?" she asked.

I fingered through the layers, assessing the damage. "What happened?" I asked.

"Carlotta!" Christine said. "She came back last night when everyone was gone, I heard she threatened the managers too."

"And you think she did this?"

Christine nodded. "I know she did. Or it was her handmaid, at least."

"Why doesn't Madame Chantelle fix it?" The theater had a seamstress for a reason, and my skills were limited anymore.

"She hates me. Her and Carlotta are really good friends. I got thread and a needle from the costume department though… And I wanted an excuse to see my friend for the day," she said. Her brows softened and eyes beamed with guilt. "I'm sorry I haven't been around." She looked away, ashamed.

I may have accepted my fate here. At least I was happy with Erique. But there were still some things that needed to be dealt with.

Reason one hundred million and one that everything was still wrong.

"You don't have to apologize," I said.

"I do," she said. The guilt in her voice was enough to eat you up. "Your friend kind of scared me a little. You know what she said about Erique. It worried me some. But then I realized I was being silly. You wouldn't choose a bad man…"

No one chooses a bad person. They choose a bad person pretending to be good until they're not.

I fiddled with the ring in my pocket. I suppose even though I knew that Erique was mostly good, he'd done some terrible stuff. Nothing that I could ignore. And the thought of him changing, or finally being who he actually was, wasn't lost on me.

"…But then you were gone. You and Erique went on your trip, right? How did it go?" she asked. "You seem refreshed and happy."

Probably the ridiculous amount of love cock I've been having.

My flesh seared again, flooded with all the memories. "Uh. It was…" I said scratching my neck, not sure where to start.

"What is that?"

Before I could look down at what she was referring to, Christine had taken my hand. "You're engaged!" she gasped.

I snapped it away and put it back in my pocket. I don't even know why. I'm not ashamed of him. But then why was my first instinct to hide it? Twice now.

"Well, not exactly," I said.

Chapter XXXVII

She sat chomping at the bit as I told her about our four days together in the cabin by the lake as I stitched the seams in the bodice of the damaged dress. Answered her questions the best I could without giving out too much detail about certain things. Like time travel.

"Erique has one too now," I said. It was amazing the jeweler in such a small town was able to get something done so quickly for us. But the Phantom can be very *persuasive*. Especially when he had enough money to have the owner close for an hour so he could go in with me.

Maybe one day it won't be like that. Or maybe he'll never be comfortable with people. Not that I blamed him. It would just be nice to walk around town together. Maybe go to parties. I don't know.

"But you won't marry him?" she asked.

"It's not that. It's just complicated."

I hated to love that word.

I still didn't know what I was going to do about it though. Someone like my Erique could only wait so long before he would start to question my love for him again. I know he wanted to be a husband. I think he'd be a really good one, but marriage was probably the most frightening thing. Well, next to everything else I've experienced the past five months.

Was that all it's really been? It'd already felt like years since I'd seen the faces of my family. Man, what I wouldn't give to see them now that I had a rock on my finger. Not that we were engaged or anything… Just the implication would be enough.

Would it be so bad to marry the man I loved? Yes.

A happy ending was something that only happened in Disney fairytales. Not stories full of murder and men in walls. No, this was good. It was the best compromise either of us could make.

I would love him forever. He would love me forever. Win-win.

Christine paused and sucked in her lip, running her teeth over the skin. "Did you… um…" she asked, turning red.

"Oh yeah. A ton."

More selfishly, I hoped he never changed his mind because I would hate to not have his love, and that mind exploding, pussy stretching cock.

My God. I was literally Niagara Falls just thinking about it. I couldn't wait to get home.

Her hands flew to her face, covering her excited embarrassment.

A knock at the door startled us both.

"Hold that thought!" she shrieked and jumped up. Before she opened the door, Christine turned back. "We're not done. I have questions."

I missed being that age. When everything was new and the world, men, hadn't ruined it yet.

Strangely enough, even with my doubts, there's just something that told me that I didn't have to worry about that anymore.

I shook off the shiver as my eyes found who had knocked.

"Ah! Raoul!" Christine said. "You're early."

"Do you wish me to leave you then?" he jested. She pulled his hand and led him further into the room. "Oh, Miss Reilly!" he said surprised, then glanced back at Christine. "I didn't realize you were busy, darling."

"Carlotta," she sighed. "Melody is trying to help me fix my costume before rehearsal tonight."

"That woman is indeed a menace," he said. "Actually, she is in part why we are here."

"We?" Christine asked.

Philippe stepped into the room. I groaned internally. Another thing I supposed I would have to deal with. As long as I was friends with Christine, Philippe would be around sometimes.

If he left me alone it would be fine.

"Miss Daae. Miss Reilly." He said my name as if he smelled something rotten.

"Yes. Philippe and I are here to ensure the woman never comes back," Raoul said.

"About time," I said.

"Agreed," Raoul replied. "There's no need for someone with half the talent when they have Christine to lead them." This young man had such a sincere way about him. It's still mind boggling that he and Philippe were brothers. They're so different.

"Oh! Something wonderful has happened!" she said. "Melody is to be married!"

"Christine," I said, shaking my head as my chest caved in. "Not married," I said quickly. "Just together. Anyway…"

I can't believe she told. I guess I didn't say not to. But she knew we

Chapter XXXVII

weren't engaged. Why would she do that?

"She's stubborn. Her Erique proposed over their romantic weekend away," she said and hurried over to me, yanking at my hand to show the men. As if they really cared. Well, Raoul might. But Philippe looked as if he were examining it for appraisal.

"Congratulations are in order then! We should celebrate," Raoul said.

"Yes!" Christine agreed joyfully.

My heart stilled as I plastered the fakest smile on my face. But even at the midst of all the unwanted attention and misinformation, there was a slight twinge of happiness at the thought of marrying Erique. *No. Stop.*

"Indeed," Philippe said, expressionless. "A grand celebration for you and *Erique.*" He cleared his throat and adjusted the scarf around his neck.

"We're very busy," I said, putting my hands in my pockets.

Philippe stepped closer. "Surely your husband-to-be can make the time to celebrate such a victory. Especially for someone that claims she would never." The tone in his voice unsettled me. He was upset. Bitter. It was obvious. Something Raoul and Christine seemed unfazed by.

"Maybe some time," I said just to end the conversation.

"Would you mind if I borrowed Christine? Just for lunch," Raoul asked. "I promise to return her afterwards."

I shrugged. "Not at all. I can have this fixed up soon enough, I'm almost done."

Christine hugged me then took Raoul's arm.

"I'll be along momentarily," Philippe said, tipping his head.

"No, you're going," I said.

He stayed unmoving as the lovebirds left us alone.

Ignoring his presence, I returned my attention back to the dress, which really was close to done. "I told you to stay away from me," I said.

"Are you really going through with this?" he asked. His eerily calm demeanor and tone was worse than his words.

I stayed silent as he stepped towards me, stopping a few feet away.

"I want to know why you chose a monster over me," he demanded.

"Excuse me?" I said, stopping my work to look up into the eyes of the human embodiment of audacity.

"Your *beloved* Erique attacked me. Threatened my life. Would have gone through with it had I not reminded him of your care for me."

"I don't care for you."

"You do not care that after I declared myself to you, despite your rejection, your betrothed attacked. Hands around my throat." He tore the scarf from his neck exposing the healing bruises around it. "A wild beast of a mad man in a mask. The Opera Ghost did this to me in your name."

"He's not the…"

"He is. Do not lie."

I hesitated, looking over the bruising on his neck, Erique hadn't told me about it. Yet, I felt nothing seeing it. I should, but I didn't.

I sighed and shrugged, laying the dress next to me on the chaise and stood up. "Ok. Well, you deserved it."

"Pardon?" he said, shock gracing his face.

"I told you no and you still did it anyway. You're lucky he didn't kill you."

The tension in my shoulders ached as he stepped closer yet again with disgust in his face. "You know he's this monster, and you still love him?"

"Stop calling him that! We have nothing to prove to you nor anyone else. Now fucking leave."

"You have not seen what he is. The Opera Ghost has killed many over the years. That pregnant chorus girl. The filthy stagehand. Many before your arrival. What would it take for you to see this man, this thing, as the abomination he is?" he said. "Here before you, there is a man that would have you despite all that. That would give you what you deserve. Give your life purpose."

"Stop!" I shouted. My heart threatened to burst through the ribs it thumped so hard into. "I am not some naive twenty-year-old girl with no life experience. I will not be told how stupid or ridiculous I am for being who I am. Loving who I do. I trust him. Philippe, there is no timeline in which I would choose you. Why is this so hard for you to accept?"

"Are you alright, miss?" a man's voice asked from behind Philippe.

Quickly, we turned our attention to the man in the doorway.

There stood Erique's friend or nemesis or whatever he was, the

Chapter XXXVII

Daroga, Ardashir. He eyed Philippe curiously as he pushed back the flap of his jacket to reveal the butt of a pistol.

"Yes. Everything's fine. Thank you," I said through gritted teeth. "The Comte was just leaving."

"You will see," Philippe hissed in my face. "I pray for you when you do."

I exhaled in slight relief as he stormed out past Ardashir and disappeared through the opened doorway.

"Are you sure you are alright, Miss? That fellow didn't seem very cheery," he said.

"Yeah. He's an asshat. Doesn't take no for an answer."

"I do not wish to bother you, but I must speak with you," he said, stepping closer with caution.

"And what is it that I can do for you?"

He removed his hat and held it to his chest. "I am Ardashir Azimi. We have a mutual… friend," he said. "It is true that you love him?" He glanced down at my ring. "Erique always did have good taste."

"Yes. And he does." This was someone I was not acquainted with; it was hard to read who he was. Even if Erique liked him, it didn't mean he liked Erique.

"I was hoping you may relay a message for me," he said. "I am afraid I owe him an apology. I was very cruel when we last spoke…" He glanced at the stool near him and took a seat. He seemed tired. But not just from lack of sleep, but a life of running.

"…I don't know what he's told you exactly, but there was a time, too long, that I was filled with hatred for him for something I did." His eyes filled with the aching memories of his past. "I tried for many years to arrest him for several crimes. The death of my family is at the top of that list."

"The King's punishment for helping him escape."

He nodded. "He told you the truth. Interesting." Then cleared his throat. "When he told me of your relationship, I hated the happiness emitting from him and that he was allowed to feel such a thing after so many years I lived in hell. One that could never truly go away. The little joy I held in my heart until I met my second wife, was that Erique was in a state of eternal misery. Knowing that no one could care for him. I kept in touch so I could relish it. As long as he was unhappy, then my family's death was not in vain. That was until he saved my life once," he said. His shoulders slumped slightly. "It wasn't until then I realized my mistake. Erique was practically a boy when my family was murdered. A young man that knew genius and self-service, nothing else. Neither of us knew what the King was going to do."

"Erique is very forgiving."

"He is, isn't he? And then he's not," he sighed. "I suppose I told you all this so that you understand that I know him. And what I say is not in light." He stared at me in silence for a moment as I listened. What else could I do. I didn't want to hear anything more about him, but this was also someone that actually knew him.

"I can see how he loves you," he said with a warm smile. "Though I do wish the most happiness for you both. I must warn you. Erique is *different*. I do not mean his physical deformity either. I worked alongside him for several years. He is obsessed with perfection. Obsessed with his work. When he is bored of things or he can't make it go as he wishes, they are easily discarded."

This man was basically trying to confirm all my fears. What happened when the boredom kicked in? Because it always did and men don't take kindly to that. Or when I wouldn't be able to get on that stage because of my own crippling fear. Would he still want me?

"Erique wants to be good, especially now that he has you," he continued. "But he can't. Death and destruction follow him everywhere. If you can live with that; stay and love him. Someone needs to. I just do not wish a life for you beneath the ground. In any way of the meaning."

I swallowed. I didn't know what to say. Did he just suggest Erique would kill me if I didn't live up to his expectations?

My lids wanted to close and stay closed. The overwhelming weight of the constant Erique bashing weighed down my head as well as Ardashir's shoulders. I just needed to see Erique. It would be fine once I did. I knew he wasn't the man these assholes thought he was. Or used to be.

"I'm sorry if I've upset you. That wasn't my intention on this visit. In a strange way I care about Erique, to my surprise, and do see him as my friend. I would like to think that you are right," he said. "I assure you." He stood and reached into his pocket, pulling out a small worn

Chapter XXXVII

notepad. "Can you give this to him? It's the least I can do. He'll know what it is. Tell him there's new information on the case. And if he wishes to speak again, he'll know where to find me."

I took the notepad and eyed it a little. It was old and worn. I flipped it open and glanced. There were city names I recognized. Paris, Toulouse, etc., but whatever else was written in a language I didn't know. Erique knew six languages. This had to have been one of them.

"Good day, Miss Melody," he said and replaced his hat on his head. "Until we meet again. I hope it is a joyous occasion then." He disappeared around the corner into the hallway.

Just so I could take a break from everything, I closed and locked the door behind him.

The chaise lounge caught me as I fell onto it and buried my face in the dress. My head pounded, wanting reprieve and getting none. My gaze landed on the giant full body mirror at the back of the room. A little ironic laugh huffed in my chest. The fucking Phantom of the Opera.

I was literally being warned, and warned, and warned about someone nobody knew. I wasn't stupid. For the first time I felt like I finally had it right. What are they gonna do when they see that?

Chapter XXXVIII

Melody

There's no place like home. Sort of. I set my little bookshelf just inside the doorway to our home and sang out his name as I closed the door behind me. When he didn't answer, I pulled the notepad from my pocket and set it on the end table as I walked further into the room.

"Erique?" I called out again.

It wasn't super common to come back and find him gone. But the fire was out, and it was quiet as I wandered through the house. He'd been gone a while.

I pulled some food from the cold storage and got the fire going again, hoping to be ready for when he returned. I couldn't wait to tell him about Ardashir. I don't think Erique's ever had someone apologize to him, other than me. I think it'll be a good step forward. Even if his friend warned me in the same breath.

I missed electric heating. Erique said we'd get some soon. Excitement was an understatement.

I meandered around Erique's organ as I munched on some cheese and ham. Sheet music was spread out over everything. I still didn't know how he kept it all together. What a beautiful mess.

Chapter XXXVIII

I gathered up the latest concoction of his mind that lay on the organ stand. He'd been nonstop since we returned yesterday. He didn't even stop to have his way with me. Until I pulled him away for bed.

The smile spread on my face at the thought as my eyes roamed some of the sheets. He loved his minor keys. My eyes stopped on the second page in my hand at seeing the title. *The Phantom's Melody.*

I didn't know he started something new. There were even lyrics written on some of them. My heart sank into a warm bath as I read the words he'd actually written down. Tears filled my eyes at the realization.

It was us. Our story.

I loved that man.

I grabbed the rest of what I could find and sat on the floor. I flipped through the sheets, playing the music in my head as I read, munching on cold meat. It was so fascinating to read what I think were Erique's thoughts after we met. Sweet, tortured man.

It wasn't until the clock chimed ten that I was pulled away. I'd been so engrossed and caught up in the draft, I hadn't noticed two hours had gone by already. It was so late and it worried me that Erique still wasn't home.

Something within my gut told me to search for him. Erique doesn't stay away long like this. There was no note. He would have left a note if anything.

I set the music aside and headed for the door. Getting to the surface didn't take long since I'd been doing it every day for the past month.

As much as I hated breaking the privacy wall, I hurried along the inner wall towards the stables. I'd looked into every dressing room along the way. Coming up onto dressing room five, I heard voices and my heart lightened for a moment.

Entwined between two very handsome, very naked men from the ensemble—who were for sure not his wife—was the uptight, curly haired manager, M. Fournier.

I was not prepared for this.

One of the guys kissed around M. Fournier's nipple while stroking his cock. The other was balls deep down his throat.

I guess the managers didn't go everywhere together.

I would rip out Erique's spine through his naval if he cheated on me.

As interesting and slightly arousing as this scene was, I needed to be on my way. I had someone I was really starting to worry about, that needed finding.

I checked the stables. Cesar and Nora were still there. The salon was lively. The passageways I knew to the stage and some of the rooms were empty as well. Still no Erique.

After about an hour of searching, it was clear he wasn't anywhere here.

He'd never leave without telling me.

Eventually I left the inner walls and walked down the grand staircase in the foyer. My head spun and my stomach told me something was really wrong. My mind said I was overreacting. I took a seat on one of the stairs and laid my head in my hands.

Some of the unwanted words said earlier in the day bled back in. Warnings I didn't want to hear in case they were true. Too much had been heard and I just wanted, needed, to have him hold me. Reassure me of what I already knew. That everything was ok now we finally let it all out.

Maybe I had missed him and he's back at the house waiting for me.

Just then a woman screamed outside the front doors of the building. My anxiety shot through the roof at the blood-curdling sound.

Fear suddenly encapsulated me as I got to my feet and ran for the door. Bursting into the late night air, I glanced around to find where the commotion had come from.

A crowd had formed on the sidewalk, staring up towards the roof. *Why were so many people out tonight?*

My hands shook with every agonizing step I forced myself to take out from beneath the overhang.

Slowly, afraid of what I was going to see, I turned and brought my gaze up.

Life left my body and my heart fell into the pit of my stomach. There, hanging from the neck of Wolfgang Amedeus Mozart, was the man that had warned me about Erique.

My hands flew to my mouth to stifle any sounds and stop my dinner from coming up.

Through trembling hands, I whispered Erique's name because it was

Chapter XXXVIII

all I could manage, hoping he'd magically appear and tell me he was alright.

But it wasn't Erique that answered.

"Melody?" Philippe shouted as he ran up to me. I recoiled when he grabbed hold of my arms. "My God, are you alright?" The smell of alcohol smacked me hard, but I didn't care. He didn't matter.

All I could see was Erique's mask sitting on Ardashir's face, as his bloody insides slapped against the thick of his thigh.

"I don't know what's happening," I said, holding onto him. "I can't find Erique anywhere."

"What does he have to do with this?"

"I didn't think he would do it. I really thought he…we," I said, trailing off. Ardashir wanted to apologize. Erique wouldn't… "No. This isn't right. I have to find him," I said and tore away from the vice grip Philippe had on me.

Panic rioted within me every quick step to the building. I ripped the door open and ran inside. "Erique!" I called out over and over.

My legs shook with alarm, trying to stop me from continuing through the hallways. Maybe he's hurt or something or scared. That's why he wasn't answering.

"No!" I screamed in Philippe's face when he grabbed me again.

"Melody. I am sorry for everything that I have done. I have never been all that well with my temperament, but this is no place for you," he said. "I want…"

"Comte de Chagny, what has happened?" M. Fournier asked, out of breath and disheveled. No doubt hurried to dress when he heard the commotion.

"It seems the Phantom has struck again," Philippe said, staring directly at me.

"You're wrong," I seethed.

"This time the investigator that was poking around." His words snide towards the manager. "We warned you about this and to deal with it. Now another is dead."

"Stop!" I spit. My wrist twisted as he pulled me along with him and M. Fournier towards the exit again.

"My God! I assure you; we thought it was handled. The accidents had been silent for months," M. Fournier said. "We can't have this get out!"

M. Fournier rushed over to the police once we reached the outside. I shook and spiraled in Philippe's grasp once we stopped. I searched the crowd of faces, the dark spots of the block. I couldn't focus on any one thing.

"Melody," Philippe said, shaking me. "Do you not see that Erique did this?"

"It wasn't him!" I said, trying to get free of his grip. Because the alternative was undeniably unbearable.

In a fight of strength, Philippe pulled me close and locked his hands against my spine. "I didn't want to be right. Truly. We must get you out of here."

His embrace felt strange. I pushed against him, not wanting to be there. My need to get back inside and find Erique, make him explain whatever this was, was stronger than the emotions coursing through me.

His fingers moved to my shoulders and dug into my flesh. "Enough," he said, shaking me. "If he's killed his friend, who knows what he would do to you."

"I can't leave. I have to go back inside."

"I will take you somewhere safe," he said as a carriage pulled up behind him.

"No, you don't understand. He will kill you if I go. And I don't want to," I cried, yanking my arm from him. He would be in danger if he helped me. Erique already hated him.

Philippe left me for a moment while I nursed my aching head, trying to make sense of it all. It couldn't be true. Erique wouldn't lie to me... He was the only good thing here. This couldn't have been him. It didn't make sense. He wouldn't hurt someone he cared about.

A hand landed on my shoulder, scaring the shit out of me. I shook it off, and readied to push Philippe away again, but standing there was M. LeBlanc instead.

"The Comte has told me the situation, dear girl. I had an idea that you may know the Ghost, but the thought was absurd in its creation. Please, for me, go with the Comte until we can figure this out. There has been enough tragedy," he begged.

Chapter XXXVIII

"I can go to the *Hôtel des Anges*," I said.

"No, dear. You must go somewhere he can't find you."

Officers were already attempting to pull Ardashir from the roof when I looked back at the building.

My pulse spun and my mind was vexed. What if Erique did do this? What if he overheard us talking and thought Ardashir was trying to break us up. I mean he was, but not…

"They need a ladder. They won't be able to get him that way," I mumbled.

"What? No. Melody," M. LeBlanc said in a gentle tone. "They will be fine. It is their job," he said. "When everything is secure, you can come back. If you want to. But please, leave tonight. We will see you before you know it. I promise."

A hand pressed against my lower back, another taking my hand. With a foggy mind I glanced up to find that Philippe had us walking to his carriage. I was on autopilot as I crawled into the box on wheels.

This wasn't real. I had everything I ever wanted… he couldn't have done it… Could he?

"*Maison*!" Philippe shouted and the cab pulled off, leaving behind the place I'd started to think of as home.

***

I was thankful for the silence for once. Philippe said nothing while we rode along. It wasn't long, or maybe it was, until we reached an iron gate that opened and let us through. I stared out past the driveway lined with flickering lanterns, into the void of night.

I hadn't noticed we stopped either until a man said something and Philippe urged us out into the cold night, and up into a giant concrete mansion. Like you'd see in any Victorian film ever.

I wish I cared.

"This is where you will stay," he said.

The room was spacious, far more than the one in the Garnier or even the one I had with Erique.

Browns and reds everywhere. Very decorated as one would imagine. It didn't matter though. None of it did.

I beelined for the large bed not too far away. It beckoned me with the promise of a warm, soothing hug. One that would ease my pain if

I accepted it.

"I am sorry this has happened to you," he said. "My home is yours until he's been found. Until then, know that you are safe here."

Safe. What did that even mean anymore? Nothing's been safe. The only time I ever felt safe was in the arms of a killer.

"What if you're wrong?" I turned and looked him in the eye. Dark brown eyes were almost indifferent as they stared back. "Erique… Once he knows I'm gone, he'll look for me. He can't help it. I mean, that is if he still wants me…"

It was like everything I feared would happen, did. All at once. Though my mind still tried to see it all as it fought in disbelief, there was a possibility that Erique did it. That he was everything everyone had said he was.

"Your worry is understandable. To be tricked by that *thing*."

Thing. "He's not…"

Philippes words drilled into me, doing their best to remind me of the decisions I had made in loving someone unlovable. Even now I still had a hard time believing I was wrong for loving him. Trusting him.

"I just know something's not right, Philippe. I mean, he hates you and didn't kill you," I said. "That should mean something. He's not like this."

"My guards are on alert at all times," he continued. "And the staff is aware of the situation and is to report anything unusual."

"I'm not scared for me," I sighed.

His eyes turned concerned. "You must rest. This whole terrible, disgusting ordeal has weighed on you long enough. If you need me while I'm here, I am down the hall, first green door. At any hour if you need of me."

My weary eyes fell to the floor and I nodded weakly. "Thank you."

"You are welcome. Good night then, Ms. Reilly."

The door closed too quickly, and I was left on my own. Left to remember every horribly beautiful thing that was now tainted.

My sluggish feet carried me to the oversized bed as my eyes checked the dark corners of the room. I couldn't feel him, but in the state I was in, I don't think I could tell if he were here.

I crawled in between the sheets, shoes and all, and pulled the comforter.

Something worse than heartache streamed down my cheeks and into the fabrics of the bedding until the sun peaked through the window and the sandman finally won.

Melody, the silly child that didn't listen. Again.

Chapter XXXIX

Melody

Crying and sleeping never changed anything; it only helped time move faster towards the end. Three weeks had passed since buildings turned into trees and open fields, since my world came shattering down again just after it was repaired. Since Erique disappeared, and Philippe brought me to his palace.

If Erique was coming for me, he would have been here by now.

So much of the time was spent going over every detail, trying to find where I missed Erique's metaphoric mask-slipping. There was nothing to find though. Erique was the most open person I knew, a little too open sometimes.

I knew I should have listened to myself. The logical, lack of empathy part that kept me trying to fight him when we met. Yet somehow, we grew into love and I allowed myself to care again, just to be ripped into unrecognizable shreds that happened every time I opened myself to it.

Even then, there was a part of me that still couldn't believe he did it.

Erique only wanted one thing he didn't think he could have, care and affection from a woman that loved him. Why would he mess that up?

I know in my heart that Erique cared for me. But it wasn't love as

Chapter XXXIX

I loved. He never loved me. Not really. It was the Phantom obsession. He stalked me, killed anyone that tried to get in the way. Clear obsession tactics.

But then why not kill Philippe too? If he didn't love me, killing Philippe would have been easy.

Sunlight glinted from the dark and light gemstones of my ring as I stared into the torn memories. Dark and light. Just like we were.

I guess he wasn't the only delusional one.

"Did you hear me?" Philippe asked.

Blinking rapidly as I fidgeted with my ring, I glanced at the man trying so hard to earn my trust or… whatever.

Lately, I had pulled myself from delusion, acting for Philippe's sake. He'd been trying to be a friend at least. Patient and kind, something I didn't think he was capable of. Even tasking me with organizing his charity campaign. Something that's kept me busy enough while loitering around the place, wallowing in self pity.

I was still an empty husk of a person though. Donning a false smile when needed, hoping no one noticed the light inside had died.

"Are you alright?" he asked.

His affections were deeper than mine, apparent by every kind gesture and grand gift, like the newest Arabian in the stables. Any girl would be so lucky. But not me, I'm a glutton for punishment and I missed my killer and our books.

"Of course. I was elsewhere for a moment. I'm sorry," I said and dropped my hands. "Continue. Please." We'd been walking around the pond not far from the house. Spring was beautiful. Barely a chill in the air anymore.

"I was only saying that you should be thrilled. My brother and his fiancée, your friend, Christine, should be arriving this evening, not long after we return actually."

The blood left my face and I froze. "What? I didn't know they were coming."

Amongst all that had transpired, Christine had learned everything. How can I look her in the eyes now that she knew the man I loved was her "angel", and how I said nothing.

"It will be alright." His voice wasn't like Erique's, not soothing in a hypnotic way, but it had a calmness to it. Something I hadn't really noticed before until recently. I still didn't like it much. It was getting better though.

I should be happy about the news, but I just wanted to take my horse and run. I'd done enough of not listening to myself, maybe this would be a good time to start.

"Yes, I'm sure you're right. That's great news," I lied through a smile, and fidgeted with my ring again, absentmindedly.

He sighed and took my hand, gently caressing it as he examined the symbol of my former love. "Perhaps it would be better if you finally took this off? Free yourself."

"No," I said without thinking and snatched my hand away even though I was done with the masked monster. Even if I missed him.

This ache. This betrayal hurt so much. I hated him. Yet, I held onto this thing as if it were the holy grail. As if it would keep me safe and grant me eternal healing.

Philippe took my hand again and placed a kiss on it. "It was not my place to suggest such a thing and I ask forgiveness."

My skin didn't know how to react. Shivering in disgust while at the same time warming under the touch.

"It's not you. I… I know I should have taken it off by now, but it's still hard to believe, you know?" I said, somewhat less pathetic than I thought it would sound. "Who wants to believe the person they love is capable of such a horrific act?"

"You knew he'd killed before," he said.

"Not like this. Ardashir wasn't self-defense." Embarrassment slithered up my spine. I didn't feel shame before and lately I was riddled with it.

"You still defend him after all this time?" he asked, calmly. My eyes fell away. I guess I was. But it'd only been a few weeks, of course my feelings were everywhere. "Finding him would be easier if you gave up the whereabouts of his crypt. The house you shared. He needs to pay for what he's done so you can move on."

I had stopped asking about updates from the opera when it was always the same. They never found him or heard anything more. They just wanted to know where his house was. Something else I wasn't ready

Chapter XXXIX

to give up yet.

"He's not there. You would know," I said.

He ran a gentle hand along my jaw. "Demons are gifted in deceit," Philippe said. "But in the end, they do what demons do. My heart is sorry for yours. I will not ask again."

If it were deceit, then why don't I feel deceived?

"…And if you have room, even the smallest amount, I would like to lend you mine," he said. "Permanently if you would allow it."

I dug my nails into my palms and my pulse jumped through my flesh. It was too soon to hear anything like this. It wouldn't be fair to Philippe either if I jumped in with him, just because it was the safest thing to do.

"I told you once before," he said. "You hold the key to my future. I need you with me."

My chest tightened as he stepped closer. He leaned down and pressed his lips to mine. His hands were warm, but even though his kiss was soft, it was empty. Like actors when they didn't find the other attractive. I've done it. That's what this felt like.

To be honest, I wasn't sure if it was him or me. Tears choked me as I held them back and prayed that I would vanish into thin air at this moment. Escape from this hollow kiss.

Flashes of heterochromia irises plagued the darkness of my closed eyes.

How I hated them.

I withdrew from the man that just poured his heart out to me. "I'm sorry," I said, and left him standing in the wake of my destruction by the bank of the pond.

Straight to the house and into my room I went, closing the door behind me. My racing heart calmed slightly at the distance, and the only thing left was the unrelenting ache in my chest.

My eyes fell to the ring on my finger. Warm to the touch, I hesitated to yank it off. The movements were there. But the strength to do it wasn't.

I sighed and dropped my hands in defeat before sliding to the floor. I was still chained by the monster that loved me.

"I'm the biggest idiot," I said to only myself.

***

Everyone had already gathered in the gallery when I finally found the will to descend the stairs.

The fear of facing Christine was worse than my feelings on Erique. My stomach stilled and clenched tight when I saw her face as I entered the room. Every part of me trembled as I plastered a performer's smile on my face. Whatever reaction she was going to have would have been completely justified. I was the worst person. To be honest, probably worse than Erique, because I knew, and didn't do anything about it.

"Ah, Melody. It is good to see you," Raoul greeted, with a sweet smile. "I see my brother has taken good care of you." Though he seemed much the same, something was a little off in his tone. There was a possibility he was upset about everything as well. I wouldn't blame him.

"I heard the news. Congratulations," I said. "I wish you both every happiness the world has to offer."

The words hurt to say. I meant them, but it still tore at my chest.

"We're looking forward to the future," Christine said.

Maybe because my body was riddled with guilt and shame, I couldn't read her, but the joy shined in her eyes with her answer. What a relief. She hadn't been completely destroyed by what had happened. At least one of us would get a happy ending. Or beginning, or however you wanted to look at it.

"Shall we? The chef has prepared a wonderful meal for us this evening. We have much to discuss," Philippe said.

At least an hour passed while I faked my way through idle chit chat. It was a good thing Philippe liked to talk. I poked at my food, not really paying attention to the conversation at hand. I was sure it was delicious, but I still didn't feel much like eating these days. The anxiety was a constant circus in my guts. And with Christine here, it was in the finale.

Every now and then, I'd catch Philippe's eye and immediately look away. I didn't want to see an apology in his face for kissing me or the disappointment for running away.

Something I wanted to forget.

I felt like I did something wrong. Like I was cheating. But *he's* not here anymore.

Why did my body feel this way? Why wouldn't it stop?

Maybe it wouldn't be so bad if I gave into Philippe. Beats being on

Chapter XXXIX

the streets. Having nowhere to go. Maybe it was the only smart decision I'd make this year.

Even if it wasn't what I wanted.

I fiddled with my ring, twisting and tugging on it just beneath the table out of sight, sliding it up and down my finger. This may go over better with Christine if I wasn't wearing the reminder of recent events.

One of the tugs went a bit far, and it came completely off. I froze thinking about it and what to do next.

"What of your campaign?" Raoul asked. For some reason the chatter pulled me from my little world, back to the table.

"Going rather well, though it is only the beginning. I think the charity event will help some," he said and took my hand, squeezing it. A sincere look of gratitude graced his face. Settling a little too kindly within my mind, thanks to my current thoughts. "And with Ms. Reilly heading the arrangements, I know it will be the most successful event."

His dark eyes glanced down at my ringless finger as he rubbed the indent from my skin. The slightest grin and hint of surprise in his eyes grew as they found mine.

"Wonderful," Raoul replied.

"Yes," he said, gazing curiously at me. "Wonderful."

I hadn't intended on him seeing me without the ring. But the sight seemed to have made his night. I clamped my ring in my other hand and slid it into my pocket. I didn't think I could let it go just yet.

He wouldn't let my hand go for another half hour or so. And I just let him do it. What did it matter anymore?

"With that said, brother, shall we retire to the cigar room for a drink? Leave the ladies to catch up?" Philippe asked.

My eyes widened and cut to his. I hoped he saw the dread in them begging him not to go.

What a turn of events, right?

Philippe leaned over, pushing his lips against my ear. "You must face it one way or another. You will be fine." He kissed my hand and pulled away.

"Come," he beckoned Raoul, and the two men were out the door before I knew it.

Just me and Christine now. Here it was. The awkward silence. Who would talk first? What would I even say? *"Hey, sorry my boyfriend and I were lying to you and he planned on kidnapping you before we met."*

I doubt that would go over well.

"When do you plan to marry?" I finally asked.

"In the fall. Seventh September."

"Not too hot, not too cold."

I kept flashing my gaze to the door either hoping Philippe would come back or possibly plotting my escape.

I'd even take Erique breaking in right now.

Christine fiddled with her hands before looking at me again. "I was so angry when I found out," she said. "When my angel was just a man. Not even a man, but a monster of a man. And you loved him anyway."

This was her moment. I had no right to rebuttal. To deflect. To defend. There wasn't an excuse.

"I wanted to hate you," she continued.

"We were going to tell you. Erique was going to..."

"The night at the *Masq*. I thought I was crazy when I recognized the voice I'd heard nearly every day for months, but ignored it because it was in fact, insane. There was no way my angel was this *man*. And you wouldn't keep a secret like that from me."

With every word my body was a hundred pounds heavier. My eyes fell away, the shame was back. "Why didn't you say anything?" I asked.

"I saw how much he loved you," she said. "And how happy you were."

My jaw quivered at the memory. At her friendship. I took a deep breath to dam up the wall to keep back the tears.

"I don't hate you. I'm not even angry with you anymore. I am sorry for you, though," Christine said. "I wasn't the only one fooled."

Her forgiveness, though I was thankful, did little to relieve the weight of everything else.

"You were right. I guess it was silly to think an angel was teaching me. You told me, and I didn't want to listen," she added. "If it means anything, I really do think he loved you. But I think that some people can't change who they are."

"There was never a time you feared him?" I asked.

Christine thought for a moment then spoke, "I always felt safe.

Chapter XXXIX

Yes, he was a little scary sometimes. Very demanding of my voice and attention during our lessons. I didn't like that he wouldn't allow me out, but it only made me a stronger performer. I miss him sometimes."

Me too.

I felt her eyes on me as I fiddled with the skin my ring used to sit, contemplating returning the metal to it.

Christine stood up from her chair on the other side of the table and took a seat in Philippe's spot next to me. I wondered if she was going to hit me or not. Throw a plate at me. But she didn't. "I know I don't know much about the world or love," she said, moving closer. "But I think that you might consider that there's still hope for you to find happiness."

Her implication turned my stomach again. No, she didn't know. And couldn't.

"I know that he has a hard time showing it, not like Erique did. But I could see tonight that he's very happy to have you here. I haven't seen him smile like that ever actually."

"I can't love him," I said meekly. Like it was a secret I couldn't let him know.

"Maybe in time you will?"

Time scared me. Would there ever be a time that I didn't love Erique?

"Maybe," I replied.

***

Christine's hope ricocheted around my mind as I sat in the crook of the large window of my room. Stars twinkled brightly above in the night sky. I pondered my situation. Options. Everything.

Raoul and Christine had gone to bed for the night. It was nice talking to her, but our conversation really fucked me up.

Fuck, I wish I had someone here to help me through this. Sarah. I wonder what she's doing right now? Probably watching Star Wars with her husband and kids. Eating popcorn and cookies. Even mom would be a good option. I'd just do the opposite of what she told me.

Mama was probably asleep though. Hopefully not permanently. Or if she was, at least she would finally be at peace.

I hated not knowing. I hated that I hadn't really thought of them. Going home wasn't an option anymore though.

Maybe Christine's right. I could do worse than Philippe. There's a possibility that if I gave him a chance, that I could love him, or at least like him enough. He had been nicer since my arrival.

It was either leave and find some sort of life somewhere, working myself to death just to get by. Or choosing this man who's very well off, kind of hot, and doesn't care who I am, or was, because he doesn't ask.

How can love stem from that?

My hand trembled as I raised it. The ring returned to my finger and twinkled like the stars above.

I forced the thing from my flesh on purpose this time. I wanted it to hurt, to remind me what it symbolized, so I could keep going.

The love was gone from it.

I jumped up from the bench and marched to the dresser before I lost all courage. I yanked the drawer open. With quivering lips, I kissed it goodbye, and shoved Erique into the void. Slammed it closed and exhaled a silent cry.

Deep, heavy breaths of relief expanded my chest.

The weight on my hand was lighter and for the moment, I thought I felt free.

Guards no longer stood at my door when I opened it. No one was there to stop me from leaving my room for my protection.

Only the voice that echoed in my mind as I walked the hallway.

'You are eternally mine as I am yours,' it said in his voice. *'Do not do this. You are my Melody.'*

"Go away," I whispered. "Go."

My stomach flipped and tumbled as I grew closer to my destination.

A shaking hand raised to the green wooden door. I closed my eyes and took a breath to calm myself again as I hovered the entrance to the end.

I guess there was a timeline in which I would choose Philippe. I wasn't happy about it though.

Knock.

Chapter XXXX

This room without windows or time held cold differently than my beautiful underworld beneath the opera. Empty and unfeeling in its touch. Cold were the rough stones against my back. Ice where I lay my exhausted head.

The growl of an empty belly could be heard as far as the Americas. Pain with every reminder of how little the swine threw scraps at my feet.

However, no amount of hunger could override the continued anguish my soul endured without her presence.

Time eludes and did not give way as to how long it has been since I was blessed to set eyes upon my cherub's face.

If not for the repeated beatings, sleep would never have found me. Rest was haunted by my friend's death. Possibilities of what has happened to my angel, worse and more creative with every vivid hallucination.

Why I was being kept alive was a wonder. Guards only taunted and mocked, never giving hint at any intended end.

How regret ate at me every moment for not having gone home with her. Pride took hold and now everything was lost.

Even the Ghost had gone silent. Perhaps too weak to help any further.

Soft glowing light reflected from the metal that tethered us together. Weakly I stared, trying to find her face. Wherever she was, on my life, I begged she was safe.

I have tried and tried, my love. I fear the worst has come.

From the darkest corner of my cage, a sound so small drew tired eyes. Slinking from the shadows into the dim light of the torch from across the room, a robust rat scurried along the base of the wall.

"You should not be in here," I said faintly. The hunger growled louder at sight of the moving meal.

Bony fingers stretched out weakly towards the rodent. "You have anywhere in this world you could be, and you choose here. You should leave while you have the chance. While I'm too weak to catch you."

My ring slid past the knuckle, threatening to come off. A small burst of strength allowed me to catch it, missing the opportunity to ensnare my furry friend.

The cold band barely fit with the weight lost. If before I did not resemble a walking corpse, I was the definition now.

"Does talking to vermin make you feel more at home, Ghost?" Philippe said, through the cell bars.

Finally, after so long, my captor had come to show his face once more.

"I will show you what I do to vermin," I said.

A rage I had not felt in some time bolted through this dying body. Just enough to bring to life a strength I no longer had. With trouble, I pushed myself onto my feet.

The last thing I would give the Rat King was a sign I had been truly beaten. The world dizzied at this height. Each step as uncertain as the last. Yet, I would not yield.

"Forgive me. I realize it's been some time since my last visit. A month," he said, counting on his fingers. "…And four days actually," he said. "I've been rather busy you see."

Had it been so long?

I stepped closer to the bars, grabbing hold to stabilize my weakened core. The swine's flinch did not go unnoticed. Insignificant pleasure to know that even now he still feared me.

Chapter XXXX

"Where is Melody?" I asked from deep within.

"I'd forgotten how horrid your face is," he said.

It was the longest I'd gone without the mask. The first thing they took from me that night to further humiliate me for letting my guard down.

"When I kill you, this will be the last nightmare you see," I threatened. "You will wish I had killed you in the parlor. Now, tell me, where is she?"

"Do not worry for sweet Melody. She is safe and happy, shopping with Christine as we speak."

To know she walked free relieved this aching mind for a moment.

"You see, I'm finally making my grand introduction into the political race. Very exciting. And I'm accompanied by my bride-to-be who has been keeping me quite busy with planning and well… other things that I won't bore you with. I am a gentleman after all."

Acid coursed through dying veins at the serpent's heavy tongue. The cretin had touched her. This diabolical scum whom she loathed more than I hated myself, had touched her with his vile, treacherous hands.

'Bride-to-be? Bride-to-be? You have not been gone long. How could she?' the Ghost said. *'She was waiting for you. Would she have taken part in this? Could she have known?'*

"No," I whisper low enough so only I can hear, surprised to hear it again.

"Alright, you've twisted my arm," Philippe said with a disgustingly sweet excitement. "Who am I to keep such a delicious secret? You see, the other night out of nowhere, your lovely little American came to my room and threw herself at me. Sucked on my cock until she cried, choking on it, and begged me to love her, take care of her. Keep her safe from *you*."

"You will pay for that filthy lie."

"Am I lying?" he said, smirking. If the devil was real, he stood a meter from me. "That reminds me, I have something for you." He reached into the depths of his trousers pocket, fiddling around.

He took no effort in hiding the mockery in his face. With nothing more to do except hope the treacherous bottom feeder took a step closer toward the cell bars keeping us apart, I waited.

"She won't be needing this any longer after tonight," he said. Filthy eyes inspected the symbol of forever that glimmered in his fingers.

Suddenly, the band around my own flesh was the weight of hell. As if to further cement the reminder it was only ever a dream. An illusion. Given to ensure my last days were the worst they could possibly be.

"Oh my. I'm so sorry. This is obviously quite devastating for you. I hadn't thought this through," he said. His tone was enough to have me envisioning the removal of his spine as he still breathed. "Please accept my sincerest apologies once again."

With a malicious smirk and a flick of his fingers, her promise fell to the earth. The ping as it hit the stone floor and bounced around, echoed in my shattered heart.

Desperately, my hands searched the darkened crevices for the sign of her love.

"How pathetic. Even now, knowing she doesn't love you; you're still desperate for her. Desperate to hold on." He sighed. "That is some love."

"You know nothing of who she is or her love. What she is capable of. I guarantee you of that."

"I don't need to. She is a means to an end. That's how love works in society," he said.

Air returned to my shriveled lungs as a glimmer of light found my eye. "She would not even say yes to me, and she loves me," I said, clinging onto the precious thing.

"I can be quite persuasive." Slime dripped from every syllable. Taxidermy was never my favorite, but a new hobby is never too late. His tongue would be a lovely addition to my wall. "Melody is absolutely the most broken thing I've ever seen. She's lucky to have me as a suiter after the turmoil you caused," he mocked, as I pulled myself to my feet once again. "Can you believe it, the American girl and the Opera Ghost fucking about the *Garnier*. A tale for the ages…"

You have no idea, fool.

"…Only later to be found out that the Ghost everyone's afraid of is just a pathetic hideous man that lives in the sewers."

I had tainted her with this repulsive flesh. My diseased mind. Fractured soul. But no vermin was going to be the judge of our love.

"And I don't need her to love me. I just need her to stay around long

Chapter XXXX

enough. Other than being the only woman in existence that is willing to take your diseased cock…" He paused and visibly shivered at his own words as his eyes raked over me with the same look of disgust I had endured many times before. "I can see why you like her so much though. And I am surprised you even still have a cock. I would have thought the fire had taken more of you than it did."

One of the most painful moments of my existence, and she would share it with *him*? Was it possible I had been wrong to believe my angel, my Melody would be loyal to me? "She would not…"

"Oh, no. She loves you too much. No, you see I was there."

My beating heart halted. The air in my body gone. Knees locked to reinforce composure.

"You seemed shocked," he said, confused. "I would have thought you knew me? You killed my friends after all. I suppose I was lucky to have been sent off to London soon after the incident or I might have joined them in the afterlife."

"You delight in such torture of those you deem less than? You would set a boy on fire, for what? Game? I did nothing to you nor your gang of beasts, yet you sought me out for fun?"

"If it's any consolation, Josephine did like your music. She just couldn't stand your face," he laughed. "What of your Melody? She's very odd, I kind of like it. What did she think of your face the first time she saw it?"

Shame at my actions in such a memory. Gritted teeth and clenched fists ached as my glare faltered. To remember her terror as I shoved *this* into her face.

"Guess love does have its limits," he said, taking a step toward the bar to further my humiliation. "It's a good thing she doesn't care about murder though. Or I'd be in trouble," he said and let out a sigh. "If she were prettier and I were someone else, there may have been something there. It's actually going to pain me to reunite you, I've grown somewhat fond of her."

Daggers were my eyes as they cut to him. Faster than he was able to react, I snatched him by the lapels of his expensive beige jacket. "You will not harm her!" I spit into his face as he strained back.

The fear in dark eyes replenished my soul and invigorated what was left of my body. The two guards who stood watch, burst from their seats and aided in their master's freedom. Sticks beat, and feet kicked as my knees met the stone covered earth.

"Make sure he stays alive. It's important," the bastard shrieked. "I want him to see his beloved one last time, just as he saw his eastern friend."

When the dogs halted their actions, crimson bled into my eye as I stared up at the soon to be lifeless thing standing over me.

"You see, monster. It's not *me* that would harm her. It will be her former lover. Blinded by jealousy. So much so, he couldn't let her live. Leaving me—the heart broken sympathetic widower that can never remarry because the love of his life was taken—behind. The same monster who killed a pregnant chorus girl. You are the villain in this story, Erique. You always will be. And your sweet Melody is just the innocent bystander."

"You underestimate her," I said, attempting breath as I held my side.

"I don't think so," Philippe quipped. "Anyway, I should be getting back. I have a charity to put on in *your* opera. Politicians and the other wealthy to impress. Oh! And someone to propose to. Fuck within an inch of her life. Then—eventually murder." He tipped his head. "See you soon."

Shaken was my body as the door to the room slammed shut and locked.

Alone once again.

Her ring burned into my palm as if calling to me. I kissed its precious metal and slipped it into my pocket.

Hope was not ingrained within me, yet something urged me forward to keep fighting for my ending.

This would be my last chance. I could not stand to watch her suffer as Ardashir did. Neither deserved such a thing.

In my last days, I could do this for her. My life for hers.

I uncurled my other fist and smirked at the sight of the iron key pressed within it. "I am coming for you, Angel."

The squeaking from my furry cellmate caught my attention as I slipped the key into the iron lock and twisted it.

"Today, God smiles upon us both, little friend."

Chapter XXXXI

Melody

A carcass rots away after death. What happens to a home when love dies? I never thought I'd see this place again. When Philippe told me the charity auction had been moved to the opera house, to say I didn't take it well was an understatement.

Once upon a time, it would have been hilarious to see what Erique would do. Now I feared it.

So, here I was, standing at the front of the door to the home that housed what I thought was love, terrified of what I might find when I opened it.

Would he be there? Would I want him to be? If he wasn't dead, I'd kill him.

Not really. Maybe. I don't know.

He's a monster, yet I was still willing to walk into the lion's den. Why?

The smell of sycamores filled my lungs as I searched for the courage to squeeze the handle.

The light in the living room was still on and everything was just as I had left it. My bookshelf was still by the front door. Ardashir's notepad was still on the end table. Our music—all over.

He hadn't been here since before I left. Was he that ashamed of what he did that he couldn't even come back?

The clock chimed, startling the shit out of me. I had to meet Philippe soon. It may not have been something I wanted to do, but I also didn't need a search party after me.

I forced myself through the room and into our… Erique's bedroom. The only thing I had on me that night was my phone and knife. I needed everything else if I was going to attempt home again.

My mask still hung on the wall around the vanity. I snatched it along with what I still had of my New York City outfit and threw it into the satchel I also thought I'd never see again.

I glanced at the wall one more time. Suppressed emotions attempted to fill my eyes as I took one last mental photo. Maybe I could just take one mask… the one with the horns.

"You're here," I said.

"Forgive my stupidity," he said, pressing his forehead to mine. *"I do not want to be that kind of man for you."*

I sniffled the ache back and stored the memory away again.

I hurried back through the living room, switched off the light and closed the door on *us* before I hurried back up to the surface. Who knew what would have happened if I had lingered.

***

I'd always wanted to go to a ball. I just wished it was under other circumstances.

Even though it'd been a few hours, I still felt the cold of the underground house on me. Where would Erique have gone if not home?

I just needed to find a moment that Philippe wasn't on me constantly so that I could break away and change. Until then…

It was nice to have been given a task to distract me from all the devastation of my life. To my surprise, the evening had gone off without issue. That almost never happened. Music filled the room as people danced and chatted throughout. Definitely a different feel from the makeshift *masq* a few months ago.

So many wealthy people showed up for the event to save face and make up for the awful things they usually did, all while wearing the most expensive things money could buy.

Chapter XXXXI

Philippe had me greeting them with him as if I were his wife. Repulsion shivered through me at the thought.

Since the other night he'd been more affectionate. Attempting to hold my hand. Kisses on the cheek.

I hoped it was something I didn't have to get used to after tonight.

"Chloe's out for a husband," Christine said of her friend as we watched from across the room, eyeing a small group of men.

I shook my head. *What innocence.* "I hope she finds a good one. She deserves happiness."

"Philippe looks so happy. You're a very handsome couple…" Christine said.

As much as I didn't want to be there, I tried to enjoy myself or at least not look like I was plotting my escape.

I swallowed the insinuation hard and opened my mouth to say anything that could remotely sound nice or close to the truth.

"Hello ladies," Raoul said, as he joined us. Never had I been so happy for an interruption. "Am I going to have to fight for your attention tonight, my beautiful fiancée?" he said, twirling Christine around and catching her in his arms.

"Maybe," she giggled as he kissed her temple.

"Are you going to sing with Christine?" he asked.

His question pulled me from my mind. "What do you mean?"

"Well, I told them we had the same teacher. And that you can sing," she said.

I stared in horror at the thought of performing live. "I don't think so," I muttered quickly. "Thank you, though."

"You can't let him win," Christine whispered. "I know what it is to lose hope. When it feels like everything's been ripped from you. But there's light at the end of the journey. Your voice is your own. It would mean so much to me."

As sweet as her words were, even after all this, the idea of getting on stage and performing wasn't something I could ever do. "I wish it was that," I said, as my knees trembled at the thought.

"Wish what?" Philippe asked as he joined our little group. He rested a hand on the small of my back and flicked his eyes to mine.

"These lovely ladies are going to sing for us this evening," Raoul boasted.

"Is this true?" he asked.

I tugged at the neck of my dress as it suddenly constricted. "I… I don't…"

"She'll be marvelous," Christine interjected.

"Well, in that case, I look forward to it," Philippe said. "You look stunning, have I told you already?" he said, leaning down into my ear. "Hard to keep my wits about me with you around."

It wasn't surprising he liked me better made up in a costume like when we first met. I'd forgotten how itchy these wigs were until he mentioned it just now.

I chuckled nervously, running a finger between the skin of my neck and the fabric of the collar again, "It's a bit high."

With a mischievous look, he placed a kiss on my cheek. I held back a groan and the unrelenting shivering in my stomach as I forced a smile while he pulled me along with him.

"I'll think about it," I said back to Christine as we left them.

Faces blurred as we greeted more people. Eventually, as luck would have it, Philippe turned his attention to another wealthy hand and I was left to my own devices again. Maybe this would be my chance to slip away and I wouldn't have to perform.

"Oh beautiful, Melody," Antoinette said hurrying over to me before I went for my escape.

I wasn't certain that they'd even received the invitation. Philippe wanted to keep the invitations open for political uses only, but I was allowed this one.

The faux diamond necklace I had given her sparkled around her neck. I chuckled ironically at the sight. I needed it, but I couldn't just yank it from her neck. My heart was lighter at seeing her. It honestly would have hurt to have left without saying goodbye.

As if she knew everything, she held my face in her worn hands. "Are you ok, *butterfly*?" she asked.

I clasped my hands around hers. "Better now."

"Happy?"

"Yes, madame. I am as happy as ever," I replied in my best voice.

Experienced eyes saw right through my words and grew sympathetic.

Chapter XXXXI

"He was broken. Your love was a blessing. But sometimes broken cannot be fixed. You will be happy, my girl."

"I just wanted to say thank you again," I said, ignoring the hurt at the top of my throat.

She kissed my cheek and walked into the giant room with Louis in tow. The woman's words echoed through my mind.

Just more words that fell into the pot of turmoil. I still didn't get any of it. Or maybe I was still blinded.

Maybe if the doorway didn't work this last time, I could just go back with her. No more ache or pretending.

"May I have this dance?" a voice asked from behind me.

My heart stilled as I turned. For a moment I swore I saw emerald and grey eyes staring down at me.

"Yes. Of course," I said and took Philippe's hand.

The band played beautifully without mistakes. Everything was perfect. Mostly.

"Is everything going as expected?" I asked, as he moved about.

"Better, actually. And I think by the end of the night there will be no doubt of my position."

"That's great for you," I said.

"For us, darling."

I hated the way he said "us". My misery was so acute that it manifested into physical discomfort, one which triggered my nausea constantly.

Even if I did like Philippe in that way, it was too fast. It was too much. I was never going to be able to give myself to another man completely, anyway. He wouldn't be getting all of me.

"*Excuse me. Excuse me,*" Raoul said, quieting the room. The party guests listened as he gave some sort of speech through his genuine smile. The room filled with a smattering of applause as they turned to Philippe.

"And now, Christine Daae' and Melody Reilly," he said.

"What?" My heart dropped and the color in my face along with it.

"It is time to join Christine on stage, darling," Philippe said, ushering me toward the stairs as the people continued to clap.

Christine grabbed hold of my hand as she met me, tugging me along.

It'd been years since I tried to go on stage. Since my embarrassing catastrophe.

The collar around my neck tightened again. "You are going to be wonderful. We will sing from the *Marriage of Figaro*."

"I haven't warmed up. I can't do this."

"It is one song, you will be fine," she said.

I stared down at the three steps up to the platform. What a stupid thing to do amongst everything.

"Calm and breathe. Reach far within. Up and out. Up and out," he said into my neck.

I may have hated him, but Erique's words created a calmness within me.

I inhaled deeply and exhaled slowly, taking the first step. Before I knew it, we were at the center of the small pop-up stage.

A thousand eyes were on us. On me.

I stared at the music on the lyre, trying to focus on just that. If I made it through this, it would just be one more amazing thing I had to tell when I got home. Mom was going to be so proud.

The small band started up and Christine began. It was the longest nine minutes of my life, but I was doing it! Erique and I had practiced this in our earlier lessons. Only this time I had a stage partner to play off of.

I did it. I did it without messing up. I did it in front of all these people and I didn't pass out. From head to toe I was euphoric.

We bowed as the crowd clapped again.

I couldn't believe that I did it.

"That was truly wonderful. I didn't know that you were capable," Philippe said.

"Neither did I," I replied, still gleeful, even with Philippe's embrace. What a powerful ending.

"Excuse me," I said, stepping back. "I must use the powder room. Too much excitement."

"Of course," he replied. "But do hurry. It's going to be an eventful evening."

I wished I could ride the high of my personal achievement. But, my smile fell as soon as my feet steppcd into the hallway and I was out of sight.

Chapter XXXXI

Luckily enough, there weren't police as I wandered. Philippe said the place was crawling with them because of Erique. But I hadn't seen any except the few near the hall. Maybe they were outside?

Still a little euphoric, I locked the door to the dressing room and leaned against it as my chest and shoulders heaved with relief for the time alone.

The satchel with all my things still waited on the vanity table that used to be the wall between me and Erique's conversations. I lunged at it, undoing the buttons to the front of my dress as I went.

As I undressed, I caught a glimpse of the woman in the mirror, someone I didn't recognize again. I hadn't realized how the sadness had eaten away at me the past month. Dark circles printed beneath my eyes if you looked close enough. I looked sickly. At least to me. No one else seemed to notice.

I ripped the stupid dark wig from my head and slammed it onto the vanity table after I got my neck free. Quickly, I got out of the dress and into my Phantom night outfit, sans my shoes and necklace. "It'll just have to work," I said, slipping my jacket on. "There."

The restroom was close enough. If I was going to be miserable, I was going to be back in my shitty time, a hundred and forty years away from this memory.

***

I hesitated for a moment, staring into the dark of the doorway. I slid the mask on and tried to envision where I wanted to go.

Home.

"Please, I just want to be home," I begged the universe, and stomped through the threshold.

My tightly closed eyes opened into darkness. I glanced around slowly hoping it was after hours in the Majestic.

My heart dropped when the hallway was the same as I stared out from the restroom. I took a deep breath and marched through again. "I want to be home," I repeated, pain straining my throat.

What hope was left had dissolved with that final step. I was never going back.

"No," I wept.

After several moments of completely cataclysmic realizations, I decided it was time to get back into costume and salvage what was left of my sanity.

Everything sucked and I was alone, forever. I never should have stopped trying. How fucking stupid. And now I would have to accept Philippe if I wanted to survive. *I hate it here.*

With the last button done on the neck of this stupid dress, I packed everything back into the bag. Not even sure why, it didn't work and I was never going to wear any of it again.

I wiped away any sign that I'd been crying and readied for the door.

Up my spine slithered a familiar sense. The little hairs across my body stood on end as a presence I hadn't felt in so long intertwined with the cold draft that crept over the flesh of my neck.

"You are the embodiment of beauty and song. My memory of your voice holds no light to what you truly are. The light of music. An angel in the hellscape of this world." His voice was soft and sad.

"Don't come any closer," I seethed, turning to meet the stare of flickering emerald green and stone-gray eyes.

He stepped into the light from within the darkness of the opened hidden door we'd walked through many times before.

"Stop," I demanded.

He halted, propping himself against the vanity table. Nothing was out of place. Mask. Hair. Dressed to impress as always... Always so *tempting*... Always. Always. Always.

"Leave now," I ordered, unable to move.

"Please, hear me, my love," he said. The thunderous voice that resonated from him was tired. Weak almost.

I couldn't be curious anymore. I couldn't care.

"No!" I said and turned back to the door.

"I didn't kill Ardashir," he said in a shaky timber. "He was my only friend."

I scoffed. Was it disbelief or denial? "Of course, you didn't," I said. "It must have been the other Boogeyman. Probably the one who killed the girl, huh? And anyone else I don't know about."

I met eyes that had found themselves closer than before.

"There's nothing you could tell me that could fix what you've done," I said.

Chapter XXXXI

"They made me watch!" he snarled, jolting closer yet again. He gripped the back of the chaise lounge. Shoulders hunched and head hung as he fought whatever was in his mind. Tortured eyes looked up from beneath the white of an old mask. "The one who did this," he gestured to his face and down his body. "Your precious Comte Philippe *de Vermin* was one of the many from my story. Beneath the city he held me. Tortured me. Told me about the girl. His plans with you…"

"Stop! I don't want to hear any more of your bullshit," I cried.

My back hit the door as he moved at me, planting his hands on the wood around my head. Locked in place, his gaze wavered about recalling whatever horrors he'd seen.

"When my friend told you to run from me. I needed to know why he would do such a thing. I had been good, Melody," he cried. "He knew, the vermin knew I'd be near you. Stayed in wait." Fear encapsulated his eyes. "There were too many. I could not save him again," he wept. "They forced my eyes…"

"You lie." My words were weak and unsure.

"I have never lied to you!"

I ducked beneath his arms and slipped away. "All you do is lie! Your entire existence is a lie. The Phantom of the Opera. One giant lie. That I fed into. What was I even thinking?" I said, catching myself in the mirror. Confused eyes met mine in the reflection. "We could never have had an actual life together. You were never gonna leave the underworld. I can't live underground. And you can't blackmail people forever to make your money. At some point they'd find you and kill you." I turned slowly, I needed to say it to him. For me. "In every scenario, we lose. It was all just a fantasy."

"You do not believe that," he said. "I know you do not. Just be with me."

"How dare you! How dare you make me love you!" I stomped around him to the door again. I was going to leave this time. For sure. "Against my will I loved you. I tried so hard not to want you, but you kept weaving your way in. I should have listened. I knew the stories. Yet, I *still* trusted you and you continued to lie to me…"

This moment tore at my insides. I should have been back in 2023 by now. Not staring into the eyes of someone that I wished were a better man as he begged me to love him again.

"You promised you'd never leave me," I said, through a cracked voice.

"I told you it would never be my decision."

"You want everyone to be as miserable as you… You…" my hands flew to the collar of my dress, clawing at the fabric around my neck. "You… I can't… I can't…"

My back hit the door as the world started to fade.

Erique's hands were on me immediately. I don't even remember seeing him move. He yanked the fabrics at my neck, ripping it open as buttons went flying.

Clinging onto Erique's arms for balance, my chest heaved as I inhaled deeply with the freedom of my lungs.

His arms were so thin beneath the fabric of his jacket as I clung. Bony fingers cupped my wheezing face. "My baby, breathe," he begged. We slid to the floor as I caught my breath. "Why would you wear such a garment? You hate anything around your neck."

The light shone against his face better where we were. Bruises colored his pale cheek and jaw. His lips were dry and cracked, like he'd been beaten and starved.

"What happened?" I asked, running my fingertips along the exposed flesh.

His eyes closed as if the touch healed him. He pressed his forehead against mine. "I would never leave you."

The gentlest kiss I'd ever experienced touched my lips. It was like ice and fire all at once and everything I wanted.

I was desperate for it again, grabbing at him as I kissed him back furiously.

How could this be so wrong?

"Come away with me, *my heart*," he begged.

"No," I whispered through a sob and pulled away. "I can't. Not again. I can't care anymore, Erique." My hand fell from his face as I forced myself to my feet. Away from his undoing gaze. "Just leave, Erique. Let this be your chance to go somewhere else. Start new."

"Life is an illusion without you," he said, struggling to his feet after me. Like second nature, I leant my strength and helped him up.

Chapter XXXXI

Something terrible happened to him. It couldn't be what he said though. Right? "You cannot go to him," he said, grabbing at me. "I do not care that you have laid with him. You are mine and always will be," he said.

"What?" I said freaking out. "No. I didn't. I couldn't…" I had chickened out and ran back to my room before Philippe could answer the door.

Relief passed through his irises for a moment before he stepped for me again. The wetness from his eyes saturated us both as he pressed his cheek to mine. "He's going to ask for your hand. And then…"

"Shush!"

Just then, Philippe's voice crept in through the door in the distance. *Oh God!*

I yanked my arm away and turned back to the door. "You have to let me go."

"Melody. My Melody, please."

"You want to live your life as a ghost, Erique? Then be one," I spit. It was the most hurtful thing I could say and I hated myself more than ever for having said it.

He stepped back as guilt stabbed me in the chest. "That is not of your mind, is it?" he asked.

Living on my pride and maybe saving us both, I swallowed, trying to ignore the utter grief and despair in those pained eyes.

"Erique, you have to go now. Please," I said, hearing Philippe's voice growing closer, calling out my name.

"He knows I've escaped and would come for you."

I rushed to him and held his face. Hoping he understood my pleading eyes. "If you ever cared about me, you'll leave and never come back. I can't stand this hurt anymore."

"Tell me you do not love me, and this world will never see me again."

Philippes voice grew nearer. I could hear my name being called now clearly.

"Please. Go you stubborn jackass," I said, urging him towards his escape.

"Tell me you don't love me."

"Ok. I don't love you."

"You lie," he said. His voice as sweet as ever.

"I hate you. Now fucking leave," I pleaded and pushed him into the dark of the wall. "Goodbye, Opera Ghost." My whisper laced in sadness.

The door swung open, hitting the wall. Philippe's dark eyes darted to every corner in the small room. "Who were you talking to?" I asked.

"No one. Just myself. Calming myself," I said.

Suspicious eyes glared down at me. "What happened to your dress and why are you crying?"

I hadn't noticed the tears had leaked again. I wiped them away. "I panicked," I said, tucking in the ripped flaps. "Christine doesn't understand how badly I fear the stage. It was so overwhelming. I panicked and needed to be alone."

He searched my face, trying to detect the lie I'd just told him. His expression turned softer, maybe seeing the sadness and embarrassment in my eyes.

I was a good actor. Ugh.

"You were gone for a time. I was worried," he said. "The world still isn't safe yet, my pet." A politician's smile graced his face. "Shall I take you back, I'd like to have one more dance with you this evening before the auction starts."

I laced my arm with his.

"Don't forget your hair," he said, gesturing at the wig on the table next to the closed passageway.

Just keep smiling. Remember, you'll be happy one day.

Chapter XXXXII

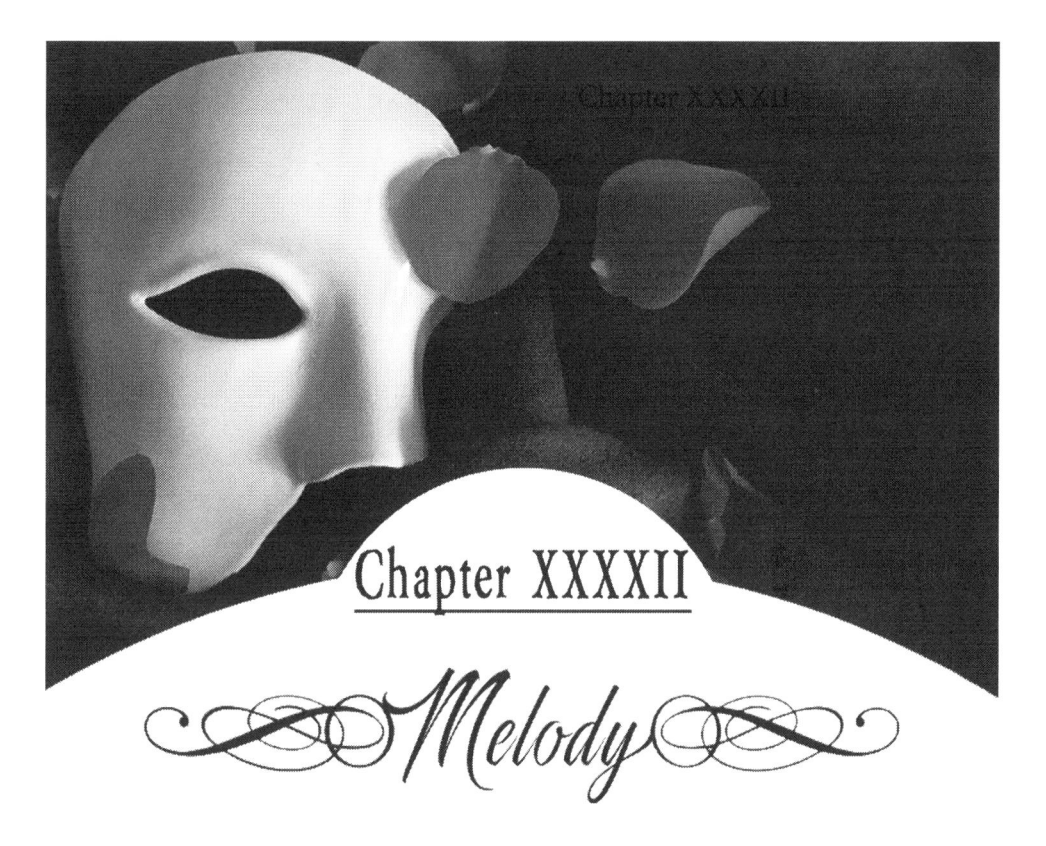

Melody

All the King's horses and all the King's men couldn't put my shattered heart back together again. But I was going to try.

Whether I believed the man I still loved, I had sent Erique away to save him. I think. Even if he didn't deserve it.

Did I really believe he was guilty? Worry was at the front of my mind. Erique didn't give up easily.

The party hadn't noticed we disappeared. Nor did they notice our return.

"There's something on your mind, darling," Philippe said. It wasn't a question. "Is there anything you need to tell me?"

Thoughts froze as I tried to find something to say. Erique had said so much. But Philippe was an asshole, not a monster. However, thinking about it, something always bothered me about that night.

How much danger would I be in for asking it?

"Silence. Silence," Raoul called over the room.

Saved by the bell. Again. Bless him.

"Hold that thought. I'll only be a moment," Philippe said and kissed my hand.

He joined Raoul on stage, charming and handsome as he could be. Guess maybe it wouldn't be so bad. It didn't matter that I wished he was someone else.

I scanned the room for signs of Erique. If what he said was true about Philippe, he'd want revenge.

"…Melody Reilly," Philippe said.

I snapped from my swirling thoughts as the crowd around me applauded. I loved singing but I didn't want to do it again tonight.

"Melody. Would you join me please?"

A shark's smile spread across his face. The pit in my stomach grew as I neared the stage.

Clammy hands took mine and guided me up. "None of this would have been possible without you," he said. "And I would like every event here after to be with you as well." He reached into his pocket and dropped to his knee.

This had to be a coincidence, right?

His words were incomprehensible as I stared down at the hideous gold ring set with a large diamond, surrounded by small, various colored pebbled stones.

Dread like I'd never felt plagued me. Not only did I think Erique wasn't lying. I knew it.

"Philippe," I said, not sure of what to say and worried all at once. "How did you know they were friends?"

Not the smartest thing, but there it was.

"What?" he asked, glancing at the crowd confused.

"How did you—"

"Angel of light in darkness of night."

That thunderous voice that ignited my soul, the one I banished, filled the ballroom with song. My pulse quickened with every sound from his lips as my eyes searched the area. It was wishful thinking that he'd leave.

Philippe gripped me tightly, trying to hide me behind him.

"Sweet. Oh sweet. So beautiful. All life flows like air around you.
Desperate, this demon crawled to breathe you in."

Scared and captivated by the voice they couldn't pinpoint, the crowd glanced around nervously. "*Cherche-le*!" Philippe shouted.

"Stop!" I yelled at the top of my lungs like I had never done before.

Chapter XXXXII

Tears welling in the corners of my eyes. "Leave this place, Erique! You're not wanted." Why wouldn't he listen? Staying was a death sentence.

"This devil, this monster, haunts and taunts, but only desires to serve this angel of light," Erique continued.

Shrieks bounced off walls. My eyes followed the turning faces. Erique emerged from the shadows in a doorway at the other end of the room as the shrills grew louder.

"She told you she doesn't want you, creature!" Philippe said.

"To you, my angel, my heart, I would never lie. From hell you pulled me..." he sang as the sea of people parted to make way.

"This soul breathes again, only for you. Deity of time."

You stupid man.

I fought the ache at the corner of my eye. What was he doing? *Run.*

"Enough of this," Philippe said and yanked me. *"Get him!"*

Erique stopped at the center of the room. Without moving, he peered around at the gawking, moved faces of the crowd.

"For air is second to the spring beating of a heart that never lived."

In a swift movement, the Opera Ghost dropped to the floor with a clink, and in his place was Erique. Head held high as the screams let out.

"Here before you I stand, humbled and me. As you wished I would always be," he finished.

"You killed Ardashir, didn't you?" I accused of Philippe.

He stilled, staring at me with hate blazing in his eyes as his fingers dug into my muscle. "You don't know what you're saying," he said.

Two officers from the hallway rushed in through the doorway towards Erique.

"Don't!" I screamed, whacking Philippe in the dick and tore away.

The officers had gotten to Erique before I could, forcing him to his knees.

I ran past disgusted faces and ignorant whispers. The officers stared, unsure of what to do as I met him on the floor. "No. No," I said, trying to cover his face with my hands. *"Stop!"* I spit at the gossiping onlookers. "We have to get your mask back on, my babe," I said, frantically glancing around for it.

"It's alright," he said, shaking his face from my hands, guiding them to his lips.

"You don't have to do this," I whispered.

"To show you, means everything," he said.

"This is appalling! Arrest it! It's committed the greatest of sins. Murder!" Philippe screamed.

"The sin is not mine, Monsieur. And we both know it," Erique said. His voice stronger than it had been throughout the night. "The sin is not mine," he repeated just for me, in a different desperate tone.

"I know," I said, and kissed him, hoping he felt the apology in my heart. In my soul.

Gasps commandeered the whispers. It didn't matter. Erique knew I believed him. That was what mattered.

With ripping pain, Philippe yanked me away. "Enough of this. You've embarrassed me for the last time, American whore," he seethed. "Now take him away!"

"He's not guilty. Stop! Stop!" I screamed as the officers grabbed at him harder. "I should have left with you, I'm so sorry, Erique!" I cried.

I reached out for him who was trying to fight against them, but was failing for how weak he was. I didn't think Erique could ever lose.

I whipped my focus back to Philippe. "The night Ardashir died. You said he killed his friend. How did you know they were friends? No one knew that except me. And how did you know the girl was pregnant?"

"Be silent!" he said.

Loud ringing and stars clouded my mind when the back of a hand met the side of my head.

The audible gasp from the crowd had Philippe looking around like a cornered dog.

"They see the real monster now, boy," Erique spit.

Through the dizziness and stinging, a gentle hand took my arm. Christine helped me upright as I looked for Erique.

"Those are not his only crimes. Monsieur," Erique said, exhausted. "How was your time in Toulouse?"

My arm stung as I scurried to him, not sure of what could be done now.

"This creature would spin lies to save himself and his whore," Philippe mocked, spitting as he spoke. "Do not believe a word of it."

"Toulouse?" Raoul asked, stepping in from the crowd. "What of it?"

Chapter XXXXII

"Hold your tongue, boy!" Philippe scorned.

"The girl's friend fell victim to the same death during your visit. Interesting, no?" Erique said, tossing the notepad at Raoul's feet. "It is in Persian speak, but the information is there."

Raoul picked up the notepad and opened it. "You were there a few months ago on emergency, do you not remember?" he asked his brother.

"This thing has brainwashed her," Philippe spat. "I wasn't even in France when the girl died."

"That's right, he was in London," Raoul answered, questioning his own mind.

"You see," Philippe said, stomping to the officers. "Nothing but a lying beast that needs to be put down."

"No, I saw you at the Opera that night. Just before act three," Christine said.

"Are you sure?" Raoul asked as she joined him.

"Yes. I didn't know he was your brother until I saw you both a month later. But he was there. Walking down the dressing room hall. I know it was him."

Philippe's eyes widened. "You lying whore." He reached into the coat of the officer next to him and pulled a small pistol from its holster. "That's all you women are. Lying whores."

"Philippe, enough of this! Please!" Raoul shouted.

"Stupid, pathetic waste of life. How dare you," he said to Raoul. "Come on." He grabbed my wrist and tore me from Erique. The officers stepped back as he waved the gun around like a madman.

"Unhand her," Erique growled, watching like a wolf targeting his prey. Ready to pounce at any moment, though he couldn't.

I shook my head, warning him. But his sights didn't waver.

"Come, we're leaving, *darling*," Philippe said. His voice heavy with disdain. "There's been a change in plans."

***

It seemed Philippe's driver didn't care that he was holding someone hostage as he forced me into his carriage.

"Well. That was not ideal," Philippe said snidely as we bounced along the uneven roads just outside the city.

"What now?" I asked, staring at the gun in his hand.

"I can't believe I was starting to like you. Even considered calling the whole thing off."

"Just let me go, Philippe," I said. "Everyone knows what you did."

"You still would have preferred that sewer dweller over a life of luxury and title?" he scoffed. "Of course you would. It just makes all this much easier, I guess."

"That's what this was all about? Rejection?" You were going to kill me and Erique, for rejection?"

Clutching the knife in my pocket, I bore holes through his head as I imagined every awful thing I would do to him. "In every life he's the easy choice," I said. At least I had the opportunity to let Erique know before we wouldn't have a chance again.

I hoped he was alright. What was going to happen to him now?

"As for this unfortunate situation," he said. "Money makes people blind. In any case. It was just a whore. And as for you, *dearest*, I do have a question before we part ways." He shifted, still aiming the pistol at me. With a twist in his face, he asked, "How could you possibly fuck that thing?" My teeth nearly cracked at the question. I was clenching my jaw so hard. "That sewer rat's face is absolutely the most grotesque thing I've ever seen. I realize that it's partially my fault, but Jesus Christ. I was nauseous just staring at it."

"That face is more beautiful than any part of you. It's also why I couldn't stomach the idea of fucking you…"

My cheek stung and my eye felt like it was going to pop from its socket as his hand landed across it again.

"You disgusting flea of American rubbish." Philippe spit in my face. My shaking hand rushed to wipe it off. "Don't forget how easy you were to convince that your precious *Erique* was the monster."

"And it's something I'll have to live with."

"Not for long." Philippe put the gun in his coat pocket. "I'm going to enjoy this." Then lunged at me.

Dark eyes filled with hate and excitement seared into me. Nostrils flared in fury. Lips mashed together in rage. The confined space and uneven road made it difficult for him to keep steady pressure as he attempted to crush my windpipe. The strain in my throat as I tried to keep breathing, tore and burned. Nails clawed at his face and hands,

Chapter XXXXII

trying anything to loosen his grip.

An insignificant man would be the one to take me out. Every fear coming to life.

Such shit.

The world faded and swirled around me as death sat on my chest.

"Phil…" I tried to say.

***

Stars faded in and out through a small opening in the dark. I tried to muster resistance, weakly fighting against the hands that tugged at me. "No!" I finally managed. My voice raspy and throat sore.

"You've found your voice, Angel."

That voice, I knew that voice.

Squinting my lids, I focused on the dark figure holding onto my arms. "Erique? How are you here?"

He huffed, helping me to my feet. "I told you, I will never leave you."

My hands clenched around his forearms, attempting to steady myself. I think he was doing the same.

I stood amazed that he was without his mask. "How did you escape?" I asked, still dazed.

"Black smoke."

Erique always had a trick up his sleeve. Almost anyway.

We were still in the carriage that had turned onto its side. With help from each other, we managed to crawl out from the wrecked car through the window.

The moon's light touched brush, sparse trees and a long dirt road. In the distance lying face down was Philippe.

"He was thrown from the cab when it overturned," Erique said, then fell back against the undercarriage.

"We need to get you help," I said, my throat ripping as I spoke. "I'll get the horses."

The horses had broken from the carriage, luckily one still hung around close by. I took a few steps, stopping at sight of the driver laying nearby.

"He's unconscious," Erique said, as if reading my mind.

Crack!

I turned to catch Erique before he hit the ground, missing completely.

"Don't worry," Philippe said, stepping up, pointing the gun at Erique's chest. "I promised you'd be together soon. I won't make her wait."

I wasn't going to lose him again. I wasn't going to stand by and have Erique lose!

"Philippe, don't!" I screamed.

The trigger pulled back, and the world stopped.

Surprise graced our faces when nothing happened.

"No!" Philippe yelled, going for a large rock within reach.

I pounced onto his back without thought as he bent over, throwing all my weight as I latched on. He stumbled forward, hitting the ground hard enough to yelp. Frantically, I found the little Smith & Wesson in my pocket and yanked it out.

"You should've just let us go," I cried and drove the blade into the side of his neck and pushed down, ripping it open. My hand warmed as the red spilled over it. Tremors attacked my body as I let go immediately. The sticky knife rolled from my hand as Philippe's lifeless body collapsed to the earth.

The worst panic came from the sight of Erique's unmoving body. Fear spread through me, weighing me down with every step as I rushed to him.

His body was heavy as I shook him, skin paler than usual. I pressed my fingers to his wrist, checking for a pulse, and then to his neck. It was faint but there.

My eyes darted around for the horses. The one that had stayed behind ran off with the sound of the gun. How was I going to get him out of there?

Tears blinded and choked my voice worse than the pain. "I'm so sorry. This is my fault," I cried, brushing the hair back from the face he tried so hard to hide from the world.

My heart stopped as a gentle pressure rested onto the crown of my head. "You'll never be free of me," he said grunting from the pain of moving. Startled, I sat up. Eyes wide with surprise and relief. "*Comte de Vermin* is a terrible shot," he said, attempting to reach for his shoulder blade.

Chapter XXXXII

I lunged forward and cradled his face, running my hand through his filthy hair. "Hi," I cried and kissed him feverishly.

"Angel," he said, as if it were a prayer.

"Stop!" I ordered as he tried to sit up.

"This isn't the first time I've been shot, my love."

"It shouldn't be too bad to get out once I find it," I said, trying to roll him over.

All that time in the rural fire department so many years ago where I never tended a wound, was about to finally pay off. Fuck.

"Breast pocket," he said, not aiding in my attempt to roll him over.

"What? No, I need to find your wound, my babe."

"Breast pocket," he said again.

Beautiful eyes stared as if he hadn't seen me in a hundred years. He's probably dying, but he'd rather sit here beneath the stars and look at me.

Reluctantly, I reached into the pocket, wiggling my bloody fingers around until I stopped on a little object. I pulled it out and stared in disbelief. In my hand was the silver ring with blue sapphires and white diamonds I thought I'd lost.

"How do you get this?" I asked.

"Courtesy of the dearly departed."

"My sister once said God himself could hand deliver the person made for me, and I'd still find reason not to believe it was true. I don't want things to change. Men always change."

The matching encrusted band he wore glimmered in the light of the moon as he found my hand. "If I change to your displeasure, send me off to dance in hell with M. *de Vermin*. I would deserve no less."

"Speaking of. If we could stop killing people, I'd appreciate it."

"If that is what you wish," he said, as his lids grew heavy.

I slipped the ring on my hand and held Erique's tired face. "I'm so sorry. I was still looking for a reason to run. That's why I think I wanted to believe you did it."

"I know," he said.

I glanced around again for the horses or anyone that could help. We were alone.

I rattled him a little until his heavy eyes refocused. "You are going to be an amazing husband. The best," I said, trying to hide the terror in my voice. I just hoped he got to be…

"I know," he said, a slight smirk tugging at the corner of his dried lips.

"Ass."

He rolled his head to better look at me. "But I can only be a husband if you say yes. Do you say yes, Melody… Amber Reilly?"

I kissed his lips and nodded. "All the yeses, Erique."

"Good. Fear had me weakened at thought of the destruction of another book. But I would have done it."

I laughed softly. "Now, we have to get back. So we can go home."

Captivating eyes dulled and rolled as his lids closed. His breathing slowed and pulse faded beneath my fingers.

"Erique. Erique, please, wake up! Wake up!" I sobbed into his chest checking for a heartbeat, yelling again for a miracle.

This was how it was always going to end for the Phantom. No matter what I did. The story was going to be the same.

We would finally overcome all our fears, mostly, then we would be ripped apart by death?

"No!" I screamed into his face, shaking him hard. "This isn't how this story's gonna end!" I slapped him.

The stomping of hooves and twigs snapping jolted me around. For a moment I thought Philippe had somehow managed to survive, or maybe the driver was ready to attack. I gasped to find Cesar, the white and gray peppered horse, Erique's favorite, barreling toward us with Raoul at the reins.

I turned back and grabbed Erique's face one more time. "This isn't how our story ends, Erique! You won't die tonight! Please! Please, wake up!"

Chapter XXXXII

Two Months Later

It's been really hard. Lonely at times.
Even though Christine has come to terms that she was wrong about Philippe, both her and Raoul have stayed their distance somewhat. I can't blame them.
What I did to Philippe—even though he tried to kill me and Erique—after Raoul saw him like that, he just hasn't been the same. I'm hoping, for Christine, he'll come around.
Even with the death of Philippe, Raoul and the few others that showed up with him helped me get Erique to someone.
It was touch and go for days, but eventually he was awake enough to not allow me away from his side, afraid he was going to lose me again.
Antoinette has been really there for me though. Now that she knows everything and understands. She finally got to see what I see in Erique. I just wish she'd seen it sooner. Maybe Erique would have felt more love before it all went bad. Though yes, it is also his fault for thier relationship.
The whole thing has been insane. Which has made the past few months suspicious. Because it's been normal. Quiet. Well. Mostly.
I think you'd really like him, eventually.
I wish you were here, but you'd hate the smell.
Though it's taken time for some to heal from his lying and stuff, it's getting better. However, the tension with the managers is still a bit intense. Erique's offered to help with productions and things in exchange for his salary instead of extortion. I think they're a bit scared still, which is why they agreed.
I'm still not sure how he's managed to stay out of jail or anything like that since everyone knows who he is now. I mean, everyone thought he was a ghost for at least fifteen years, and he's killed people.
Our opera, The Phantom's Melody, is almost complete. It's definitely different from the stories we know, especially because he doesn't die at the end. We're just putting some finishing touches on it before presenting to the house as a possibility for the next season. And guess who's trying out? It only took me falling into the scariest thing in my life, to finally get what I've always wanted.
Oh, by the way, we're getting married…

"What are you writing, *my heart?*" he said, breaking my concentration with a kiss to the temple. I didn't even hear him come back from his outing.

Erique still rarely went out, especially in the day, but it was getting better. Though people stared—because he's wearing a mask—they *only* stared. Nothing much else. Whether they knew the stories of the Ghost or not, he's found most people just stayed away.

"A letter home," I said. "I thought I'd try it. I've seen it in movies and thought maybe there could be a way. It's stupid."

My body ached staring at him. I bit my lip, forgetting what I was doing before. I hated when he unbuttoned his shirt. It was worse when he let his wavy hair free instead of slicking it back.

"Don't do that," he warned, running a thumb over my top lip. "There are several banks along the way to London. We can see if there is something to be done." Butterflies tickled my body as he kissed my hand and pulled me to him. "We are going to need a deposit box anyway."

His soft kiss had my knees weak. I couldn't wait. We were leaving in the morning to travel for a few weeks. He was taking me to places he wished he could have seen in a better way. Through my eyes, as he liked to say. I couldn't be prouder of him.

"I have something for you, my darling wife," he said, pulling out a folded paper.

"Not for a few more weeks, turbo," I said. Even though the word was kind of growing on me, it was still a little weird to hear.

"We were eternal the moment you kissed me."

Gentle lips seared along my neck, and goosebumps spread over my flesh. Tingling trailed behind fingertips as they traveled along the length of my arm.

Poorly, I ignored his advances and unfolded the sheet of paper. It seemed to be a title or deed of some kind. "What is this," I asked.

"No more managers." His lips moved to my ear, caressing like a breeze over wild grass.

"Did you buy us a theater?"

"Mmmm," he purred.

"What about this place?" I said, glancing around the living room to our underground home.

His lips moved to my jaw, nipping and kissing at my hypersensitive

Chapter XXXXII

skin. My eyes rolled back, giving in just enough to the sensations coursing through me, urging me into submission.

"We will elevate the theater in London. Where our music will play. In our theater. Starting with *The Phantom's Melody*," he said.

"We aren't coming back?"

"Only if you want to. I belong wherever you are."

Our tongues laced together in slow passion, but I was still trying to focus on the surprise. *We're moving to London to run a theater. Holy shit.*

I attempted to look over the paper to our future again, landing on the names at the bottom. It was signed with a familiar last name. One I'd heard all my life.

"Where did you hear this name?" I asked, staring more intently at it.

"It means reborn. That is what we are. Life has offered us rebirth, my Love. And we will embrace it."

"I… I don't know the first thing about this," I barely uttered under his touch.

"We can do anything. Don't you know that by now, Mrs. *Renaître*?" he said and pushed my legs open to settle in between.

Hearing it out loud almost made me laugh. The name my mother had told me over and over since birth. Sure, why not? Of course, I would be named after myself.

Guess she was wrong about the French part though. That was my soon to be husband. And not exactly a playwright. But close enough.

I chuckled at the irony though as the man of my fantasies continued his exhibition of my body.

The stories were written. But it could still change. There's so much unknown. So much that could happen. I never looked into the story of Melody and her mysterious husband. I didn't know how it ended.

The sudden fear of losing Erique again weaved through the shield of love that had formed around me. "But what if…?"

"Shhh…" he purred.

And just like that, the spike of fear and the future melted away under his scorching kiss, and all was forgotten.

Epilogue

"How do you walk into a bathroom with twenty people and just vanish? How does that happen?" Sarah said to me as we entered through the door of my home. "I'm sorry Mom. I'm still in disbelief."

I hated that I had to leave New York without my little Melody. Without any answers. It had been a week of unending questions and watching the same footage over and over again just to see her walk into a restroom and never come out, until we couldn't afford to stay anymore.

"I don't know," I said, drained of any remaining life in me. Sarah was just as tired. She was the one consistently bombarding the police throughout our stay.

"Alright, Mom. I have to call Clint and let him know I'm here now," she said, as she helped me into my bed. The only other thing that saw me the most, outside of Melody. "Get some sleep, we both need it. I'm going to the couch, ok?"

I nodded and turned to face the wall. Like a projector, I replayed the videos again and again, trying to make sense of it. She walks in, and walks out. Then poof. Gone.

"Hey Jules," my friend, Roger, said walking into the room. I bolted upright at his voice. I had forgotten he was coming over. "I'm sorry to hear what happened, any news?"

I laid back down, trying to muffle the sobbing in my pillow. What a dumb question. Like it was something I would keep silent.

Epilogue

"I know this really awful thing happened. I wish I could make it better for you." he said. I just continued to stare past him. He was a great friend, but I just wanted to be alone. "You got some mail while you were gone," he said, trying to lift my spirits. "Mostly junk. Do you know anyone in London?" he asked, handing me a yellow stained envelope.

"I don't care what you do with it."

He smiled a pity filled smile and rubbed my side. He set the pile of mail on the nightstand and left me. "She'll pop up, kid. Don't worry."

I closed my eyes tight, wishing and praying to God that she would. That the phone would ring, and she would be asking for a ride home. That she just got lost or was in hospital and safe.

I missed my hardworking daughter. The one that, despite everything, still always loved her mama. Even when I wasn't easy to deal with.

The dreams were enough to keep me tossing and turning. I even thought I heard her calling out at some point. Of course, when I opened my eyes, she wasn't there.

Unable to sleep, I turned back over and reached for the light. My phone still had no missed calls or emails.

I stifled a sleepy, tired sniffle and looked at the pile of bills. The yellow stained envelope sat right on top. "London?" I said, and reached for it.

It had been stamped and restamped a handful of times with a requested delivery date for a few days before we returned back to Washington. With the return name above the London address M.R.R.

I flipped the thick envelope and tore it open. A key and photos fell out from within the folded papers into my lap. I picked up one of the photos curiously. They were in black and white. A man in a mask with black hair and bright eyes stood next to what looked like my smiling daughter.

"Sarah! Sarah!" I shouted, unfolding the papers as quickly as my aching hands could.

Hey Mama. This is number six out of ten copies of
this that I'm sending, hoping it gets to you.
That is if this actually reaches you. I'm alright.
And I have the craziest thing to tell you…

"What's wrong?" she yelled, bursting through the door. "Mom?"

"It's Mel!" I said.

She rushed to join me, taking the papers from my hand. "Where did you get this?" she asked. "Is that Melody? Mom, what is this?"

"It was in the mail."

"I'm so confused. What's happening?"

"Give them back," I snapped, and snatched the papers. I continued to read out loud so that both Sarah and Roger, who'd joined us, could hear.

Every sentence was as crazy and impossible as the last. It took almost an hour to read it because I couldn't stop crying.

My sweet little girl wrote of her arrival to this place she claimed was the year 1880. That she'd killed some people. Sang on stage. Everything all the way up to a marriage? *My baby got married?*

> *Hopefully the photos are still good by the time you get this. It's Erique and I on our wedding day. I thought you'd like that. It was really hard to get him to take one without the mask so there's two. Don't freak out.*

"Oh my God," Sarah shrieked, looking at the other photo from my lap. "What the heck is that?"

"Stop," I said, taking the photo from her. "Oh…" The man behind the mask was jarring, but the love on my daughter's face took away any doubts I may have had. "She looks so happy."

"I swear, her taste in men is so awkward. As long as she's happy I guess. But how is this possible?" Sarah asked as if I would somehow magically know the answer as to why we were receiving mail from a hundred years ago with my daughter's face on it. "Does this mean that she's…"

"Don't say it. Not right now, Sarah."

"So, do we tell the police?" Sarah asked.

I shrugged. "Tell them what?" What could they do? They would think we were out of our minds if we came to them with this story.

"What's this to?" Sarah asked, picking up the key from the blanket.

Epilogue

...This is the key to the safety deposit box. It's at the C. Hoare & Co. London's oldest bank. It was the only one I remembered being around long after the wars. You just have to get there. It's gonna have the story of my life in it. And some things to help you guys out when Erique and I eventually... anyway.

If the story of the Phantom is different from what you remember after going over the letters and things I've left, then good. It's the real story with a crazy twist, I guess.

Maybe Google search me? See if I come up. I miss the internet almost as much as you.

Mom, you're gonna love the next opera we're doing. It's called The Dream of Julia. I think you might like that one.

I'm sorry I couldn't be there. But I have to say, my heart is whole. And my soul is healed. I'm not hiding and I'm not scared anymore. It's fucking crazy.

If this does reach you, I hope it helps.

I love you.

Melody Reilly-Renaître

Acknowledgments

To my Mama, Kande, And other mother Kate, and everyone else in my life for the unending support and thinking I'm the bees' knees.

Thank you to my Beta readers—Sharon, Maloree, Adam, and Michelle. Without you, I wouldn't have the amazing story I do now. Beta readers are in fact, the bees' knees.

And seriously, thank you, the reader, for showing interest in this little indie author adventure. This is the coolest thing I've ever done. You are also the bees' knees.

About the Author

In 2017 Australia D. Kincannon had just seen Star Wars: The Last Jedi and that was when her writing journey began.

So in love with the story, she went to Ao3 to start her first fanfiction, which she never finished. But, not too long after that, she wrote her first screenplay and continued down that path for a few years. Horror and thriller being her favorite genres to write at the time.

Never had she imagined writing would be the thing she loved more than any other form of art she had done throughout her life. Her high school teachers would be just as shocked.

It wasn't until her first time to New York City with her mother and sister to see The Phantom of the Opera on Broadway in its final few months, that she was inspired to write a novel.

"What would happen if I fell into the story I loved so much?"

To be honest, she knew she would probably die right away. But she decided to write a suspenseful romance with a "Happily Ever After" instead.

Made in the USA
Las Vegas, NV
28 February 2025